Eaglets

Book Three of the Story of Ele

Part of the Heirs of Ana

By G. Lawrence

This book is dedicated to Fe,

who makes a dreary day bright.

Prologue

Fontevraud Abbey

Poitou – Anjou border

1200

We stand with the dead. Their tombs before us, I wonder, do we do this, make such monuments, that we might demonstrate dominion over death? This show we put on, this honouring of our dead with markers and statues, with their names carved in eternal stone, is it a last cry of defiance against the shadow of death?

True, the majority of the dead lie in the ground and that is below our feet, yet some we place in tombs higher, which stand tall, eye to eye with the living. Do we do this to show that some, even in death, remain unvanquished?

Of course, only the rich can make tombs so high, can build in marble or Caen stone to make monuments that all look upon and marvel. That is why we build them, so others will come before them in the future and stand breathless at the grandeur of the person there entombed. We build so high and so prettily, so the person who lies inside will not be forgotten. Tombs, are they monuments to the dead, in truth, or to our own fears?

Perhaps we all fear this, not to die, but to be forgotten. To be remembered, our names still spoken by our ancestors, this is the victory we seek over death. But to be remembered, truly, we must do one of two things. We must be very good, or we must be very bad. Those are the people our ancestors remember. Never those in between. There must be a story to be told of us, one people will want to hear.

"How do we know if what we do is good, or if it is bad?" I ask the child Isabella at my side. "How do we know that what we choose to do in life is for the best?"

"We have intentions which are good." Her tone is obedient, as if I am her tutor. I suppose I am, in a way.

"But how do we know our intentions are good?"

She pauses a moment. "We wish the best for others, perhaps for ourselves."

"Then are those actions not selfish?"

She bites her lip a little, suspecting a trap. "Perhaps all actions are selfish," she says. "There is always a measure of self-interest in what we do, but just because our actions are selfish in one way does not mean they are not good for others too."

"An answer befitting the great Queen you will be." My eyes glimmer with approval as she beams. "Balanced and ambiguous. You should always keep people guessing, child. Become easy to predict and that is when the mouth of the world catches you, bites you down to little bits. I was too easy to predict once, and I was caught, a rabbit in a snare." I touch her shoulder as we look down on the tombs of my son, his father, and, not far away, my daughter.

One of my daughters. My other children, so many of them now, those I birthed and those I raised, they lie in graves set about the world. What patch of the world on which we walk, I wonder, is not a grave to something? Life springs everywhere, and it grows, like the roots of a tree, or of a flower, through the skulls of those who lie beneath. A womb and a tomb is the world, death and life entwined in a dance which never ends.

"The truth is, child, we never can know if what we do is good or bad, even if we start with the very best of intentions. I have seen lives ruined because someone intended something good for another, witnessed wars begun and fought fierce because someone believed themselves to be right and others wrong. I have seen a saint made and martyred because two men believed theirs was the true, right way. I have watched an empire torn apart, because no two men could agree how it was to be ruled. Even if we wish the best for others, we cannot in truth offer them such. Even if we wish the best for ourselves, we cannot bring that best to be. There is chaos in this world, and, as a drifting storm cloud so it floats about the earth, darkening lives and lightening others. We prepare for the storm; we follow its path with our eyes, feel the pattern of the wind on our skin, but even if we have watched it with care all our lives, we can never know what thunder will break over our unwary heads as we stand in the path of the tempest."

"So, what do we do?" She looks fearful. I suppose no one has ever had the heart to tell a child such as her the truth of life. It is, indeed, a frightening thing, and yet it helps us more to be prepared than not.

"We do the best we can, and we understand that sometimes that may not be enough, that sometimes we can do our best, do all right, we may win every battle, yet lose the war." I smile and place my hand on her shoulder. "But we are forgetful creatures, so when people have forgotten the horror of war, there will always be another. As long as men want power, there will be another chance to fight, and there will be another chance to prevail."

I look down. "Until it ends, here," I indicate to the tombs. "The last understanding we must come to is this: Death has the last word, one we all must listen to."

Chapter One

Poitiers

Poitou

Christmas 1168

Upon the thick glass pane of my small window, I traced the flight of a snow speck in the sky outside. My fingernail, light yet hard, flowed with the dancing fragment of ice and light through the air, pausing as it came to rest, joining others on the stone windowsill outside. Not many would get to see such a vision this night unless they stepped outside. Glass was highly expensive, used only by the rich or the Church, but in my private chambers I had installed it, an indulgence so I could witness the world outside from the comfort of the inside.

Light snow was drifting in the air, tiny dots of light floating in dove-grey skies of the gloaming, coming to rest on the ground. It was not a heavy enough fall to make travel or life a hardship, just enough to make the world prettier for a while, as if a thousand stars had descended from the heavens to cover the world with a glittering blanket. I stood at the window, watching those specks of brilliance prance in the soft grey light of the fading day as my women combed my hair, set my gown straight, ready for another night where I would preside as Duchess of Aquitaine, over my own court.

It was a relief, not only that I was home, home where the spirit of my family, my ancestors and all the stories of my childhood were sung so strong, but I was, at least most of the time, living in this world without a husband too. Oh, we were still married, of course, and oftentimes in the past fourteen years we had lived apart for long periods, but now, truly, we seemed separated, not by law or Church but because I had come home, because we did not have to meet to procreate more children, because I could rule my lands and he his, because I had decided to immerse myself in my own lands and people and stand just a little away from Henry and his choices.

It was liberating, in so many ways.

There was a sense of intense freedom in being so far from Henry and in being home, a sense of satisfaction in being able to, and indeed trusted to, govern my own lands, my own people. In truth Henry could not manage the people of Aquitaine or Poitou as well as I could. I could understand instinctively the moments when diplomacy was required and times when a show of force was necessary. Henry was always ready with the fist and sword, and that was not always the best way. I had been raised here, my people made sense to me. To King Henry of England, the feared Duke of Normandy, the folk of Aquitaine and Poitou, Gascony too, were odd, alien, always troublesome. To my people, Henry of England was the one who was odd, a curious, brutal outsider they resented as their lord and master. But me, they had great affection for, perhaps even love, and finally I had come home as long they had been asking me to and as I had promised. With me I had brought their future, my son, Lord Richard, one day to be their Duke. They had rejoiced in my return and continued to do so now, though I had been many months at home.

And I, freed in what some would term the winter years of my life – although I would say I was more glorious golden autumn than stark, white winter – was joyous too, for I was finally able to do as I wished. My time of breeding was not over, I knew that for I still had regular courses, but Henry and I had agreed that in order to preserve my strength and life we would share a bed no more. Freed of the necessity of bringing heirs into the world, and having done my duty many times over in this regard since we had four sons and three daughters living, I was at liberty to live the life I had dreamed many times of, a life where I chose where I dwelt, where I wielded the power conferred upon me by my ancestors, where I was no more called on every day to calm or appease the wild mind that existed within my husband.

He was happy enough with his mistresses, and I was merry with my people, and my children.

Many of my children were here now, at my court. I could hear them not far away, trooping down the stone corridors by flickering torchlight, coming to my chamber to escort me to the hall where the rest of my court would be gathered, as they did on any good occasion. This night we would hear poetry and song, we would feast and dance, we would share laughter and affection. It had been this way since home I came, every night we were surrounded by the warmth of a central fire blazing in the middle of the hall, by incense billowing blue and white into the air, and by the chatter of a hundred voices of people come to court to petition or talk to me. Some arrived at my court just because it was one of refinement and beauty. People had spoken of my father's and grandfather's courts with wonder perfuming their breath, and I was determined that that would be the way people spoke of my court for the rest of time too.

In the tranquil days of summer, we had roamed the gardens and ridden in the forests of my lands, surrounded by the verdant beauty of Poitou and Aquitaine. My heart had ached to contain so much happiness. At night, spices filled the air, rising in clouds from incense burners and braziers of scented wood, and the long, light evenings had been awash with the dusky blue light of the falling day, and the talk of cultured tongues rippling through the gentle petals of the flowers, carried on the sweet-scented breeze. Now it was winter, we gathered sooner in the evenings in the great halls of my palaces, listening to stories of old which troubadours sang clear and true. We watched dancers twist and writhe to tell a tale using body and bone. Drums beat in the shadows and musicians played for feet that did not tire of the dance, no matter the hour. The light of candles and torches illuminated the darkness, casting golden light onto welcome faces of hearth and home. Wine flowed and ale was plentiful. Often the nights would stretch long, and yet feel short, for the lively company we kept.

My people were enamoured of me and my return. They loved my children, and my children returned their love. We were of one heart, my lands and my family. It was the way I had always wished I could live, and now I did.

Richard, my heir to Aquitaine and all my lands, was with me almost all the time, when his father did not need him. Richard was at my elbow every hour, learning how to be ruler of these lands when I was gone, and often, looking at him as he observed how I came to a decision or chose to speak to a troublesome baron, I saw a little frown of concentration formed between his eyebrows. That frown I adored, a sign of diligence upon his young brow.

Eleanor, Joanna, Geoffrey were with me too. But not John or Henry, nor Matilda either, she being married and in Saxony now. Young Henry, my eldest son, was often in England, sometimes Normandy when his father remembered his existence and needed something of him, and John was at Fontevraud, learning how a life was to be dedicated to God, since we had sworn to offer him to the Church. I saw my absent children when I could, but my younger children as well as my people were my daily life, and my most treasured responsibility.

"Maman?" There was a polite, firm knock at the door.

"Come in, Richard," I called. "I am ready."

My third-born son, yet now second eldest living, stepped into the chamber, and smiled. "You look beautiful, my lady." He swept into an elegant bow which made my heart twitch with pride. Eleven years he was about to turn, and he had more charm and grace than many men twice his age.

"You look well yourself, my son," I said, admiring his well-combed hair and smooth skin. My ladies of court had taken my son on as a kind of pet, giving him potions for clear skin because they admired his good looks so. Richard, in his frequently slightly aloof way, had been enjoying their attentions. "You have news?"

"King Louis sends another raiding party to the Vexin." Richard came to the window to stand with me. "But Father is seeing the King of Francia off with ease, so I am told."

I had in fact already been informed of this, but I liked to bolster the confidence of my son by making it appear he could bring news to me. We were not quite at the moment when he could become co-ruler in truth with me, he was still too young, but we were not far off the time it would be appropriate. I wanted him to believe, however, that he was already in this position. If I should die, a sudden fever or an attack perhaps, as were common in our world, Richard needed to be ready to step in, even at eleven years, and take on the mantle of ruler. He therefore had to believe he could rule, had to have the confidence to do so. If he did not, then powerful barons and lords of this land would crush my son like a weevil in a biscuit.

Instilling confidence in him meant a little fakery at times on my part, pretending I knew something not, or that he had had an idea which had not occurred to me, but any playacting on my part was done with the intention of making him self-assured and bold in this, his destiny.

I tugged on a brooch of enamel and garnet at my chest, slightly askew as I made it straight. "Your father is at Argentan, my son, so it is his men who see Louis off."

Richard frowned. "They act in his name, my lady."

I nodded, wanting him to understand the distinction. "And yet *they* are not *him*. Always remember the debt owed to those who aid us in holding our lands, my son. One day you too will need such people, men or women you can leave in one area to hold your territory as you travel to another, and you must appreciate these people in whom you place trust. Men or women who are not appreciated grow tired and rancorous and look for a new master who will share acclaim with them. Men turn rebel when they think their acts and deeds go unnoticed by their lord and master." *Women even more so*, Petronilla whispered in my mind.

Richard nodded. "I understand."

I smiled. Of course he understood. Richard was, of all my children, the one who knew how to listen. I was glad he had finally been granted to me as the heir to my lands, as I had long been asking. Training him in the role was not only easier than it might have been with headstrong young Henry, or my slightly slippery younger son Geoffrey, but was a pleasure too. Richard was one to heed lessons, listen to my advice, yet always he had his own thoughts to share too. I had wanted a promising child to offer to my people as their future lord. Now, in part thanks to King Louis and his treaty with Henry in which my husband had promised to give each of our sons lands of their own – something I had suggested years before yet somehow this had been forgotten by my husband – my people had their promising future, in my son.

This treaty between the two kings was supposed to be in place now, yet still King Louis sent men to raid, and Henry responded. They were due to meet in January to secure their pact, at which time Henry would agree formally to divide up his empire upon his death between his sons. In the meantime, each king still appeared to believe that until the treaty was secured, raiding was permitted. When the two kings came to meet again it had been agreed my three sons would be present to pay homage to the King of Francia as their overlord, as was traditional. There was something odd about the sons of my second marriage paying homage to the husband of my first, but the ways of the world are often curious.

"Father wishes still to crown my brother Henry as his heir?" Richard asked, heading to another subject. "I thought it might be done this Christmastide."

"To my sorrow, I think we are still a way from young Henry's coronation," I said, my eyes travelling out to watch the snow again. "Until the rift between your father and Archbishop Becket is resolved, we have no one of suitable rank to crown your brother."

It was something I supported, the crowning of young Henry in the lifetime of his father. It was a tradition well practised in Francia, to crown the heir as a second king, a king of the future, within the lifetime of his father. The ceremony offered a country stability, unity, allowed the son to learn at the side of his father, even to rule segments of land himself whilst his father was still alive to watch over him and guide him. It was a sensible apprenticeship. In many ways, the same had been done for my husband. His father, Geoffrey of Anjou, had handed over the title of Duke of Normandy to his son whilst Geoffrey still lived, which had allowed Henry to begin his rule with his father standing at his side, there to support him. We, the present rulers of this empire, were training our replacements, were securing the succession. When Henry had suggested the coronation of our eldest son, I had supported it wholeheartedly, thinking it a step on the path we were forging of a future bright for our people.

But my eldest son could not be crowned, not yet.

The troubles between my husband and his once greatest friend, Thomas Becket, Archbishop of Canterbury were still ongoing, and the Archbishop was not even in England as he was still a fugitive in Francia, along with most of his family, because Henry had exiled them from England in revenge for the Archbishop refusing to do as he wanted. Henry had thought his old friend and once-Chancellor Becket would aid him in curtailing the powers of the Church in England if he made him Archbishop. This had not transpired as my husband had wished. Until the rift between them, one formed of Henry's prideful desire to dictate all the Church did, and Thomas's refusal to allow the Church to be so controlled, was resolved, there was no one of sufficient rank to crown young Henry.

"Do you think they will resolve their quarrel?" Richard turned eyes of blue, so like his father's on me. I had blue eyes too, of course, yet it was Henry's eyes which shone in the faces of our sons, lighter and colder than the blue of mine.

I breathed in. "I know not, my son. The truth is, your father elevated his friend to the position of Archbishop, supposing that since Becket had been his friend and loyal servant once, he always would be so, but your father misread the man. He thought him his friend in truth, but Becket has always and most dutifully served the master he possesses and the personal glory he seeks. Once that master was indeed your father, and once the glory Becket sought was worldly, but upon Becket's elevation his master became the Church and his glory became the spiritual, to all outward appearances at least. To my mind, the man is as avaricious as ever he was, he simply hides it better now, behind chalice and under cowl. Your father wishes to command all, even the Church itself, but Becket will not allow that now for it would harm his new master and reduce his own magnificence. One must submit to the other, and neither wishes to. Both believe their power, their opinion to be the righteous one, and this argument is their way of proving who is right. And it has spread further than just two men for now it is a question of who has the most power, a king with all his worldly authority, or a servant of the Church, backed by the papacy? This question consumes them both, and the fire that burns in them, over this, has kindled in the hearts of others too."

Richard paused a moment, considering his next question. "You do not think the Archbishop is supported also by God, not just the papacy?"

I laughed a little. "Does God choose only His servants of the cloth?" I asked. "Kings and rulers are set in place by the Almighty just as servants of the Church are, so your father could argue as persuasively that he has God's approval as Thomas Becket could. The truth is, we cannot know the will of God until a choice is made as to who prevails, but we do know that Becket, at most times at least, has the support of the Church and the Church is a powerful creature. Had your father elevated a man to Archbishop who was more malleable, or as would have been more advisable, had compromised with the Church rather than tried to subdue it utterly, this matter might have been resolved long ago, then we would have crowned your brother by now and he could be already ruling a portion of the empire. This argument, all it has done is wasted the time of everyone involved."

"Father was foolish in this matter." Richard sounded scathing. I did not correct him as he insulted his father. I praised my husband where it was due, especially in terms of warcraft for few were his equal, but Richard had to understand that even great warriors, even his father, could make mistakes. It was part of his education. Besides, he spoke only the truth. Henry had been a fool.

"He was," I agreed, "and continues to be so, and Becket is a fool too because for the sake of spite and revenge neither will let the matter rest. It is a mistake I hope you will learn from. Many of my ancestors too tried to go against the Church, my own father was one of them, and they were beaten back. The Church is a power as great as any prince, any king, perhaps more so since they hold power not just in one kingdom but in every land where they operate. It is better to compromise, to deal with them, than to try to flaunt them openly."

I sighed a little. "What is it, Maman?" Richard asked.

"I do wonder at times if your father – even if we crown your brother – will allow young Henry the independence he needs, will trust him to rule, even partially, within your father's lifetime," I said, frowning. "Your brother writes to me often, frustrated, for he is not permitted the power he wishes for. Your father holds tight to all that we have built. I understand, for it can be hard to relinquish what you have so carefully nurtured, but a time is coming when some power at least must be released into the hands of the next generation, to our children. It is important you and your brothers learn to rule, to stand as men of power, whilst we, the elders of the past, are still here that you might come to us when in need."

"This does not seem to worry you, Maman. You share much with me though I am young and green."

I smiled, taking his hand. "When you come to rule my people, *your* people, Richard, I would have you ready for it in all ways, but I will admit to you this; there is still hardship in releasing my authority to you. It is a little tug paining my heart, a selfish impulse urging me to hold on to what I have. I recognise and release that little pull of covetous jealousy I feel, knowing what is best for my people is not for me to hold on to all and release nothing. I know that tug is wrong, pulling me in the wrong direction, so I defy it. I understand that you must learn at my elbow now, so the future is secured, but your father... I know not. I think sometimes he is becoming as his grandfather was towards the end of his rule, holding on to everything too tight."

"So, Father cannot let go?"

"Perhaps, time will tell, but you will understand one day, my son, power is not like a sword or spear that one may grasp tight, it is more like dough."

"Dough?"

I chuckled a little at his incredulous tone. "Yes, dough. Hold the dough to make the bread lightly in the hand and it may be formed into any shape, but squeeze it too tight in the fingers, and it slips out, sliding through every gap, forming a mass of spidery threads. In the same way power may be abused, transformed into chaos. The good baker knows to take care, to dress his hands in oil of the olive, to knead hard and shape gentle so the dough will be fashioned with slippery ease into a work of beauty which will feed and sustain many people. The bad baker, he tries too hard to hold on, the air is pushed out of the bread. The dough is mishandled, and the bread is ruined."

"Power like dough," Richard mused, that crease of concentration back between his eyes. "I believe I understand."

"As you must, for one day you will be the baker." I kissed his hand.

"We will travel again, after Christmastide?" Richard asked as we moved towards the door. Outside I could hear my other children jostling in the hallway. Geoffrey was trying to command his sisters, but they, Eleanor and Joanna, were spirited creatures. I smiled to hear Eleanor scold her brother for his ungentlemanly ways. It was good my daughters learned young that there was more than one way to be a woman in this world. Submission might be what was taught by the Church and many lords, but it was not the best way for a woman to exist if she wanted to be heard.

"I believe we will stay in Poitiers until January at least," I said. "And remember, you are to join your father after Christmastide, along with Geoffrey and Henry, so you might all do homage to King Louis for your kingdoms."

"Yes." Richard looked a little forlorn to leave my homeland. He also did not truly like his father a great deal. Henry was a person who had appeared in Richard's life, in all the lives of our children, briefly and then left again. Often, he was sweet to his offspring when he needed something from them, and then ignored them the rest of the time. People say that children should love their parents, and my children did love their father, but they were quite aware of his lack of love for them. I had spent more time with all of them than Henry had, and even though my duties too had called me away from them for months or even years at a time, my children were in no doubt that I loved them, because I told them I did, and because I proved by my actions that I did. It was not the same with their father.

I touched Richard's hand. "You will be back soon, and this is necessary, so you can secure your place as the future ruler of these lands I know you love as well as I do."

A rare smile came. "Yes," he said. "You are right, Maman. And then we may travel again?"

I chuckled. Richard enjoyed seeing all of my lands. We had been on the move a great deal in the months we had been home again. It was necessary as well as pleasurable. After years of French rule then more under my husband, after a succession of misguided Norman or English lords ruling my lands, officers who did not understand my people truly, I had had a great deal to put right with my people. Richard and I had travelled here, there, and everywhere restoring old markets and fairs, giving back land which had been confiscated, welcoming the exiled home and receiving homage from those who had remained. I had restored peace and offered hope in the months I had been home. It was not perfect, no realm is, and the oldest wounds would take the longest to heal, but I was applying a balm everywhere I went, and taking Richard with me so my people could see their future lord and so he could understand his people. He took to the task well. Aquitaine was in his heart and my homeland was fast taking my son into its heart too. I was to be forty-seven in the New Year, and I knew not how long I had left to live, though I felt fine and fit. Plenty of people never made it to my age, and there was always the chance some petty, piqued fit of fate could steal me away. I knew if my son was to care for these lands as I did then he had to love them, so I had undertaken the part of matchmaker, had made it my duty to make them fall in love, Richard with Aquitaine and Aquitaine with Richard.

It was a match I was certain would end in joy.

All I wished for was to protect Aquitaine, Poitou, Gascony, to offer my people a good future through my son. My own dreams I cherished too, of liberty in my homeland, of friendship and love with my children, of a life ordered and controlled by me, and, at least somewhat less frequently having to be mother not only to my children but to a husband. There was, in this autumn of my life, the most gloriously coloured season of the year, a reciprocal, mutual blending between the dreams I conjured for myself and those which always had been my duty. I was more aware of all I wanted and needed, all I required in order to be content, than I ever had been. The life I had carved out for myself here was satisfying, and all I needed to be content.

I had come to understand that contentment is a greater thing than happiness. Happiness is sweet and good, mistake me not, a glorious silver spike in the memory, but it is brief and transitory. To be content, steady in life and purpose, satisfied in accomplishment and daily tasks, to work and have enough to occupy oneself with but not feel overwhelmed, to have love and to know love is given by one's own heart in return, this is contentment, a steady, golden light, warm as a mother's embrace. Contentment is a great accomplishment.

Perhaps this was wisdom, falling on a headstrong young daughter of the sun as the dusk of her life came, although to me even if this was the dusk of my day there was time left to do much. There still was all the glorious night to come yet, her shining stars, her merry moon. I was older than many could ever boast to become, yet I was far from done with my life. I had many plans.

I took the arm of my son and out into the corridor we came. Geoffrey, Eleanor and Joanna were there, standing in line, as was Marguerite, one of the daughters of my first husband. Marguerite had been birthed by a wife other than me, of course, and was now married to my eldest son Henry. Young Henry should perhaps have had his bride with him, but they were too young to live together. Besides, I had wanted Marguerite with me. Young Henry was a headstrong boy, like me and his father in many ways. He needed a strong woman to guide him. If Marguerite lived with him, Henry would find ways to bully, charm or cajole her whilst she was young, and her character was still forming. He would mould her into just another admirer, one he could control. I wanted this not. If with me, I could teach her all the ways I knew to rule at the side of a man. Admittedly, I had not always succeeded, but Marguerite was intelligent enough to learn from me, and to make her own choices too.

I smiled at my husband's half-sister, Emma of Anjou. One of the bastard children of Henry's father, she had been with my court for many years and was one of my trusted women. "Your children are prepared, my lady," she said with a smile. "Though I cannot promise they will be as decorous in behaviour as they are in their dress."

I laughed. "I would not have it any other way," I said as I turned to inspect them. "As long as they do not disgrace me utterly, I would always have them in possession of spirit and substance over obedience and silence."

"Father is promising to convert to Islam if Thomas Becket is not deposed as Archbishop," Geoffrey burst out as I was inspecting their clothing one by one. Evidently, he had taken me at my word.

I gazed into his eyes. It was obvious he had been storing this gossip up and it would not remain contained any longer, and, just as obviously, he had been saving it to tell to me and had not shared it with Richard or the others. Geoffrey wanted to feel important, to show off in front of Richard.

I felt for Geoffrey at times. Although John was the youngest boy, he was many years apart from the three eldest. Geoffrey was the youngest of my three elder sons and felt left behind, at times, by his brothers. This led him to have a grappling, clutching sense to his nature. Always he was seeking to be noticed, to be more, not understanding this led to him being seen as less, or as lacking, by some. It was a thirst to prove himself, I supposed. Yet it remains a sad irony of life that those who always are trying to prove themselves never seem to be as easily believed as those who simply are themselves and try to prove nothing.

"Your father is a Christian, and never would do such an outlandish thing as converting to Islam," I said. "Thank you for telling me, my son, but mention this gossip to no others. We do not need your father facing false accusations of heresy along with all the troubles he has with Archbishop Becket at the moment, nor would such a rumour reflect well on you, as his children, either."

"Yes, Maman." Geoffrey looked crestfallen.

I took his chin. "It is good you told me," I said, staring into his blue eyes, another set so like Henry's. "Always tell me when you hear any rumour, but do not always believe them, Geoffrey. I have not raised you to be a dolt, and only a dolt believes all they hear." I smiled. "You are no dolt, my son, are you?"

"No, Maman," he grinned.

"Of course you are not, for you are *my* son. I only produce intelligent children." I smiled at them all, my daughters, bright and spirited, my sons, ever a mixture of vice and virtue, and they grinned back at me.

As we started to process to the great hall, I exchanged a worried glance with Richard, who was on my arm. I might have said to Geoffrey that my husband would not do something as foolish as to decide to take up another religion in order to get what he wanted, but in truth Henry was capable of many an idiotic, impulsive idea, and also more than capable of acting on it in haste, leaving all the time in the world to regret it later.

"You will send word to my uncle Raoul le Faye this night," I whispered to Richard. "Tell him I want to know the truth of this rumour Geoffrey has told us."

Richard nodded, not saying a word as the huge wooden doors to the great hall swung open and into a cloud of warm incense smoke billowing, and a din of many mouths cheering me and my family, we walked.

Chapter Two

Poitiers

Poitou

January 1169

I breathed out, a fog of mist emerging from my mouth, drifting away into the skies.

The gardens were crisp and cold, small flakes of snow glittering as they fell, lighting on the faces of stone saints carved about the Maubergeonne Tower. With ice covering those faces formed of stone they seemed blue, ghostly.

As I looked up to the Tower, I could almost see two young girls, ghosts of the past, of me and Petronilla, as we stared out from the apartments of our grandmother, Dangerosa, watching the world go by below. How we had wished as children to be part of that world so full of excitement, yet now, looking up rather than down, back rather than forward, I envied us as children. We were loved and had been sheltered as best those who loved us could, and as best they could those people had shown us their love. What more can someone ask for? I hoped my children felt this way now, even though some, like Henry and Richard, like Eleanor, were almost classed as adults now.

At least, if we are not children anymore, you are still here with me, I said to my sister's ghost. I could feel her so strongly in our homelands. Her voice was ever on the breeze of summer in Aquitaine, her soul in the creeping mists of autumn which hung in the violet skies of Poitou. Her spirit was in the peaceful, glittering lights of stars peeking into the world of day as dusk fell. I saw her in a sparkle of mischief in the eyes of my children, heard her in their laughter. I felt her in any thought of wisdom which came to me, and I missed her every day I lived after she had died.

I will always be here, Petronilla whispered through the falling snow. *Where else but at your side would I be?*

I nodded, walking on, my hands stuffed deep into a muff of rich, white wolf fur, a present from a lord who had travelled far, far north in the winter before this one. My ladies scurried behind me, Emma at my side, appreciating that I needed silence. My women had not wanted to come out, but I had needed to think and thought came easier to me when my feet were busy.

I suppose it was the notion of my children being almost adults which was part of what troubled me that day. Just as I could lift my nose to the wind and tell you snow would soon fall heavy, so I could tell trouble was on its way for my family. Richard and Geoffrey had left the palace, travelled to their father, and he was to take them to do homage to Louis of France for their lands. Geoffrey was to have Brittany, Richard Aquitaine, Poitiers and Gascony, Henry's possessions were England, Normandy, Anjou and Maine. John had no lands assigned to him, for he was to enter the Church.

This homage as well as other terms of the treaty with France would make my sons the legal rulers of their duties and domains, and they were expecting to be able to act as such, but I knew, in my heart I knew well, that my husband was not about to relinquish control if he could. I hoped I was wrong, but I did not think I was.

With my lands, he had small choice. I was ruler here even if Henry was my overlord because he was my husband. Officially, Louis of France was still my kingdom's overlord, if my father's will was still taken into account, which was not often. But I had been trusted to rule my lands as I wished by Henry. If that meant including Richard in every decision, that was up to me. Brittany was a small territory, and it was likely Geoffrey might begin to rule there, albeit under close watch by Henry's trusted men, soon enough, but as for our eldest son, I could not see any lands falling with ease into his hands. My husband had fought his mother's foes for England and Normandy, and Maine and Anjou were his father's lands. He had reasons aplenty to cling to all of them, in his own mind. The possession of them was personal. This I could understand.

But my husband had also proved long ago, when the troubles between him and Becket began, that he had trouble sharing power. The struggle with Becket and indeed the Church itself had all been about who held the power in England. Henry was King, but even kings must share power, delegate to lords and make deals with other lands, including Rome. As the squabble with the Archbishop dragged on and on, it seemed to me my husband was becoming increasingly unwilling to cede to the notion that anyone else should have power other than him.

This was a problem if our son was to be crowned and was going to learn to rule at his father's side.

I was starting to suspect that my husband saw our eldest son not as an heir to be guided to follow him, but as a threat, an unwelcome reminder of his own mortality perhaps.

I had another concern that morning which was troubling me, as my husband was due to meet not only Louis that January, but Becket too.

Rather than convert to Islam, something my uncle Raoul had informed me in a missive Henry *had* said aloud, but apparently only to threaten the Pope with, my husband had agreed to meet with his troublesome former friend that January. He and Becket were to reconcile, that was the plan. It was part of this longer, larger meeting with Louis of France, trying once more to come to terms of peace, but to my mind the meeting with Becket was more significant than the one between fellow kings.

It was more significant because it was the one more likely to not go well. History may teach us much if men would pay attention to it, and the history between these two men was acrimonious, raw and deeply ingrained.

I was not invited to this meeting. I never was when Louis and Henry met. I think it was easier for Henry and Louis to meet and not think on me, the woman they both had been wed to at different times and the woman they both had sworn they loved, also at different times, although admittedly those times had overlapped somewhat. If they met as friends or enemies, something which altered constantly, that was easier than meeting as men united by the fact they both had bedded the same wife.

I sighed as snow started to fall heavier and thick, giant soft flakes settling on my cloak, making it wet and chilly. It was time to go in and yet I had no wish to. There was something comforting about being out in the still air of a winter's day. If only the frozen world could stay that way, then nothing bad would happen for the world would remain ever the same, trapped as this one moment.

And I had a feeling bad things were going to happen, soon.

*

The meeting took place at Montmirail Castle, on the border of Maine, near Chartres. Of course, our three eldest sons were there to do their homage to Louis, so he could in turn recognise their rights to those lands, securing them in a secondary sense, just as their blood had secured them once. Louis probably supposed this act of homage might make the Angevin Empire easier to manage, with all the inheritors to that empire sworn to obey him as their overlord. In truth, it meant little. Louis was my overlord, through the will of my father, and Henry's due to France granting the lands of Normandy to his ancestor, and we had always done as we wished without reference to Louis. Yet traditions exist in the hope that they confer meaning on the chaotic happenings of life, so we continue to honour them, and this way Louis could always enjoy being outraged, or have a reason to start war with us, when one or all of my sons disobeyed him. Rulers like to have a reason to start war, it makes them appear reasonable.

For my part, I hoped rather than believed that this ceremony of homage might allow Henry to slacken his grip just a little that he might witness what his sons could do were they offered a little power and authority of their own. I did not think he would immediately hand their inheritances to them, as his own father had done for him, but I did hope he might learn to trust them a little.

After the treaty had been confirmed, young Henry did homage to his father-in-law Louis for Brittany, which Geoffrey would rule eventually in his stead, and Louis received young Henry's fealty with pride. The French King confirmed the betrothal of Geoffrey to Constance, daughter of the last lord of Brittany and his only heir, as well as another match, which granted Louis's daughter Alys to Richard. Alys was to be handed to my husband, then to me, to raise at my court much as Marguerite was being raised. Young Henry was named seneschal of France, and Richard too did homage for his lands. Perhaps enough homage had been paid, or the hour was growing late, as it was agreed Geoffrey would do homage to Louis and to his brother for Brittany later, when he was closer of an age to rule alone.

"I have concerns about Richard's bride," I said to my uncle Raoul who had come to update me on the meeting.

"You object to Alys of France?" He adjusted a smart patch of black cloth he now wore over one eye. On a hunting trip with my husband some months ago at Woodstock, my uncle had fallen from his horse into a bush and was blinded in one eye by a sharp twig. Members of the clergy told him it was his own fault for hunting on the Sabbath. Raoul pointed out he had, in fact, been blinded on a Wednesday, but the tale still endured. Wrapping his wound in mouldy bread and a certain kind of wood mushroom recommended by a cunning woman had aided his recovery, though he was still struggling a little on a horse and with his bow especially, as his vision adapted to the loss of the eye. Raoul, being the man he was, however, was not one to gripe about misfortune. He told all who would listen how fortunate he was to be alive, and that his lost eye was now in Heaven, watching over him from above.

"The girl herself I have no objection to, a daughter of the King of France is a good match for the future Duke of Aquitaine, but possible plots behind it I like not. Louis once ruled my lands when I was his wife. It was his right to do so whilst married to me, and he was loath to lose my territories when our marriage was annulled. His reluctance to set me aside in fact kept us married much longer than I ever wanted, all so he could keep his hands on my rich, productive lands. He always protested it was because he loved me, but Louis in truth only ever loved one entity who was not himself, and that is the Church."

"You think he is trying to take back Aquitaine and Poitou by covert means?" Raoul nodded to Emma with thanks as she filled his goblet with a fine red wine from La Rochelle.

I tapped a fingernail on the armrest of my high-backed chair. "Indeed. I suspect this marriage might be another way of trying to draw my lands back under French control. With a son, half of Richard and half of Alys, on the ducal throne of Aquitaine, France might try to grasp back control of my lands, but I have faith that Richard would bring up any son to put our lands first. The girl will be raised in my household too, and therefore I can ensure she has but small loyalties left to her homeland, and more to mine, by working on her."

Raoul grinned. "It seems you have solved your own problem again, niece. Whatever do you need me for?"

I smiled. "I need no men to solve problems for me, but I do need them to aid me. I cannot be everywhere, and I only have two eyes. Your eye I trust, uncle, to see where I cannot."

He laughed. "I would offer you two, if I still had both."

"Your one eye is sharper than those of many a man," I told him.

When it came time in that meeting for Becket to meet Henry, all held their breath. "I wondered at the sight of the man," Richard told me when he returned home. We sat at my fireside, wine in hand as we talked. "He ever was thin, but he looked gaunt, skeletal, almost."

"I suppose life as an exile has had some ramifications. The splendour he used to dwell in is much depleted, I would think." I ran my finger about the rim of my goblet of silver. "I hear he still fasts and whips himself, or has his brethren do it, on a regular basis."

"Daily, I would think, Maman," Richard grimaced, "by the look of him. I think the years and constant fright for his life have taken as hard a toll as the punishments he inflicts on himself. He did not look well."

"Before we get to this meeting of your father and former friend, tell me, what did you think of Louis?" I asked.

"I thought he seemed a strange, soft man. He has eager eyes which edge on madness, for the heart which lights their clinging fires is so keen to latch on to anyone, to anything. People say I am still a child, but there was something about Louis that made me think him the infant. He seemed to be always seeking something to comfort him, like a baby looking for a breast."

I laughed. "He always has been that way." I patted my son's hand with approval. "God did Louis a disservice in making him a king, had he been bound for the Church he would be a saint by now for his devotion would have been given slavishly, wholeheartedly, and someone would have martyred him by now for simply being vexing." I sat back and took a pull on my wine. "So come," I went on. "Tell me of your father and his once friend and their ridiculous shared, offended pride which so defames all the rest of us by association."

"You speak as if they too are children."

"Are they not?" I asked. "Adults must find ways to resolve things without throwing toys at one another, children just continue to lob trinket and doll across the chamber. This spat, all over which man is the more powerful, Archbishop or King, it is a fool's game and has been going on far too long. They act like infants, and all the rest of us are forced, too, to take part in this war because they cannot make peace."

"We thought they would try," said my son. "It seemed hopeful for a short while."

"It always does, and then one of them opens their mouth a little too wide so the truth slips out." I lifted my eyebrows. "Who was it this time?"

Richard laughed. "Becket."

It did not surprise me. Becket and Henry had not seen each other for four years. Had Henry not needed to reconcile with Becket in order to crown young Henry, he probably would never have agreed to the meeting even though Canterbury was calling out for its leader and England too wanted their spiritual head returned. That meant nothing to Henry, but now *he* needed something, and there always was a promise of love to be restored if Henry wanted something from a past friend. I should know, often enough he had tried that trick with me. In the days when I had loved him it had worked. I saw the truth now, as I suspected Becket did too. Henry offered love to those who had something to offer him. It was a trade, with him, rather than tenderness.

As for Becket, he had hardly been idle in those years of separation. He had lived at various courts and gained a reputation not only as a solid, loyal son of the Church, but for the penances and harsh flagellations he inflicted upon himself too. He had also sent perhaps a thousand letters to Henry, reminding him of the Church's position as the King's overlord, calling himself Henry's spiritual father, and lecturing the King on his duties and obediences. His letters had flowed as waters swollen by the spring thaw full of grief and self-pity, and they were not only sent to Henry, but all over the world. All kings and dukes of the world had heard the tales of Becket's sorrow, and by that time were no doubt sick of hearing them too. I certainly was.

By that time the papacy was also sick of dining on a sumptuous feast comprised of the self-pity of Thomas Becket, and had told him to make peace with the King of England. Henry went to that meeting because he needed something important from his former friend, and Becket went because he was commanded to. In truth, neither wanted peace, reconciliation, or to see each other. It was not an auspicious start.

The trouble with these men is, Petronilla whispered in my ear, *they are too alike in pride and self-pity.*

"It seemed hopeful for more than a moment," Richard told me. "Becket came before the kings, and Louis was smiling because he thought all would go well."

"Louis has always suffered from a chronic sickness of misplaced optimism," I said dryly. "It is a foe he has carried all his life, thinking it a friend. Always it bolsters his confidence, and always it lets him fall."

"It let him down again, indeed. Father had said he would forgive the Archbishop and bestow the kiss of peace if the Archbishop retracted his accusation that the Constitutions of Clarendon were heretical," Richard went on. "And it seemed this would go ahead. The Archbishop came before Father and prostrated himself, begging for mercy, which pleased our father but then..."

"Becket decided to say something?" I interjected.

"You have heard this tale already? Did Geoffrey write ahead of it?"

I shook my head. "I have not heard the tale, but I have met Becket before. The man never can stop getting in his own way, especially when everything is going as he wants."

"Becket offered to submit to the King in all things... save the honour of God," said Richard.

"Ah, which your father did not welcome for he knew that statement negated all else."

"He did not welcome it, but I do not quite understand why it was such a dire thing to say."

"What is the will of God?" I swirled the last of my wine in my goblet.

"It may be many things, unknowable to man."

I nodded. "Exactly so, so saying this is adding a clause to Becket's agreement of obedience to your father. That clause allows Becket to disobey the King and to defy him anytime Becket fancies, for he can claim his disobedience is required in order to sustain the honour of God. That makes all apologies for the past or promises for the future null and void. Becket was trying once more to prove that the Church is mightier than the Crown."

"But that is exactly what he did say after." Richard was gazing at me as if I were a sage. "He said it did not become a clergyman to submit to a layman."

"And in that one sentence he has the whole argument laid out. Your father never should have elevated that man to this office, for it made him a prince of the Church. Now Becket thinks he is the overlord of all kings and may even rule over the King who made him." I paused. "I imagine your father reacted with his usual good humour and calm control of temper to Becket's clause?"

Richard laughed. "I thought he might kill the man. He went purple in the face and exploded at him, although, Maman, he was not alone. Even the King of France was scolding Becket as we rode away, and he seems like a man to keep his temper."

"When it suits him," I said. "I remember many a time when that milksop on the throne of France made me think he might use his fists on me."

"He threatened you?" Richard's chest puffed out, ready to defend me.

"He was cleverer than that," I said. "But when there was something to throw, that something always belonged to me, often was precious to me. There was a wall to punch, and frequently it was close to my face. There was a punishment to be doled out, and it was one of malice directed at me. Louis is a child in more ways than one, my son. He never laid a hand on me, that would have disrupted the image he has of himself in his mind as a knight and a noble man, but there are ways more than physical, more cowardly ways, to try to intimidate a person."

"He never could intimidate you," Richard said. "You are the strongest person I know."

I smiled sadly. "Thank you, my child, but I was not always as I am now. Once I was young, a child myself, and surrounded by men hostile to me. When a person is alone, unsure, isolated, it is easier to make them fear you. My first husband knew that. He did not win over me, did not make me afraid of him all the time, only at certain times, but his behaviour was unworthy of a lord and husband. Even though he did not scare me into submission, there were reasons aplenty beyond our lack of sons that I wanted to be free of him."

Hearing more from Richard and others, I came to think Henry had been quite fair at this meeting. When Becket had delivered his now-famous retort about "saving the honour of God" Henry, when he had recovered his temper had turned to Louis and said, "My lord, this man foolishly and vainly deserted his church, secretly fleeing by night although neither I nor anyone else drove him out of the Kingdom…" – it could be said this was not entirely true since Becket had fled in fear of his life but I suppose Henry had not sent any express order to exile him, so on some level it was true – "… I have always been willing and am now to allow him to rule over his church with as much freedom as any of the saints who preceded him but take note of this, my lord, that whenever he disapproves of something he will say it is contrary to God's honour and so always will get the better of me. Let me offer this so that no one shall think me a despiser of God's honour, let him behave towards me as the most saintly of his predecessors behaved towards the least saintly of mine and I will be satisfied."

Many men had agreed with Henry and cries of, "Hear, hear! It is a fair offer! The King has humbled himself!" sounded across the plain. Louis had turned to the Archbishop, who uncharacteristically had remained quiet during this protest of Henry's and said, "My Lord Archbishop, the peace you desire has been offered, why do you hesitate? Do you wish to be more than a saint?"

"Perhaps he does," I said to my uncle Raoul, who had come to the Tower the next morning. He was there to tell me more about our other domains, those I could not be in at this time, and to see Richard whom he had missed. The two men liked each other. I had already been forced to tell him, however, that seeing Richard would have to wait. I heard my eldest son sometimes slept until noon, but Richard was up with the cockcrow each morning, and into practise with the sword or with the bow he would go.

"Perhaps," Raoul said, pouring himself wine. "Though none can tell me what Becket's response actually was, I think if he said anything it was muttered to the King of the Franks."

"Perhaps he said nothing, but Louis's words gave him something to think on," I said.

"What do you mean?"

"What step is higher than the one Becket is on now? Sainthood would indeed be the next rung on this ladder he climbs. Some make it there before death, after all. Hildegard of Bingen, who I write to at times, is seen as a living saint and Bernard of Clairvaux was honoured in a like way when he was alive. Perhaps the troublesome Archbishop seeks to make himself into such as they and be thought a saint in his own lifetime."

"I am sure he thinks thusly of himself." My uncle sat on a stool opposite me, his grey hair glinting silver in the sunlight from the window, its ornately carved wooden shutters open so air and light could reach us. "He and Foliot, Bishop of London are now engaged in a war of paper, each trying to reprove the other."

I stretched my arms before me. "They were rivals for the Archbishopric of Canterbury, and Foliot lost because the King favoured the wrong man. Foliot always hated Becket; he thinks him a fool."

"The man is a fool."

"In some ways," I glanced into my goblet, long since empty, "but in others, he knows exactly what he is doing."

"I thought you did not like him?"

"I do not, I think him a wastrel and a scoundrel, more obsessed with his own glory than anything else."

"But yet you speak somewhat warm of him?" Raoul took a long pull on his wine.

I smiled. "It is possible to admire how good someone is at the game without liking how they play, uncle."

Chapter Three

Poitou and Aquitaine

Winter's End – Summer 1169

That March my husband was in my lands, riding out to crush rebellious lords I could not ride against personally. Trouble had arisen and our forces were not enough. Richard was too young to head our armies, and the timing I thought was excellent, as my husband needed something on which to vent his rage. There had been another round of talks with Becket in February, which had gone just as smoothly as the first despite the Pope writing to Becket, telling him to make peace at whatever cost with the King of England.

The counts of Angoulême and La Marche had been making trouble for me, so Henry rode out to meet them, forcing them into submission. This was what he was good at, and having quelled the rebellion, he left again in the summer, leaving my dominions to me once more to rule.

"I believe you to be doing well," he said to me, on the one night he rode to meet with me and see his children on his way back to Normandy. "There will be times when I am needed, of course, like now, but know that I am content to leave you in charge of these lands. You do well here, Lenor, for the most part our lands here are clement and content, and all speak well of you."

He sounded a little surprised, but something else too... envious? It was possible. Many were happy to criticize him at that time for the ongoing spat with Becket. Perhaps he did not welcome me being spoken well of when he was being often condemned.

"A change from the past to find people speaking well of me." I offered a sideways smile, trying to remind him if I was spoken well of it was deserved, and it had certainly not always been the case. France had tried many times to reject me before I actually left. "And thank you, my lord, for bringing your sword arm and armies to remind such rebel lords what happens when they give me trouble. There are times I wish I had been born a man that I might deal with these rebels myself, but God thought me better born a woman."

"I like you better a woman too," Henry said with a smile which spoke of the desire he still held for me. The envy vanished from his face as a flicker of lust removed it, but I wondered if it still burned in his heart.

"You go from here to see our eldest?" I moved away to the window, wishing to divert him from thoughts of the bedchamber. Henry was always ready for a woman after a fight. I did not want to be that woman. He was keeping his mistress Rosamund in England. She was the one he went to now, and I had no wish to play second woman to anyone, especially my husband. Besides, let him into my bed and I might risk yet another child, and that was too much a gamble at my age. With John, my last child, I had bled much. I feared if it happened again, the bleeding might never stop. Sex and any pleasures that came from it were simply not worth my life.

"At Angers I will see Henry." He scowled a little. "Henry needs to spend less time with his friends and more understanding how to rule."

"Then perhaps you should give him something to rule?" I suggested. "He learns nothing of responsibility, because he has none."

"Henry is too young," said my husband.

"Richard learns at my elbow how to rule these lands, and he is younger than our Henry," I pointed out. "And you were around the same age as our eldest son if not younger when your father was taking you on campaign."

"*I* was responsible at his age."

"Because you had been trusted to be so." I tried with all my might to stop myself sighing out loud. My husband had a bullish nature. He could not see that the reason he had been responsible and able to command at our son's age was because his father had done with him what I was advising my husband do with our son. "There must be give and take in any relationship, my lord husband, and most importantly with the man who is to follow you on your throne."

"He is too young." Anger rode his voice and the bull of his nature stopped short in his soul, refusing to move. With that I knew the conversation to be done. There was no point going over and over arguments with Henry. Sometimes something I said would sink in. It would lie at the bottom of his mind a while and arise, floating, presented as his own thought to his mind. Sometimes that thought would come out into the world, and my will would be done. It took time, of course, this sequence of events where Henry claimed my thoughts, any good ones, as his own, but sometimes it worked. It was the only thing to be done with someone so stubborn.

I sighed inwardly and continued on another subject. "I am told you are considering a husband for Joanna."

He nodded. "William II, King of Sicily."

"Were you thinking to inform me of this?"

"You clearly *are* informed. He is a good match, Lenor, she would become a Queen and Sicily is a country with an advantageous position, good for trade and war." He looked thoughtful a moment. "I am to meet with Louis again in the autumn," he went on, "and I hope to persuade him, at last, to recognise your claim to Toulouse."

"Louis would never hand that land to me." I narrowed my eyes, wondering what my husband was up to this time. Toulouse was in the hands of Louis's vassal and brother-in-law Count Raymond.

"No, but he might to our son Richard. It would make sense to add that land to Richard's, since the lands he is to inherit from you border Toulouse, and indeed because he inherits *your* lands, and Toulouse is one of your ancestral territories."

I nodded. "That would be agreeable to me." I knew it would hardly matter if I disagreed. Let him press again for Toulouse. If won it would be a great thing for Richard and if not, we were in no worse situation than before. "And what of Becket and crowning our eldest son?"

Henry made a low noise, like a growl. "I understand," I said, "and this time, truly, I hold you not accountable for the continuation of your argument, but something must be done."

"The man refuses to cede any ground, even though the Pope has commanded him to, and even when I am tricked into thinking he will, he goes back on whatever he has promised to other lords about being reasonable."

"The Pope is telling him to back down, perhaps he will to the Holy Father listen."

"That man hears no one but himself."

That is why you fight so hard, I thought, *because you are so alike.*

*

They met again that November, but Becket still, and despite urgings from his papal master for peace, refused to cede. He stated he would not agree to anything which could be seen to be at odds with the honour of God. "But what does that mean?" asked Geoffrey, there with me in Poitou again and now with his future bride, Constance.

"Whatever the Archbishop wants it to mean," I said, examining the needlework of Eleanor and Joanna, who had brought their pieces to show me that day. "Becket wants peace, for he wants to return home, but he wants power too, and will not surrender his path to power, and greater power." I smiled at my daughters and bade them to sit and listen. They needed to know the machinations of the world of politics just as my sons did, perhaps more so because there was every possibility their husbands or powerful lords of their countries might exclude them from such discussions as these in the future, and therefore they would need to know how to gather such information themselves and understand much from limited sources.

"I hear Father refused to bestow the kiss of peace again," Richard interjected.

I adjusted my headdress. Several of the pins had come loose. "He did, but I begin to think he will have to, for we never will have your brother crowned if no peace comes, and only with Henry crowned will your father offer him any of the power and responsibility that he needs."

"Father says I am too young to rule Brittany alone." Geoffrey sounded offended by his own youth.

"You are too young to rule alone, but not too young to learn how to rule," I corrected. "And you are the Duke now or will be as soon as you pay homage to Louis of France."

"I would have at the last meeting, but I was told not to!"

"It will come soon, Geoffrey. Fear not, and in the meantime, you may learn much here, from me and your brother."

"Richard has all he needs," Geoffrey said sulkily. "And at least Henry is named the Young King by some."

"You will rule on your own one day and may at that time think back to this moment and marvel at how you could have been so miserable when you were so carefree and without responsibility." I narrowed my eyes at my son. "Dedicate yourself to learning now, and it will aid you in the future. Think of what you have and not what you have not, learn well and do not pout like an old woman with no teeth trying to suck up stew, my son. Such an expression does not become a lord."

Geoffrey laughed out loud, and his siblings joined in. "You will be this Christmas at Brittany with your father and promised wife," I went on, nodding to little Constance who was in the corner sewing and trying not to look as if she was listening in. She was, of course.

She was eight then, a bright, pretty little creature with dark hair and hazel eyes. Officially she was Duchess of Brittany, taking the title after her father's abdication had been forced by my husband. Although as a child, and effectively a prisoner, albeit a politely held one, she could not wield power in her homeland. "When you are with your father, Geoffrey, show him the promise I know is within you. Do not pout or sulk or demand, for this will annoy your father, but listen to him. Question, certainly, but always defer to him. This will please your father, and he will feel happier about handing more power to you."

"This you should say to Henry our brother, Maman," Richard chimed in. "He irritates Father continually, bleating for his inheritance."

"I have said such to him, in letters and when I have been able to see him," I replied. "And I have asked William the Marshal, his guardian, to say the same. The trouble is your elder brother chooses not to listen to me."

Indeed, I wondered if my eldest son listened to anyone. There was too much noise in his mind created by his own mutterings and grumblings to hear anyone else. Like Geoffrey, he wanted more authority, and young Henry had more cause to complain about the lack of such since he was the elder, but alternately sulking and demanding from his father was not likely to bring about the results he wanted.

That Christmas my husband celebrated at Nantes in Brittany with Geoffrey and Constance. I remained in Poitou with Richard and my other children, all but Henry and John. After the feast on Christmas Day, I took little Joanna aside and told her of her future husband.

"It will not be for a while yet," I hastened to inform her, seeing the dawning panic on her face. I was relieved as I watched it subside. "But I want you to know, so you can prepare yourself." I smiled at her and put a hand on her slim shoulder. The frailness of her tiny frame hurt my heart just a little. How could Henry speak so easily, so carelessly, about sending creatures as light and small as my daughters out into the world to be taken in by other people? My youngest daughter was only four. "But also, so you can take a moment in such times as these, and be sure to store memories of your family, to keep your heart warm when you rule your own lands."

My little girl thought a moment. "I would be a Queen. Like you, Maman?"

I smiled, seeing a little ambition in the eyes of my daughter was good. "You, daughter, will be a greater Queen than I."

She giggled. "That is not possible, Maman."

"I will show you how to believe it is not only possible," I said, "but inevitable."

Chapter Four

Caen

Normandy

1170

"I know the truth. Father will not make peace with Becket because he does not truly want me crowned," whined my eldest son, lounging at the window seat, wearing a stunning blue robe and a petulant expression. "He does not want me crowned, Maman, for he wants to hold all the power of our kingdom until death and crowning me would give me the same powers that Richard and Geoffrey already have in their lands."

Geoffrey complains about Henry, Henry about Geoffrey and Richard, the only one of my sons not complaining about the others is Richard, I thought.

Because he has the power from you which your husband denies to his other sons, said Petronilla.

I suppose I could have said John did not complain, but that was only because he was so young and still ensconced at Fontevraud.

I gazed steadily at young Henry. My eldest son, now fourteen, was a most beautiful creature, that could never be denied. Glorious to look upon he was. Sadly, that meant he got away with much that others not so fair would not have, even had they been princes. It is the way of things that we think that which is beautiful is good, is true, and is trustworthy, and frequently, despite all evidence to the contrary, people continue to hold this belief in their hearts.

Young Henry was, in form, the best of all I and Henry had to offer. His hair was golden red, his skin clear, his frame tall and his face so handsome he could cause men and women to stutter when they locked eyes with him. I exaggerate not, I had seen it with my own eyes. Others were struck quite dumb as he turned his manifest charms on them. Such beauty as he possessed, there was power in it, and he used it well. Many fell to his charms. Sadly, his father was not one of them.

My eldest son also had a great deal in him that was good and welcome too. He had courage when he called on it, cleverness when he thought to use it, and he could make any person his devoted disciple through his abundant charisma. He possessed natural grace, fluidity of movement and a smile that was like the magic one feels standing under the first glimmering rays of a winter sunrise, but it was also true that in youth he had been indulged. He had been taken from my care when still young and handed to Becket. Then, the provision of his own household too young, when my husband had snatched him out of Becket's guardianship, had led to young Henry being surrounded by those who were his social inferiors, and as such he always had got his way. At the same time, he had lacked a strong role model. Young Henry had indulged his whims and wants as head of this own household, and now, almost grown, my son was as full of vices as he was virtues. He was vain and extravagant, decadent and although he wished for power and kingship he shied from work and accountability as a bat does from sunlight. He wanted the crown for he had been promised it, yet at the same time did not fully understand the responsibility which came with its power.

But that, to my mind, could be put right by giving him what he wanted now. Young Henry was old enough to have learnt poor ways, true, but he was young enough that these vices could be largely drained from him before he came to rule alone. No king is perfect, after all, and I did not think I would get out all that was bad in him, but certainly some could be worked on. He also had William the Marshal as his guardian and tutor. Marshal had been a good influence, encouraging the best in young Henry and at least partially reducing the worst.

The trouble was, although my son's accusations about my husband and Becket were fanciful and a touch paranoid, I did in truth wonder if he had a point. My husband desired the status that crowning his heir in his lifetime as the French did would offer, but as I had thought many times in the past months, I did wonder if this coronation would lead to young Henry being treated more as an adult by his father. My husband might, in fact, start to consider our eldest son a serious threat if he was crowned, for young Henry would have an equal claim to the very throne his father sat upon, and even if he had been given that claim by his father, my husband was likely to start looking on him as a rival.

My husband had seen off a few rivals in his time. None were alive now.

"Your father, despite constant troubles with Becket, continues to try to make peace." I attempted to reason with the part of my son that possessed intelligence and sense. It was there, it was simply that one had to dig through layers of querulous arrogance first, something which I always thought he had picked it up from Becket. Young Henry's propensity to self-pity was, too, rather akin to the show Becket put on at times. Just how many ill traits had he inherited from his time in Becket's care? "Your father does want you crowned, my son, as I do. If your father were trying to avoid that ceremony, he would simply let the Archbishop go, to remain an exile. He would not continue on with the talks."

Young Henry swung his leg back and forth, that expression of petulance not gone from his face, and I thought suddenly how young he indeed seemed, much as his name defined him. Richard was two years younger yet far more mature than his elder brother.

"I hear your father is in fact to disregard Becket, since they cannot make peace," I went on. "He is to ask Roger de Pont l'Évêque, Archbishop of York, to preside over your crowning."

Young Henry stopped swinging his leg and stared at me. "But... would that be accepted?" he asked. "Would that be legal?"

"Your grandmother, the Empress Matilda, was crowned as the Holy Roman Empress in Rome by a cardinal rather than the Pope, for her husband and the Pope were warring at the time, and her coronation was accepted." I did not add that the cardinal in question was excommunicated afterwards. It would hardly aid my point.

"But would the people of England, and conservatives most of all, accept me as the Young King?"

I smiled, for at times, when my eldest demonstrated he had a canny mind, it was pleasing. "I believe so," I said. "And if not, there are ways to persuade them."

Henry smiled at my insinuation of violence, but he was busy thinking. "And Father would then offer me the power I wish for, such as Richard and Geoffrey already wield?"

Richard and Geoffrey did not have as much power as young Henry seemed to believe they had, but we are ever wont to see the lives of others as more favoured than our own.

"If you were crowned as the Young King, you would have to be recognised as the king in waiting." I smoothly sidestepped the issue at hand, or so I thought.

"By *Father*?"

I sighed. As I said, sometimes his mind was sharp as that sword he carried and only used in tournaments against his friends. "It would be a step on the way," I admitted. "Remember, Henry, you are to inherit more land than your brothers, and you will take on the crown of a king, not just a duke. Your titles will be greater and so will your power. Perhaps this is what makes your father hesitate, but, Henry, you must dedicate yourself to such a role and not just the pleasures of it."

A sigh of impatience came from his pretty lips. He had heard this criticism many times before, from his father. "Maman, what more am I to do with my time when Father offers me nothing to do? I play with my friends, yes, but in doing this I also nurture relationships with nobles, I am seen and loved by the people I will rule, I show that, were I tested in battle, I could perform better than all other men."

"William Marshal has taught you well," I concurred, for the knight I had sent to my son had indeed taught Henry much. Most of the better aspects of my son's character had, in truth, been nurtured by William. "You will make a fine knight and I have no doubt a good king, but your father must see more sides of you than the prince of pleasures you show him."

"Father sees what he wants to see." He leapt from the widow seat and came to me, a leopard could not have been more graceful. "You have always seen me clearer than he." He held my hands and as I stared into that beautiful face I smiled, understanding how all his many friends fell so deep in love with him. "I can be more than I am presently allowed to be, Maman, but Father will never see that. You must help me."

"You are my son." I touched his cheek. "Of course I will do all I can for you, and I agree, you know that, about your power and your crowning." I drew him to me and kissed his forehead. "Let us get you crowned, and when you are the Young King your father will have a harder time denying you the power, and responsibility you seek."

*

The custom of crowning the heir during the father's lifetime was indeed a French one, first brought about by the Emperor Charlemagne. It meant that the succession was safeguarded, for the heir already crowned would have a God-given right to the throne on which he sat, he would already have been anointed and sworn to his country and his barons would already be bound to obey him, so when the time came when he was to assume the throne, everything would be in place for a smooth succession.

"A smooth crowning is all I would wish for," I muttered to a letter, sent by Uncle Raoul. It did not hold good news.

It was the office of the Archbishop of Canterbury to crown the sovereign and although Henry had asked for the Archbishop of York to carry out the service instead, it seemed that Becket had heard of this and was greatly offended by the gross insult this afforded him. I know not how he found out, but Becket, as Head of the English Church, forbade both my husband and the Archbishop of York to go ahead with the coronation of young Henry on pain of excommunication. The Pope, who no doubt heard of this from Becket, also had sent word forbidding the ceremony.

This letter, or a succession of them, came after my husband had left Caen for England. Henry was determined to carry out the ceremony despite the ordinances of the Archbishop of Canterbury. Raoul's letter told me that the Pope's prohibition of the ceremony had arrived in the form of a letter to the Bishop of Worcester who was on the Continent at the time. My husband, in ignorance of the fact that the Bishop was carrying this command to stop the ceremony, ordered him to attend the coronation.

Something had to be done.

I closed all the Channel ports so that men working for Becket, or indeed Becket himself, could not get to England to stop the coronation, then I sent word that the Bishop of Worcester was to be forcibly detained in Dieppe. On my orders was he held so that he could not prevent the ceremony.

"Maman," Richard laughed. "Surely this is illegal?"

"When the time comes, I will deny having known it was illegal." I cast a look at my daughters. "Sometimes, the ignorance supposed to belong to women can work in our favour," I told them. "Men will suppose you to be foolish, so sometimes you may plead you knew not something was wrong or illegal, simply because you are a woman."

"Do we want them to think us foolish, Maman?" asked Eleanor. Little Joanna still looked baffled.

"Those who matter will know already you are not a fool. Those who do not matter will suppose you to be a fool in any case; you may as well gain something from their ignorance," I told her. Emma laughed a little.

"We should always have something in reserve, should we not, my lady?" Emma asked.

"Indeed so," I said. "Heed your aunt, my daughters, for she is wise in many matters, and this one especially."

In the meantime my husband, unhindered by everyone who was trying to stop him, had already set out upon the sea. On the 3rd of March, sailing into the mouth of a turbulent storm, he crossed from Barfleur to Portsmouth leaving me in charge of Normandy and our other dominions as he arranged the crowning of our son.

Once the bishops of England had agreed to crown young Henry, my husband summoned our son to England. On the 5th of June he set sail, escorted by the bishops of Sees and Bayonne. Upon young Henry's arrival in England, my husband knighted him in the presence of a great assembly of lords and prelates, a stepping stone on the way to his crowning.

"I am glad to hear it goes so well," said my daughter-in-law Marguerite of France. She did not in truth look pleased, as I read her the letter describing events in England.

"Your time will come," I told her. "And it will be less controversial than this moment."

She inclined her head, but I could see suspicion rising in her. It was not directed towards me but my husband, and I could understand why. It had been a surprise when Henry had ordered our daughter-in-law to remain in Caen with me rather than to go with her husband and be crowned at his side as Queen. My husband sent word that he thought crowning her now, in light of the papal prohibition of the ceremony, which officially Henry knew nothing of, might offend her father, King Louis, leading to another bout of war. Henry thought, in fact, that crowning her without the approval of the Holy Father might well offend Louis more than her not being crowned at all.

It was a risk either way, in truth, and Marguerite had been left behind. She had also been left with the notion that there might be another reason she was not being crowned. She and young Henry had not been bedded; they were still just a little too young. I believe suspicions that her father-in-law might seek to replace her as his son's Queen might have galloped through her mind when the command came for her to stay behind.

"My husband will have my son crowned a second time and you with him," I said to Marguerite.

"If you say so, my lady."

"You doubt my word?"

She smiled, a sad smile. "I never doubt *your* word, my lady."

I comprehended her meaning perfectly. "Even if my husband does not keep his promise, your husband will. Young Henry adores you; I can see it in him."

She shrugged. "We barely meet, I do not know what he feels for me."

"That is a good thing, the not meeting much before marriage. To be a little acquainted is a good thing, but you have the rest of your lives to be together. It is good to have time to be alone, to be you, now. In time, your husband will take up much of your life, your children too. Men, and women also, they tire of the one they are always with. There are exceptions to this rule, of course, but they are the most fortunate of people. That you are apart allows your husband to see your virtues more, and you his." I took her chin in my hands, drew her eyes to mine. "You will have all the time in the world to grow tired and weary of each other later in life," I teased, and she chuckled. "Then you will look back and wish for this time, now and here, where you thought of him so often and he of you, because you were apart and not always in each other's lives so much you grow sick of one another."

She laughed again and kissed my cheek. "I wish I had known my mother more," she said. "But I am glad I was given to you, my lady."

"You *are* my daughter for you are wed to my son," I told her. "So, though you lost one mother, know you always have another in me." I touched her face again with affection. She was a beauty, this little girl of twelve. My husband wanted her and young Henry bedded, but I wanted to put it off for a while. I thought her too young, though I knew at twelve girls were considered women. Marguerite was small of frame and hip. It would do her no good to try bearing children so young, it could kill her. I thought of my daughters, who would go to other courts to be raised by other women who would prepare them for marriage to their own sons, and I hoped those other women would take the same care of my daughters as I did for the children of other women granted to me.

"Let us go and find your sister," I said. Little Alys, eight years old then, had been sent to my court to be raised alongside her sister, in preparation for marrying Richard. "She will cheer you."

"She always does."

Alys, in truth, could cheer all people. She was a merry little thing, with a quick but never unkind tongue. She never had had freedom to use such a thing in Francia, and certainly not near her father, but women and girls of wit and poetry, of cleverness were encouraged in my lands to use all they were freely given by God. If Alys was to wed Richard, she had to be an ideal duchess of Aquitaine, nurturing wit in her court, inspiring the songs of troubadours, and encouraging other women to do the same. I already had high hopes she was to turn out just as I wanted.

"We have come seeking you so you may cheer your sister," I told Alys as we came to the schoolroom. The time for lessons was long passed, but she was often still there after the others had fled, reading. She loved books and she loved to learn.

"Why does my sister need cheering, Your Majesty?" Always she was respectful. I think, in truth, she was glad to be at my court.

"She is sad that her coronation will not occur now."

Alys looked shocked, but then she grinned. "But, sister, just think, if yours takes place now you always would be in the shadow of your husband and would not be seen, but if later, then even if the Young King has been crowned, everyone would know the ceremony was in truth all yours."

We laughed.

"Come and see this book of tales I have, sister, and you will not be sad anymore," said Alys. "For in here there are stories of deeds so powerful they may make you forget all else." She looked up at me and smiled. "The Empress Matilda is in here, my lady."

I nodded. I had, many times, told them tales of Matilda. She had taken on a divine element in their eyes. "Will you tell us of how she escaped Oxford again, my lady?" Marguerite asked.

"And then, my lady, tell us again of how you escaped the men trying to capture you, on the road home when you left France," said Alys. "I like that tale even more."

"You would not have liked it had you been there," I noted.

"I do not doubt you, my lady, but because I was not there and because I know it turned out well, I do like it."

I laughed again. When I looked on this little girl, with her clever eyes, quick tongue and pretty skin, I was glad she was to be Richard's wife. She was worthy of him, of my people. It was the highest compliment I could pay, but Alys deserved it. I thought she would have a glorious future as the Duchess of Aquitaine.

Sometimes we can become tortured by a hope of the past, when someone intervenes with fate, and makes it so what we thought would come to pass never does.

Chapter Five

Caen, Normandy and

Poitiers, Poitou

1170

On the 14th of June, a Sunday, my child Henry became the Young King. My oldest living son was crowned King of England in Westminster Abbey by Archbishop Roger of York with six bishops assisting him. The succession was assured, the heir named and crowned, but from what I heard from England my fears about my husband had been justified. The Old King had no intention of handing any of his power over to the Young King.

"You make him resent and even hate you, Henry," I spoke to the pages of a letter which came soon after the coronation from Richard de Lucy, the Justiciar, who I often had worked with. The pages told of the coronation, and an event during the feast afterwards which troubled many.

Although the Young King had already exhibited a measure of contempt for his father as well as distrust in private, my son made this most obvious at his coronation banquet in Westminster Hall. The Old King had insisted on acting as a server to his son in order to highlight the importance of his new status. My husband carried a boar's head on a platter to the high table where young Henry sat with the Archbishop of York. As he came to this table my husband jested, "It is surely unusual to see a king wait upon table."

"Not every Prince can be served at table by a king," agreed the Archbishop.

"Certainly, it can be no condescension for the son of a *count* to serve the son of a king," my son replied.

Although de Lucy did not record the response of my husband, I cannot imagine it was a temperate one.

As I travelled back to Poitiers to put on a similar ceremony for Richard, I heard that many people were offended and angered by the coronation ceremony. It was not just my husband's anger about young Henry's words, insulting his heritage, many were up in arms about the event. The Pope and Archbishop Becket were referring to the crowning as "this last outrage" and other people were speaking with fear, claiming that my husband had set England upon a path to war. King Louis was offended that his daughter had not been crowned, so perhaps cared more in truth for worldly power and prestige than papal approval.

"But it is done now, and none can undo it," I said to myself as I rode along the path to the gates of Poitiers with my men.

When I arrived, there was already a letter from Henry waiting, clearly both written and carried in haste. Breaking the red seal of the King, I opened it and found commands. I was instructed to send word to Louis that young Henry and Marguerite would be crowned together at some future date. Duly, and that very hour, I did indeed sit down to write an assurance to my former husband on behalf of my present one, and oddly, not long after, I had a polite reply in which Louis informed me he would trust in my word, though he would not in the word of many others.

It was so similar to what Marguerite had told me that I could only think in her letters to her father, which she was of course permitted and encouraged to send, she had said something of our conversation. Most of her letters were read when they went out, a necessary evil. Louis already had spies in my court, and I hardly wanted to grant him more ways to steal information, but I did not remember reading anything of this sort in any letter she had sent. "It could be Alys," I said aloud. I had not taken much time to read her letters, since she was younger and greener than her sister, but perhaps I would have to start paying more attention.

After his coronation my son the Young King had been assigned his own household in England, still under the control of his guardian William the Marshal but also under the governance of tutors and other legal advisors. Henry was fifteen, an age which most people considered adult, yet he was not able to be the head of his own household and was not being given the power which his father had promised him once he was crowned. I had not liked to say to our eldest son that the promises of his father were often forgotten as soon as they left his lips. He had already realised this in any case. If one paid enough attention to my husband, to his words, one would hear the vagueness of the promises he made. Quite often people supposed he had sworn to offer them all they wanted or needed but listen close to the words he used, and Henry swore nothing of the kind. Were it not so annoying a trait, I might have admired it. Were it not used against me and my children, I might have lauded it as a worthy skill of a cunning king.

I suppose many of us excuse evils if they are not directed at us, even more so if they benefit us.

"In absence of power, your eldest son again pursues pleasure," my uncle Raoul told me. "I hear he keeps a splendid court where he dispenses lavish hospitality and lives beyond his means, which most people might think a thing impossible for the son of a king, yet young Henry proves it is not."

"Any amount of money can be spent," I said. "Even the largest pile can be frittered away."

"And he fritters well, my child. Your husband, hoping to curtail him, has actually granted your eldest son an allowance most meagre, but your son simply requests more from the Treasury, and he is victorious in many tournaments in jousting and the sword, and in winning, he gains the prize money."

"At least he is doing some training for combat." I was grasping at any reason to think well of my son.

"Indeed, but his nights are filled with drinking and women, so I hear. He is being wasted, my lady."

"I agree, but I have nothing to offer him here. My lands are for Richard to inherit, that was the agreement, and I have tried talking to his father, tried getting him to release something to young Henry, but he will not. My husband sees our son drinking and playing at war all day and thinks this is proof young Henry cannot rule for he is too immature, but the reason young Henry pursues such things is because he has nothing else to occupy him all day. They are stuck in a paradox, my husband and son, where until my son proves himself responsible my husband will hand him no power and my son cannot prove himself responsible because he has no opportunity to do so. I admit, I do not know how to solve this riddle."

Not long after, my husband, with the approval of the Pope, banned tournaments in England on the grounds that too many young knights were being killed. It was a move no doubt intended to punish my oldest son, and indeed it did. It took away the only thing young Henry was good at that he was allowed to do. Further he sank into bitterness and lowness of spirit.

"Many of the King's men are condemning the Young King," my uncle told me as we walked in the gardens one day.

"I understand, my son is doing much that would attract censure." I pulled at a strand of rosemary in my fingers, releasing the oily scent onto my skin. "But those who see only the bad, they do not look far enough into him. He has so much potential, and he is not the only one wasting it. His father is too. What is saddest for young Henry is that his father cannot see how much promise he has, and I do not believe anyone should ignore the pain within the heart of a son who knows his father has no faith in his abilities. It is a heavy cross for any man to bear, to know his father does not believe in him."

I glanced to the other side of the gardens, noting Richard strolling with Alys. I smiled briefly. I had told my son to spend time with his future wife, so they might know each other, become friends, long before they married. Although he had of course taken my command to heart, I could see by the look on his face that he was enjoying her company in truth. I had taken Alys under my wing of late, teaching her much that Dangerosa had taught me, and Alys was, without any outside aid, a witty, engaging girl. When they were older, they would make a fine couple and a great Duke and Duchess, I was sure of it.

Alys too looked pleased with Richard. She glanced at him often when he was looking another way at feasts or dances. She tried not to show how deeply her feeling ran, but I could see it. If things continued as they were, I thought they might become very much in love by the time they married.

Raoul sighed. "Your oldest son has many virtues, but his bad traits are being allowed to fester. He is gaining a name for being weak, idle, a reputation for untrustworthiness and being a man of a violent temper."

"He inherited that temper from his father," I said.

"I also hear he can be cruel much as his father can be."

I threw the rosemary to the ground, as if it were responsible for all these ills. "In truth what my eldest son is, uncle, is a restless young man. There are many of those in the world, and often they turn out to be fine men, good soldiers, lords and knights. If his father would only believe in him, take him under his wing as his true heir, I think England could have a great Henry III as its king."

Perhaps that was just what his father feared. To be outdone by the one who comes after you, it is an event most monarchs never live to see, of course, yet here, with his son panting to step up to the throne, my husband could live to see it, and could be outdone, outshone, in his own lifetime, by his own son. That could be dangerous.

Would others look on the Young King and want him to rule instead of the Old King? If my husband allowed young Henry power, would old Henry be forced to step aside, to stand to one side of events, looking on but unable to control them? Would he be forced to endure the shame of becoming impotent as a king, before he had even left life? I think all these potential horrors were in my husband's head, and to him they were horrors indeed. Henry was not accustomed to taking a lesser position; was this not indeed what he had battled Thomas Becket over for years now? He feared to surrender any part of his power in case it led to the loss of all. That was how he saw this, not a smooth transition of governance, which was the duty of any ruler, no. Henry saw this as a mountainside which has endured too much rain, and with the slip of one rock so the mighty mountain will fall.

I did not fear our children. At the same time as my eldest son was being crowned as the Young King of England I travelled south to Poitiers for the investiture of Richard, then twelve years old, as the Count of Poitou. It was a stepping stone across the waters which one day would lead him to the ducal throne of Aquitaine.

Much as the ceremony for Young Henry had made him heir to England and Normandy, so this one made Richard heir to my lands. This ceremony took place on the 31st of May in the Abbey of Saint Hillarie. Richard received from the Bishop of Poitiers and the Archbishop of Bordeaux the holy lance and standard of Saint Hillarie, patron saint of Poitiers. Then at Niort he was presented to the lords of Poitou as their future overlord, and they paid homage to him. Richard did well despite his youth, managing to keep constant on his face throughout the ceremony a grave expression, reflecting the magnitude and honour of the situation. I have no doubt it was not a mask worn for show but a true reflection of his feelings, for Richard seemed to understand the burden of power as well as the potential pleasures of it. There were banquets and dances to mark the occasion afterwards and it was as we were celebrating these that I had a most unexpected and most welcome visitor.

"Marie," I gasped as the young woman stood before me. People milling at the corners of the hall stopped in their quiet chatter and stared at this, the first petitioner brought to me that day. I had been handing out favours, granting requests, as had Richard, in honour of his investiture all that week.

Richard, at my side on a throne of his own, stopped for a moment too and stared at me, as did the young woman.

She blinked. She had been about to curtsey but froze. She had not been introduced to me formally as yet, so she was obviously unsure as to how I knew her name. Marie sank into a curtsey before me, but from my throne on the dais I rose immediately and went to her, putting my hands out to take hers and lift her up so she stood before me.

"My lady mother," she gaped at me, "how did you know it was me?"

"You think I would not recognise the first child born to me?" I asked. "You, who I held under my heart? You think I would not know my eldest daughter, my eldest child, amongst every other woman in the world when brought before me?"

In truth, I am not sure how or why I recognised that she was Marie Capet, Princess of France and Countess of Champagne, my eldest child, born to me from my marriage with Louis of France. She who I had called my miracle Marie and sang Ave Maria to in her cradle. She had been an infant still when Louis and I separated. I had never seen her grow into a woman, as she was now. Yet the moment I saw her I knew it was her.

Richard was gazing curiously at his older sister.

Tears sprang into the eyes of my daughter as I held her hands and I embraced her, kissing her on each cheek. "What fresh miracle is this, my miracle Marie, that you are brought here before me?"

"My father has asked if I might join your court a while, my lady."

She did not need to say more, and I smiled, understanding her instantly. To my smile, she offered a small blush. Louis might write that he trusted me where he would not trust others, but it was not entirely true. I had not expected him to trust me again so swiftly and it seemed he did not, for clearly his daughter, the Countess of Champagne, had been sent in order to spy, at least a little, on her mother and the goings-on of my court.

I could understand. Louis wanted his eldest daughter to check that one of his younger daughters, Marguerite, was to get the crown which my husband had promised her. Perhaps Louis thought he was being subtle by sending Marie to me, thought that I might be so overwhelmed by seeing my eldest daughter once more that I would not enquire as to why exactly she was there suddenly, with me. But I did not care that she had come as a spy, I did not care that she would write to her father. In truth, given the way that she was staring at me, with all the life and love of the world in her eyes, I did not think she would present me badly to her father in any case. Even if she did, Louis could not be persuaded to think any less of me by any person than he did already. And it was worth any risk of information leaking to France to have my daughter in my arms again.

"You have come at an auspicious time and must meet your brother who now is the Count of Poitou." I swept out an arm to Richard. Marie dropped to another curtsey.

"I am pleased beyond all imaginings, to see you at last, my lord," she said.

"Our mother has often spoken of you, and your sister, Alix." Richard came from the dais and kissed his sister. "I am honoured to meet you at last."

"I am sure your half-sisters, Alys and Marguerite, will be pleased to see you too," I said.

"I will be pleased to see them again, and those I have not met. I have followed the births and doings of all my siblings since first they came into the world," Marie told me. "I would dearly love to meet every single one of my siblings."

There was indeed a hunger in her eyes, born of a kind of loneliness we all share, the loneliness of being born into this world. However supported we may be, however much family we possess, we always do stand alone. Love, I often have thought, is a way to bind us to others to ensure the survival of the body, the blood, and so we might, for a while, ignore the aching thought that we always, and ever, are alone in these shells of flesh into which our minds are born.

"I have followed all your doings all your life," I told my daughter, "you must never think that leaving you and your sister was not the hardest thing I ever had to do in my life, I still dream at night of the time I said goodbye, asking you to take care of Alix and of yourself."

"I understand why you had to leave, Maman." Marie clutched my fingers. "I did not at the time, I cried often and every night, but there are many things I have come to understand since I have become grown."

I was sure she had. Her husband was no easy man to live with, I was sure. He had caused untold trouble for my husband, joining often with our enemies. She had pleased him by bearing a son, Henry, named for his father, however, and I understood he trusted her much now, even allowing her the freedom to support art and music. His court was famed for sophistication, being a gathering place for poets and writers, and Marie was at the centre of much of this. Her husband was eventually called Henry 'the Liberal' because of his court of culture, but in truth a great deal of the credit for the refinement of that court should have gone to his wife.

However much freedom she had, though, Marie looked indeed as if she understood why I had left her father, and that meant a wish must have occurred about leaving her husband at some point, futile though it might be. Louis had betrothed her as a child, when she had been unable to protest, but there was something in her now that would have protested, if it had a chance of being heard. I could see it in her eyes. She had been married when she was nineteen. That, at least, I could thank Louis for, that he had insisted she be a woman grown before she went to her husband's bed. Louis had not, of course, done the same for me but men tend to be more protective of their daughters' entrance to the wedding bed, rather than their wives. Alix had been less fortunate too. She had been fourteen when she married into Blois.

"I wish I had been there to see you grow," I said, holding her hands as if I never meant to let go, "but had I stayed there would have been nothing of me left."

"You may not have seen me grow up, Maman, but you can see me now, a woman grown and a friend returned."

Tears welled up in my eyes too and I pulled her to me again. "Come then," I said, "let me introduce you to your brothers and sisters. And you must tell me too, of your son, little Henry, my grandson! What a thing that is to think of, that I have a grandson alive in the world. Did you bring a likeness of him? And your poetry, I hear grand things about all the ideas you infuse the troubadours with in your lands, so they write the stories you tell to them and set them to music and bring them here and..."

Marie laughed, pulling my arm closer. "Maman." It made my heart almost break to hear her call me the same name as my other children did. "You must choose one thing for me to speak on first, for I cannot tell you all at once. Only one mouth do I have!"

We laughed, excusing ourselves to Richard, who I left to take care of the petitioners – it was a good thing for him to do this alone in any case – and we made for the gardens where my other children were, some of them at least, along with Marie's half-sisters.

For weeks Marie and I did not stop talking. There was a great deal of life to be caught up on, a great deal we had missed, and by the end of that first month, the end of long mornings where we came to each other's rooms to sit by the fire or window, or walk in the gardens arm in arm, I knew that even if she had been sent to spy by her father, she was now more mine than she ever would be his.

My other children adored her too, Richard and Geoffrey in particular. Whenever Geoffrey was at my court it was Marie he sought. He loved her tales of the French Court, and she offered him a kind of attention I think he was lacking, for when Marie was in conversation with another person, they had all her attention. There was no one else in the chamber. In a world so often indifferent, it was a powerful virtue to possess, and Geoffrey loved to be the centre of attention. Often, he was a little overlooked. I will admit I was at fault in that respect. It was hard to grant equal attention to so many children. Richard had to be my first priority, and the troubles between the Young King and his father often came next to my mind. My daughters were being promised in marriage, so I was trying to train them as wives and queens, and the business of my lands took up a great deal of time, so I admit, Geoffrey, already betrothed and with a land of his own promised to him, often was not the centre of my attention. I was glad, therefore, that he had his sister now, and that they were so close.

And every day I was glad and gave thanks to God, for something I had asked long ago finally had come true; that I might one day get to see my children again. I had wished this, but never expected it to come true.

Sometimes life is kinder than we expect it to be.

Chapter Six

Poitiers, Poitou and

Falaise, Normandy

1170

A little after Marie first came to court, I visited Fontevraud to give thanks for the restoration of my daughter to my life. It was not something I took for granted. Most royal parents, when they sent their children away to be wed to another country, would never see them again. I had been given this chance to know my daughter.

There is always much for us to complain about if we choose to, and it is a choice to complain about our lot in life. It is not a requirement, as some people seem to think. But there is another choice and that is to try to weather the storms we are granted without constantly bemoaning them, and to take a moment and thank God for the good times whenever they occur. Marie was one of those times, something to thank God for, something to rejoice in and however long or short our time together was, I would treasure it.

She was a swift favourite with all my other children. Perhaps I had primed them all too well over the years, for I had spoken often of my children of my first marriage to those of my second. They were already prepared to love her and welcome her as their elder sister long before she arrived at our court. Emma too took to Marie at once, and they spent many an hour walking in the gardens together, talking of music and writing. It was a pleasure to see them, graceful women arm in arm, their minds afire and tongues busy sharing everything they knew. Little made me happier than to see such a thing. At times I could almost see ghosts of Petronilla and me, walking beside them in the same manner.

At Fontevraud I put my seal to a gift made to the chapter by one of the King's stewards. Whenever this was done Richard would be present too as a witness, or would add his seal, as much my heir as young Henry was my husband's. More so, in truth, for Richard did more in the art of ruling than poor young Henry was permitted to. I journeyed to Falaise after, where I was joined by my husband who had returned from England that summer to the Continent. I found him in a stupor of outrage.

"What is wrong?" Having just that moment entered the room I nonetheless could see he was in high dudgeon about something. Months could pass, years even, and I could read Henry of England like a book left open with but one easy word printed on the page, and more often than not that word would be "anger".

"The Bishop of Worcester is a knave!" he shouted.

When finally I had the story I wanted to laugh. On the way to Falaise Henry had managed to meet with the Bishop of Worcester, he whom I had detained at Dieppe, and, not knowing I was the one who had sent the order to detain him, Henry embarked upon an argument with the man, denouncing him as a traitor for not coming to the coronation of young Henry. As the argument went on the Bishop had unveiled that it was in fact me as well as the Justiciar who had had him detained, and that was why he had not attended. Henry refused to believe him, thinking this but a way for him to escape from accusations of treachery.

Bishop Roger, despite his irritation at me, gave an answer which I much welcomed. "I do not cite the Queen, for either her respect or fear of you will make her conceal the truth so that your anger at me will be increased, or if she confessed the truth your indignation will fall upon that noble lady. Better that I should lose a leg than that she should hear one harsh word from you."

"The man was indeed telling only truth. I detained him," I told my husband after he had trotted out the tale entire, expecting me to deny it. "I am rather impressed that despite me being the reason he was held back, he sought to defend me."

"So, it was you?" He stared at me with wild eyes. "You were the reason he did not appear in England when I explicitly commanded him to be present?"

"Bishop Roger was carrying an express, written order from the Pope, forbidding the coronation," I explained. "I detained him and prevented his going to England so that he could not give that order to you, or the bishops who were to crown our son. Since you knew nothing of what I did, you cannot be held guilty for the holding of the bishop and since, officially at least, you did not know the Pope had forbidden the ceremony on pain of excommunication, you cannot be blamed for it going ahead. I will take the blame for this, and do penance if the Pope demands, but either way, we have managed to crown our son and you cannot be held accountable for going against the Pope."

Henry paused for a moment, pondering my words, then he laughed. "I thought Bishop Roger a simple traitor for not attending the coronation," he said. "But now I find he is a complex one, for he meant to put a stop to our plans, and now our plans have gone ahead he seeks to protect the very woman who foiled his plans and those of this master."

"The Bishop understands I was acting as a natural mother, concerned with protecting my child." I smoothed my gown, rumpled from the ride to Falaise. "And in the few times we have met, I have always had the impression he respected me."

"I begin to think him a little in love with you," said Henry.

I shrugged. "Even if he was, what harm would it do us? It would be a benefit, perhaps."

Henry nodded. "You do have a habit of making men fall in love with you."

I rolled my eyes. "I do nothing, and they do not love me, husband. They know me not a whit, and care for me not at all. If such men harbour any emotion for me, it is because they see a vision of something they believe they want or need, and I become melded with that vision. It is a dream, nothing more."

"A useful dream," he said.

"Men's fantasies often are useful, to the one who knows how to manipulate them."

"The Pope has sent another order insisting that Becket and I make up our quarrel," Henry suddenly blurted out, starting to scowl. I thought how he resembled an aggravated hog, one who has lost all the truffles to another.

He was starting to look a little portly, and there were more lines on his forehead than ever I had seen before. Years of riding under the hot sun on campaign was starting to make his face look like wrinkled leather, and years of quarrel with Becket too had done little to aid this appearance of aging. There was a crease between his eyes, just where Richard's was when he was concentrating on something, and even, as my son's was, it was a little wonky. The one on Henry's forehead had been created solely by Becket, I was sure.

"The Pope demonstrates wisdom in this matter. Surely it is time, husband," I said, "this argument, if it goes on for any longer, will be the longest one that ever man had with another man. Men laugh about it, you know, tittering at you and Becket and your inability to make peace like adult men. Rather than us all look like fools, perhaps it is time to simply send the troublesome tick back home to Canterbury. I hear from many people that the man is not well and looked entirely gaunt at your last meeting. Perhaps you will not have to wait long until you can appoint a successor to Becket, one more malleable."

I can barely describe the look that crossed his face then; there was savage joy at the thought of Becket's death, as there was sorrow so deep the oceans of the world could not fill its gaping maw. In that moment I knew there was still love there, from Henry's heart reaching for Becket's, still that man was his friend in certain, hidden parts of his soul, yet at the same time there was a part of Henry that wanted the Archbishop dead. I could see it.

"I have responded to the Pope and told him that I am ready to make peace," said Henry. "It was not me making trouble the last time, after all, and King Louis and Rotrou of Warwick, Archbishop of Rouen, have offered their services in mediating."

"If one of them could simply tell Becket to keep his mouth closed, all would be well." I smiled. Henry burst out laughing.

"I could take a bung and stop his mouth as one would a flask of wine," he said.

"Perhaps what you should try doing, my lord," I gathered all the patience I had, "is to remind the Archbishop of your old friendship and love for one another and rather than going again over the arguments which have kept you at war, to dismiss those arguments, agree they never will be resolved between the two of you, and start peace anew."

"A fresh start," mused Henry. "I like the idea."

Of course, many of us like ideas we are entirely incapable of seeing through, but at least he was willing to entertain it. The truth was, Henry had a vengeful temper. People disobeying him led to great fear in his heart. Henry had always relied on having the last word and here he might not have it.

As a king he might have seemed like the most secure man in any room, yet he was only too aware that a throne is a chair, like any other. Take an axe to it, and firewood it becomes.

He might well pretend to make up with Becket, but it was unlikely that the friendship would ever be mended in Henry's heart. There were too many wounds there to sew up.

Chapter Seven

Falaise

Normandy

1170

King and Archbishop met on the 22nd of July at Fréteval, where the Archbishop of Rouen and King Louis acted as mediators. Taking my advice, Henry put his arms about his once friend and declared, "My Lord Archbishop, let us go back to our old love for each other and let us each do all the good he can to the other and forget utterly the hatred that has gone before."

Admitting that he had wronged the Church over the matter of his son's coronation, Henry asked Becket to return to Canterbury and re-crown young Henry, this time with Queen Marguerite at his side.

Becket, to everyone's astonishment, agreed.

The Constitutions of Clarendon were not mentioned, and the King and Archbishop retired from the meeting with everybody breathing a sigh of relief, for it seemed they had entirely reconciled. Henry had not however given Becket the kiss of peace. He promised he would do so after Becket had returned to England.

After the meeting Henry fell extremely ill at Domfront with a tertian fever.

"My lady, you must prepare yourself," the messenger said to me in a grave tone, "it is thought the King may die."

"Prepare myself?" I shook my head. "Go to the stables and tell them to *prepare* my horse. That is what shall be prepared here, good master!"

The shocked man scampered away to do my bidding. Within an hour I was on the road with a party of knights for protection. Prepare myself? What did that little milksop think I was about to do when my husband and King was at death's door, sit and wait for an opportune moment to faint in my chamber?

Not one for swooning, I rode out to my husband. Though there was not between us anymore the great love that I had once hoped might come from our relationship, I did not want him to be alone at such a time. They say when men die on the battlefield that the one person they cry out for is their mother. I could not offer Henry his mother to comfort him as he faced death, but I could offer myself, the mother of his children. I would not have him die alone. That is truly why men call out for their mother when they are mortally wounded on the field of war, because their mother saw them into this world. In a moment of darkness and confusion and pain she was the one who was there with them. As they die, men want once more the feminine presence at their side to guide them in this moment of utmost darkness. I could be that for my husband.

It was of course also important that I be there in the event that Henry did die, and we needed to set young Henry up as King.

In the event however when I arrived at Domfront, Henry was already past the crisis point of his fever. "We wrapped him in blankets, Majesty, and set him before the fire," a monk told me, "his fever was entirely perilous, but we took a risk, and we decided it was one worth taking in order to save the King's life."

"You broke his fever with more fever," I touched my husband's skin, slick and unpleasant, "it was a risk indeed, but it appears to have worked." I put a hand to Henry's forehead and, while still warm and clammy, it was not burning with a raging fire that I had been told was within him previously. When he woke two days later, I was at his bedside.

"I dreamed that you were here." He fumbled for my hand. "Lenor... my Lenor."

"It was not a dream," I said, setting my hand into his. "I am here, I was here. I did not want you to be alone."

"I think I was always alone," he said, sounding drunk as he tumbled into slumber again. "Until I found you."

I watched him fall asleep, touched for a moment by his sentiments, yet I knew well enough that this moment of truth was fleeting and brief. When he woke and recovered his strength, he would go back to his old ways, keeping me and all others at bay so we could not get close enough to harm him. It was the way Henry was, the way he had survived all these years as King. The only person who had been truly close to him was his mother, perhaps his father too, but they had died and left him. Perhaps that only redoubled his unwillingness to be close to anyone else.

To Henry, to love people was to have a weakness. His mother, his father, Becket, his brothers, all these people he had loved, and some had left, and some had betrayed him. That was why he had never let me in, why he treated our sons and daughters as he did, as pawns rather than people. He was afraid to lose power, certainly, but even more so was he afraid to allow himself to love. That meant he was always alone, more so than so many others who risk their hearts. When this sickness was over and he forgot his need for me, pushed it down into his stomach once more so it could not hurt his heart, he would go back to his mistress, and I would go back to my children.

That was the way it was and no matter how sad it made me at times, or regretful at others, I could not change him. We cannot ever change other people. They are as they are. Nothing we say or do will alter them. We can change ourselves, but others, never. Sometimes we are fortunate, and they take heed and change themselves, but more often than not they do not. People have their own paths, we only join them for a brief while as our paths intersect.

I set Henry's hand down on the bed, and pressed my fingertips into my eyes, feeling the flesh there burn. If Henry was not to die, there was other work to be getting on with. When he woke, I wanted much to be in order for him, so he did not exhaust himself in trying to catch up on the affairs of the realm.

Into his chambers I walked and called his pages to me. "Bring me the missives and commands he was working on before he became ill," I told them. "And any men in the castle who know what the King was working on, I need them too."

They ran off, more than pleased to be helping me. Within a week, we had the empire running smoother once more.

*

It was the end of September before Henry was recovered fully and, deciding to give thanks for his recovery and being snatched from the arms of death, he went on a pilgrimage, taking me with him to the shrine of Rocamadour in Quercy. We came through Aquitaine where Henry spent time attending to administrative business that had fallen to one side during my absence and his illness, and we dealt with local disputes such as sending in his troops to deal with an unpopular provost at the town of Souterrain.

"I am thinking of retracting the betrothal between our daughter Eleanor and the son of Frederick Barbarossa," Henry said one day as we rode side by side. I had been admiring the flowers on the wayside, fluttering in a happy breeze.

I inclined my head. Relations between my husband and the Emperor had been cooling for some time. "Do you have a different bridegroom in mind?" I knew that when he said he was thinking of doing something, it was as good as done. Henry rarely hesitated and even if Prince Frederick knew it not yet, he had lost a bride.

He did of course have someone in mind, a man who was much closer to Eleanor in age. He intended now to give our daughter to the twelve-year-old King Alfonso VIII of Castile. "I would like her to have Gascony as her dowry," Henry said to me.

I blinked in surprise, had to restrain myself from slapping his face. This was what Henry did; it was being coaxed into a trap, talking to him at times. He would lull you into a place of friendship, use your affection for him, get you to welcome part of his plan – the part he knew you would welcome – then he would spring the last on you, the part he had been preparing for all the time the conversation had been going on. I had fallen for it, again.

"That land is promised to Richard." My tone was stiff as a corpse.

"And for now he would indeed rule it," Henry agreed, "but in order to make our daughter a queen she will require a greater dowry than she presently has. I would propose that Eleanor would receive Gascony as her dowry, but only upon the death of the present Duchess of Aquitaine."

"How gracious of you," I snarled, "not to give away my lands until my death."

"You seem a hale woman, my love," Henry grinned, "and whilst you were living, Gascony would not be handed to another king, so Richard could continue to rule it."

"Richard will not warm to this," I warned him, "and I do not either for eventually my lands of Gascony would belong to another Kingdom and not to the lord I had chosen in order to watch over my people. You should take care, husband, in so lightly giving away lands which you have already promised to your sons. You will cause men, and women, to think your promises are flighty things which have no weight behind them."

"Those lands are in truth mine until my death." An edge of metal was entering his voice. Tell Henry not to do something and he would, just out of vindictiveness. "And I can do to my lands what I will."

"You can of course do with your lands, *my* lands, as you will. They are yours as overlord. You can do as you will with land, just as you can do with your children and with your wife, too. You can promise one thing and do another, swear to uphold our rights and then ignore them. You *can* do as you wish, that is your right as King, but what comes to be nurtured for you in the hearts of others is something you cannot control, and the more you disregard the feelings and wishes of those who follow you, of those who always have supported you, the more alone you will become. If men cannot trust their King, trouble comes."

"You seek to threaten me?"

My voice was harsh as a sandstorm. "I try to warn you. You little know your sons. Too often in their lives you have washed in when you wanted something of them and then flowed back out again. Your sons are growing, my lord, and all of them are full of ambition, all of them you have made promises to. Be wary about what you choose to do to them now, for all men have long memories when it comes to matters they resent."

"Our sons love me," he said.

"At the moment that might be true," I said. "But will it always be true if they learn they cannot trust you? Will it always be true if you show no concern for them and only for your own self? And a man should not rely on love alone. You did that once before, with Becket, and love did not save your friendship, did it?"

Henry kicked his horse and rode ahead, his face thunderous. I sighed. In truth I had no doubt that eventually Henry, because he did not want to lose any land, would find a way to snatch Gascony back from Eleanor's proposed husband – just another broken promise to add to all the others – but all the same I could see this idea was going to cause trouble. He had done this before, changing who was to inherit what.

Henry did not see, could not seem to understand, why lands promised to our sons *had* to be promises that were kept. He thought that because those lands belonged to him now, that he could chop and change any time he wished, carving out this land for Geoffrey or that for young Henry, or swapping those lands with the ones Richard held, but our sons were old enough that they were starting to find their homes in the world, the people they wished to rule, the places they felt like lords.

To have that sense of stability always threatened by the notion their father might snatch those lands out of their hands at any moment and hand them all to another brother, leaving them with nothing to call their own, would make any man feel insecure, frightened and angry, and that is the most dangerous kind of man.

And we had four sons, all about to become men in truth.

*

That October Henry finally issued a formal safe conduct for Thomas Becket to return to Canterbury and resume his duties as Archbishop. He wrote also to young Henry in England to confirm that the Archbishop's return had his approval and said that he and Becket had made peace in accordance with his wishes. He ordered our son to see to it that Becket and his followers would have all their possessions in peace and with honour. Not long after this my husband and Becket met at Chaumont near Amboise, to confirm their agreement of peace, and it was there that Becket made an extraordinary statement.

"God speed," said Henry, and went on to say he soon would follow, and be in England too.

"My Lord," said the Archbishop, "my mind tells me that I will never again see you in this life."

Henry was affronted, supposing Becket was implying that Henry's intentions were treacherous. "Do you think I am a traitor?" Henry asked, frowning.

"God forbid, my Lord," said Becket.

"What in God's name do you think the man meant?" Henry asked me later.

"Perhaps he thinks you less a traitor than he believes himself to be," I said.

"You think he is going to wage another battle in this war against me once he reaches England?" Henry's face was turning red with rage again.

"I think it entirely possible," I replied. "I see not what else he could mean. He spoke of his own death, surely, and not yours. I think there may be a reason he has made peace so easily this time. Everyone was surprised, were they not, by how malleable the intractable man had suddenly become? Either Becket thinks himself sick unto death and that is why he might not see you again, or he is returning to England to begin another stage of his attack upon you, and thinks he will die in this last attempt."

"God's eyebrows, I wish that would come to pass." Henry stormed from the chamber, slamming the door so hard I thought it might leap from its hinges.

*

On the 1st of December Becket set foot once more on English soil when his ship landed at Sandwich. Once he was on English soil some overzealous port officials tried to seize him in the name of the King. They released him as they saw the seal of the King upon the safe conduct issued for Becket.

He rode to Canterbury where people lined the streets, cheering and crying out his name, welcoming back their beloved Archbishop. Becket had made himself popular with the people of Canterbury in his short time there. When he wished to charm, he had an abundance of it to use on people.

His welcome was not entirely warm however, for several royal officers made it clear that they were not happy about it and young Henry, who once had called Becket his second father, refused to receive him at his court at Woodstock. The Archbishop had brought horses, fine chargers, to give as a gift to my son, but hearing Becket had left Canterbury to see him, young Henry sent men to stop him on the road. They told the Archbishop to return, take his gift with him and not leave his city again.

Becket admitted himself baffled and confused, but I do not think he could have been so lost. He thought my son would welcome him with open arms, since they had once been close, but young Henry was more than aware that Becket wanted to use him against his father. He also had another, more personal, reason. Becket had refused to crown my son, and young Henry had a temper like his father's, one full of resentment.

My son was correct not to take his gifts, for Becket had already decided that rather than make peace he would continue his war.

Before he had even sailed, so we later learned, he had dispatched a messenger to England, sending word to the bishops who had conducted young Henry's coronation that they were suspended from duties, pending possible excommunication. His war became public on Christmas Day that year. From his pulpit at Canterbury Cathedral the Archbishop publicly denounced the bishops and published his sentence of excommunication upon them.

On the 30th of December he confirmed this by sending a messenger to deliver letters which excommunicated the bishops. The Pope had given him these letters but had told him they were for an emergency only, meaning if Becket was attacked then he could use them to strike back. Becket thought it best to come out fighting, rather than to defend.

Becket wanted to win against the King and punish those who had disobeyed him. The bishops, however, had left upon receiving their very first letters, and were already on their way to Normandy to see the King and protest. They might even have crossed Becket on the water as they sailed in opposite directions.

When Henry heard, there was no ancient God nor imp of the Devil who could match my husband in his furious rage.

Chapter Eight

Bures, Normandy and

Poitiers, Poitou

Christmas 1170 – New Year 1171

We were at my husband's hunting lodge at Bures in northern Normandy when rumours came of the bishops and Becket. Full news arrived with the bishops themselves, as they descended upon court on Christmas Day.

It had been a fine Christmas until that time, the dark halls of the hunting lodge alive with the sound of laughter and music, each night we had watched mummers and performers. "When I was a child," I had told my children as we watched well-paid tumblers from Egypt make an elegant, arching tower from their bodies, "and my sister and I were growing up, we would tell each other tales that we had run away from our ducal palace in Aquitaine and become as travellers on the road, preforming for a few coins so we could feed ourselves that night, sleeping under the stars." I smiled as they chuckled.

"You never would have enjoyed such a life, Maman, you are too fond of your bed!" Richard teased.

I smiled. "It is true, I do love that bed." It was a most comfortable one, with a soft mattress of hay and one of goose down too. Warm hangings surrounded it and I had it taken apart and transported to every castle or palace I stayed in, but that was not unusual for royalty. Beds were highly expensive pieces of furniture, and as such were prized possessions. "But when I was younger, many a time I slept in tents and on beds far less comfortable. On Crusade we all did, sometimes upon the ground, and the ground at times then, it was frozen."

"Tell us of Crusade," one of my children, usually a son would beg, and I would tell them. I was not kind about our feeble second crusade and I spared nothing of detail in the battles. If they wanted to know what it was like, then they should have an honest picture of it. Too many settled for heroic lies. One day my sons would be old enough to take the Cross, my daughters to become pilgrims, and if they did, I could not stop them. I did not want them marching off as I, as Louis, and as so many men and women no more with us had done, thinking we were marching to glory. The crusades, any wars, were so full of dust, bones, blood and entrails that there was little space left for glory.

So, the season had passed with tales and company and joy, since most of us were together, but then came the bishops, carrying news of Becket and his fresh wave of war on the King of England.

Almost all our family were present that year, Richard, Geoffrey, Joanna, Eleanor and John as well as Constance, Marie and Alys. Young Henry was holding his own Christmas court at Winchester that year along with his wife. He had no doubt heard the news before we had.

The bishops of London, York and Salisbury arrived at court and immediately altered the mood of my husband from joviality into blind rage. He had been sitting back, enjoying yet another goblet of wine – he had already had more than I dared count – his belly bulging bigger with every cup he took, and then they came into the hall. Explaining that even before he reached Canterbury, Becket had issued the sentence of excommunication upon the bishops, they secured Henry's worst fears within his mind and proved my suspicions of Becket's curious words to Henry before he had left.

"So, he did mean to cross you again, my lord husband," I said.

Henry glanced at me. "You were right, again." He sounded rather irritated at me too; for being astute? I knew not. "I should never have trusted that devil, nor allowed him back into my kingdom! God's Blood! Will he ever rest in his vengeance against me? Am I to be hounded all my days by that priest?"

"My lord King, while Thomas Becket lives you will not have peace or quiet or see good days," declared one of the King's barons, his cheeks hot and outraged. Henry nodded, those blue eyes as frozen fire, for he was too furious and indignant by that point to be able to form words.

Had that lasted we might not have had the trouble that we had, but eventually words found the tongue of my husband and were let loose. "A curse!" he screamed, "a curse on all the false varlets and traitors I have nursed and promoted in my household who let their lord be mocked with such shameful contempt by a lowborn priest!"

We knew it not, but that night, men listened and, hearing the words of their King and thinking it their task to rid him of that priest, four knights of Henry's household left quietly in the night and made haste to England. Their names would be whispered by history: Reginald Fitzurse; William de Tracy – who was Becket's former chancellor; Hugh de Morville – who had served the King in the north as a justice since his ascension – and Richard de Brito.

When Henry noted they had gone the next morning he realised with some alarm what they had in mind before any of the rest of us did. At the time I knew not why he was so disturbed. Henry sent messengers to summon them back, but they had already taken ship and sailed to England.

"Why are you so concerned?" I asked Henry later that same day as he paced back and forth in his rooms. He was never a still man, but I could not remember the last time I saw him so agitated. "You think they will do something to Becket in your name?"

He did not answer but walked to a window, staring out into the darkness through the translucent ox horn pane.

Something dawned in my mind. "What have you said to them, before that meeting in the hall, to make you think they would do such a thing?" Suspicion was growing, like a scared cat it arched in my mind. "What have you been saying to your men in private about Becket?"

"I have said nothing," he said.

I did not believe him, his voice was too quiet, and his eyes which would not meet mine told me he had said something, something he now had time to regret. Henry had a habit of speaking wild when annoyed, and Becket had made him furious on more than one occasion. I feared then, and feared rightly, that it was not only that one night, those few words, which had caused those men to take up arms and sail to England, but many more words spoke on many more occasions.

What had been said? More curses from a king about men who would not aid him in getting rid of an enemy? Promises perhaps, if a man could humble Becket for him? More than one of the men who had left had loved Will, Henry's brother. They had been his companions. The whole court had adored Will, of course, but these men had been close to him, beloved friends. More than one person about court blamed Becket for Will's death, saying that Will had pined to death for love of a woman who Becket would not let him wed. Had Henry spoken of that too? How many reasons had he given men to fear and hate Becket? What had he said when deep in his cups, about this once friend?

"Incautious man," I said in a whisper as I left my husband. "What have you done?"

Soon enough we heard.

It was the afternoon of the 29th of December when the four knights who had escaped our court went to Becket in his study at Canterbury and made various wild accusations against him. They threatened him with punishment if he did not leave England.

"Stop your threats and stop your brawling," Becket shouted at them. "I have not come back to flee again."

Indeed, he had not, but neither had they. The knights withdrew into the courtyard, angry, muttering against the Archbishop. They put on their armour. There were plenty of witnesses as to what happened next.

That evening as monks went in procession into the cathedral for vespers, the four knights followed them, walking fast. As the Archbishop entered the church the monks stopped their celebration of vespers and ran to him, fearing what the knights might do. The knights were already advancing upon the Archbishop. Monks hastened to action, bolting the doors to the church to try to protect their Archbishop. Becket however, perhaps understanding that this was his moment of true glory even if it was also a moment of mortal peril, ordered the church doors to be opened. He said, "It is not meet to make a fortress of the house of prayer, the Church of Christ."

When I heard that, I knew. He had already determined that he would die that night and meant not to go quietly. History would ring with the sound of his voice. The pages of the records of the world would be writ with his blood. That was how he saw it.

Perhaps he was right, considering what happened after, but personally I think what he did was commit an elaborate suicide. Only those who live long enough may write their own stories, those who die have no more control over the quills of men. Becket thought he was writing himself into history, and perhaps he was, but never again would he be able to speak for himself. Others would put their last word into his mouth.

I doubt that would have pleased him. He always had plenty to say.

As soon as the doors were opened the knights entered, swords drawn in contravention of the law that no man was supposed to bear a naked sword within a church of God. Already the others present understood what their aim was and started to shout in horror. Crowds that gathered were frozen with fright, all except Becket, who stood composed at his altar. He must have understood that they meant to kill him but perhaps he welcomed death, knowing how much trouble his life had been. I came to think also that he was ill, just as Richard had said more than a year ago. I believe Becket knew he had not much time left in any case. If he was to leave life, should he retreat into death with a whimper, or go out in a blaze of saintly glory? The man had always chosen grandeur in life, so why not in death?

I believe he knew that in dying, in becoming a martyr such as he was sure to become if they cut him down in his own church, he could finally best Henry, for who is the greater? An archbishop and a king matched upon the earth, or a king upon the earth and a saint in heaven? The King had made Becket his equal, and now Becket was to raise himself only higher.

"Where is Thomas Becket, traitor to the King and realm?" cried one of the knights.

"I am here, no traitor to the King but a priest," replied Becket, "why do you seek me? I am ready to suffer in His name who redeemed me by His blood." As he said this he turned away and began to pray. The knights closed upon him.

"Absolve and restore to communion those whom you have excommunicated," they commanded him, but Becket refused.

"Then you shall die!" one of them shouted.

Becket, to the amazement of all he stood before, remained utterly calm. "I am ready to die for my Lord, that in my blood the Church may find liberty and peace."

They sought to grab him, pulling and dragging him so they might kill him outside of the church, thereby saving their souls.

"Touch me not, Reginald," Becket shouted at Fitzurse, "you and your accomplices act like madmen!"

Perhaps Becket would have helped his own cause had he not also called one of them a pimp. They ceased trying to drag him outside. I think they cared not for their souls by that point, rage had blinded the four men too far. Even in facing death, Becket was not humble. It enraged them.

Fitzurse lifted his sword and Becket fell into prayer, lifting his hands and commending his cause and that of the Church to God, Saint Mary and the blessed martyr Saint Denis. Fitzurse swept his sword down, slicing the skin from the top of Becket's head. As the sword descended a man named Edward Grimm sprang to the Archbishop's defence, but it did not work. The blade nearly severed his arm. Seeing blood bright upon the ground, the other monks fled but Grimm remained by the Archbishop's side, using his uninjured arm to attempt to support his master.

Becket was still on his feet when the knight struck again, a second sword swipe to the head which astoundingly also failed to knock the Archbishop down. A third blow managed what the first two could not. Becket fell onto his knees and elbows, muttering, "For the name of Jesus and the protection of the Church I am ready to embrace death."

This was a good thing, for death was coming and his pace was fast.

As Becket lay on the ground Richard de Brito inflicted a mortal wound. His sword broke against the floor. The blow was so vicious, the crown was separated from Becket's head. Blood and brain slopped from the open top of Becket's head, spilling upon the floor of the cathedral, heaping in pools of puddled, warm gore.

Hugh de Morville had been preventing monks from returning into the church as his companions murdered the Archbishop. A man who had aided them, a subdeacon named Hugh Mauclerc – although I always wondered if this name had been given to him after the murder for it seemed too fitting otherwise – came before the Archbishop and put his foot on the neck of Becket. He extracted the blood and brains from the hollow of the severed crown of Becket's head with the point of his sword and scattered the gore on the pavement. Perhaps he was in wonder at the deed, or perhaps he simply wanted to ensure Becket was never coming back.

He called out the others, "Let us away, knights, for he will rise no more."

In so many ways, he was wrong. Dead the Archbishop might have been, but in death he would ascend higher than life.

Thomas Becket, Archbishop of Canterbury, former Chancellor, ambassador, warrior and negotiator, and once the greatest friend of the King of England was dead, yet it was Henry, King of England who had lost this final battle. And he knew it. The moment he heard of the murder, Henry knew he had lost not only a friend, but this war. One cannot beat a martyr. Now the Church had one, they would use Becket against him for the rest of his life.

"What have you done?" I asked my husband, my voice barely more than a murmur.

Blank eyes turned up to me, or seemingly blank. He looked stupefied, but I knew it was an act.

In the centre, in the darkest part of his pupil I saw not blankness nor sorrow, but a flame which had a long time burnt, of rage.

Chapter Nine

Bures, northern Normandy, and

Poitiers, Poitou

1171

"Do you not see that it was your temper, your incautious, foolish words which led to this?" I shouted at Henry. I had to shout; he did not seem to hear anyone.

It was a few days after the news had come of Becket's grisly murder. Since we heard, Henry had been denying he gave the order to kill Becket, either on the night the knights had left or on any other. The mention of *any other night* made me think he had indeed said something just as I had thought, perhaps not a direct order but something close enough, and this had led those men to believe their King would be more than pleased if Becket were dead. Henry was not a man to go against, not a king any man would dare disobey without some serious consideration. These men would not have simply taken it upon themselves to go and murder a man so prominent, so powerful, no. Henry had said something. I believed he had given an order, perhaps when angry, probably when deep in his cups.

That was why he knew immediately what those men had gone to do, because at some point he had told them to do it.

At first, Henry had just sat there as the grisly tale was told. He looked as if his soul had absented his body. Arnulf, the Bishop of Lisieux had in fact touched my arm and whispered to me that he thought the King might be suffering a fit of apoplexy. This was proved not so a moment later when Henry had burst into loud lamentations and started to take off his royal robes, tearing them from his body as he wailed and wept, which made men about him think that he had fallen to insanity.

When he exchanged those robes for sackcloth and called for ashes which he rubbed upon his face, I knew it was a feint. It was all too much to be real grief. Real grief is not so overdone, especially not at first. Grief is shock and silence, not this wild, theatrical performance Henry was engaging in. I had seen widows wailing at funerals, of course, there is a time when grief and sorrow become most noisy, but not in the first moment. Henry had been expecting this, he knew Becket was dead the moment those knights left. He had planned how he would react so he might appear innocent.

It was important no one saw his true feelings. There was a part of Henry which was overjoyed at the news Becket was dead. He might even have desired the brutality of Becket's death, seeing it as justified because of all the trouble the man had given him.

I felt a little nauseous, thinking of this. Henry did not care, I realised, what we would face, as his family, due to this event. He had thought only of himself in this matter, whenever and wherever he had given those orders. Not of us. Not of how this would stain his children, his daughters, his sons, me. No, us he had not thought of.

For days after, he had easily fallen into a stupor, after which he would again recover only to utter groans and cries louder and louder and more vehement than before. For three whole days he remained shut in his chamber and would accept neither food nor water nor admit anyone within to comfort him. People were soon saying that he would die from the excesses of his grief, or that he meant to bring death upon himself by these actions. In consequence, men started to fear that we would lose the life of the King, which was, I had no doubt, Henry's aim from the beginning. He wanted to convince the world he had wanted this not, and to stun them with his sorrow. He wanted people to pity him, and to believe him innocent.

I believed none of it.

Oh, I had no doubt he mourned his friend. There had been moments aplenty when I had realised that Becket meant more a great deal more to Henry than I ever would, or our children, or possibly even his mother who had been the closest person to him in his life. There had been a friendship deep and irrevocable between them and when that friendship had been betrayed there was instead a loathing deep and irrevocable between them. All of these things Henry would grieve about his friend, but this act was put on for the court, for the Pope and for every man who might challenge him now, in the name of the Church, and it *was* an act, make no mistake about it, it was performed because he realised how deep and heavy was the accusation of guilt for this crime that would fall upon him.

Upon *him*. This was all about saving him and his reputation, not us. We were already tainted by association. Even my grandfather and father, no friends of the Church, had never gone so far as this.

He had brought the wrath of the Church, of the people, the possibility of invasion from other lords and lands upon not only himself but me and his children, all to rid himself of a man he could not vanquish by honest means.

Henry was not alone in 'grief'. When my son, the Young King, heard, he was taken by sorrow, yet not so taken that he could not add a hasty, poor remark. "What a pity it is," he declared, talking of the Archbishop's death. "Yet I am glad it was kept secret from me, and that no liege man of mine was involved in this."

Insensitive though his comments were, it was clear my son also thought this a plot of his father's.

For my part, I had no reason to grieve Becket save one. The man had never liked me, and little had I ever warmed to him. This was no death of a friend or man I respected and might grieve for in that way, no. This man had been nothing but trouble for my marriage, my husband and my children, my country too, since we had first met. I could not conjure a single thing I would miss about him and could only think on his passing from life with relief, though I admit, no one deserved the way he had died. Yet I had reason to grieve, for this death would be used by all, every enemy and even possible friend against not only Henry but me, our children and our hopes, and it would never go away. The floor of the cathedral was already wiped clean of the blood of the martyr by common people dipping their cloths into it, using the blood and gore to cleanse wounds and bring about miracles of healing, but the stain upon us, on our bloodline, that would never be wiped clean.

All because at best my husband had not learnt to control his tongue, and at worst because he had ordered this, and cast a curse upon all of us.

I left the next day for Poitiers, and I made sure all knew I was going. I took my children with me. Anything I could do to minimise their association with this crime I would do. If distance might make people understand we stood not by the King in this, his moment of shame, then distance I would use.

I was livid with Henry, a rage beyond all anger ever I had experienced was upon me as a fever. He was a liability to all of us, not something which made us safe but something which added to the insecurity of this already unstable world for us.

Perhaps the true reason I was so furious however, was because I was angered at myself. For many years, though we had fallen from love, I had supported Henry in his schemes, even knowing that when he made promises he did not keep them, knowing that he would swear much to our children only to retract it as soon as it was of advantage to him.

I was almost certain that we had all been brought to him for that Christmas so he might present another face to the world when this scandal broke, the family man, the good husband whose wife and children were at his side. Perhaps he had known what Becket was about to do to the bishops. Perhaps he was already preparing for his next move in their war when he had commanded us to come as a family to him.

I had been a pawn to him, so had my children.

Why had I managed to marry a thoughtless child each time I was wed? The first time the man had been older than me, yet a child Louis was and still remained, and this time, wedding a lord younger than me yet one versed in ruling and warcraft I had thought I would marry a man, yet again there was a child hidden underneath.

And I was done with that child, done being a dressing pressed to the wounds he made in our empire, in our family, in our marriage. Over and over I was forced to absorb all the harm he did, but no more.

"No more," I muttered as we rode into my lands, an oath. "No more, Henry, will you use us as you wish."

Chapter Ten

Poitiers

Poitou

1171

"The news is everywhere," my uncle Raoul told me.

I nodded, closing my eyes. I had known it would not take long, of course, but the speed at which the ill news had travelled had surprised even me. Bad news is like that, it has a swift foot which the fastest destrier would envy. Good news is a slow, lumbering beast. No one cares about passing on the good news of this world, not when the bad is so delightfully shocking.

And this was the greatest scandal for decades, generations perhaps. The highest man of the Church in England was dead, murdered, by men acting for the King of England. The layman had slain the spiritual man, it was an event of Biblical importance.

"Some even have declared it the worst crime since the crucifixion of Christ," my uncle went on, taking off his cap to smooth his hair, now almost all white, back from his brow. I glanced up at him, since he seemed to have read my mind. That was how people would speak of this, was it not? Henry was as good as Pilate.

I wondered if, in time, men would find a way to blame me for this. Oftentimes it had happened. Louis' disastrous command on the second crusade had often been blamed on me. Perhaps as Herod's wife asked for the head of John the Baptist so I would be found in rumour, begging my husband to send knights to cut Becket's head open. *Curse you, Becket,* I thought, *and curse you, Henry!*

"I wonder if Christ would agree this is the worst crime since he was slain." My tone was waspish.

"I would be careful, niece, about expressing any word thought sacrilegious, even in private." Raoul poured a hefty measure of wine, clearly as much for bolstering his ragged spirits as quenching thirst, and drank deep. "The world is watching you all now, just waiting for another slip."

"I would hardly call what my husband has done a slip, uncle."

"All the same, you must take care not to be tarred by the same brush."

"It is too late for that." I threw my hands in the air. "Guilt by association. We are all painted red with Becket's blood, by Henry's hand."

"William, the Archbishop of Sens, has asserted that this surpasses the wickedness of Nero, the cruelty of Herod, the perfidy of Julian, and the treachery of Judas, and King Louis has written to the Pope."

"You are doing nothing to comfort me, uncle. Do you know what he has written to the Pope?"

"I am not here to comfort but to counsel, and indeed, my men tell me your former husband has been quite outspoken in what he has written to the Holy Father. In fact, niece, he has said that 'such unprecedented cruelty demands unprecedented retribution so let the sword of Saint Peter be unleashed to avenge the martyr of Canterbury'." My uncle paused. "Your husband has managed to set the entirety of Christendom against him with this one act."

It was true enough. Henry was loathed throughout the kingdoms which followed the word of Christ, his reputation had been dashed upon the floor much as the head of the Archbishop had been, and just as the brains and blood of the Archbishop had flowed out, spilling upon the floor in an ungodly mess of gore, so the honour of my husband lay in tatters too.

"What I want to prevent is the entirety of Christendom being set against my children with this one act," I said.

"It is said that already there are miracles taking place about the body and blood of the Archbishop," continued Raoul.

"Of course there are. In no time at all they will have made him a saint." I did not doubt my words even though they were spoken in cynicism. If there was anyone less godly I could imagine than Thomas Becket they were few and far apart but that is how martyrs are made, is it not? By reputation. By tale and story they are created, made by others. It matters not what they were actually like.

Whilst I took my children away in the hope that I might manage to salvage something of their reputations even if Henry had destroyed his, Henry remained in seclusion and there he stayed for six weeks, refusing to attend to any business or take any exercise or indulge in any activity other than wailing and moaning. The Archbishop of Rouen was eventually summoned in despair, by men hoping to bring the King from the brink of death. In his presence the King had called upon God to witness for the sake of his soul that, "the evil deed had not been committed by his will nor with his knowledge nor by his plan." Henry submitted himself to the judgement of the Church and with apparent humility promised to undertake whatever it should decide as penance. People were amazed at his self-effacement. I was not.

"What other choice does he have?" I said when I heard.

"None," my uncle answered. "This is the only way to be forgiven, and to stop every lord and prince and king coming for his lands."

"His people might rise against him too," Richard added. "Many could take this as an excuse for rebellion."

We had already reinforced the garrisons we had stationed in our lands. That, as well as distance from Henry, had been one of my primary aims in coming home. "I want reports on all our measures to prevent uprisings in the south," I said to Richard. "Send out messengers tomorrow."

"I shall get them to observe and listen too in markets and squares," he told me. "If there is whisper of rebellion, we might hear of it soon."

Through all that was going on with Henry, through all of my intense disappointment and rage with my husband, I felt a surge of love, respect and pride in my son. I put my hand on his shoulder. "You will be a great lord," I said. "No, let me change that. You *are* a great lord."

Richard smiled. "I had a good teacher, in the lady who ruled before me."

"I am not gone yet, my son."

"Something I am grateful for. I would not have you go ever, Maman. There is much I know I am still in ignorance of."

"I will be here for as long as you have need of me," I said. "But it is a wise man who knows he has much yet to learn. Fools think they know everything."

Henry sent envoys to the Pope to protest that he had never wanted Becket's death nor ever had commanded it, but Pope Alexander refused to speak to those envoys for a week. They were forced to hang about the halls of the Pope's court waiting for a moment to have an audience whilst all other ambassadors there shunned them. The Pope placed all of Henry's dominions under an interdict which was nevertheless soon lifted, and the Pope began to behave towards Henry with an excess of moderation which many found surprising.

For my part I did not. I had no doubt the Pope was delighted. The Holy Father had long wanted the King of England obedient, no more trying to oust the Church from power in England, and now here Henry was, under the Pope's papal boot for he was the only one who could deliver absolution for this crime. Becket had delivered the life-long obedience of the King of England into the hands of the Pope. No doubt the Holy Father lauded the blessed brains of the murdered Archbishop every night. But of course, a show had to be put on. Gloating in public might make people think the Pope was just another man, full of vices like the rest of us.

For some months the Pope apparently deliberated as to whether to excommunicate Henry as most of Europe expected him to do, or whether to extend the interdict upon all of England but in the meantime the Pope merely forbade the King to venture onto consecrated ground until he had been absolved of his guilt.

Young Henry, still at Winchester, announced that he "has better control over my men than my father does over his."

"Can no man in this family learn when to keep his mouth closed?" I asked no one, one day in my chamber. Richard, who was standing near me came to me, took my hand, and said nothing, making me smile for the first time in weeks. "I speak not of you," I said.

He continued to say nothing but embraced me.

On Easter day that year the Pope finally excommunicated the four knights who had undertaken the murder of Becket, calling them "those satellites of Satan". For one whole year they remained in Knaresborough Castle in Yorkshire fearing reprisals that might come upon them. There were no reprisals, which led many to believe as I did, that Henry had ordered them to kill Becket. Later some of them would make for the Holy Lands to take a pilgrimage and to fight in the Crusades for which they received absolution. One, Hugh de Morville, was eventually restored to royal favour. William de Tracey, however, went on pilgrimage but died before he could reach Jerusalem.

And by that Easter more people were claiming that miracles were taking place at the tomb of Thomas Becket in Canterbury. His blood had cured the blind and his brain matter had been brought to cripples, causing them to walk again. To stand near his tomb was to feel the hand of God upon one's heart, so people said.

"That man is looking upon us now from wherever he is in God's afterlife," I said to Emma, "and by God, how he is laughing at us all."

Chapter Eleven

Poitiers

Poitou

1171

That year my youngest son John was to turn five years old and despite the fact that it might have gone well with the Church to dedicate a son to them at that time, Henry decided he had changed his mind.

He had received an envoy, Benedict, the Abbot of Chiusa, who came from Count Humbert of Maurienne with an offer. Humbert ruled over a wide expanse of land but was not wealthy and had no son to succeed him so was seeking a son-in-law to rule when death came for him. He had a daughter and was willing that his line be carried on in blood, if not in name. The Abbot came to my husband and offered the hand of the Count's eldest daughter Alice to John, the only one of our sons as yet un-betrothed or already wed. It was a chance to grab more land, and this Henry would not pass up without consideration at least.

This offer meant John would in time inherit domains all his own and our family would control the western Alpine passes, both good things, yet I heard of these negotiations through my uncle rather than from my husband. Much as when he had offered my daughters to men without consulting me, Henry did not think he needed to inform me that he had altered our youngest son's destiny. His children were his property, not mine, that was how he thought.

Perhaps that was part of the problem in truth. When we cease to see people as people, as living, breathing entities with thoughts and hearts, emotion and opinions, it is easier to do with them as we will, but never will we be close to people we treat like that. Perhaps in seeing his children as possessions to be haggled back and forth for his own greater advantage, Henry was rendered blind to the distance growing between him and them, all of them.

John was not taken away from Fontevraud whilst the negotiations continued however, as my husband wished to make sure that he was getting the better deal by releasing John into the world rather than keeping him back and offering him to the Church.

"It seems curious your husband would not offer John to the Church, especially now. It might appease the Pope," Raoul said.

"I doubt the Pope is displeased about anything at the moment, he probably is having trouble not skipping about the Vatican, laughing," I told him. "He was growing tired of Becket, as anyone would, all the constant griping and whining and endless refusal to make peace was making the Pope's job only harder, and the Holy Father wanted the King of England to stop trying to restrict the powers of the Church in England. Now, with Becket dead and the King's soul in the Pope's hands, the Holy Father has the best of both worlds. I cannot imagine he could be happier with the way things have turned out."

Raoul arched an eyebrow, snowy white upon his brow. "You make it sound as if the Pope might have engineered this death."

"It is possible. Were it not for the theatrics Henry put on, I might think it was so."

That summer the Pope sent two cardinals to hear Henry's side of the story of Becket's death and to discuss with him terms of his penance, so that he might receive absolution, but Henry, fearing they had come to excommunicate him, did not meet with them. Instead, on the 6th of August he sailed for England, having decided that this would be a good time to begin his long-delayed conquest of Ireland, a land granted to him by Pope Adrian IV in 1155, and the very same conquest which his mother as well as the rest of us had told him was foolish and unnecessary. Now the Pope wanted to talk to him, this conquest had become entirely necessary, apparently. On the 16th of October he set sail from Milford Haven with a large army, landed the next day at Watford and rode north into Dublin where he established headquarters for the winter. Hiding there from the Pope, whilst apparently fulfilling the wishes of another Pope, my husband remained in Ireland throughout the winter, isolated by tempestuous weather. He did not emerge until the spring of the next year. It was hardly his finest moment.

"Of all things I have thought your husband, timid was never one of them," Raoul told me.

"I like it not," said Richard, "Father looks like a coward on top of being a murderer."

"He makes a tactical retreat." I hoped this was indeed the truth, and at the same time was not quite sure why I was defending Henry at all. "Space and time will allow tempers to cool so that when the matter of Becket's murderer is next raised people will be more temperate. He also evades the Pope's men to show them that even now he can still bargain over his penance, he can still exact some control over his empire. It is, in a way, a show of courage."

"An odd one. I would stand and talk to these men, not hide on an island pretending to be a warrior and leader," sniffed my son. "He is doing little to conquer Ireland and all tongues everywhere are talking of his timorousness."

"My son, you would not have spoken without caution and caused the death of the Archbishop in the first place." It was true enough. Richard had the same hot temper as his father, it was true, but he was a man of few words, and all words he spoke were necessary ones. He was not given to share his emotions with any but a few trusted people either. The unbounded carelessness of his father was not in him. Richard was colder, more precise, an arrow shot on a winter's day into the frozen skies. Henry was heat and fire and impulse unrestrained, as a fire burning in a dry forest.

If he was hoping for an easy time, however, Henry did not get one. The Irish were not enamoured of Henry coming to their lands and were resentful of his distribution of various lands surrounding Dublin to his followers. Henry had no quiet winter hiding away, for all the time he was there the Irish people remained in a constant state of rebellion against him. Henry seemed somewhat surprised by this, having perhaps thought that they might welcome him as their lord and master, but Henry was always a man who, if he did not understand people well, understood how to wage war perfectly. He imposed his power over a vast swathe of Ireland through violence, and in another bid to regain the Pope's favour he instituted reforms of the Church in Ireland, bringing it into line with those of Rome.

And that December we heard of more miracles occurring at the tomb of Thomas Becket. People were already claiming the man was a saint.

"It would have made you happy," I said to his ghost. "In death, Thomas, you have become all-powerful, as always you wanted."

Somewhere distant, over the snowy fields before me, I thought I heard a laugh, of triumph.

Chapter Twelve

Aquitaine and

Poitou

1172

It was not until April of that year that Henry returned from Ireland, and when he returned, he learned that the legates sent from the Pope the year before were still waiting. I suppose he thought he might be safe by that time, but as he learned they were ready to make a reasonable settlement for his penance, Henry became convinced this had come about because of the delay in his return. It was not. They had been quite prepared to be reasonable from the very beginning.

Henry returned to Normandy in high spirits in May with young Henry in tow, as well as Marguerite. Ten days later at Avranches Cathedral, having already declared yet another oath to God that he had neither wished for nor ordered Becket's murder but at the same time admitted that he *had* in anger spoken words that had led to the four knights going forth to avenge him, Henry was absolved by the Archbishop of Rouen of complicity in the murder of Becket and was formerly reconciled with the Church.

They were not quite done with him, however. Penance in various forms was demanded, and after this ceremony Henry was stripped of his outer garments and clad in a hair shirt. The King was brought out to kneel on the pavement outside the cathedral, where he was flogged by monks as young Henry and the legates watched. The legates wept but my son did not shed a tear. I imagine he might well have enjoyed the spectacle.

After this the King was to make reparation for his sins, one of the conditions of absolution, which required him to restore to the See of Canterbury all the possessions he had confiscated and to make amends to those who had suffered at the King's hands as a result of defending or championing Becket. Henry was also required to take the Cross for three years against the infidel. The Pope however excused him from this obligation at present in return for a promise to found three religious houses, and Henry kept this promise, establishing a Carthusian house at Witham in Somerset as well as re-founding Amesbury Abbey as a cell of Fontevraud and re-founding and greatly enlarging Waltham Abbey in Essex.

"The Pope makes much of all he is given," I said to Emma when I heard. "The Church grows richer and richer through Henry, feeding from his need to be forgiven."

"And there is much to be forgiven," she replied in a quiet voice. The events of Becket's death had shocked her a great deal, as they had many people, but Emma had always looked up to her half-brother. It seemed that time might have come to an end.

I sighed a little. It was as when my father had tried to defy the Church, he had failed, and they had grown only stronger. The Church fought few battles itself. Oh, it had knights and orders dedicated to it, but they were as the military arm and used only on those who worshipped other gods than ours. But just because we did not see the Pope leading armies out as kings did, this did not mean the Church did not fight, did not conquer. It did it in a different way, by manipulation, by words and threats and promises and politics, and because enough people believed the word of the Church was synonymous with the word of God. They had power enough to bring a king to his knees, could cause him to be whipped in public, could extract what they wanted from him. What king could do that to another king? The Church was a fearsome opponent, truly, and those who did not understand this learnt later, often fatally, and always to their peril. It was far better to be pragmatic about the Church, accept it as a necessary evil and move on. And yes, I did mean evil. God, Mary, Jesus and most of the saints, they were good, but the institution representing them on Earth was not always so.

If only men would cease to think of the Church as godly and appreciate it was just as worldly, just as vicious and blood-soaked as the rest of the world's rulers, they would understand its power better. The Church was not an institution of purity or piety, but power, pure and simple.

"Your husband is also required to do a public penance in Canterbury at some future date which was not mentioned and also is to renounce any laws that he has introduced which are detrimental to the Church," Raoul said, reading from a letter sent by my son, the Young King.

"They mean, of course, the Constitutions of Clarendon." I was sure that was what all of this had been about, and this was why when I said Becket had won, I meant it truly. In death Becket had served his last master better than all the others, had given the Pope the power and means to subdue the King of England in all ways, a power the Holy Father never would have had had Becket remained alive.

"It is said your husband, however, has reserved to the Crown the right to protect its interests if it is threatened by the processes of the Church," said Raoul, "and in this he shows himself to indeed be Becket's friend, perhaps his apprentice, for was it not Becket's endless refrain that he could not go against the honour of God? Now your husband protests he cannot go against the honour of the Crown. He has learned the power of such a clause."

"I wonder sometimes if my husband has any good ideas that are his own," I said ponderously, "quite often his own ideas, such as when he first decided he was to march into Ireland or when he decided to war with Toulouse, were foolish ones, born of malice or avarice. Many of the decisions which he is most lauded for in fact came from his mother, or from Becket or me, and now he steals again from his dead friend so that he might always protect the power of the Crown." I shrugged. "I care little, most of the time. What I am pleased about is that this sentence falls on him alone. His people have not been punished and our family not included in this. Most view the King as having acted alone. I have not even been mentioned as a source of blame for Becket's death, which is a situation almost unique. Usually, I am the first one blamed when a husband of mine or a son does something untoward."

"Your efforts to distance yourself from the situation seem to have worked well." My uncle rubbed his chin. He needed to shave. "You did it in time, and with haste, so others did not associate you or your children with this crime."

"We will always be associated with it," I said. "In the future, when my sons are grown, when they make a mistake, as all leaders will, this action of their father's will be brought out and thrown at them, to see if the mud will stick to them. They will never escape it, just as I did not escape the affair of my grandfather and Dangerosa following me, causing men to question my morals and my virtue. People stare into the past, looking for a reason for the events of the present, seeking a course for the future, and because we like patterns, for they make life simple, we will find them. Of course we will. Look close enough and there are patterns everywhere, and so people will say one event was fated because of another, because of the blood within a man, the bones which hold him upright, the father and mother that made him, but the truth is the past is only as powerful as we make it. We grant power to many a thing through belief. If we believed just as hard in the power to be something other than what our past thinks we should be, our destiny would not be fixed, but ever changeable and always able to be changed, by us."

"Then you can alter this destiny you think you are bound to," Raoul pointed out.

"Perhaps," I said. "But I would need to alter the way the whole world thinks on it, not just the way I think of it. If we could leave Henry behind now, all of us, we would stand a greater chance, but I am bound to him for life, by marriage, by our shared children, and those children will always have a bond to him, no matter how much he ignores it, which he often does unless he needs something of them."

"Do you have any affection left for him?"

"None, uncle. We both were given a field to tend, to sow seeds in and water, but one of us neglected our duties and the other could not keep the field going alone, nor did they want to. So, the field has fallen to waste, and weeds and bracken grow there now. I cannot waste more time on it, so I plant my own field, and I will see it flourish where our shared one died."

"That sounds lonely, Lenor."

I chuckled. "Does it? There is an odd truth to be learned in life, uncle; sometimes it feels lonelier to be with someone than it does to be alone."

"I would be named Duke of Aquitaine," Richard said to me.

"Your father has replied to my letter," I said. This idea, to name Richard Duke in my lifetime was similar to that of crowning young Henry. I had written to the present Duke of Aquitaine, for we could hardly have Richard start to use the title without his permission, and Henry had agreed that our son be named Duke. It was, however, pointed out that Richard would be under my supervision, and the lands he ruled would remain his father's. Richard would become the young Duke; his father however remained his overlord.

Richard was fifteen, eager to be released into the fullness of his inheritance, eager to rule, and yet he could not, not fully.

Geoffrey, although younger, was already ruling nominally in Brittany, although I had heard many whispers that this land so much smaller than the portions ascribed to his elder brothers might not satisfy him for long. Like Richard, young Henry was chomping at the bit to be allowed to be King in more than just name, yet his father still did not seem willing to give up any of his power. For my part, I could do something for Richard, but young Henry I could do little for, for I could not convince my husband to give up one part of his empire, England, Normandy or Maine perhaps, that young Henry might rule it. But my lands were still mine and therefore I could move Richard into a position in which he was formally recognised as my heir and also as my co-ruler whilst I was alive.

"There are things we can do," I said. "Things of tradition and custom which will mark you as my co-ruler and indeed the next ruler, in the eyes of the people. Your father might try to maintain all control, but if the people believe you to be their ruler, then you will be."

I considered Richard old enough to exercise power in Aquitaine. I had been thirteen when I became Duchess. He was two years older than that and had been trained far more intensively that I ever had. My father had done all he could, but I, being more aware of all the dangers for a young ruler than my father had been, had done better. I say this not out of arrogance. I am sure, had my father met Richard he would have agreed that my training had been superior.

I did not mean, of course, to relinquish all my authority to my son, but his position needed to be formalised so the two of us could rule together. If anything happened to me, he needed to be already prepared to step smoothly into my place and my people needed to be ready to accept him. I was satisfied of his intelligence and also because of the fact that he still came to me for advice, so I knew he was not about to attempt to go above me as I elevated him. My husband had no such trust in our eldest son however and kept young Henry firmly in place.

On the 11th of June that year, Richard, wearing a silk tunic and gold coronet entered the Abbey of Saint Martial in Limoges and was invested with the ring of Saint Valerie. Valerie had been a Roman martyr and was the city's patron saint. Investing him with her ring was as a form of marriage, binding the Duke of Aquitaine to the saint, to the city, and to the country.

And there he was proclaimed Duke of Aquitaine.

It was an old ceremony which I revived to emphasise the continuity of our ancient ducal line, and I decided it should take place in Limoges for a reason. We had had trouble in that area not only because of rebellion by restless lords but also, and mainly, I thought, because of Henry's oppressive rule. The people there had suffered more under his hand than many in other parts of our empire. This ceremony honoured them by creating the next Duke in their lands. It would give them a future with a lord who would not treat them so brutally as Henry had, or only if it was deserved. Richard was their Duke, part of their blood, part of their past as he was their future. After the investiture and Richard's symbolic marriage to the saint there was a banquet held, the like of which had not been seen in the city for many years. People danced all night in the streets enjoying the largesse which flowed from our house.

I gazed upon my son proudly that night. Richard was tall and although he was shooting upwards faster than the sun rises in summer, he had never seemed gangly. One day he would stand six foot five inches tall, a giant of a man, yet he was ever graceful of figure. His hair shone golden red, and his limbs were straight and strong. His arms were slightly overlong for his frame but were never outmatched in their ability to wield the sword. Richard was born to be a warrior. He had inherited his father's bright blue eyes, yet he had none of that restless energy Henry so often displayed which seemed not to know what to do with itself. Richard always knew what to do with himself. He had purpose.

He was my child more than any of his siblings, because he had been my apprentice and I his master. He spoke the *language de oc* as his native tongue and was intelligent; he had even mastered Latin. Of late he had started to compose poetry in verse and songs in both French and *provincial* and he loved music and had a fine voice.

I knew he was not an angel. Richard could be stubborn and headstrong, that was true enough. He possessed a certain singlemindedness and a determination never to break his word, which I admired and found annoying at the same time. Bertran de Born, an influential troubadour and courtier, gave Richard the nickname *Oc-y-No* which meant yay and nay, to reflect this singlemindedness. Yes or no, there was no other answer, nothing lurking in between for Richard. Only years after his death would people named him *the Lionheart*, it was not something they called him during life, though in many ways I thought it true enough. If there was something Richard never lacked, it was courage.

Richard had many abilities, some of which I was only just beginning to see. He was a warrior indeed for it was in his blood from his father and grandfathers, and one could say his grandmother the Empress too, but also possessed a good mind, was capable of making more rational decisions than his father and my father had been willing to entertain. He was a natural leader, inspiring many a man with a kind of controlled charisma, which spoke of confidence beyond his years. It was true he had inherited the hot temper of his father, as had all my sons, although in Richard it took longer to break. He had the potential to be ruthless, unscrupulous at times, but in many ways, in the world in which we lived, these were qualities necessary to survival. And whilst he was certainly ambitious, he had no interest in the inheritances of his brothers, indeed the more time he spent in Aquitaine the less he cared for England, Normandy or anywhere else, and the more he cared for my lands. I think this was due to my love for them; I managed to install in my son a shard of the love I had ever borne for my homeland.

*

Whilst I honoured my heir, another did the opposite. My husband appeared to have become obsessed with making young Henry obey him in all things. Rather than leave him alone or hand him any responsibility, my husband was keeping young Henry under his eye and his boot at all times. He carted our son from Avranches to the Auvergne on a trip young Henry was not needed on at all, when the Old King went to meet Count Humbert who had arrived for the final negotiations over his daughter's betrothal to John.

Whilst they were there, Henry made things only worse between him and his son when he told Humbert that upon his death John would inherit three castles, Chinon, Loudun and Mirebeau, as well as some estates within England. Since all these castles and estates had been previously assigned to young Henry my eldest son was furious. To add to his humiliation young Henry was forced to witness the marriage treaty, thereby giving away his own property to his youngest brother.

"John is Henry's favourite." I stood from my chair after long hours of work and set my hands to my back, feeling a stretch which brought pleasure and pain in equal measures spread over my muscles. "He chooses the youngest son to favour, for John poses the least threat to him, for now. This is why he brought young Henry along, dragged him there like a child, so Henry could witness his father giving away land and property promised to him, and force him to sign to witness it as if he agreed with it. Young Henry probably thinks he might be formally made a prisoner if he did not go along with this, rather than being made a prisoner in all but name by his father keeping such a close eye on him."

"Your husband does not appear to see that this will cause resentment between your sons," said my uncle.

"I wonder sometimes if he cares," I said. "Perhaps he hopes it will drive a wedge between them, so they will fight one another and not challenge him. All Henry seems to wish for now is that people obey him, we saw this much with Thomas Becket."

On the 27th of August that year, young Henry was crowned a second time at Winchester, this time with Marguerite of France at his side and with her own crown, but it meant no more than the last coronation. This one was carried out simply so Henry could appease Louis of France, and perhaps his son a little too, thinking to mollify young Henry with yet another outward show of his rank, whilst denying him all true possession of it. Perhaps he thought a second coronation might make up for his handing young Henry's lands to John.

It did not. Our eldest son wanted no toy crown to play with, and that was all his father was offering him.

The Bishop of Evreux officiated, since the position of Archbishop of Canterbury was still vacant after the murder of Becket, and the Archbishop of York as well as the bishops of London and Salisbury had been forbidden by the Pope to attend this second crowning after having illegally crowned our son in the first place. Even my husband, the Old King as most people now called him, was not present at this second crowning, having gone to Brittany. Soon after this the Young King and Queen Marguerite began living together as man and wife. Old enough to start producing children my son was, but not old enough to be responsible for his own country, apparently.

That November King Louis invited his daughter and young Henry to Paris, saying that he wished them there so they might have a family reunion.

"Speak to me plain and true," I said to my daughter Marie who I had called to my chambers to talk on this, "do you think your father really wishes to see his daughter Marguerite, or do you think he wishes to cause friction between my eldest son and my husband?"

"My father is well aware of the rift between your husband and my brother Henry," said Marie, "and to own the truth, Maman, my father never has been particularly interested in any of his daughters. He may be more interested in a son-in-law, but I would think your second suspicion is the correct one."

I nodded. "And trouble will be easy to stir, for young Henry resents his father already, and he has the temper of his father in his blood."

"He is also your son, my lady, and has many good qualities."

"I know that well enough, but you are wrong when you say he is my son. He is more like his father than me, aside from in looks, and that is why, I think, his father doesn't trust him. He sees his restless energy and knows that young Henry could become much, as he himself has become. When I look at my eldest son, I see what could have become of my husband, had all that energy not been poured into war and conquest. I suspect Geoffrey of Anjou saw this too, the possible outcomes of fate for a man as restless as Henry of England, and that was why he harnessed that power early, taught my husband how to be a king and warrior, a leader, gave him an endless stream of matters to attend to and things to do, wars to fight and lands to conquer, so he would never sit still and always would be occupied. Geoffrey of Anjou knew that my husband needed such a life, so as not to run mad, or do impulsive and dangerous things. But my husband will not do the same for his own son, and that is why young Henry is becoming as he is. All that energy has nowhere to go."

Before leaving for Paris, young Henry and Marguerite visited my husband in Normandy and once again young Henry demanded his inheritance. Once again, the Old King refused, this time even reproaching his son for his boldness in asking again, which only provoked more bitterness in the heart of the Young King.

Whilst young Henry was in Paris it was widely rumoured that King Louis was indeed nurturing deadly hatred between father and son and was advising young Henry to demand, on pain of war, a share of his own dominions. Hearing this, my husband summoned young Henry back to Normandy for Christmas to join all his family who were likewise summoned, and yet when I arrived, I found my oldest son had not come to the family celebrations but instead performed a strange and extravagant gesture, whereupon he ordered his heralds to summon all knights in Normandy whose name was William to feast with him.

One hundred and ten Williams turned up for Christmas dinner with the Young King.

"People are calling it, and him, preposterous," Richard said.

"I believe that to be the point." I massaged my temples. Why can family bring a headache like no other upon a mind? "Your brother tries to demonstrate to the world the ridiculousness of his situation by feats such as these." In truth, I hoped I was right. That this was a point young Henry was making. If it was as pointless as it seemed, my son was more a fool than I had taken him for.

When I joined my husband in Normandy, I attempted to convince him that young Henry was only asking for what he had been promised and what he was due. "He should have somewhere," I protested, "England, Maine or Normandy, wherever you decide that he could reign and start to understand kingship properly, but he must have somewhere, Henry! Our eldest son is right to feel he is not being treated fairly. His brother Richard is coming into his inheritance, Geoffrey too rules his little realm, although sometimes I wonder if that is simply because Brittany is an unstable place and you need someone there all the time. Even John is being handed estates that belonged to our eldest, and all our other sons are younger than the Young King. It is only natural that he should start to resent that he has not been offered the same as his brothers."

"I will not allow it," said my husband.

"Why *not* allow him this?" I asked. "By his age you were ruling with your father in your dominions. Do you wish him to be untried for the task of kingship when you come to leave life, or would you rather set a wise King, practised and versed in the task of ruling, to follow you?"

"He is a child." My husband looked not unlike an infant himself, his cheeks red with indignant fury at the notion of sharing any of what he saw as his lands. To my mind, they were not his lands, neither was Aquitaine mine in many ways. We had been set here as guardians for a time to rule lands and people and one day we would not be here anymore and the light of this torch of destiny would be handed to another. I was already handing my torch to my son Richard, but Henry would not share. Greedy and grasping had his hands become, clutching his crown and lands so tight that I thought they would one day pop from his fingers. He would lose control, in this attempt to control all.

"By law and by age our eldest son is a child no more," I said. "But if you want to keep him as one the best thing to do is to deny him all that should be his."

"He is not ready to rule anything. He is flighty, careless and seeks only pleasure and play acting at war in tournaments."

"You do not allow him to do anything else, so why should he have learned gravitas or care? He has never been taken to war. Why should he not practise in tournaments if he is denied the test of knighthood in real life? Your father tested you in all ways, and when you were younger than our eldest son. Do you not think you should start to do the same with your heir?"

"I was an entirely different kind of man to our son," he snapped.

"The two of you are more alike than you know, and that is why you struggle to know peace."

"I am nothing like him!"

I sighed. "You will make him resent you, Henry, you will turn him from you."

"I am his King and father," he retorted. "In all ways he owes his loyalty to me."

"You are his father," I agreed. "Would you not rather have his loyalty because he loves you?"

Henry left the chamber.

That Christmas was a sullen one in Chinion Castle. We spent it with Richard and Geoffrey. My husband resented that I was attempting to impose my opinion on this tantrum he and young Henry were throwing at each other and that I was supporting our son rather than him. Henry began, in fact, to blame me for the way that our eldest son had turned out, ignoring the fact that young Henry had been taken away from me and placed in the household of Becket, then placed in a household of his own, so I had had little to do with his raising. Henry started to say that I had been too indulgent with our son and had spoiled him.

"And yet Richard is turning out fine," I argued, "a good man, and Geoffrey too is ruling his lands without this fuss, and I had more hand raising those two boys than our eldest."

Henry ignored me when I pointed out truths like this, not wanting to see that the decisions that he had made for our son had led to this, not any indulgence on my part. When people feel guilty about something, particularly when it comes to their children, they prefer, rather than accepting accountability, to find someone else to blame. If my husband wanted to find the root cause of the immaturity of our elder son, he would not find it solely in actions I had taken. He needed instead to look inside his own heart and find the child within which young Henry was mirroring with his own behaviour. I was happy to accept some responsibility for young Henry, but the way he was turning out had a lot more to do with his father than me. Richard, trusted to step into his power and role by me, was turning into a man I knew I could leave my lands to in perfect trust. That was my doing, my way of raising a future leader. My husband was going down another path, one most perilous.

And the truth was, it was not only young Henry who was harbouring resentment. Many of the vassals and subjects of my husband were too. Henry's grasping control of power coupled with his violent and brutal rule led people to name him an oppressor. The murder of Becket appeared to have sparked something amongst many vassals throughout our empire, particularly in my lands. Already resentful about the way they had been treated and looking at the evidence of how Becket had been killed, they were now looking on Henry as a tyrant rather than a mere king.

Something was coming, I could feel it in the air. As the wind grows warm before a tempest hits, so I could feel a change in the world.

Chapter Thirteen

Limoges

Aquitaine

February 1173

When one knows that there is a storm coming, there are choices to be made.

One choice is to stand still in the path of the storm, watch the pregnant, grey clouds roll towards you, feel the rain start to fall and the angry wind begin to rise, and do nothing. You can stand in the path of the storm and let it wash over you, eventually falling to your knees under the power of the rising wind, body sodden with water and eyes blinded by the storm. But there is another choice.

The other choice is to survive.

There was a conflict on its way, I did not need to wet a finger and hold it up to the wind in order to know that there was a storm coming. I knew my sons, and even though I was far from young Henry, I could feel his anger rising, his resentment building. I could almost hear the plans forming in his head.

And I knew they would fail, without help.

My husband would not give his sons what they wanted and what they deserved, and they were getting to an age where they would not accept anymore this refusal, especially young Henry. My eldest son was being treated even more like a child than his younger brothers. Vassals in many areas of the kingdom were ready to rise and it would not be long before one group or another went to young Henry or his brothers and offered to support them against the Old King. A rising with a true king, not just a rebel lord at its head, would likely be more successful, and some men, especially since the murder of Becket, were willing to do anything to get the Old King off his throne of tyranny and set up a new king in his place. My husband had plenty of enemies, and even ones who claimed friendship at the moment, like Louis of France, would support another king, particularly if that other king were married, as young Henry was, to his daughter.

My husband would not hear reason and was engendering only acrimony and hatred from his own family and from his people. He did not see the storm he himself was creating.

When one knows that there is a storm coming there are choices to be made, and I made my choices.

I did not take them lightly. I knew what I was doing, was well aware of the danger I was putting myself and my family into, but I thought this test of loyalty I was granted was a fair one. Henry did not have my loyalty anymore, not if a choice came between him and my sons. They were my blood, and he was not. They were the future of my people, our empire, and I loved them as I no longer did love my husband. I would not leave my sons to stand alone against a foe so dangerous.

If their father would not stand with him, then their mother would.

That meant putting into plan much that people would later condemn me for.

And yet would they not have condemned me had I stood with my husband and not with my sons? Whichever side I stood on in the end people would find fault with. If I had stood by my husband, they would call me unnatural for disowning my sons. I might as well make the choice which made the most sense to me. I would be condemned either way.

The eyes of the world are ever censorious, and they love to judge the actions of others. People do not consider what they would have done, truthfully, were they set in such a position as I was put in, where I had to choose between loyalty to two branches of my closest kin. I would suspect that many women would choose their offspring rather than their husband. That might shock many men, but if so then they understand not the heart of a mother. It was my duty to protect my children against all foes until they came of age and could rule by themselves. All foes, even their father.

We could not let the storm break over us. Preparations had to be made. It was through Marie that I contacted King Louis of France, my former husband, and still officially my overlord, to ask for aid for my son. Since young Henry was his son-in-law, I did not think Louis would refuse me. And he did not.

It was done carefully, so carefully that in the future when my husband looked for ways to accuse me of what I had done, he found nothing, no evidence, no proof, only rumour that I was the one who instigated the pact with France. In truth, when I first made this move, I was not thinking of war outright, but of giving young Henry a way to escape his father so he could bargain from afar, in a greater position of power. I knew there was a possibility of war, of course, I was no simpleton, but we must ever hope for the best and prepare for the worst when we make plans, particularly of this kind.

My husband was keeping my son almost as a prisoner at his side and I knew that in order for young Henry to truly press for his rights he would have to be free of his father. Young Henry was being forced into a submissive stance and that would never allow his father to see him as anything but a lesser man. I knew there was a danger that once set free and sent to France young Henry could well return as a rebel against his father, but if he was not set free then my husband would squeeze the life out of our son, or young Henry would find a way to rebel too close to my husband's power so it would be quashed immediately, or perhaps would anger his father so greatly that the Old King might dash his son's head against the wall. No, my son had to get out and away, that much was clear to me, and so it was that I contacted Louis of France. I told him I wanted an escape route for young Henry.

"It is a dangerous path, Maman," said Richard. I had of course told him everything.

I squeezed the bridge of my nose. A headache, one I had had for days as the pressure of this action weighed upon me, was paining me again. "If we leave your brother as he is, I think it will be more dangerous still. The young King will find a way to either provoke an argument most dangerous with your father in person, or he will try to raise a rebellion right next to him, within his own lands, which will immediately be crushed. Your father is not to be underestimated in war. For young Henry to have a chance he must be at a distance, and he must have powerful allies. Your father does not take him seriously at this moment, so therefore is unwilling to offer him the inheritance which should be his, but I mean to make him take your brother seriously. I mean to force him to accept Henry as his heir in truth, not just in name."

"I do not doubt Henry will get away, but you are putting yourself in danger." Richard rubbed his forehead, a wound there from training against other young men healing and itching him.

"Who should put themselves in danger for their own children if not mothers?" I asked, sitting back in my chair. "I risked my life birthing every single one of you into this world and I would again. Anytime any of you needs my life I would give it up for you."

"If only father was as reasonable as you are there would be no issue with Henry," said Richard, "you are not threatened by my sharing power with you in Aquitaine, Poitou or Gascony."

"Perhaps it is because I am a woman," I smiled, "and so have become accustomed, by experience, to people sharing my power or trying to take it."

"I think it is not because of that," my son said in a quiet voice, "you are not afraid, as father is, of us. Sometimes I think he resents us being born."

Oh, how telling a statement that was. It spoke to the wisdom of my son that he could see into the heart of all his father's actions and understand it was not pride, it was not truly a belief that his sons were not ready to rule, it was not confidence within his own self that he was the only one who could be monarch of our empire, but that it was fear that drove the Old King to restrain his sons so greatly.

Fear is in truth a curious thing, for it wears many faces and has many masks. A good trickster is fear, for we may think it anger when it comes in one guise or confidence when it appears in another, yet always at the root of each costume there is fear behind the mask. It sits inside us as a spider, its legs on each strand of a web which reaches out to grasp us and pull us in. My husband could not see that he was in this web, so deep he could not see the strands.

But I could see, could see much heading in a direction I liked not. So, I would alter the direction events took. I would betray my husband, to save my son.

*

Close to the end of February that year Becket was canonised by Pope Alexander III. We had all known it would happen, for by that time a cult had come into being around his name, and not long after an order of Knights of Saint Thomas of Canterbury at Acre was established in the Holy Lands.

Miracles of all kinds have been attributed since the moment of his death to this man I had known well and had also known was no saint. So many churches came to be dedicated to him as well as a hospital in London. By the end of my lifetime, his image was everywhere, and people prayed to it. In short time the shrine erected to him at Canterbury grew rich and remained one of the most popular places of pilgrimage in all of Christendom. It was a lesson to learn, how a story may grow and grow, becoming more powerful than the truth.

It would have been a thing impolitic to point out there had been nothing holy about Thomas Becket, so when people asked me what he was like, as often they did in my lifetime, I told them his good points and I did not lie, for though I had liked him but little he had some redeeming qualities. I never wanted to disturb anyone's image of him as holy, ridiculous though it was, and who would have believed me in any case? Myth is so much more enticing than truth and all people need fictions to tell, tales to believe in. Life is dull and brittle without stories. The man was dead and there was little more he could do to interfere in my life, so I let him have his glory in death. Perhaps it made him happy in Heaven, to hear how many worshipped him on earth.

Around that time my husband and I, as well as Richard and young Henry, were hosting a week of lavish banquets and festivals at Limoges in honour of Alfonso II the King of Aragon as well as the King of Navarre, Count Humbert, and Count Raymond V of Toulouse. If you remember anything of my story, you will remember that Count Raymond was the man my husband went to war with some years ago in pursuit of taking Toulouse as part of our empire. That had failed, but now Raymond had finally agreed to cede those lands to Richard and me. Raymond was there to pay homage to Henry and his sons and acknowledge them as his overlords. He had decided to ally with my husband because he had fallen out with his overlord of France, Louis. The main problem had occurred when Raymond repudiated Constance of France, Louis's sister. She had never had a great deal of luck with husbands, her first being Eustace of England who had died before he could inherit a crown and her second being Raymond who had set her aside.

"I do not understand why Raymond is here to pay homage to Henry and to the Young King rather than just to Richard," my uncle mentioned as we stood in the hall, watching the flames of the central fire lick higher into the darkness of the roof. "Toulouse is Richard's, his claim inherited through your claim, which has been supported in the past by your husband, by King Louis and was first envisioned by your father and grandfather as part of your empire. It sounds as if your husband is once again thinking of stealing Toulouse for himself or deciding perhaps to give it to young Henry, which will cause only strife between your two eldest sons."

"That is why we are here, uncle," I said as I sipped my wine, "that I might use my mouth to speak for my son if necessary, and so I might use my eyes to watch what my slippery husband is up to next."

"There was me thinking we were here to celebrate alliance."

"That we are, but not the one my husband makes. I celebrate those alliances I hold dear with my children."

It was not only this issue causing problems, however, for during that week young Henry spoke out publicly about his father's refusal to assign any power or lands to him as well as his brothers, and also spoke in anger about Henry's decision to give to John the castles and estates in Normandy and England.

I supported him and once more attempted to talk to his father, a last chance, if you will, to make the man see sense. My plans for aiding young

Henry to escape his father were in place, but if he did not have to use them it would be better. As I said, I did not take this lightly. "You act as though all we have built is yours alone, not belonging in any part to your sons, or to me," I said to Henry when we were alone.

"They *are* mine," he growled.

"And yet you have promised these lands to your sons. You have sworn they are to follow you as your heirs, you have promised much to them. What would you have done had your father handed you Normandy and then taken it apart to grant to other men, even if those other men were your brothers? Your father was wise, teaching you to manage men and land in youth, but you do not grant your sons the same chance."

"They are but children."

I sighed. The same fight we kept having over and over. "They are the same age, if not older than you were when you started to take on responsibility. If they act as children, it is because you refuse to treat them like men, and it will not stand, Henry. Not forever will they accept this treatment."

"The Count of Toulouse said you might try speaking this way," Henry narrowed his eyes at me, "and he advised me to beware of you and our sons."

"The Count of Toulouse has every reason to dislike me, since I am the reason he may be giving up his lands," I retorted, "so I am not surprised he would try to sow discord between us. Surprised I am more that you would listen to slander against your own sons and wife. All I am trying to do, all I ever have done is to offer you just and sensible counsel as once you said that you would always welcome from my lips."

"*Sensible* counsel always will be welcome," he said, implying that was not what I was offering.

I already knew that the Count of Toulouse was not to be trusted for in private he had come to young Henry and to me, and Richard, all individually, speaking with sympathy and offering his services to gain my sons the inheritance they wanted. I had not believed in his sincerity then and now to hear at the same time he was setting Henry against me and warning him there was a possible plot against him showed that he had two faces, and neither was trustworthy. I did not think Raymond knew of the arrangements I had made with France. He was simply guessing or trying to spread discord in the family which was poised to claim his lands.

*

All through Christmas the arguing raged on, at every feast and celebration, and then my eldest son made one great and fell mistake, by pointing out that it was King Louis' wish as well as that of the barons in Normandy and England that he take more power than he was presently given by his father.

"I want you to return to Poitiers with Richard and Geoffrey," Henry said to me that night, "you, I need there."

"And what of young Henry?" I asked.

Young Henry was to be once again all but taken captive by his father as my husband pressed on towards Normandy. This was not to be borne. I went to my son.

"You should not have mentioned King Louis and the barons," I said to young Henry, holding his hands. "You have alerted your father to the fact that there are forces aligning against him."

"And he has decided he once more will take me captive," said my son, "he means to take me to Chinon and keep me ever under his heel. Maman, you must help me now."

I nodded. "This is unacceptable, and I will not stand by and allow it."

"You will help me escape him?" Henry pressed my hand with his. There was something desperate in his grip and my heart hurt to feel it.

"I will." I took my hands out of his and put them to his face, drawing his blue eyes up to stare into mine. "Keep watch for the signal, cast by my men. We will get you from the clutches of your father."

"Thank you, Maman." My son fell into my arms.

"Once I was a prisoner too," I said, pulling back from him and looking into his eyes. "No one then stood for me, but I will stand for you." I pushed the hair, a little long, from his eyes. "Keep watch for the signal," I said again. "And be prepared to ride hard. Do not underestimate your father or his reach. If you are to escape, you must keep going and do not look back."

"As you did, when you outran all those men coming for you when you left France," said my son. "I am your son, and I will not fail you."

"As I am your mother and will not fail you. In all I do, I am yours."

Chapter Fourteen

Poitiers

Poitou

March 1173

The storm had come, over our lands it had broken, trees heaving and the soil tearing up, flying into the tempest, but for now my husband was still abed, snoring through the rising winds. Whilst he slept, it was time for my plans to be put into effect.

My husband took his son to Normandy and on March the 5th they stayed at Chinon where Henry even insisted that young Henry sleep in the same room as him.

That evening, having seen a signal from the hilltop, the Young King managed to sneak from his shared chamber, protesting a need of the bladder to the guard on the door, and from there he managed to persuade the castle guards to lower the drawbridge which allowed him to escape. In the morning Henry woke to an empty room, his son gone. He sent messengers after our son who returned with information most unwelcome; young Henry had already crossed the Loire and was riding north in the direction of Normandy, heading for France. The King gave chase through Alençon and Argentan, but to no avail. My husband raged, unable to comprehend how his son had outstripped him.

It was because of me. I had commanded a string of fast horses to be positioned perfectly every five miles, so that they could be ridden close to gallop, each and every one of them, so my son did not have to slow down. I had men watching to bring news to young Henry too, at each stop. My son knew that when his father started to reach him, he was to swing east across the French border and make his way to Paris from there. Fresh horses, yet another string of them, had been provided by King Louis of France from the border onwards. On the 8th of March young Henry crossed that border, fleeing into the arms of my first husband. His father did not catch him.

"Father will know that it was you," said Richard when we heard Henry had made it safe to France.

"He may guess."

"Who else could have organised it so well?" asked Richard.

I laughed a little, though it held small humour. "Your father has underestimated me many times during our marriage. He may well underestimate me again, though I think you are right, and he will realise it was me. He could never believe your brother could do this alone."

Safe in Paris, young Henry and King Louis pledged themselves to be each other's allies, calling Henry their common enemy. My husband sent a deputation of bishops to Paris to urge Louis to return his son, and Louis, never the bravest of men, decided it was time to prod the already angry bear of England by taunting him from afar.

"Who is it who sends this message to me?" Louis asked when Henry's men arrived.

"The King of England," said one of the bishops.

"But that cannot be so," said Louis, his eyes wide, "the King of England is here with me, but if you still call King his father who was *formerly* King of England, know that he is no longer king. Although he may still act as king, all the world knows that he resigned his kingdom to his son."

When the bishops returned to Henry, they warned him, telling him to look to the safety of his castles and security of his person. Henry interpreted Louis' words quite correctly as an open declaration of war. Soon afterwards many of Henry's vassals declared their support for young Henry, abandoning the Old King. William the Marshal stood by young Henry, so did Bertran de Born, and soon after this the younger Henry made his way secretly to Aquitaine and to me.

"It is time for my brothers to join me," he said to me and I agreed. It was safer for them to be with him than it was for them to be with me. Besides, my eldest son was to make war and who better to be his generals than his brothers?

"You should join me too, Maman," urged young Henry. "Father will find out it was you who aided my escape, and he will come for you."

"It is true, Maman," Geoffrey chimed in.

"I understand that you wish to protect me," I smoothed my gown, "but I cannot abandon my people."

"Then I should not abandon them either," interjected Richard, "they are my people too."

I shook my head. "You must go. By going you would not be abandoning our people. Your father will seek revenge after this, suspecting that I had a hand in helping Henry escape, and if he is not fully occupied with France and Louis and you three, then your brother is right, he will come for my people, take revenge on my lands. I will remain here in order to aid our people, hold our lands in your name, Richard, but you must go with your brother, not only to support him but so that one of us will not be captured even if the other is. I am the present of this land, it does not matter if I fall or am captured, but you are the future, and it would be a disaster if you were." I put my hand on his arm. "I know, if anything does happen to me, you will stand for our people."

"Of course, Maman," Richard said.

"And all of you must promise if I am captured, you will not bargain anything for me. Ask for my release, by all means, but give up nothing valuable for me."

"Maman, you would be safer with us," pleaded young Henry. "I do not want to leave you here, alone."

I smiled. "I have stood alone more times than any of you could count, and I am still here."

"The danger is greater this time," said Geoffrey.

"That is why I must stay," I said. "It will be better for our cause if I am here and able to aid you by sending men or distracting your father in the south.

I have raised all of you to be good men, to take responsibility for your actions. We embark now on a very dangerous time. Do not underestimate your father's skill in warfare nor the depths to which his pride will force him to go when he is challenged. Do not lean either too heavily on Louis of France, for while he is presently your ally, he may not always be. Lean instead on each other, for your siblings, all of you are of the same blood and of the same bone. That must bind you in loyalty more than any other cause or man who asks you to rise in his name. Hold fast to one another and we will prevail." I looked at them. "You need me here. If we are to succeed, many areas of this empire must rise. Aquitaine, Poitou and Gascony, they will revolt against your father at my word."

They nodded; they knew I spoke the truth.

"Besides," I went on. "If all of us go to France then people will say it is a French plot, but if I remain here then I can protect my people and I can stir up the south against your father. If he is forced to face war on two fronts, or more, it is more likely that you will win."

I watched my son Geoffrey as I spoke. My third living son was dark of hair and short of stature and was not good looking, unlike his brothers, but what he did possess in abundance was charm and cunning. People would later call him treacherous and grasping and I suppose he had those elements within him, but it was also possible that he was even more clever than Richard, perhaps cleverest of all my sons. I thought Geoffrey would be a worthy ally to his brothers as long as their interests aligned with his. I understood later why people would call him treacherous and unscrupulous, for when he was engaged in warfare he would raid even abbeys and shrines. He had few scruples and could be ruthless, but so could all my sons be. Speaking of sticking together, of loyalty to each other was however aimed more at Geoffrey than my other sons.

My sons left for Paris as my uncle and I sent messages to the lords of the south, asking them to rise up in support of my sons. Upon hearing this, there was great celebration in many quarters of my lands. My husband had never been liked and the fact I was now inciting my own people to rebel against him brought me much favour. There was even a verse composed about it by the troubadour Richard de Poitevin which went, *"rejoice O Aquitaine, be jubilant O Poitou, for the sceptre of the King of the north wind is drawing away from you."*

People sang it in the streets, everywhere, that was how greatly Henry was hated by my people.

*

"I want you in Paris, with my sons," I said to Raoul as tales of armies being gathered by my sons grew.

"I should be here with you."

"No, I need an intermediary there, to stand between my sons and Louis, someone I can trust. I need someone to advise them who is not of the court of France, for I know the people there. They will do all they can for Francia and that is not what will be best for my sons and their lands. They need an elder with them, uncle and it must be you. I cannot leave here yet."

He scowled. "I am loath to leave you, what if your husband comes for you?"

"If he comes for me, at least you will not be here. Me he will have to treat with at least a little dignity but you, you he has always blamed for much. If you are here, he may try to blame you for my rebellion and take your head. At least if I am alone here, there is only one person he can blame, and that is me." I went to him and kissed his cheek. "I need you with my sons," I said again. "And I need eyes in Francia. You can tell me what is unfolding there."

I looked to Emma. "You should go too," I told her.

"I will do nothing of the kind," she said. "You need me here, my lady, to aid you with the court. Your daughters remain, so I remain."

I nodded. I did need her there, it was true, more so if I had to go anywhere. I needed someone to keep order over my court if I had to travel south to gather men for our cause. I had gone back and forth over whether to send my daughters away or not and had decided they would be safer with me than with Louis. Only God knew who he might try to wed them to if I sent them to France. "Your brother will resent that you stood on my side," I warned her. "More so will he resent you for you are his sister. His daughters and daughters-in-law he will suppose were corrupted by me, but you he will blame."

"I stand on the side of righteousness." Her voice was hard as sea stone.

I knew it would not take Henry long to find out what I was doing and so I acted with speed. I knew I could not evade him for long, but once my people were roused, they little needed a general to guide them. If I was captured, they would still fight on. It might, in fact, be more effective to set them loose and wild upon Henry's men, for they would be less predictable without a leader. Many times, he had only held these lands because of my intervention, and now he had that not, I expected my people to give as much trouble as possible.

It would not be long until he knew of my betrayal, and he was not a man to forgive. This was as bad as the betrayal of Becket, perhaps worse, but in truth the man who is constantly betrayed by those he claims to love should look about and wonder why it keeps happening. Is he surrounded by faithless people, or does his lack of faith in those around him create foes to surround him?

Henry had spies at my court, that I knew, and they must have reported the visit of young Henry and the fact that Richard and Geoffrey had united with him. I knew this for certain when I received a letter from the Archbishop of Rouen, who asked me to use my influence upon my sons to bring them into submission to their father. He threatened me with excommunication if I refused to go along with the plans of my husband.

"Pious queen, most illustrious queen," he wrote, *"we all of us deplore and are united in our sorrow that you, a prudent wife if ever there was one, should have parted from your husband. Once separated from the head, the limb no longer serves it. Still more terrible is the fact that you should have made the fruits of your union with our Lord King rise up against their father. For we know that unless you return to your husband, you will be the cause of general ruin. Return then oh, illustrious queen to your husband and our lord. Before events carry us to a dire conclusion, return with your sons to the husband whom you must obey and with whom it is*

your duty to live. Return lest he mistrust you or your sons. Most surely we know that he will in every way possible show you his love and grant you the assurance of perfect safety. Bid your sons, we beg you, to be obedient and devoted to their father, who for their sakes has undergone so many difficulties, run so many dangers, undertaken so many labours."

There had been the cajoling, the guilt and reminders of my place as a wife, and then came the threats.

"Either you will return to your husband or else by Canon Law we shall be compelled and forced to bring the sanctions of the Church to bear upon you. We say this with great reluctance and shall do it with grief and tears, unless you return to your senses."

I ignored the letter. I did not welcome people who called me lunatic because I had an opinion different to my husband's, or who tried to tell me that I, Queen of England by marriage and Duchess of Aquitaine in my own right, should obey this man who happened to be my husband even if he was wrong.

I believed I was the one who was in full possession of my wits. I had no faith in any of the promises of my husband and I certainly had no faith in his love. That commodity he had given to so many other women, spreading it so thin there was only a sliver left for me. And that was not enough. Saying that my husband would in every way show me his love was laughable. Did Henry think I would be so desperate for his love by now that I would faint away, surrender all my plans for my sons, just for a scrap of that love?

He knew me not at all, not anymore.

At first, with astounding arrogance, Henry did not really appreciate the gravity of the situation he was in. For a foolishly long time, he thought the flight of his son and the rebellions being raised nothing. He had never taken his sons seriously, then suddenly he was forced to. It made me chuckle.

Swiftly he gave up hawking and sending letters to me filled with bribery of emotion and threats of the Church, and hastened to action, abruptly understanding that masses of men were rising against him, from all areas of his empire. His sons, me, Louis of France and his own people he had never seen as threats, but together, combined, he realised we were.

On the advice of King Louis, my eldest son and his brothers were making allies by promising lands and income to anyone who was willing to join with him. Philip the Count of Flanders had become their ally in return for the promise of the earldom of Kent as well as the castles of Rochester and Dover and one thousand pounds per annum. His brother Matthew, Count of Boulogne, had been promised the country of Mortain, and the Count of Blois had been offered great estates in Touraine. Louis had even had a new kingly seal made specially for young Henry so he could solemnize these grants to his new followers. In his haste my son had left his seal behind, but this new one was one created for a king, and he used it often and well. When my uncle arrived in Paris, he counselled some restraint on these grants and thankfully they listened to him. It was all meet and good to make allies, but one should not hand out all land at once. The Crown needs some too.

That spring Louis held a great court in Paris which was attended by my sons and there all the lords of France vowed to fight for the Young King, who, along with his brothers, promised not to make peace with the Old King without the consent of Louis or his chief vassals. After this ceremony Louis was the man who knighted Richard.

"The rebels now include..." began one of my men, come to give me a report, and I held up a hand.

"We fight on the side of the *true* King," I corrected him. "The rebels are on the other side, supporting the Old King, the tyrant old Henry."

The man tried and failed to smother a smile. "Those fighting for the *true* king, my lady, now include the King of France, Geoffrey of Brittany and Richard of Aquitaine, the Counts of Flanders, Blois, Boulogne, Champagne, a number of English lords as well as lords and barons of Maine, Anjou, Brittany and Poitou, and now the King of Scots, William the Lion, has sent word he is with them too."

I nodded. "So England will come under attack as well."

"It seems likely, Majesty. If the Scots have joined, they will invade the northern borders of England. Much land there they claim is theirs, stolen from them by England. Their first priority will be to take it back, but they may well press on, invade the north of England too, perhaps beyond."

"So, the Old King will not know where to turn, as all sides press in on him at once."

It was as I had hoped, for Henry was a fearsome warlord and only eruptions from all sides of his empire at once could possibly unseat him. The swiftness with which so many had turned on him was a measure of how unpopular he was at that time. Of course some were simply out for land, that is the way of many men, but many were ready for change, and they believed young Henry could give them what his father could not.

Lords were rising in every part of the empire, and the only ones of our family who were still on Henry's side were John, who was a little boy still, and Geoffrey his bastard son, who recently had been elected Bishop of Lincoln. That May the Young King and his brother Richard, backed by the Count of Flanders, attacked Pacy in Normandy, and King Louis, aided by Geoffrey, bore down upon the Vexin with men and fire.

But news came.

"My lady, though he cannot send armies, there is news that the Old King has promised much to any man who will take you prisoner. With many of your lords away, already gathering arms or fighting, we cannot guarantee your safety here. An assassin or kidnapper may well infiltrate the castle."

I nodded to the steward of my palace. "I know, you are right. I must to France go, and meet with my sons. There, I can be safe with them."

Henry was sending men into my lands. He meant to find me.

It was late in the hour when I made my escape; I should have left before I did, I knew that, but I did not want to abandon my people to the whims of my husband. When I left, I realised there was little chance I was going to evade him. His men were already in Poitou, but I would do my best.

If I could reach the border, I was promised safe conduct by Louis, who sent me a last missive through Marie before she was recalled to

Champagne that he was eager to see me again. I wondered if that was true. In truth the notion of going back to France, to this land that had hated me, whilst I was in direct conflict, inciting uproar against my second husband, was not an entirely welcome one. I had no doubt people would cast further aspersions on my reputation, but another part of me said, what of it? We have carried such slanders all our life and the repeating of them has never made them true. What should we care what people say, when we know what is truth and what is not?

The only reason I cared was if it should impact upon my sons.

I was, in a way, curious to see Louis again, to see what the years had done to him. It had been a long time since I had left him. He had had many wives since. Perhaps time would have mellowed his feelings for me, those of love and those of contempt, enough for us to meet at a mid-path. I also believed he had a genuine affection for my sons. Louis had a habit of idealising people, falling hard for them. It did not mean he always would feel that way for them and certainly did not mean he always would be loyal to them, but in the moment, as he was flushed with that emotion or a myriad of them, he could be zealously devoted. My sons were charming boys, all of them. I was sure they could work that to their advantage.

I called my women to me. "I must leave here," I said to them, my eyes on Eleanor, Joanna, Emma, the most, but Marguerite, Alys and little Alice, to be the bride of John, tugged at my heart too.

"Take us with you, Maman." Eleanor sounded as if her heart would break.

"I cannot," I said. "The road is too dangerous. You will be safe here. My husband sends men after me, but they want only me. If I can get away, this country will become safer for you. Taking you with me would simply put you where his mercenaries are to aim."

I clutched Emma's hand as she came to me. "Take care of my children," I whispered. "As you are sister to my husband, you are my sister. I entrust you with them, who are most precious to me."

"I will not fail you," Emma said.

In May I left Poitiers to follow my sons to France, accompanied by only a small escort. In an attempt to evade capture, I dressed as a man. I was tall enough to pass as one at a distance and I rode my mount astride. Speed had worked for me in the past, and speed I used now. But we could not run our horses fast forever.

We took paths not often travelled, and perhaps that was my mistake for I had done the same when coming home, evading the men who were bent on capturing me when I left France. Henry knew much of that story, of my methods. Perhaps it had made me easy to predict.

We were not four leagues from my palace when men apprehended us. We had slowed our horses to walk, and then they came from the bushes on either side of us, bows loaded and arrows pointed at us. There was nowhere to go, and my men had not even had time to draw their swords. "Stay your hands," I commanded, looking about. "They would have you dead before you could swing. Senseless, pointless death is not something I welcome."

As I looked at the knights who commanded the men surrounding us, my heart dropped. I knew every one of them. "William Mangot," I said, staring him in the eyes. He had the decency to look away, to the floor, where the shreds of his honour lay writhing. "Portedie de Mauze, Foulques de Matha and Herve le Panetier...." I went on, naming all of them. "Men of my own lands, sworn to uphold me and yet here you are. You have abandoned ties of loyalty to me and taken instead the coin of my husband, have you?"

They hardly needed to answer.

"The last circle of Hell, my lords, is where betrayers end their days," I told them. "Remember that, each time you spend one of the thirty pieces of silver my husband handed you, remember that."

"You too have betrayed your lord, my lady," de Mauze said quietly.

"I have offered my loyalty to the Young King, my son," I retorted. "*He* is my lord. And where I may have betrayed my husband, one man, you, sirs, have betrayed the lady sent by God to rule over you, as well as your people and the future of your lands. You have betrayed all this not to uphold your lord, your blood or your own son but to fill your purses. Tell me, what gold or silver is there on earth which can settle the guilt in your hearts? Tell me where in all the lands we together have called home will you be welcomed after this?"

I hoped it might be enough for them to let me go, but life is not as it is in stories where men respond to the call of valour and honour sounding in their hearts. They took my men's swords, and they took me.

They said little as they escorted me from my lands into those of my husband. I was quiet too. I was trying to think. What would Henry do with me? Keep me prisoner, or would I vanish from the pages of history this day, my body left to rot in some unmarked grave? I had been in this situation before of course, but I was older now, and I had actually done what I was accused of this time.

I was now the prisoner of my husband.

Chapter Fifteen

Chinon

Touraine

Summer 1173

"I would not have believed it until now." Henry was staring at me as if I had crawled out from under his blankets, a bug sent to bite him in the night. "Until I came to see you here, captured, after inciting my sons to rebel against me. I never would have believed it."

"You never did have much imagination when it came to those you underestimated." I looked around. "Why bring me here? I know you love this dark, dank old castle, but we are in the middle of an area infested with rebellion. Do you seek to taunt my sons?"

"They are my sons too."

"Not anymore. They have chosen a new father, the King of France, who will aid them to get what they wanted and you would not permit; their rights."

"They are my sons, and they will obey me."

I laughed; a dark sound devoid of happiness. "Good, try shouting that to them across the battlefield, I am certain they will simply lay their arms down and come to you weeping." I curled my lip in contempt. "You expect people to offer you love and devotion with nothing in return from you, but that is not the way of the hearts of men or women, Henry. You think you can simply order the world to do as you want, but that is not how the world works."

"Educate me, then, crone," he said, gazing furiously at me. "How does the world work?"

"By compromise, *boy*. By give and take, by barter. You should have learned that with that fool of a man you called friend and raised too high, you should have learned it with your sons, to whom you promise all and give nothing, and you should have learned that with the wife you took and chose to ignore."

"So that is why you do this, because I took mistresses." His voice was dripping with scorn.

I chuckled again. "Oh, tell yourself that if it makes you feel better," I said. "Tell yourself all this came about because a woman was jealous and in her jealousy she set your loyal sons and loyal subjects against you. It is not the truth, but you have ever been good at finding a story to follow instead of the truth. The truth is, Henry, I do not care about your mistresses. Long ago I stopped caring. There could have been much between us, the greatest love for generations I think, but you denied me your heart. That was your choice. I doubt you have given it, either, to any of these other women, and just as you have denied love to women, whilst making all the promises under the sun to them, you have done the same to our children. Slights to me I can forgive, but not to them. You have sought to keep each one of them children, dangled lands and titles under their noses and then snatched them away. You have taunted them with their destinies, and then stolen them back, time after time. You play with people, my lord husband, with their emotions, with their dreams and with your love, and now you have done that too many times. That is why all the empire rises against you. Your own people, your own family loathe you. They want no more of this Old King, this tyrant who never keeps his word. They want a new King, and that they have, in our son."

He stared at me a long time. His anger was cold now. He did not like being told the truth. "I would not have believed that you of all people could betray me thus," he said.

"You find it hard to believe that someone could make a promise to their children and keep it?" I shrugged. "You do have small experience in such matters, it is true."

"What of your promises to me? To love, to obey?"

I chuckled only harder. "You left our vows behind long before I did. You have never forsaken all others. Once a king has broken his word, his followers may too. But my children have never broken faith with me, and I never with them. I swore, the moment each was born, that I would keep them safe against any foe, even if that foe be their father."

"You are my wife, and your loyalty is owed to me first."

I shook my head. "No, my lord. You are mistaken again. My children are my blood, my bone, my kin. You are a stranger I was bonded to by a ceremony. Those sons we have made together, they are part of me, as close to me as my own flesh. They are my first loyalty. For them, I will risk my life and my freedom. I would not do such things for you."

"You are my wife!" he screamed.

"And they are my blood!" I shouted back. "They mean more to me than you ever could!"

He reeled backwards as if I had slapped him. "They mean everything to me, and you nothing," I went on.

"You have said enough," he said. "Do not get comfortable here. You will not be in one place long enough for your rebellious sons to find you."

I smiled. He thought to punish me with moving, with travel, with denying me luxuries. I knew already what waited for me. I had considered he might kill me, but I thought not for if I died my lands would pass to Richard and he would not want that. "When my sons prevail over you," I said. "They will set me free, and we will dance together, welcoming in the new reign of a glorious king, and the death of one who has become rotten and obsolete."

He rose up as if he might hit me then, his hand rising. I lifted my chin and turned my head. "Go ahead," I said. "Nothing you do has meaning now."

His hand fell and he marched out of the room. I did not see him for some time.

Captive I was. My location was kept secret for more than one reason. Henry could not risk my children freeing me, this was true enough, but it was done for other motives too.

I wanted more than anything to know of my children, and keeping me in seclusion, away from the world and information, was torture. He used this to pain me. And as for my children, it was used to harm them too.

To all intents and purposes, I had simply vanished on the road to France. My sons would wonder where I was, if I had been captured, if I was hale or being punished. They might think I was dead. It would distract them, perhaps only a little but a little might be enough. If Henry wanted to use me thus, I was a valuable piece to bargain with.

But I had already told them not to bargain for me. I had commanded it. I wanted to be nothing but a strength to them. I would not permit myself to become a weakness to my sons.

That meant that for however long I was to be a prisoner, I could not let it diminish me.

Chapter Sixteen

Chinon and

Falaise, Normandy

Summer 1173

I was moved a lot. Chinon was my first prison, then a hunting lodge nearby, then another house of a loyal lord, then to Falaise we went. All the time I was on the move. I was given few servants, only people to bring me food or drink, or water to wash. They were commanded not to talk to me.

Those first weeks were miserable ones for me. They were engineered to be so.

My accommodation was always basic. Even the best rooms of the best castles, ones I had stayed in many times, had been stripped down so only the essentials were there. There were no people to talk with, no books to read, no occupations like sewing, even, to do. The idea, I supposed, was to drive me to distraction, so I was more malleable.

I was never mistreated in my imprisonment and yet I was. My husband did not order me beaten or raped, did not keep food from me, and always I had just enough to wear, enough bedding to sleep under, so many a prisoner kept worse might say I was lucky, and I suppose I was in some ways, but I knew my husband. The manner of my keeping was not intended to honour me but chastise me in ways Henry probably thought subtle. I was teased with comfort, but never handed it, shown what freedom was but never given it.

He gave me just enough but sought to strip everything from me that had made life worth living, my children, my pursuits, my country, my people. He thought to destroy my mind through tedium and punish me with stringent living. He thought to hurt me in all ways but bruising my body, and no doubt some would say I deserved far worse for betraying him. Henry certainly thought I did. This imprisonment, this lack of knowledge, this separation from my sons, all of this was my husband's spite made manifest. I lived in a prison made of his pettiness.

I knew little of what was going on in the outside world in those weeks, and I knew altering this had to be the first mission I undertook. My husband thought to deprive my mind of all that could occupy it, but I would occupy myself.

Henry had told his guards and the women who were serving me not to trust me and not to talk to me. I knew this from the start when they came into the chamber, placing a meal, simple and plain – which was intended as another punishment since Henry knew I loved spices and sauces – on the table. They would not look at me and left as soon as they could. For drink, I was brought boiled water, or milk. Sometimes there would be ale, but never wine. Not in those early days at least. This was meant as another chastisement.

These people will not speak to me, I said to my sister in my mind.

You have always known how to get to people, sister, Petronilla whispered in the flames of the fire.

That was true. Henry had never understood others, but I did. Tell someone not to do something and that is all they want to do, so when people are commanded not to talk to someone, they want nothing more but to talk to them. So, I remained silent, aside from thanking the servants gently for their pains. When my servants entered the room, I would be sitting, demure and good, on a stool. When I rose, I tried to limp a little. I was still beautiful, I was well aware of that, but I also could look my age if I chose. If I remained straight of face and did not smile, for a smile always lights the face, if I hung my head and did not stand upright, I could look older than I felt. That was something I would use now, not only the wits and knowledge I had amassed in my years, but the supposition that when we age we must become infirm. I stiffened my muscles, hunched my shoulders, looked pained from time to time. I had no pains, not many considering my age in any case, but I wanted to appear fragile, so I would engender pity and also so my captors would think I was less physically capable than I was. If there were a chance of escape, I would take it.

Pity worked, swifter than I thought it would. One day, setting down a bowl of water and a cloth to wash with, one of the maids glanced sideways at the door then whispered to me, "Your sons, all of them, are alive, my lady. Your daughters are safe, and your people call out for you to be restored to them."

"Thank you," I said, barely moving my head in case the guards outside the heavy oak door were watching us through the tiny window. "Thank you."

"My father was of Aquitaine," she muttered, pretending to be wiping the table. "And as I am of your country, my lady, I am one who, at heart, calls for your release."

"If you can bring me any news, any at all, I would be most grateful," I murmured.

"I will do all I can, my lady." And with that she was away.

I smiled as I washed. Henry knew it not, but I had friends.

*

Her name was Joan, which made me smile for sometimes we called my daughter Joanna Joan too. Her father was of Aquitaine indeed, but upon his death her mother had wed a lesser baron of Normandy and they had come to my husband's lands in Falaise. Her stepfather's name concealed her identity enough that a daughter of my homeland was allowed to wait upon me. Had Henry known she had the blood of Aquitaine in her, Joan would not have been allowed to serve me, but I doubt anyone checked too deep the backgrounds of people such as maids in the castle. Men frequently suppose women to be unimportant. Joan moved with us, to each castle I was taken to, and through her I found out much.

On the 29th of June the Castle of Aumale had fallen to my sons and soon after that of Driencourt had too. "King Louis has pressed into Normandy, they say he means to take Rouen," Joan told me as she tidied the chamber. It hardly needed cleaning, there was so little in it, but she made a great job of pretending to be busy. "The Flemish troops set siege to the border fortress of Verneuil, but the Count of Blois died of injuries from a crossbow bolt, and in order to take his place as Count of Blois, Philip of Flanders has retired from the war."

"Have there been many battles?" I murmured, my head down as if I was praying. If I stayed in this position, my lips were easily concealed by the headdress I wore. Even if the guards looked inside the room, it would probably appear that I was merely muttering in prayer.

"Not many outright, more sieges and skirmishes, my lady."

I soon heard more. Louis had tried to take up the place left vacant by Philip of Flanders in Rouen, but when my second husband advanced on my first, Louis did what he did best, tucked his tail and ran back to France.

Many castles were besieged and villages and towns too numerous to count were set to flame and sword. My sons waged war on their father with vengeance, laying waste to his lands on every side. It was a tried and tested policy to scorch the earth and burn crops, one often employed in war. The Count of Flanders put it succinctly when he had said, "first destroy the land and then one's foe." If men could not eat, if there was nowhere for them to rest, they were easier to annihilate.

There were uprisings all over the empire. "In Anjou and Maine, the King's vassals have openly renounced their loyalty to him," Joan told me and as September came she had more news; Count William of Angoulême as well as Guy and Geoffrey De Lusignan and lords of Poitou had risen up in support of me. "They are calling for your release, and demand to know where you are, my lady," she said.

I bit my tongue. I had almost asked her to get word to them, and that was too much a risk for Joan. I was too well kept here, in so many prisons. I was too well watched to escape. There was more a chance on the road as I was moved place to place, but I did not want to put Joan in peril, end up with her captured, which would leave me knowing nothing of what was going on. Joan would no doubt lose her tongue or her eyes, if not her life, and I would lose my only contact to the world. She had risked everything to bring me this news, I knew that. I did not want her to lose her life for it.

Besides, it sounded as if my imprisonment was having an effect upon my people which would be useful to the cause of my sons.

But the defiance of my people was not to be. Henry sent in a mass of mercenaries to Poitou. They burned the vines of the wine regions, tore down castles, laid my homeland to ruin. Crops were uprooted and people starved. *My* people starved. My people suffered, but I was the true target, for Henry would know how guilt would assail me when I heard. I had failed to protect them, and they had been punished for my actions. It was his way of showing me what happened when I, his wife, dared to step out of line with his wishes.

The rebellion in Brittany was short-lived, more mercenaries were sent against them. We heard Breton prisoners were being kept in the Castle of Dol.

"The Old King has the support of the Church," Joan whispered one day as she swept out my fire. The guards, by then, knew that she was taking too long in the rooms I was in to truly be cleaning, and they did nothing. I had talked to one, asking of his family, and another, recommending an ointment for an aching knee. I was gaining their trust and they felt sorry for me. Knowing I was having a little conversation with Joan, they allowed it, out of pity.

Pity is a useful thing. I doubt they knew she was passing on such valuable information.

"Of course he has the support of the Church," I whispered. "They could have no other King so firmly under their control as he, after Becket's death, so he is useful to them, and it is better for them to support him. He is their puppet. They do not want his strings broken."

She looked puzzled. I had to remember not everyone knew the details of Becket's death as I did.

"The Church refuses to back the Young King," she went on. "He has petitioned them for support, but the Pope denies it. England too, most of its men and lords at least, they are in support of the Old King." She hesitated. "My lady," she went on with clear reluctance. "They say the Old King is winning."

Much as I had hoped events might turn out otherwise, I had expected this. The truth was, Henry was better at war than the men he faced. He had more experience and more natural talent for it. I had hoped they might take him by surprise, and they had, but the surprise was not enough. My son, the Young King, was not experienced enough to coordinate all these opposing armies who had risen in his name and so frequently King Louis took command, but Louis had ever been inept as a warrior and sadly, despite all their many allies and their just cause my sons were set down. In September Henry came to me again and told me all of this with glee in his face and his eyes.

"Your sons wish to sue for peace," he announced, "as does King Louis. Your rebellion, madam, has failed."

I said nothing, looking at the wall rather than at him.

"Do you have no message that you wish to send to your sons?" his voice mocked me, "when they come begging on their knees before me?"

"Tell them I love them more than I have loved any man," I said, staring straight at him. "Tell them I am proud of all they have done, and all they will do, in the future."

He glowered and I knew he would say no such thing. I smiled. "You think you have won, my lord, but all you can do from this moment on, is lose."

"I understand you not at all, I have vanquished my enemies. They bow to me."

"Of course you understand not, but you will, one bitter day." I smiled again.

"You are gone insane." He was staring at me as if he knew not what I might do.

"My wits are perfectly hale, and my eyes clear," I said. "That is why I can see much that evades you. But fear not. The day will come, lord husband, when you will see all. I long for that day."

*

That September they met, and Henry did his utmost to humiliate his sons. He never was gracious in defeat or victory, and as age pressed upon him this became only more pronounced.

On the 25th of September he met his sons and King Louis at Gisors under the branches of an ancient elm tree, a traditional meeting place of the kings of England and France when they wanted peace. Henry offered his sons castles and allowances. Most reasonable, one might think, but it was the amounts that were humiliating, for Richard was promised half the revenues of Aquitaine, Geoffrey the same for Brittany, and the Young King was offered a pittance of an allowance. Henry made no mention offering any authority or power to them. They would not rule the lands that had been promised to them. On the advice of Louis my sons rejected their father's offer.

I was proud of them when I heard.

"England has been invaded from the north by the Scots," Joan whispered to me not long after. "William the Lion, King of Scots, who is sympathetic towards your son Henry but also is desirous of regaining Northumbria, so I hear, has joined with your son upon the Young King's promise to return that county to Scotland. Scottish forces have laid waste to the north of England, setting everything to fire and to sword, kidnapping women and children. There is great unrest there. The war may not be over, my lady."

I thought for a while this invasion from Scotland might bring hope to my sons' cause, but an army commanded by English lords marched out and drove the Scots back across the border and attacked too the lands of the Scots. King William was forced to sue for a truce which was to last until January 1174.

"There has been an attempt at an invasion of England," Joan whispered to me as she set my dinner before me. Plain meat, a roll of bread, a small hunk of cheese. "Robert de Beaumont, son of the last Justiciar who died not long ago, is behind it, along with a Flemish army sent by Philip of Flanders."

For a while it seemed Henry would have to go to England to see off this threat, but not long after, at Farnham, the Flemish forces were routed by a peasant army, raised and led by Richard de Lucy and others. They said few men were left standing and whoever did remain alive ran. Men who had marched in favour of the Flemish, like the now ancient Hugh Bigod who had fought in the civil wars decades before, were captured or became exiles. After that only pockets of rebellion remained in England.

That November Henry and his mercenaries were south of Chinon, bearing down on my uncle's castle at Faye-la-Vineuse, which they managed to take after a short siege. I was panicked for a while until I heard that Raoul was still was in Paris. At the same time my son Richard made an attack on the port of La Rochelle in Poitou, trying to take it from Henry's mercenaries, but it was unsuccessful.

As winter came both sides were forced to negotiate a truce, for that season was no time to be fighting a war when snow and rain were constant visitors. As they made peace, I was left in a kind of limbo. My sons could not sue for my release, if Henry would even consider it, and Henry could not be persuaded to release me whilst his sons still warred with him.

All that winter in my cold prison I prayed to God for my sons, prayed that they would hear me, prayed that they would use this time well to make plans against their father, for I knew Henry would use this time. His resentment and sour hatred towards his sons would only grow with every day that passed as the snow fell and the wind wailed.

And it was in that winter that a change began to fall on me, one Dangerosa had told me of long ago. My monthly courses became erratic, my nights were full of what felt like fever, and yet I awoke with nothing of such things in my blood. Sometimes words would fail me, slip out of my head so I could spend half a morning — there was so little to do in my prison — trying to recall the word I had lost somewhere in my memory. There was a darkness there, in my mind, and it felt at times as if it would swallow me.

My grandmother had said this time could come to women if they were fortunate to live long enough. "Heat rises in the blood, and changes fall upon us," she had said long ago. "It is a time when the body leaves behind the time of childbearing, and woman, who has until that time been at the whim of nature, alters."

"To become what, Grandmother?" Petronilla had asked.

Dangerosa had smiled. "To become not a servant to her nature, child, but instead the master of nature. To become free of the destiny life puts upon her in youth and take up a life all her own in age. Not all women are given the gift of this time of life, for many die young, bearing children, or of fever or war, but those who are favoured, fortunate enough, they come through this time of change, where they must face the darkness and the fire, and on the other side of change, is something new."

"Does it hurt?" I had asked.

"It is a struggle, and a hard one, I will not lie to you, child," she had said. "A long darkness we all, if we are fortunate to live so long, must go through. It burns us, and it alters us. The alteration carries pain, the fire can scorch through to the bone and the darkness can at times seem never-ending, but at the end, child, at the end of the darkness of transformation, there is light, and, like a butterfly a woman emerges, to see where she may fly on the other side."

She could have as easily been speaking of my imprisonment as the changes in my body.

This would not be easy. There was a struggle upon me already, but if I could wait it out, there was another life to be had on the other side of this long darkness.

Chapter Seventeen

Falaise, Chinon,

Normandy

May 1174

"With thaw, comes war," I muttered, remembering this old saying of my father's.

That spring, the moment the weather improved, fighting broke out again on all fronts. My informant told me that Henry was busy in Anjou and Poitou. He crushed the supporters of my son there, and on the 12th of May he personally visited Poitiers. He wanted more hostages, you see.

"My children, my court," I murmured to myself, feeling a sick worm of guilt and rage bury itself in my heart.

I could not protect them, could not stop Henry doing whatever he wanted to do to them. He knew that, and sent word to me, a letter, telling me he was dismissing what remained of my court. My daughters Eleanor and Joanna would be set under "his protection" as would Marguerite and Alys of France, Emma of Anjou his bastard sister, Constance of Brittany and Alice of Maurienne.

He also stripped my palaces of many valuables which he knew were precious to me, items owned by Dangerosa, my father, by Petronilla. It hurt to think of him touching such treasured memories with his soiled and greedy hands, but things could be replaced. People could not. I feared for my daughters and for my daughters-in-law. All these women now were hostages as I was. He hoped to keep women like Constance, Marguerite and Alys to use against his sons. I feared how he would take revenge on Emma.

Yet it did not all go well for him. His enemies still had not given up despite their losses. For a year this war had raged, and there was no end yet, for in June Henry received news from England. "The King of Scots has once more crossed into England. He lays siege to Carlisle," whispered Joan, tidying my plates away. "The north of England is under attack from his lords, too, and the North and Midlands some say are alive with rebellion. The Castle of Nottingham has fallen, and it is said the Count of Flanders as well as the Young King plan another invasion. Richard de Lucy sends men to plead with the Old King for aid to reinforce England, and the Old King has been ignoring them, until now."

"What is being said of the Old King by the people?" I whispered. "Are they still opposed to him?"

"Many are, my lady, but many are not. It is said the Old King is seeing these disasters as punishment from God for his failure to do penance for the murder of Becket and has decided that this penance must be his priority. For this, some laud him as pious."

"That is simply a move to make sure the Church stays on his side," I muttered, "Henry has never held himself truly culpable for the death of his friend, he thinks Becket deserved death for defying him." I shook my head. "He thinks to win the public to his side with this demonstration, thinks to convince them that he is virtuous and godly for putting penance before war. It is all a show."

One day I was suddenly shipped to Barfleur. I did not even get a chance to say goodbye to Joan, no chance to thank her, to clasp her hand in mine and tell her she had been the sole reason I had not gone out of my mind with worry. There was nothing, no time and no goodbye. Much as I vanished on the road to France, I did again, from her life. To many people we become as ghosts, and I did to her as she did to me.

Perhaps someone besides the guards had heard her talk to me, or perhaps no one ever knew she was my friend in that dark time. I never knew, never found out what happened to her after I left. One morning I was roused by guards, and they told me to dress. I asked for water to wash and was told there was no time. From my prison I was bundled into a litter, and I was carried to the port town. It was then I knew, I was being sent to England. Henry could not risk me on the Continent. I would be harder for my sons to find in England.

But I was not alone.

From a prison chamber in that town, I saw at a distance my son John, as well as my daughters Joanna and Eleanor. I saw Alys, Emma, and all the other prisoners of the Old King. Henry was sending all of us to England.

There were forty ships there to transport the entire royal family, all these noble prisoners, and our personal servants, as well as the King's household, his court and his army of mercenaries. I wished I could face him, but Henry came not to me. I wished I could have told him that stealing away the brides of his sons was lower than even I had thought he would stoop, but I had not the chance.

Yet I wondered anew if God did at times intervene in the events of man. Often, I have thought this but a fiction created by men who believe themselves, their lives and destinies, to be more important than they truly are, but at times, especially upon the sea, there have been moments I have wondered.

Perhaps the sea is closer to the heart of God. People often look upwards, to Heaven above, to see His mind, to try to find what He is thinking, but I see the ocean as the heart of the Almighty, for there I ever have felt His emotions. God was angry that day.

As we were setting out the waves started to become rough, white foam splattering our faces, wind rising. I was bundled downstairs, to the cabin. From above, through the rickety boards of the ship I could hear many of the sailors asking the Old King to delay but when Henry learned that the wind was blowing against us, and the strong gusts were getting worse he urged his men on. Later I was told he lifted his eyes to the skies and cried out, "If the Lord of Heaven has ordained that peace will be restored when I arrive, then in His mercy may He grant me a safe landing, but if He be hostile to me, if He has decided to visit the Kingdom with a rod, may it never be my fortune to reach the shores of my country."

It was a wise gamble. If his ship was sunk in this tempest, it would hardly matter what he said for he and all the crew would be dead. If he arrived safe, no matter what beating his ship took, it would seem that God was with him. And since his ship made it, Henry could, no matter what evidence to the contrary there was, and there was plenty over the years, claim God was on his side.

One could, of course, have taken note that whilst the King's ship made it, plenty did not. Many a ship was lost in that storm, and many stomachs were emptied too, of their contents, but the ships containing the hostages made it. I knew, for I saw the women who had been part of my court, my daughters and my daughters-in-law, as we landed.

Briefly did I again see them, for we were sat at a table and made to eat a simple meal of bread and ale. We were told not to talk. Guards stood close, to ensure this happened, grim men with grim faces.

My daughters Joanna and Eleanor, as well as Emma and all the women who I had raised more than their own mothers had, kept glancing at me, noting my frame which had grown thinner in captivity as well as the pallor of skin, since I had not been allowed to see the sun for months. When the guards looked away, my little girl looked straight at me, as if she would burst into tears, but I shook my head and smiled at her. "Be strong," I mouthed to Joanna. "I love you."

She nodded and looked back at her plate, where her uneaten bread was. Eleanor took her hand and nodded to me, tears in her eyes. Marguerite and Alys glanced at the guards and Alys mouthed, "Are you well?" to me. I nodded once before the guards looked our way again. "No talking!" one of them shouted, evidently understanding something had passed between us.

"There has been no talking," I said calmly, breaking my bread into bits. He scowled at me, made a move as if he meant to threaten me with his sword, and I simply stared at him.

He lowered his hand. Even if I was a prisoner, he could do nothing to me. Touch me and he would be punished, he knew it.

After we had eaten bread and ale, I was taken away under guard to Sarum Castle near Salisbury and there I was once more confined again. The others did not come with me. Later I learned that Queen Marguerite, along with her sister Alys and Constance of Brittany, had been sent to the Castle of Devizes when they were to be kept no doubt until Geoffrey, Richard and young Henry could be brought under my husband's power. I heard not long after that Alice had died, I knew not what of, but John's bride to be was no more. Emma of Anjou was given that year in marriage to Dafydd ap Owen, the Prince of eastern Gwynedd, in return for his loyal service to the Old King. She went into Wales. I doubted I would see her again. Even if peace lasted between this Welsh prince and Henry, Wales was hostile to the English invaders so Emma would not be allowed out. I did not think she would have an easy time in her new country either, for although she was of Anjou she was likely to be viewed as at least allied with the English if not one of them.

She had stood with me, and this was her punishment. I hoped her husband was a good man, kind to her but I knew it was a distinct possibility he would be neither of those things.

As for me, I was shown a brief vision of my daughters, all of them, and then it was snatched away. And I was to be kept in England. He knew I hated the cold, the rain, he knew I loved my own country. He meant to take the sun from me, the light from my world, the warmth from my bones and from my heart. He meant to crush me.

*

Now that all his rebellious womenfolk were imprisoned in various houses about England, Henry went off to do what clearly mattered more than making friends with his sons. He would do penance for his great friend.

On the 12th of June, a Saturday, he dismounted near the city of Canterbury and laid aside his insignia of kingship. Clad in only a woollen smock, as pilgrims might wear, the King of England walked barefoot to the chapel and prostrated himself before Becket's ornate tomb, where he remained long in prayer. Bishop Foliot delivered a sermon to the watching crowds who had come to ogle at the notion of a king humbling himself before a tomb, explaining yet again that the King had not ordered the death of Becket.

The more someone says something, the less it makes sense. Try it with a word now, repeat it over and over and you will find that the word becomes meaningless, unmanageable in your mouth. It was the same with Henry and his repeated protest he did not order the death of Becket. Repeated over and over it became meaningless, because it was. It was not true, and he did not regret his actions at all. The more I heard that protest, the more I was sure of that.

Henry received absolution from the bishop and, baring his naked back, received three to five lashes from each and every one of the numerous body of churchmen who were there assembled. Seventy monks participated in the flogging, yet I doubt any of them hit him hard. I suspect everyone wanted to have a go, however. How often does one get to strike a king with impunity? It was quite something to boast of afterwards.

When the monks and prelates were done lashing him, Henry remained lying before the tomb, praying all day and night. He gave a good performance, neither took food nor went out to visit the jakes, and would not permit himself to be covered by a rug or a blanket or anything for warmth.

On the Sunday he heard Mass, drank water from a well dedicated to Saint Thomas and was given a vial of blood from the martyr's body. He departed from Canterbury rejoicing, cheered by the people, reaching London on the Sunday evening.

"Well, I am sure one evening of hardship was so taxing for him." I gazed about at my stark chamber in Sarum. Deprivation is hardly onerous when it lasts one night, or when we know there will be an end to it. I did not know when my punishment would end.

But at such times when I came to think on this, I told myself another tale. I had a bed, I had food, I could not see my children, but they were alive in the world. There were others in this world who did not have food in their bellies or a place to sleep. There were people who had lost their children. When I came from this place I wanted to be as I had been, not bitter and twisted from the things Henry had done to punish me. Indeed, if I let him turn me into something I was not, then truly he had won. So, every time I started to delve into sour tales of my neglect and imprisonment, I told myself another tale, a tale of plenty, a story of what I had and what I needed to thank God for. It was hard some days, but it was always good for me, I knew that for it made me feel better.

That night, exhausted apparently from being flogged and from fasting for a whole day, Henry had to summon his physician, who let his blood. Then the Old King fell into a peaceful sleep with his head resting on his elbow and a servant rubbing his feet, those *poor* feet, cut by the hard stones on the walk to Canterbury.

But he was not to sleep long. There was a banging on the door. The keeper of the room told the person outside to be gone and come in the morning for the King was asleep, but Henry soon was awake and in came a messenger who carried news most marvellous to the King's ear. An army led by Geoffrey his bastard son as well as the Sheriff of Yorkshire had achieved a victory at Alnwick. The King of Scots himself had been captured and was being held at Richmond Castle. Henry was so merry that the messenger, named Abraham, was immediately rewarded with an estate in Norfolk. The Old King ran off to tell his court the fine news. All the bells of London were rung that night, pealing on and on in the darkness, and Henry cried out, "God be thanked for it, and Saint Thomas the martyr!"

I rolled my eyes when I heard of this, knowing that now Henry would use Becket as his personal link to God. Once more he had proved the man he was. In life he had loathed Becket, he had caused his death, but in dying the man had become useful to Henry. He would use Thomas Becket, now they were 'reconciled' to demonstrate he was godly. Becket the Saint was looking down upon him from Heaven and rewarding him, that was the message Henry was trying to offer.

What was saddest of all was that some people believed him. The corpse of Becket had come to be wrapped about the King as a cape of righteousness and protection. It was foul, and I loathed Henry for it. Becket would not have wanted this, and for all the man had done to me I hoped he was not looking down from Heaven to see this. It would have horrified him.

But the dead cannot speak for themselves, and neither can a prisoner. Henry could use us any way he wanted now. Or so he thought.

Men believed God was on Henry's side, and the confidence of his foes fell away. Soon enough the rebellion was quenched in England. It collapsed, and upon hearing of this Louis told young Henry and the Count of Flanders to call off their planned invasion of England. It was too much to risk without support from within England itself. Louis joined them instead in an attack on Rouen which went not well from the very beginning. Henry's enemies were indeed losing their confidence, as more and more people became certain that God and Thomas Becket were on the King of England's side.

By the end of July, England was once more under his full control, the King of Scots was in his custody, and on the 8th of August I heard Henry had returned to Barfleur with his mercenaries, as well as Welsh troops. With this force he advanced on Rouen, apparently reducing King Louis to a state of utter bewilderment, and on the 14th of August Louis gave up on being a warrior once again and ran back to Paris with the Young King in tow.

My sons were forced to concede that they had been beaten.

Against overwhelming odds, the Old King had prevailed.

Chapter Eighteen

Sarum

Salisbury

September 1174

Some are gracious in defeat or victory, but as I have mentioned Henry was not one of them. Riding high on the elation of having won against so many foes, he decided to subject his enemies to humiliating terms. In Falaise, William the Lion of Scotland was forced to sign a treaty which surrendered Scotland to Henry as an absolute fief, which would mean the King of Scots had to pay homage to the King of England, recognising him as its overlord every year. He also had to surrender to Henry the castles of Edinburgh, Stirling, Roxburgh, Jedburgh and Berwick.

Realising they could do nothing more, Louis and Philip of Flanders attempted to heal the breach between the King of England and his sons. They persuaded young Henry and Geoffrey that they had no choice now but to sue for peace and submit to their father.

Richard did not cease campaigning against his father until the very end, and finally when he came face to face with him at Montlouis, near Tours, at the end of September, he threw himself at Henry's feet and begged his forgiveness, but only because it was his last resort. People said he wept but I would doubt that very much. Richard was a man who could weep, most often for fallen friends, but his father never stirred much emotion in him apart from contempt. Yet those who win the war get to tell the tales, and Henry had won.

For now.

The Old King raised Richard up and gave him the kiss of peace, so the story went. On the 30th of September a full peace was reached at Montlouis. The Old King assigned young Henry an income of £3,750 per annum as well as two castles in Normandy. Richard was given half the revenues of Poitou and two castles, and Geoffrey was given half the revenues of Brittany with the rest to follow up on his marriage to

Constance. Many said the Old King was generous, but he was not. These settlements were less than my sons had had as income before the wars. The idea was to limit their ability to rise again, but Henry also wanted to punish them.

Most humiliatingly he had not delegated any aspect of his power to his sons and had forced young Henry to accept the original settlement of estates and castles which had fallen on John.

John now had an inheritance substantially increased by the addition of properties in England which should have been his brothers', as well as ones in Normandy, Anjou, Touraine and Maine. My husband was rewarding our youngest son for being the only one who had not risen against him. The truth was, John probably would have, had he been old enough. He was only seven.

My sons were forced to offer promises that they would never demand anything of their father beyond this settlement and would withdraw neither themselves nor their service from their father. Henry blamed the King of France and me for the strange, strained relationship that he now possessed with his three eldest sons, and whilst he gave the kiss of peace, he never again trusted them. His bastard son Geoffrey he loved more than all the others. It was a widely told tale that Henry had informed Geoffrey, that he had proved himself his lawful and true son. My husband said that his other sons were really the bastards. From that moment onwards Geoffrey was one of the King's most valued and trusted counsellors.

I was glad there were no executions of rebel leaders. The Old King, having given orders for the destruction of all rebel strongholds and the release of all hostages, proclaimed that there was to be a general amnesty for all who had risen against him.

That did not include me.

All others were released. I was not.

Chapter Nineteen

Sarum

Salisbury

1175

Henry spent Christmas of 1174 at Argentan, as I was left to rot in Sarum. Amnesty for all. For all men, but not for his wife.

In truth it was in some ways a compliment that I, considered the most dangerous of his enemies, was not released. In other ways I knew it was personal. He knew, knew only too well, how I had hated being a prisoner of Louis when I was married to him, and so, venom ruling his heart, my second husband did the same to me now.

Our love once had been soft, sweet fruit, ripe, the flesh yielding gently under the fingers, whispering of joy to come in nectar, pulp and juice, but now, teeth had bitten through that sweet part, had eaten all the syrupy, soft flesh to reach that which hugged the central stone. The flesh there was bitter, a mean contrast on the tongue.

I had one maid, the same one now but only ever one. Her name was Amaria, and she was my sole companion in those barren years. People cried out, protesting about my imprisonment, for they said I should be released since Henry had ordered there to be peace now within our family. But he meant peace between his sons and himself. Not me.

The war of his sons was over, but ours was not done.

He had not won yet, you see? He knew that. He must have been having reports of me and my behaviour from those who watched me, and although they no doubt reported I was thinner than before, that I was paler, they would not be reporting that I wept in my chambers, for I never did. They would not be reporting that I wailed or moaned, for I would not give Henry the satisfaction. I went about my days with routine and ritual. Where I was given no books, I would sit by a window and remember the tales told to me by my grandmother. I would remember the births of each child, their games and all they had said to me. I spent time in prayer, and I made plans for my future. He had not won, because he had not crushed me. That meant he would need to keep me prisoner for longer, but we would see who out of the two of us possessed the most endurance.

I admit, though, Sarum was a test.

The town of Sarum was perched atop a windswept hill, dominated by a Norman keep and cathedral and surrounded by a deep ditch. It was a bleak, inhospitable place. At night, the wind had voices in it, wailing, calling to me. In dreams they shook me, woke me, so I would lie there in the dark staring at the canopy over my bed which rattled and shifted in the draughts blowing through my chamber. Often if I woke, I would lie there for hours, remembering the past, the people I had loved and lost. Sometimes I would feel arms reaching about me, and I would smile and fall back to sleep, knowing that even if I was alone, a prisoner, a captive, Henry could not stop the ghost of my sister reaching me. Petronilla was always here, he could not keep her away.

Water was scarce and hard to come by in Sarum. The city was overcrowded, smelly, and the wind was so strong that it was said the clerks in the cathedral could hardly hear one another sing. Sarum was a city where many there suffered from rheumatism, aches in the joints and bones, swelling in the fingers and knees, and the cathedral was repeatedly damaged by severe gales. I was fifty-two when I was sent there and whilst I was in fine health with the sun of Aquitaine in my bones and the change of women raging in my blood, I knew Henry had sent me to Sarum hoping my blood might chill, my bones might freeze, and I might crumble and become less of a threat to him. He thought to make me a ghost to the world, so the world and my children would forget me.

He thought I was weak, you see, because I was a woman, because of my age, because the change was upon me. He knew nothing.

There were other punishments than the cold Sarum wind and the bitterness of isolation. I had little money. Henry by that point had sent money, but allowed me only a pittance knowing that I loved luxuries. It was not a very creative punishment. I imagine he sat in his chamber chortling to himself about this one, but I had lived in far worse conditions than he offered me then. What made me sad was I could not reward those who served me well, but there was little I could do about that then. In the future, I told myself, much would alter.

My household was very small, it was true, Amaria my only companion. We shared a bed, as much to keep warm as because I had only one bed, yet I was treated courteously by the men who guarded me. I was cut off as much as possible, as much as Henry could manage from the outside world. He meant to deprive me of any means of plotting my escape or further conspiring against him, that was true enough, but he also meant to punish me by trying to ensure that I would hear nothing of my children.

It did not work.

Had it worked this would have been a true deprivation, but I had ever had a talent of making friends, and I made them in Sarum. Amaria was soon enough my good friend, no two women can share that much time and cold together without becoming so, and she was young, being only fourteen, and already much impressed by me before we even met, so winning her to me was easy. Henry forgot not only that women make peace and friends easily where men often struggle, but that I had raised many daughters, some of my blood and some the children of other women, and all had come to respect and have affection for me. It was the same with Amaria.

When I noted her olive complexion and almond eyes and mentioned she seemed to resemble women I had met in Constantinople she smiled, telling me she had been born there and her father was a native of that city, but when he had died her mother had wed a high standing merchant from England and brought her and her brothers and sisters to this land. "You must miss the warmth of Constantinople," I said.

"I do, my lady, and scent of the evenings in summer."

"Jasmine," I said, my voice almost a caress as I remember the soft, sweet scent.

"Yes, my lady." She was delighted that I knew something of the place of her birth, and it was pleasing too to think that we now had something to converse on with ease.

"I am glad to have you, child," I said to her often, and she opened to me in friendship as a flower does on a warm summer's day. In the chill of Sarum, I became the sun to her, and as for Amaria she was as the North Star to me.

The guards who watched my door, too, came to be fond of me, for I enquired about their wives, families, their lives. People like it when another shows an interest in them, it makes them trust, and in truth the wide world is so busy and the people in it often obsessed only with their own concerns so someone paying attention to your doings, your troubles, seems remarkable. Perhaps it is, and perhaps that is why it works so well to disarm people.

It did not all happen at once, of course. I had to move with care for I was a prisoner, and they were primed already to distrust me. So, a question here, a heartfelt word of thanks there, and soon enough I had the guards telling me of their children, and Amaria telling me her dreams.

And I was, in truth, not disinterested. It was not all an act to gain their trust. Prison life is dull, ask anyone who ever has been held captive. Anything of the outside is interesting after a while, and even if I had not wanted to gain friends and convince them I was no threat for escape – which was not true, if there was a chance I would take it – I would have listened to their tales in any case. It helped to gain sympathy too outside of this castle and this town, for in time if stories of the good Eleanor and her clemency, her humility, her virtue whilst kept in prison leaked out, then the public might be able to put pressure on their King to release me.

My custodian, Ranulf Glanville, came at first only from time to time, but in less than a month he came to my chamber each night, to talk to me of the events going on in the world. He was not supposed to, but I shared plenty of ways that he might find paths to elevation, told him of useful men to contact, good skills to know, and in response he shared with me news of the world.

That was how I came to know that my people of Aquitaine and Poitou still protested about the imprisonment of their Duchess and wailed in grief and anger, but they had Richard still, that part of my plan at least had not gone awry. I was happy they had him. I did not fear to leave my homeland in the hands of my son. I only wished that I could see my son as well as his brothers and sisters, as well as their wives. Those women had been as much my children as any of those I had birthed.

It was said there had been a prophecy which I had fulfilled, that an eagle with two heads had raised her eaglets. They had flown from their nest and lifted talons against the king of the north wind. My second nesting, this rebellion against Henry, had failed and I had found myself without my eaglets. They called me the 'Eagle of the broken alliance', yet it was also said there was a last part to this prophecy, that the day was approaching when I should be once more delivered unto my homeland and to my sons, when the eagle would fly free.

"The gyrfalcon is sometimes mistaken for an eagle," I mentioned to Amaria.

"Then one day perhaps this will come true," she said, shaking back her dark hair, like strands of night curling about dreams of man it was. "You will see your homeland and your children again, my lady."

"These prophecies are part of the prophecies of Merlin as recounted by Geoffrey of Monmouth," I told her. "They could mean anything, of course, for the wording of such stories is left vague, and people attribute any event which has come to pass which seems similar to such prophecies, but I am willing to believe. I rejoice to think there might come a time when I would be free to return to my native lands, to see my children. To be taken from them, it is the hardest punishment." I smiled at Amaria. "That is why I am glad I have you," I said to her again. "You remind me of my daughters."

"Which of them, my lady?"

"All of them." My heart sang as I thought on each and every one. "You have the decorum of Matilda, who is gone away now and is married. You have the sweetness of my little Joanna, who is the youngest, and you have the spirit of Eleanor. You hide it more than she does, but I see it in you."

I wanted Amaria confident, and not just for her own sake. I wanted my maid bold enough to find out much for me, and to share it with me.

At the moment there was nothing I could do to free myself, and my sons, though I heard they protested my continued imprisonment to their father, could not do anything either. They had little money and no power. It would not last, though, I knew that. They had come very close to succeeding, very close indeed. Such things give men ideas. This would not be the last time they rose against him. If there came a chance in the future that I might be freed by them, I had to be ready to take it.

My husband, merry in his triumph, was living openly with his mistress Rosamund de Clifford. Rosamund did not preside over court in my place, such would have been an affront to the Church, and they would have removed their support for Henry, so young Queen Marguerite was trooped out to stand in for me on official occasions. She must have done well, done all she was told, for I heard that her income was increased to a level which far exceeded anything I had ever been offered, and in time she was released for a month or so at a time to be with her husband on the Continent or in Paris. In those times Henry presided alone over his court and went at night to bed his mistress.

With me safe at windy, barren Sarum, Henry sailed back to Normandy with young Henry, his bastard son Geoffrey, and his court until the following spring. Whilst he was there the King was putting pressure on the Pope for two things, firstly to confirm Geoffrey's election as Bishop of Lincoln and secondly to be rid of me.

"I hear the King is asking, discreetly of course, if an annulment could be brought about, my lady," said Ranulf, my custodian.

I smiled.

"You would accept?" His voice was incredulous.

"I smile because it will never be allowed," I said. "Not on the terms my husband will want, which would be to rid himself of me and yet retain my lands, and not by my sons, who, by this action, he seeks to bastardise."

"That would be insanity, surely, my lady." My gaoler looked shocked, as if the possibility of this had not occurred to him, but he did not know Henry and he did not know the power spite had over the man. "To try now to bastardize his sons, who are grown men? If the King sought to wed again, if his suit to the Pope to end your marriage was successful, a new child, even if he managed to have another boy, would be an infant when the time came for him to come to the throne. His sons now, there are four, and all but John are grown, ready for the throne."

"And yet that is what is in his mind," I said.

"But the kingdom would be plunged into war, anarchy."

"The King has left caring for others behind in this stage of life." I crossed to the window to look at the bleak landscape outside. I often thought it was intended as another punishment. Even the view here was ugly, but I had found beauty in it. Often when the wooden shutters were open, I would stand at the window, feeling the breeze on my face. The stark hillsides and threatening skies had their own magic, if one learnt to find it and I had all the time in the world to find such things. "He once was a great king, but that time has passed. He now is a tyrant, and he is filled with malevolence. He might make up with his sons by me for now, for peace, but he will seek to disinherit them, no matter the damage to his kingdoms, in order to pay them back for their rebellion. This peace he offers, even the kiss of peace, they are just that, peace, but not forgiveness. Henry wants to make them pay, everyone who ever has defied him."

Ranulf left that day looking most disturbed.

Fresh news came within a week. Richard and Geoffrey had been sent away to minister to their dominions. Geoffrey went to Brittany whilst Richard returned south, where he was forced to subdue angry vassals of Poitou and Aquitaine. They were still fighting the Crown upon my past orders, and now because I was imprisoned. Some of them, since Richard had made peace with his father, had come to think of him as but a puppet of Henry's, so they fought Richard too, but Richard was not a man to be crossed. Savagely he worked to repress them. He ravaged the countryside, castle after castle fell to him. It was said by some he would not hesitate to stoop low, for he ordered maimings, blindings and mutilations, and had women raped by his men in front of their husbands. "Such things as these done to women, I hope are not true," I whispered when I was told.

I knew not if they were, though. Perhaps I should have been shocked at all the crimes, it was not nothing for a man to lose ears, a tongue, an eye, and yet, and probably because I was a woman, the idea of rape was more horrific. Men can strip something away, a limb, and go on living well enough, but as I knew from what Louis had done to me under direction of the Pope, some other wound is formed in rape. It is like a shadow which comes, stronger in the early days, after it happens, but never without power no matter how many years have passed. And it never goes, all your life it is there, even when you think you have vanquished it, even when it no more is your first thought when you wake and last as you go to sleep, even when your dreams are no more always hunted by visions of what happened.

Always, it is there, hiding, waiting to leap from amongst other shadows. It shocks you on days where nothing seemed untoward, comes back in dreams. It sucks life from you at times, sure as if someone had cut your throat and hung you upside down like a calf so the blood may drain onto the floor. The shadow makes you distrust people you have no cause to distrust, and sometimes it sends you, trusting like a fool, towards people who want to hurt you, all because the pain they offer has become so familiar it feels like home. It reminds you of a time when all power over everything, even your innards, your body, was stripped from you, and it whispers in your ear that it could do it again, and laughs.

In some ways, being a prisoner of Henry was a constant reminder of that time. The shadow was all about me here. My control over life had been taken from me, my freedom, my liberty. Yes, here the shadow was strong, and it laughed in the darkness with glee.

It had been years since Louis had forced sex on me, years, yet I remembered every moment of it, and of carrying his child after. With all my heart, I hoped my son was not capable of doing this to people. But I did not know for sure.

Sometimes tales are told of men in war which are false, and sometimes men in the grip of war do awful things to their foes. None of my sons were angels, some were not even good men. I had always had more faith in Richard than any of them, but I did not know for sure if he was capable of such evil.

From this time onwards Richard would ever be engaged in a succession of campaigns against his turbulent vassals, and I would hear reports of him, hoping with all that was within me that my son was a better man than the one men spoke of in the missives Ranulf received.

And when the shadow came to me, chuckling in my ear, I did not shrink or hide from it. I turned to face it, for there was a darkness of transformation within me that was stronger, harder and deeper than the shadow which had followed me.

I turned my own darkness on the shadow, and watched it flinch from the restless, changing power which raged inside my heart.

*

In October of 1174, Henry had made peace with Louis. Richard and Geoffrey swore fealty to their father as did young Henry later on. On that second occasion of swearing fealty, Henry raised up his son who was weeping before him and assured him of his love. "He also assigned him a more generous allowance from the treasury," Ranulf told me as he placed his knight on a square of the board with a satisfying little clunk. Ranulf had brought chess with him, a game I often had played in the Holy Lands, as I had told him. He was a fair opponent, but I was better. I let him win from time to time, however. It was good for his confidence and our friendship.

"I doubt young Henry was weeping out of regret." I moved a pawn to higher ground. "Unless it was regret that he did not win."

"You think your son deceives the King?"

"I think the King deceives young Henry and young Henry, the King." I watched as he toyed with his bishop and moved to a foolish position. All his attention was on the conversation. This was why he was only a fair opponent; he could not concentrate on the game and on talking at the same time. "In truth, perhaps I speak ill of my son for no good reason. He wanted, all his life, for his father to recognise that he had something of worth in him, and the King never did. He never has thought young Henry was worthy of his crown, that is why he keeps him a child. Perhaps he fears what the man will become when treated as an adult."

"I never thought the King afraid of anything."

I surveyed the board. "He fears his sons, you can see it in every action he takes, trying to subdue them, to hold them back from their true potential, trying to keep all for himself and share nothing of his lands with them. And they, all their lives have been waiting for this man so often a stranger to them to come and approve of them, just a little, and never has it happened. Henry fears his own children and his children resent him." I sat back on my stool. "And the reason he is terrified of his children, my lord, is because he fears the future."

"The future?"

I nodded. "For what lies in the futures of all of us? What is the one thing all the living will do, the thing which unites us as one?"

Ranulf looked confused. "One thing we all will do, my lady? All of us?"

I smiled. "We all will die, my lord. The living, every one of us, every flower, bird and stem of wheat, all will fall to dust one day. The King looks at his children and he sees the future; he sees the time that he is dust and it terrifies him. The King looks on his sons, and he sees the face of Death."

I took his bishop and added it to the growing pile of his men at my side of the board. "Now, pay attention, my lord. If you become too distracted by the King, you will lose this battle."

Ranulf laughed and attended to the game.

Chapter Twenty

Sarum

Salisbury

1175

In May of 1175 two kings of England, one old and one young, crossed to England in a single boat together, no doubt so the Young King could not sail away and escape, and together went on pilgrimage to the shrine of Saint Thomas at Canterbury. The Old King stayed up all night in vigil and in prayer, fasting and scourging himself until the third day. After leaving Canterbury the King and his son went on a progress through England. Hearing this, I did hope at that time I might be permitted to see my eldest son, but I was not.

"I am sorry, my lady, but I hear from court that your son has not even requested to see you." Ranulf looked uncomfortable and aggrieved.

I nodded and looked to the window, allowing him to see the glimmer of tears in my eyes. They were real, it hurt that my son, for whose sake I was imprisoned, had not asked to see me, but my grief could be useful too, in gaining more sympathy. I had to use all the weapons I had, for I had so few.

In some ways I could understand why young Henry had not asked to see me. It could have been mere thoughtlessness. I knew my son well enough to know that I might well have simply slipped from his mind the moment I was not of use to him anymore, he could be like his father at times, but it could be more than this too. Petitioning for me might threaten the new, fragile peace between father and son, and young Henry needed that peace to last if he was ever to get out from under the boot of his father. He was as much a prisoner as I was, for Henry kept our son almost tied to his waist, he was on such a short leash. There was also the possibility that young Henry *had* asked to see me, but this was not the tale being told at court. My husband no doubt wanted people to forget me and for them to think that my sons had forgotten me too, reducing my importance in the world. If that was the idea, it was no wonder the news that would come from court was a tale of my son's indifference to me. Henry was good at spreading misinformation.

That, I wanted to believe, but I did not know if it was true. That is the trouble with knowing people well, you know what they are capable of.

"The news is, my lady," Ranulf went on, rushing on to fill the uncomfortable silence and evidently hoping to distract me, "That the Young King spoke much with friends about the fact that once again his brothers are permitted to rule their kingdoms and he is not, but he has not shared his indignation with the King, or in public again."

I inclined my head. "He will." I continued to stare out of the window with tears shimmering in my eyes. I wanted it reported by Ranulf to Henry and to others that I was sad, but I faced my sadness with courage. It was, after all, only the truth, so I should get some acclaim for it from the outside world. "My son is trying to be politic, which is good considering it often does not occur to him, but resentment will spill out of him in time." I turned to Ranulf. "We are as goblets, my lord. There is a certain volume of emotion any of us can hold but when the limit is reached, over the side burbles what we cannot contain."

"Some say the Young King says nothing because he and his father are closer than ever, never are they away from one another."

I chuckled with dark humour. "That is not affection which so binds them. My husband keeps the Young King as his prisoner, but rather than send him to windy Sarum, like me, he ties him to his belt. Both may be pretending it is for love of each other, but it is not. Hatred may bind men just as tight as love."

Ranulf pushed his cap back, a fine one of black velvet, and scratched his forehead. "I did hear the Young King was requesting to be allowed to go to France, go on pilgrimage in other lands, and was not allowed."

"His father has him under his boot once more, and now the Young King is going nowhere unless his father knows of it. I am sure another reason my son did not request to see this prisoner of the King..." I indicated to myself "... is because he is a prisoner himself."

It was around this time that Henry took steps to have his marriage to me annulled. There had been whispers already of course which I had heard through Ranulf and my maid, but now there was an addition to the first rumour.

"People are claiming, my lady, that the King is enamoured of Alys of France," Amaria told me. She had been to the market that day and had picked up as many rumours as there were dried pippins on the apple stall.

"Alys of France?" I whispered. "The girl I raised in my household as my daughter, the girl promised to Richard as his bride?"

Amaria nodded, her eyes wide. "Yes, the very same. People are saying the King is in love with her."

I was silent a moment, more than a moment. It is an odd time when you think you are immune to shock, that you have heard all or seen all, and then you learn something, some fresh evil, and it takes your breath away.

I felt nauseous. The girl was now fifteen and had blossomed over the last year into a beauty, so I was told. I did not doubt this was true, Alys had held great potential when I had last seen her and many times girls transform in beauty during the age she was now. She was also a wit and came from a great house, but I balked at this notion, not only because she was Richard's affianced, not only because Henry was trying to set me, not to mention my children, aside, but because I had brought the girl up. She was like my daughter, and he meant to try to wed her? Oh, it was not incest, but it felt like it all the same.

"This is another punishment," I said, feeling my heart shudder at the thought of Henry taking this girl who could have been his granddaughter to his bed, "for me, for Richard. Young Henry he has on a leash and now he strikes for Richard, trying to take his bride from him, trying to take revenge, and he knew that Alys and I had an affection for one another, he knew that I was training her to become Duchess of Aquitaine. He would try to steal the future from my people in this way, try to strip her from the husband she should have and the future that was promised to her."

Amaria brought me a cup of ale. I must have looked pallid. I sipped it, wishing it was wine.

Closeness of blood, a dark irony, I learned, was how Henry was thinking of being rid of me. It was true Louis had used consanguinity to end our marriage and I was, in actual fact, closer in blood to Henry than I had been to Louis, so it should have been an easy way to object to our marriage in one respect. But there were problems. Henry did not want to lose my lands. In ending our marriage, they would leave his hands and go back to me, then to Richard and he would have no say over what our son did or how he ruled. Henry would be setting up a man he already saw as a rival with vast power and resources. The second problem was almost amusing, for if he ended our marriage, he would have no hold over me anymore and would be forced to release me. Henry did not want that.

A woman at liberty, I could go back to Aquitaine as its ruler and start war against him all over again, and this time we might well win. Quite aside from this, Henry did not want to let me go because he was enjoying punishing me, and because he never liked to let go of anything he thought he had power over.

That did not mean he was not going to try to rid himself of me as a wife. During the summer of that year, I heard that Henry had asked Pope Alexander III to send a legate to England to hear his case against me. He did not want this widely known though, and therefore when the legate arrived, the man came on the pretext of resolving the quarrel between the Sees of York and Canterbury. This was not, however, his only purpose.

"The King seeks to curry favour with the Cardinal in order to separate from you, Majesty," Amaria told me, as rumours flying all over the market had come home in her basket. Foreign merchants had been there that day, ones who had travelled far bringing news from many a country with them. News traded as well as silk or spices most days. Amaria had been speaking with two Moorish merchants who had come to trade that day, and they had picked up this gossip on the road from Rome. When they heard she was my companion, they bade her tell me of it, telling her further that they, along with many people of many cities they had visited, deplored the way I was being kept prisoner by my husband.

"So, he will try to cajole and charm this man into agreeing to have me cast off as a wife and Queen," I said.

"But if you separated from the King, he would own your freedom no more, my lady, you could go home, be with your sons." Much as others did, she deplored the windy castle in which I was kept, the poor allowance I was permitted, and believed my age was enough to grant me more privileges even had I not been the Queen of England and Duchess of Aquitaine, yet Queen I might not be for much longer, if my husband had his way.

"He would never release me into full freedom, child, and there is more at stake here than simply my liberty. He seeks to shame me, through this loss of power, but I think he wishes to strike at my sons too," I said, holding out my hands to the fire. We had one lit even though it was summer, Sarum was cold that day. "Henry is trying to cast not only me off, but is trying to set aside all I have given him over the years of our marriage. He seeks to rid himself of the threat of his sons. He will try something devious, like keeping me in an abbey, perhaps, forcing me to take religious orders. That way, if I have retired voluntarily from our match, he might be able to get the Pope to name him overlord of my homeland, he might keep my lands and take a new wife."

"But the King is much older now," said Amaria. "Even if he managed this, my lady, separating from you and perhaps marrying Lord Richard's bride, Alys, any child she gave him would be far younger and less experienced than your sons."

I tapped her knee in approval. "You have a good, quick mind, child, and you are not the only one to be fearful of this with good reason, and yet there are many that might support him in his attempt, Louis of France for one. He might relish the notion of the chaos this would cause in England and beyond, and if he thought he could place a grandson on the English throne, thereby giving France a foothold not only in Henry's lands but mine too, he might support this. Louis has wanted Aquitaine back, all my other lands too, since we separated and he lost them."

"But King Louis has ever supported your sons, Majesty."

"That might change if he saw a way for France to win more than ever seemed possible before."

*

On the 1st of November, the feast of All Saints, my husband met Cardinal Uguccione Pierleoni of Sant' Angelo at Winchester and whilst nothing was said publicly, I had no doubt Henry was talking to the Cardinal about an annulment. Henry, who was never noted for his generosity, gave the legate a large amount of silver. Many understood this was a bribe. At Sarum we heard rumour that the King was asking that he be permitted to separate from his wife, and I would to a convent go, for the rest of my life.

I held my breath, thinking I might be bundled into a religious order before I could protest, might be shut away from the world and forced to become a nun, that Henry might steal my lands and marry Alys.

But I had reason to be grateful to the Church because their legate refused to even listen to Henry's plea for an annulment and instead warned him of all the risks which were involved in setting me aside.

"No doubt soon we will hear that Henry is fallen out with the Church again," I chuckled, feeling light as a flea, to Amaria. "But then again, I doubt it. Because of Becket he cannot now go against the Church ever again, all men would call him wicked beyond redemption, and the Pope would grant free rein to any to take his lands." I laughed again and clasped my hands together as if in prayer. "Saint Thomas," I said in a voice full of mocking benediction, lifting my eyes to Heaven. "I never thought I would have cause to be grateful to you, but I am this day, for due to your dying for the faith, my husband is unable to use the faith against me."

Mocking I was, but if Becket was anywhere listening, I was grateful to him. He would know that, if he heard me.

Amaria laughed with me, though she crossed herself at my sacrilegious talk over a saint. We celebrated that night. There was nothing special to celebrate with, but we toasted each other with the same thin ale we drank every night, and to my palate the bread and meat of the evening meal, served plain as always, tasted rich as the costliest spices, because on my tongue was the sweet spice of victory, making all taste of glory.

I was in prison, it was true, and Henry was free, but I knew one thing then.

He was not all-powerful.

The Cardinal left England soon afterwards and upon his leaving plague fell upon the country and famine followed soon after. That winter was the coldest in living memory and at Sarum I suffered greatly.

That Christmas Henry and young Henry were at Windsor together celebrating as the land was lashed by snow and covered in ice. It was a long winter indeed and the thaw did not begin until Candlemas of the next year.

It was a hard season for me and for Amaria. We had a fire in our rooms, but fuel was sent irregularly and the wind which whipped through the tower in which our chamber was, was cruel and cold and bitter as the heart of my husband. My hips ached some days and my head on others. Much of the day we spent in the bed in our chamber for it was warmer than sitting even near the fire. There was no need to dress up as Queen for no one was permitted to come and see me, and although at Christmas my servants of my tiny household tried to cheer me by bringing in greenery and decorating the halls, it was a hard, mean Christmas we passed that year. There were a few comforts, a little wine was sent, some extra flesh from animals slaughtered in November we were permitted, but the coldness of Sarum and the thought that I was separated from my children and could not see them at Christmas as always I had, weighed heavy upon my soul.

Yet one of the ghosts in the winds of Sarum was my sister, and in the cold nights, my arms wrapped about Amaria, trying to keep both of us warm, I would see my sister, hear her talking to me so many years ago. One particular memory kept coming back. She had been laughing, preparing me to be crowned as Queen of France. I could remember so well how the gold of my dress had shimmered on her beautiful face, as if she was a thing of light, a creature made of the illumination of the sun.

It was, in truth, how she had always seemed to me.

"I am also telling you to not only look at the darkness about you." My sister spoke in my memory, her smile warming my heart. "There is always light, there are always good things. Nights come, and they are long and cold at times, but the sun always rises. If you stare at the darkness alone, you forget what it is like to be in the light. Do not forget to observe also the good things about you, no matter how small they are, things that bring joy. You are naturally of a merry disposition, and I would not have you lose that by taking the world too seriously. Arm yourself against the world with your laughter, sister, and with your light."

Petronilla was right, I could not allow my spirit, which had been one of joy, to be so damaged that I would see only the darkness of the world. Even here, even so far away from all that made me *me*, I still was Eleanor. I still was a mother, a ruler, a sister. I still was a wife, and I was not about to be set aside so my husband could take another woman to bed and disinherit my children.

I am sure Henry thought to break me that winter, force me to accept any deal he offered when the thaw came, when I had suffered through much coldness of bone and blood and soul, but even though he had lived with me for many years, even though I had borne his children, there was much he did not know about me.

He did not know about another long winter I had faced in France before I separated from Louis when I was pregnant with Alix. He knew not the long wolf winter of my heart where I had hunkered down amidst the cold, both inside me and outside, and I had made a promise to myself that I would survive and escape.

I made the same promise now. I would survive, I would escape. I would find my children again. Every day when I was forced to go back to bed in order to keep warm, every night when I listen to the wind howl about Sarum, in every moment when I took to my knees in my chapel to pray, I prayed the same thing: let me endure, let me go to my children again or by the wrath of God I would make all men pay for what they had done to me.

Perhaps God heard my prayers, for whilst He did not permit me escape, the Almighty allowed respite, in the form of a guest.

Chapter Twenty-One

Sarum

Salisbury

August 1176

"Rosamund is dead, lady mother," said my daughter Joanna.

Due to endless pleas to see me before she was sent away to be wed – the finalities of her match I had of course not been consulted on – my eleven-year-old daughter had managed to prevail upon her father and was permitted a short time to see me. Joanna was my first guest, the first person I had seen who was not of my household for a year. I was no fool, however. Happy I was to see my daughter, but I knew that she had not been allowed to see me merely because she had pleaded to. Henry wanted something of me, and this favour was allowed because of that.

In the New Year he had sent me a letter, trying to tempt me with an offer that I might retire to Fontevraud, become Abbess perhaps, if I agreed to end our marriage. He thought to disarm me with my own desires for sunlight, the warmth of the south, the chance at future power, and he thought I would have been weakened by my time in prison during an English winter in the raw cold of Sarum, but I was only stronger than before. I was a Queen, a Duchess, a ruler and I would not be demoted to the rank of Abbess, still less would I allow him to harm my children, using me as a weapon against them.

I had rejected his offer outright and sent word to the Archbishop of Rouen, which reached him at Easter, telling him I was being pressured to enter a religious order against my will, which caused outrage within the Church, much to my delight. I knew what Henry was up to. Even the offer of Fontevraud was not freedom. Fontevraud was within Angevin territory, therefore still under his power. He would still be my jailer. The man thought he was clever, but he was a grand old fool.

I had chosen the Archbishop of Rouen for I knew he was an advocate of only those with a true vocation entering the Church. The Archbishop had refused to allow me to be sent to Fontevraud against my will, and so Henry had appealed now to the Pope, but the Pope had no reason to indulge his little lapdog, the King of England, and he did not want his servant to lose valuable possessions such as my land. The Pope wanted his puppet wealthy, so he could use that wealth, and so he wanted England to keep my domains. I have no doubt the Pope would tell the King to wait, have patience. I was an old woman now, after all. I was in prison in a barren keep with few luxuries. I would die soon, and he could get on with his plans then.

But I had no intention of dying. I would live just to spite him.

"Of what did my husband's mistress die?" I asked Joanna.

"I was told she simply wasted into death," said my daughter. "Yet the illness was a long one for she retired from court a year ago, entered the convent and there she died. People said she knew the end was coming a long time before it arrived."

"Then I am sad for the child, for she never truly had a chance to live." I stroked the back of my daughter's hand. Her skin, so soft, I tried to imprint on my memory, so I could recall this moment again and again, in case we never were allowed to meet after this.

"There is more, Maman, and I think you will not like it."

"Your father has taken Alys Capet into his bed and means to try to wed her in my place," I said calmly, still looking at her hand.

Joanna blinked. "How did you know that?"

"Even here, so cut off from the world, there are people willing to tell me much." I looked up at her.

In truth I had not known he had started to keep Alys as a mistress, it had been a guess, but I knew Henry and he was not a patient man. If he wanted a girl in his bed, and girl I would call Alys for she was not to my eyes a woman grown, he would go ahead. If her father Louis found out, there would be war. It was a disgrace that a daughter of France was being so abused as to be kept as a mistress of the King of England, when she was supposed to be kept safe in order to wed his son. I felt sick again.

Louis had never been the most attentive father to his children, but I had sworn to keep his daughters safe and now at least one of them was under threat from her own father-in-law.

I breathed in and let it out slowly. "I know your father's plans and he will not prevail. He sent me an offer as the year turned and I refused, as I am sure you heard. I knew then that he would have a bride in mind, and many have whispered Alys is already his mistress. I hear the papal legate would not countenance his plans to send me to a convent and set me aside, and my good friend the Archbishop of Rouen intervened too, at my urging, therefore the Church is not in favour of your father casting me off. Not that I think this is due to any papal affection for me, but they understand, as I do, the fullness of his plans. He will try to wed Richard's bride, something the Church and others would look upon with horror, and from her he will try to get a new son, who might supplant Young Henry. He will then have revenge on both eldest sons who rose against him, and on me. On Louis too, I suppose, since he makes his daughter his whore."

"The whole family suspects this too," muttered Joanna, glancing about.

"Amaria, the guards here, none of them will whisper of what we say," I told her. "They may be paid by the King, but they are my people. When the day comes that I am free, they know they will be rewarded."

She smiled at me, shaking her head. "We feared so greatly for you," she said, "and yet here you are, Queen of all you meet, as ever."

"There is reason to fear," I warned her. "My keeping here is not overly harsh, but I am not as young as I was and if fever or plague get here, I will be at risk. My wrists and hips ache when the snow comes and there is little to entertain me, but I keep my mind busy by imagining what I will do when I am free, when I may see all of you again."

"My brothers, Richard most especially for he seems to grasp what our father is up to best, urged me to ask that you do not surrender when Father asks you to agree to an annulment again."

"I never had any intention of doing as he wishes." I smiled. "And you may assure all my children of that. No matter if your father takes my bed or all my firewood, I will shiver on and keep myself warm with malice against my husband, and love for my children."

Joanna laughed a little. "I feared to come here and find you broken, sad and alone, yet nothing he has done to you has touched you."

"I am sad and much alone, but men have been trying to break me all my life and they have not managed to shatter the whole." I took her hand. "There is something to remember, when a part of you breaks, when you lose something, when something in you is torn, it is not you in truth. Dreams, illusions, plans, love, all these things may break inside us, this is true enough, but these things are not all of which we are made. When something we cared for does shatter, we can take a moment, stand apart from it, and look down at what remains. What is valuable, what we need, we can stoop down and pick up, we can carry that which is of value with us still, and what we need no more may remain on the floor at our feet. Every time something we care for breaks, we leave behind what has become useless to us, and we take on only what still has value, so each time we break, we grow stronger, not weighed down by the burden of the unnecessary anymore. We go ahead carrying only the vital. Each time we break, we become more completely what we are intended to become."

My daughter stared into my eyes. Her lip wobbled, but she nodded sternly, and lifted her chin.

I squeezed her hands. "Your father can do as he wills, he can hold me here, keep me a captive, keep me alone of all his former foes as his prisoner, yet he cannot command my heart, my mouth or my mind. My body is his prisoner, but my mind is as free as ever it was, and I will not be set aside. My children will not be named bastards or disinherited, and I will not step aside so he might claim his own son's bride as his own. I will not to a convent go, and I will stay strong. Tell your siblings this and tell them I remain undaunted. You, and all of them, are my first concern, and I will never cease to stand for you all. I may be reduced in authority here, but with all the power I still possess, I will fight for my children." I smiled. "As far as I am concerned this war is not over, nor will it be until the rightful king sits upon the throne."

I took Joanna in my arms and embraced her, wrapping my arms about her, holding her tight, hoping to absorb so much of her into myself that I would be able to call on this memory, in months or years to come when I was alone here with only the cold and Amaria to keep me company again, and this memory of my daughter would feed me, sustain me, just as memories of my sister did. I wanted to be able to breathe in, as I did then, holding her, and smell her scent even when she was sent from England and was so far away, married to a man of another country.

"Tell me of your brothers," I said eventually, pulling back. "What are they doing?"

"Richard is stamping out rebellion most effectively," said Joanna. "Sadly, Maman, he is forced to fight men loyal to you, for they rise in your name."

"Well, that is partially true. I would suppose my people feel it a great insult their Duchess is imprisoned, especially since I am the last prisoner left of all who rose against your father, but I am also an excuse. Those men would rise anyway, I have no doubt. Your brother must keep order in our lands. Tell him I understand what he does and approve, though I would caution mercy to be as useful as violence, at times."

"My brother Henry is in Flanders, and not behaving well, by all reports."

"Are those reports ones of your father?"

She grinned. "His, and others, Maman."

"I am surprised your father allowed him out of his sight."

"Father did not want to let Henry go but was persuaded eventually. Henry wanted to see his wife, and his father-in-law, and had Father kept refusing it seemed people might consider my brother to be a prisoner in truth."

"So, your father let him go that he might prove he is not," I mused. "I wonder if the same might work for me?"

We both laughed at that dark little joke. "My brother, the Young King, went to France, most briefly, then to Flanders he flew, to his old friend Count Philip, and there Henry is dedicating himself to tourneys and to pleasure. He wins large amounts in the joust and the sword and spends it just as fast. Father says he never has learned how to be a man." Joanna pulled a face which suggested her father was the one who needed to grow up, and I agreed.

"Young Henry will always be a child until he is permitted to become a man."

"I am going to ask Father that you be allowed to come with me to see me off in the late summer when I am to be sent away to wed," she told me, her face so earnest. "I will demand it, Maman. Richard thinks that if you are seen more in public people will not forget you, so we must make it so you are seen."

"You mean to draw me a little at a time from this dull and bitter place?" I tapped my lips with a finger as I thought. "The plan has merit. I shall try to look as wasted and pitiful as possible when I do appear, whilst forgetting no attentions to my appearance, so people may be moved to tears to see me so beautiful and fragile at the same time." I laughed. "If there comes public sympathy for me, your father might well be forced to let me out."

I thought a moment. "Do my sons ask for my release?"

It was a question I feared to ask. My daughter was there, with me, so at least one of my children had not forgotten me, but I wondered about the others. Richard might be enjoying ruling alone, and my other sons might well have forgotten me for they had their own concerns too. Perhaps I had faded from memory, perhaps I was embarrassing to them.

"They did at first," she said. "But, Maman, we talked about it and Richard said it would do no good to keep asking, for the moment Father hears your name or a request for your freedom from my brothers he suspects them again of treason... not that any of us consider what you did to be treason, of course. Richard and Geoffrey both want to find other means of freeing you. Geoffrey is now enjoying high friendship with the Prince of France, Philip, and thinks there may be a means, pressure from another source such as France which might aid you, and when I marry, I shall do all I can for you too."

"When you are away from your father's power, you mean."

She nodded. "We are, all of us, under his boot here, but in other countries his power is thin. There may be means, Maman, and do not think for a moment we are not all thinking of you every day. Henry says you are a prisoner in body as he is by power, and all of us talk of you every day when we are together. We are well aware that you are in this present trouble because you gave yourself to your children, heart and soul. Our loyalty is bound to you, even if we are forced to bow to Father, for now."

"I understand." And I did. They were, none of them, in an easy position and from all I heard, my husband was starting to lose himself to tyranny most complete.

As my daughter left me there was another 'request' sent that I retire to a convent, although this one was couched in more threatening language.

"The King grows desperate," I said to myself, reading it. I smiled.

Henry, you see, was running out of time to be rid of me and get a new heir on a new wife, but if I had nothing else at Sarum, I had time. If I had no other way to prevent his foul plans for Alys, I could wait them out. He could not wear me down, so all he had left was to wait until I died, but I was not about to step into the grave to appease him.

I would wait, I would endure, and we would see who still was standing when this ended.

Chapter Twenty-Two

Sarum

Salisbury

Summer 1176

From my daughter I had learned that Richard and Geoffrey had been in England that year, and obviously were not permitted to see me. At Easter they had been at Winchester with Henry. I doubt not that my husband had tried to pull them into his plans to annul the marriage between us, for why else would he want his children near him other than to give him opportunity to try to extract something from them for himself?

There was no reprieve with our eldest, either. The Young King had come to suspect his father would keep him a prisoner all his days and then exclude him from the succession, and perhaps his complaints, or the fact he was too close to the truth for comfort, had annoyed his father, for as Joanna had told me the Old King had finally allowed young Henry to go on pilgrimage to visit the shrine of Saint James of Compostela in Spain. This was when young Henry had instead gone to France, then Flanders, and, having escaped his father for a while, spent his summer in the lists, jousting and competing at the sword.

After this incident, the Young King travelled south to assist Richard with the rebels there, apparently in accord with his father's commands. In order to ensure that this happened, my husband limited the allowance of our eldest son even further, trying to force him to go and aid Richard. But in Poitiers, young Henry met with some men his father would not like and I doubt his brother was warm to either.

"It is said the Young King has been meeting with rebels of the past uprising," Ranulf told me as we sat before another game of chess. I was letting him win this one, but he did not know it just yet and was sweating at the game more than a little. I had to make it challenging, or he would know I was playing him, rather than our match. "And the King is unhappy about this, for he has sent his vice-chancellor Adam Chirchedune to keep an eye on the Young King."

This did not go well. Chirchedune found that young Henry was indeed meeting with past rebels of Poitiers, many of whom regarded the Young King as a hero who had tried to lead them to freedom. Considering this, and young Henry's reluctance to return to England, the vice-chancellor sent word he thought the Young King would rebel again. Well aware of what the vice-chancellor was up to, my son had set men to watch him, and they caught him with this letter on his person. This led to my son ordering the vice-chancellor be stripped naked and whipped in the public square at Poitiers, then sent home. My husband, so I heard, descended into a fit of wrath so great that he chewed on the floor rushes in rage when he heard.

"I hear my son and William the Marshal made quite the names for themselves in the tourneys in Flanders," I mentioned to Amaria some days later, after hearing it from Ranulf. "And now they will go to war, arm in arm with Richard. Mayhap this training at fighting will become useful to young Henry now." I hoped this, more than believed it. He was my son. I wanted to believe in him.

For the next three years young Henry decided to all but set aside his ambitions for power, knowing that his father would not offer him anything, and he used that time in tournaments and in spending money. Even the conspirators he left behind, apparently giving up on the notion of rebellion. He became a highly talented knight, famous in all the lands of Christendom and beyond for his skill in the tournament. Were he of lower station, were he not my son, I might have rejoiced, but whilst these dreams were good enough for a mere knight, a baron of the country or a third son without much to call his own, my son could have been so much more than just a man playing knight.

If I knew he was happy it would have been one thing, but I knew he was not. No man who devotes himself so wholeheartedly to pleasure has found joy. No man who gives up everything he could have had and settles for what he can grasp is content.

*

That August, Joanna was formally betrothed to William II, King of Sicily. My daughter was at Winchester at the time, and she must have petitioned her father well for that August I travelled there under guard from Sarum to say farewell to my daughter, most spirited of all my children. If this leniency was not enough to rouse my suspicions, I was astonished to find I was further permitted to accompany Joanna to Southampton where she was to take ship for France on the first stage of her journey to Palermo. Her escort was to be headed by John of Oxford, the Bishop of Norwich, my husband's envoy to the Sicilian court.

"Thank you for all you have done for me, my daughter," I said to her as she was to embark upon her ship. I knew, in truth, that it was not only her pleading with her father that had brought this about. This much freedom, this much contact with a child all at once? No, this was not some guilty strain of Henry's heart plucked by the urgings of his daughter. He wanted something.

Joanna, however, did not need to know that. Better that she thought this was all down to her, to infuse her with confidence in her abilities to charm and cajole before she went off to become a bride to a foreign king. She needed all the help I could offer her.

"I would I could do more," she wrapped her hands about mine, "and I will try with all I have within me to make sure that one day, Maman, you are free."

I was taken back not to Sarum but to Winchester after saying goodbye to my daughter. After Joanna's departure there was more money allotted to my household and even new clothes; two cloaks of scarlet cloth as well as two grey furs and one embroidered coverlet for me and Amaria arrived.

"I believe that your daughter must have pleaded with her father to alleviate some of the dire conditions you have been placed in as a prisoner, my lady," Amaria said, touching the cloth with something approaching reverence. I doubt she had ever owned anything so expensive.

Scarlet was a luxurious cloth, although there was a covert insult included here, since I was allotted one and my maid was granted one of the exact same cost, colour and type, so I could not demonstrate my rank. We were only allowed one coverlet, too, so that meant even at Winchester we still were sharing but one bed. But these new things, this new freedom, all this sudden and touching attention I knew did not come without something desired in return.

"We are being trussed and plucked for the pie," I said dryly as Amaria tried on her new cloak, the twin of mine. "My husband is not being kind for kindness's sake, nor because he cares so much for his daughter's opinion or happiness."

Amaria stopped admiring her cloak. "You think he will try to get you to agree to a separation again, my lady, that is what these things are for?"

I nodded. "You start to see him as I do."

Amaria began to take the cloak off slowly, looking at it with a touch of disgust. "Do not do that." I got up and put it back on her shoulders. "It is not the cloak's fault, nor yours, that my husband sent this gift in such bad taste. We have need of new clothes, do we not? And this cloth will keep us both warm."

"It feels tainted," she said quietly.

"I understand," I said. "Try to imagine now what years of your life, so many memories you thought were happy might feel like when spent with such a man. But he cannot ruin everything, not if we do not allow him to. This is the same man I made my children with, and I will not allow him to spoil my thoughts of them, or my love for them."

Had Henry ever really loved me? He had sworn he had when we had promised to wed and many times after that but perhaps none of it ever had been true. Perhaps I had been duped, and he had just wanted my land and that was the secret of his attraction. The fact I had been easy to look upon had simply been a boon, made the task of creating sons and daughters more a pleasure than it might have been with a rich, ugly bride. Certainly, he treated his children and me as if we were commodities to be traded rather than people he had any affection for.

I trusted nothing he ever had said now. I had seen too much of the other side of my husband to believe in the one he had presented to me for so long. Which was real? It did not matter, what mattered was which face was watching over me, and this time it was the ill one.

I smiled. "We have had little, so let us enjoy this slight offering we are given. The cloth is warm, the furs too. This is a grand treat after shivering our way through last winter, but it is not so grand a treat that I will forget myself as I pull on this cloak and allow my husband to cast me off." I laughed. "He thinks I am so easy to buy with a little luxury after so long without, but I am not so shallow. He will have to learn this the hard way, for he never took the easy way once in his life."

These gifts were given not out of a genuine concern for my well-being but to soften me. He had tried to crush me with bad treatment, and this had failed and so now he gave me a small taste of what might be mine if I surrendered and gave him what he wanted. Fine cloth, better housing, the ability to see my children, all this was a tease, a worm on a hook. He expected me to bite, and perhaps I would but I would not bite where he expected me to.

*

At the end of September that year my youngest son, Lord John, was betrothed to his cousin Hawise. She was the daughter and heiress of William, Earl of Gloucester, one of the most powerful of English magnates. He was also the son of Earl Robert who had supported the Empress Matilda, Henry's mother. Upon marriage, John would acquire estates in England which were vast and plentiful. It was more land than his father could offer him, so it was a good match but I was angry to hear of it. John was still my son. I should have been consulted on his match.

It was around this time that I heard the King had erected a beautifully decorated tomb to his former mistress Rosamund de Clifford. It stood before the high altar in the abbey church at Godstow and it was said it was a place of wonder to look upon. "They say it is a fine tomb, covered with silk and cloths and surrounded by candles, and is tended well by the nuns," Amaria told me.

"She was a child," I said sadly, "children should have good graves. They pass too brief from life and should be remembered."

"Do you not resent her, my lady?" Amaria asked. "She was your husband's mistress."

"She did nothing to me. The King wanted her, he beckoned, and she came. I have no doubt her family would have forced her into his bed had she not gone willingly, and Henry can be charming, when he wants something. I understand how she fell for him, for I did too, once." I breathed in and smiled at Amaria. "Rosamund broke no vows to me, Henry did. He is the one to blame for their affair."

My husband however had not mourned long. He was now openly keeping Alys of France as his mistress. He had not bothered to wait until he could annul his marriage to me and wed her, but instead had simply taken her into his bed. Waiting might have indicated he had some respect for her, but he did not. Rumours were spreading about the two and soon enough I had no doubt King Louis of France would hear how his daughter was being used by the English King. When Louis heard, the world would know too. It would be a grand disgrace and Alys would never be allowed to wed Richard if she had lain with his father. No other man would want her, either, after this.

I did not blame the girl, I blamed Henry. I had no doubt she had been eager to go to his bed because he did not like women who were not enthused, but just how had she been made eager? She was in a foreign land, his prisoner no matter how politely held, and he was much older than her. In so many ways he had all the power and she none. I had no doubt that she had been talked rather than forced into her new position, persuaded and charmed, promised and appeased. In such means of making a woman into a mistress there is manipulation.

She was too young to defend herself against such an onslaught of charm as Henry could bring against her and therefore she had been talked into ruining herself, perhaps on the promise of becoming a queen rather than just the Duchess of Aquitaine, which she would have been through marriage to Richard. Perhaps she was promised love, which Henry would never be able, truly, to offer her. Alys had possessed an ambitious streak, and she was a clever young woman in some ways. These qualities might have been used against her by my cunning husband for often the clever think themselves cleverer than they are. She might well have thought she was entering this pact in full knowledge of what it might bring her and had not considered all she might lose.

Alys was known as the mistress of the King of England. Whilst I and many others of Aquitaine would not look down on a woman who took a lover, even in our lands when this was done it was discreet. This affair was not discreet, and the eyes of the world were far more judgemental than mine were. The world would look upon her with loathing for surrendering her virginity. That same world would excuse Henry his sins. She would pay the price for this, not him.

It was too late now, however, unless the French could force the match between Alys and Richard and make the world forget she had bedded his father.

When the Church heard of it, too, there would be trouble. Henry was too busy racing ahead with all his plans to see that he was creating problems of other kinds for himself in the future.

In truth, I did not need to conspire against him. No one did. He was his own worst enemy.

Chapter Twenty-Three

Winchester

Hampshire

Winter 1177

That February my Joanna was married to William II, King of Sicily, and I heard it was a magnificent event attended by all the dignitaries of Sicily and beyond. After the ceremony Joanna was crowned Queen of Sicily and then from public view she vanished.

Probably her father had known that her new husband had adopted many of the customs of his Turkish subjects which included maintaining a harem of women to attend to him and keeping his wife in seclusion in a household of her own. My daughter, the one of all my children who had managed to talk her way into seeing me, was now as much a prisoner as I was. I wondered if her father had known this would happen and this was why he had chosen this King for her to marry. She could not help me and could not speak out now that she was shut away from the world.

Oh, how my heart seethed at that time.

Impotent rage is such a vile thing to carry. It has no outlet. Where can it go but back into the body, writhing as a snake in the heart, on fire with rage and fury and frustration, its skin curling from its flesh, and in the heart does that snake grow cold, and there it becomes a hard stone within the soul, waiting for a chance to be unleashed, to spark to fire again, to be at liberty.

Such was my anger and my soul; such was the wrath of Eleanor. And such was my waiting. I was waiting to see my children, and I would wait for my revenge to come upon my husband too. Even then, I had no doubt it would. Sometimes in dreams I did not see my revenge, did not see Henry dead or in disgrace, but I felt it. I felt a bliss come upon me of satisfaction, a cool water upon my heated brow, driven almost to madness by the actions of this callous man I had married. When I woke from such dreams I felt satisfaction. And I knew, somewhere deep down, that he would not prevail, not in the end. Something was coming for him, and I would live to see it devour him.

I was not alone in growing angrier and angrier with Henry. By that time my husband's affair with the daughter of France was becoming notorious about Christendom. King Louis had certainly heard the rumours, everyone else had. I doubt not word came to his ear from his daughter Marguerite and her husband, young Henry, for suddenly and without warning Louis demanded that Alys' marriage to Duke Richard was to be celebrated without any further delay. She was sixteen now, Louis barked from France, more than old enough to be married. To ensure that my husband complied with his request Louis appealed to Pope Alexander, asking him to enforce the marriage or if Henry disobeyed, to place all the King of England's dominions under an interdict. "Louis is never so assertive," I said to Ranulf when he told me this. "So that means the King of France is aware that the King of England is keeping his daughter as a whore."

*

That summer, on the 19th of June, Marguerite of France bore her husband a son. My first grandchild of this side of my line was named William. He was born in Paris but just as soon as I received word about the birth of the heir to the Angevin empire, I received another letter. This one informed me that the infant, three days old, had died.

"I of all people could have comforted her, for I know there is no comfort to give," I said to Amaria. "I have lost two children. One, a child who died before they were born, and the second was another William, my first-born son."

"You say there is no comfort to give, my lady, so how would that bring comfort?"

"Because people tell you all kinds of foolish nonsense, when you lose a child." I sat, my soul shuddering, into a chair. "It is not their fault, they are trying to cheer you, trying to drag you out of the dark hole you fall into, but none of that nonsense helps. People say that you will heal when you have another child, but the hole caused by the death of one child is not filled by another. The hole always is there, the grief forever is. You learn to cope with it, to carry it, day by day but it never goes, and one child cannot replace another, and you *know* that, you, the mother who has lost her baby *knows* that the moment someone says these things to you.

"So, there is no comfort to give in words, but it is a comfort sometimes for someone to simply take you in their arms. It is a comfort for them to tell you that there is nothing anyone can say, there is no way to make this better, that you always will grieve for your lost child and that is as it should be. That is normal. It is a comfort to know that others have stood where you stand, that they managed to carry on, that they bore the grief and the pain and the sorrow, and you will too. It is a comfort to know there is no comfort, for that is how it feels when you lose a child, and it is good to know you are not mad to think so. It is a comfort to know that others know that too, that they have felt that weight and they still survive, which means you too can survive this thing which feels like it might crush you alive." I sighed, looking to the window, wishing that Marguerite could hear me. Through the ornate window screen glimmered small shafts of light, dancing on the rushes on the floor. "A woman should be with other women, at such a time," I said. "I doubt my eldest son, or Marguerite's father, are much consolation."

My husband sent this word on from Woodstock, and whilst he was there, he had another unwelcome letter for it seemed that the papal curia had again rejected his request for an annulment of his marriage to me. This was not all. A cardinal was on his way to ensure that Alys of France was married to Richard with immediate effect, otherwise the King would find his lands under an interdict.

"If Richard will accept her still, it would be better for her if Alys was married to him," I said to Ranulf. "The poor girl, the world knows she is the King's whore. He has ruined her name."

"Do you think Lord Richard would accept her, now?" Ranulf asked.

"Richard was growing most fond of her, perhaps he even loved her, when she was in my court," I said. "If he reaches for those feelings rather than ones caused by his father's usurpation of his bride, it is possible he might accept her."

In July there was an odd occurrence. "The skies opened, and what came was not rain but blood, my lady!" said one of the guards to me through the door. "The Isle of Wight was covered in blood, for two hours it fell and before that the day had been bright and clear, so people had hung out their washing which they took in then, red with gore!"

A remarkable occurrence it was. Everyone spoke of it and had a reason as to why God had caused blood to fall from the skies. "It is a tiding of things to come," I said to the guard and later to Amaria. "Blood as plentiful as rain. It means something ill is coming."

*

In August my husband went to France attempting to straighten out the matter of Alys with Louis face to face. I suppose when a man has taken the daughter of another into his household as a babe and promised to raise her as his own and marry her to his son, then when she grows up a little has taken her into his bed without promise of marriage and has made her a whore, and had the world know of it by living openly with her, it is something that should be explained man to man.

They met on the Norman border on the 21st of September and Henry somehow managed to charm Louis into standing down that day, with an extremely vague promise that as soon as legal formalities to do with the transfer of her dowry were complete, Alys of France would be married to Richard. It was said that good friendship was restored between the two kings, and they also agreed to go on a new crusade together. After this, Henry travelled to Aquitaine where he was due to inspect Richard's conquests. I have no doubt he was also heading to his son to offer excuses about what had been happening with Alys, since it was impossible Richard had not heard that his own father was bedding the woman who was supposed to become his wife.

"He cannot marry her now even if he wanted to," I said to Amaria one day. "I have been considering the matter. Alys is now his mother, of a kind, in the eyes of the Church, for she has bedded his father, so if he were to wed her now it would be incest."

Richard at that time was busy in any case enforcing his authority in the south of his territories with the aid of his brother, young Henry, when the Young King could be persuaded out of the lists, that was. Richard had subdued Poitou and the north of Aquitaine but there was still trouble in other areas.

But perhaps Richard did have words with his father, for after this time and upon his return my husband took more care to attempt to ensure that his affair with Alys was kept private. Perhaps Richard had assured my husband he still would marry Alys if this was done, but even though the affair was quieter kept everybody knew the secret of the King of England. A bell cannot be un-rung after pealing loud into the night, shattering the silence. Henry probably thought he was subtle but during the next few years Alys would bear him a son and a daughter, and all of England heard of it. The daughter did not survive but the son did. Both were kept secret. Henry wanted this girl in his bed, this girl who should have been his daughter rather than his mistress, this girl who should have borne his grandchildren rather than his bastards, and he kept his bastards secret, just in case he might one day be able to set me aside and take her as his wife. I know not how they thought to explain the son then, perhaps he would be brought out at court when Alys was Queen and called a cousin. I wondered if she would be happy about her son being disinherited so.

*

It was in this year that Henry decided that John should be given Ireland. That land would be his, and he would be crowned King, but for now he was simply named the Lord of Ireland. My son was only ten years old, so his sovereign duties were to be carried out by Hugh de Lacy, his viceroy. This was not the only plan for our children. That September my daughter Eleanor was sent to Castile for her marriage to King Alfonso VIII which had been agreed upon long ago. This time, perhaps as punishment for continuing to refuse an annulment, I was not permitted to escort my daughter across English soil to the ships that would take her away to her marriage.

I sat in my chamber, my prison, and I imagined I had gone with her to say goodbye, that we had been in Aquitaine, and I rode to the border with her, so I could see her to the edges of the world I knew. At the gateway to another country, at the start of another life, I had to leave her, just as I had left her sister Matilda, her sister Joanna, and just as I had left William, their brother, as he travelled on to the kingdom of the afterlife.

Someone should be at our sides, at such times. Someone to face the darkness with, someone to bolster our courage when it fails, someone who loves us so we might remember love is present in all places, even those we fear in which to walk. When we look about and think we stand in a place devoid of love, we do not. The reason we cannot see it is because it is inside us. I would have my children remember this, no matter how far and wide about the world they were scattered by their father, my love for them was always with them, escorting them just as I escorted my daughter to her new country, if only in my mind.

Her marriage would secure the border between our countries, reducing risk of invasion, yet I hated to be parted from her. I had not seen my daughter for years and now she was gone, and I would not see her again. Oh, other mothers had been forced to give their children up to my household far earlier, that I knew. I was lucky to have the years I had with my girls, but still, all the time in the world would not be enough.

Henry, so I learned, laid down nothing on paper or parchment to say that Gascony would belong to Eleanor upon my death. It was pledged as security, in case the full amount of her dowry was not paid, but never was it promised, although reading some of the correspondence between King Alfonso and Henry later, I could see how Alfonso might think the land had indeed been promised.

That night I dreamed of my Eleanor.

"You must keep safe, and when you are able, write to me," I said to my daughter in my dream, as we dismounted near the border. Guards on the other side, as well as a party including the King of Castile, had ridden there to meet her. I was glad of that; it showed some respect and I hoped she might have a man who valued her as her husband. He was young at the moment, of course, which I was also glad of. Hopefully she and he would have time to grow up and know one another before their courtiers and advisors threw them into bed together. "I will be depending on hearing from you often. The lands of Castile are beautiful, I am told, so you must describe them to me, and every doing of your day, too, you must tell me of. No detail is too small. I am interested in everything."

"Yes, Maman," she whispered, tears rising to her eyes.

I took her chin and lifted those eyes. She had my shade of blue there. "You are my daughter," I said. "A strong, beautiful and wise woman you will become. Do not cry here and now, for you are about to begin a life extraordinary, Eleanor. Dazzle me and the pages of history."

"Yes, my lady," she said, drawing herself up and blinking back her tears.

"That is good." I kissed her cheek. "My love travels with you, Eleanor, wherever you may go, it is there, about your heart."

"As mine is with you."

As I watched my daughter ride away to the border, in her procession of servants, a hand stole into mine. Marie smiled at me as I looked into her eyes, mine awash with tears. She had insisted on coming with us to have more time with her sister, in my dream I remembered this. "Too many daughters I have been told to say goodbye to now," I said. "You, Alix, Matilda, Eleanor, and Joanna."

"My sisters are canny little things all," said Marie, "and if I found my way back to you, Maman, they will one day too."

"I fear I will not see my other daughters again. You are the exception in finding your way back to me, but then, you always have been a miracle."

As I stared into her face, the world I stood in began to fall apart, like ice on a pond shattering, so the skies and the earth cracked, the sun fell to the earth, the earth slipped away beneath my feet. "No," I said. "Do not go. Do not leave me here all alone again. Marie! Eleanor!"

From the world of dreams, I fell and yet as I did, I could hear their voices.

"You are not alone, Maman," they said in one voice. "We always are with you."

I woke with a heavy heart. All that day and many after I could feel my blood aching for my daughters. All I wanted was for my arms to find them, to pull them to me, to feel their hearts beat against mine. It took a long time for that feeling to subside. It was agony to me.

That Christmas Henry and his three eldest sons kept the season at Angers. Many spoke of it as a marvellous occasion, talked of how the celebrations had gone on all night, how sweet the food was, how delicate the decorations. I remained at Winchester, and I spent much of the day of Christmas upon my knees praying that Eleanor my daughter would have a good marriage, praying that she would know more power than I did, praying that I might one day see her again, to tell her I was sorry that I never had a chance to say goodbye.

Chapter Twenty-Four

Winchester

Hampshire

Summer 1178

It was summer, the sun high and hot, the lands alive with birdsong and crops ripening gold and silver in the fields, as if the English farmed not wheat and corn, but metal most precious born from the earth. When I was allowed out, as I was sometimes now, I would stand in silence near such fields, and listen to the faraway noise of the world, to the chatter, indistinct and broken, of workers in the fields, to laughter which would ring out, sudden and brash, over the skies. In the distance I could see women gathering wild plants for food and medicine, some leaving their babes hanging from swaddling robes in cool bushes where the sun would not reach them, some carrying them bound against their bodies so the babies could feed as they needed to. If all went silent, I would listen to blackbirds trill and sparrows chatter, and sometimes, leaning in close enough, I would hear the crops crackling, the stems and seeds ripening, goodness flowing into the world.

Summer was harder than winter in some ways, as the change came stronger upon me. In the heat, I found it taxing to cool at all and would lose words faster, they just fell from my mind. For some time, Amaria thought I was losing my wits in age, but I explained it was but part of the change and she seemed assured. She would remind me of the words I had lost, and all was well. Sometimes my mind would feel hazy, as if I knew not what was going on, but in such times I had to just sit a while, collect what thoughts had raced away and re-centre them.

Sometimes I thought it was a blessing in a way that I had been put aside, into prison, at this time of change. There was much to concentrate on with my own body, preparing for something, a new time of life, a new phase of being. I remembered once, when a maid of mine had been with child and she apologised often for she kept forgetting things. She called herself foolish, but I had shaken my head. "It comes upon all of us, when with child," I had told her. "You must not be hard on yourself during this time. Your body is growing a person, child, a whole new soul is being made in your belly and it takes many resources to do so. That is why you forget things, your body is using its energy elsewhere, and that is as it should be."

It was the same now. My mind wandered at times, because my body was busy, bringing an end to the time of childbearing. Women I knew had lived long since this time, Dangerosa for one, and they had thrived, living on with a purpose beyond bearing children, a purpose of passing on wisdom gleaned from so many years of life. Few men reached great age, too many died in battle, or of disease, or of stupidity in many cases, but women who survived the time of giving the world children, they could live on many years. I was looking forward to that time, and I knew in order to get to that time, I would be tested now.

Summer was harder because my blood now was always hot. I slept little, the sheets were soaked each night and I pitied Amaria, so I petitioned for a second bed for her, and eventually it was granted. At least she did not have to wake each night soaked through as my body raged its way through the change.

Sometimes I dreamt wild dreams, of the past, of people lost, of my children. Sometimes I thought I had been shown portents, but when I woke, I could only remember brief images. Sometimes I dreamt of fire, of feathers in flame, of an eagle who was not truly an eagle but what else it was, I did not know.

Often at night I would be awake, my blood hot and mind racing. Sometimes I sat in bed and sometimes at the window, its pane made of ox horn, watching the still world of darkness. I came to think that night was my element in this phase of change. The night, cooler than day, allowed my mind to think better, to roam through memories pleasing and displeasing. Dangerosa was right, there was a darkness in me at this time, a place of transformation like the womb we all are grown in. The night echoed this darkness, letting me know it was not an enemy. If I embraced it, it was a friend.

I remembered a letter Hildegard of Bingen had sent to me. The great Abbess was known for handing out advice, and once, many years ago I had written to her, disturbed about the troubles brewing between my sons and their father and troubled in mind. To my letter she had responded, *"Your spirit is like a wall, past which various clouds drift. You look around everywhere but have no peace. Flee this! Stand firmly and consistently, toward God and toward humans. In all your difficult times God will stand with you in support."*

Finally, I understood her words, for no more did I look around everywhere finding no peace. I had learned to look inside me and there find both the struggle and the answer.

I was still at Winchester when I learned my husband had returned to England on the 15th of July, and on the 6th of August at Woodstock, he knighted Geoffrey. I was not permitted to attend once again but outwardly, at least in appearances, relations between the King and his rebellious sons had become peaceful. Whilst young Henry was not appeasing his father by rushing around all over France attending tournaments and winning them, his popularity amongst the knights of Christendom had made him famous and that his father did like. Richard was doing well in Aquitaine, Geoffrey restored and ruling well in Brittany. It was said the Old King was happy during this time, admiring the victories of his sons. He returned in full the Young King's possessions which had been taken away after our rebellion.

I was not fooled, however. Henry's gifts always had a price.

Chapter Twenty-Five

Winchester

Hampshire

Winter – Autumn 1179

On the 26th of February that year the Young King returned to England and by all accounts was received with honour by his father. I had no doubt this was true. In part his father liked that our eldest son was now king of the tournaments upon the Continent. It brought glory to my husband's name yet did not strip any of the power of his own positions from him, so it was an ideal arrangement. It also allowed Henry to continue to treat his eldest son as if he was a child, for my husband could claim young Henry was only a warrior in *games* before *spectators*, using the thing our son was best at against him.

Richard however was not playing at war in any sense but was fully immersed in heavy engagement. He had decided to set his forces against the proud Geoffrey de Rancon who had declined to do homage to Richard, refusing to recognise my son as his overlord. Richard collected a force and besieged the Castle of TallieBourg on the 1st of May. The siege was a success although it was at the time regarded as the most desperate venture that any man had ever done, since it had seemed that fortress was impregnable. Yet after only nine days that stronghold was razed to the ground on Richard's orders. People looked on in wonder and horror at the feats my son achieved. This was a great triumph for him and afterwards his reputation as one of the most formidable generals of our time was established. The news of it caused alarm in those who were still standing against Richard in the south, and further alarm fell upon them when, one after another, more castles submitted, defeated, within that month. Having achieved everything he wished, Richard crossed the sea to England and again, according to reports, was received by his father with great honour.

And, I imagine, not a little jealousy and trepidation too.

If Henry had managed to infantilize one son, the next eldest was becoming a man to be reckoned with, a warrior to be feared, and Henry feared the men closest to him the most. Becket had taught him that lesson.

Richard was not the only visitor to England that year, for I heard that King Louis, now fifty-eight years upon this world and in ill health, visited England for five days to make a pilgrimage to the shrine of Thomas Becket. He was received graciously by my husband at Dover and the next day they travelled together in a solemn procession to the newly rebuilt cathedral at Canterbury. There had been a fire a few years before that, which had burnt down the choir, and so it was decided that since this place drew so many people to it – and gathered so much wealth – it should be rebuilt with all the glory that Thomas Becket deserved. Considering how much he had loved material things when Chancellor, I am sure the attentions to his grave and cathedral pleased his spirit.

Louis gave handsome gifts to the shrine which included a huge ruby, known as the Regale of France, and Louis who ever had been a pious man spent three days undertaking vigils, prayer and fasting.

I have no doubt he was asking much for his son. Philip of France had been due to be crowned, but in the days before the event he and his father and their men had gone hunting at Compiègne. Chasing a boar, Philip had become separated from his friends and lost his way. For hours he was alone in the forest until he stumbled upon the cottage of a poor charcoal burner, who guided him back to his party. The prince was returned to his father, but fell ill of a fever not long after, and his people despaired of his life. In grief, Louis knew not what to do, but on three consecutive nights he dreamed of Thomas Becket, and so, thinking this a sign from God, had come on pilgrimage to ask Becket to intervene and save the life of his son.

It seemed this worked, for after visiting the tomb of Becket and placing a golden cup filled with gold coins on top of his grave, Louis returned home to find that his son had recovered completely. The coronation was planned then for the 1st of November, All Saints, an auspicious day to crown a king, but Louis could not attend that day to see his son crowned. Soon after he arrived home, he suffered a fit which left him unable to move down the right side of his body, and effectively put an end to his reign.

Young Henry attended the coronation of this boy who could have been his brother. As the seneschal of France, as he had been appointed by Louis himself, and since young Henry was also the husband of Philip's sister, he had the honour of preceding Philip in the coronation procession, carrying the crown into the cathedral. Richard and Geoffrey were also present and at that time swore fealty to the new King of France for their domains. My husband stayed away so that he could avoid having to pay homage to this fourteen-year-old boy who was now his overlord. After the coronation there was of course a grand tournament near Paris, and in that tournament young Henry and his knights were victorious over all their opponents, as I knew they would be.

"I think that, if his father would ever allow him to do anything with himself, such victories as these show that the Young King has much potential," I said to Amaria as I read an account of young Henry's wins. "Even here, in games of war, he has ambition, bravery, vitality, determination, enthusiasm, he will deal with those he fells with admirable chivalry and does not resent those who beat him." I sighed, setting the paper onto the table in my rooms. "So much he could be, and nothing is he allowed to be."

In that letter I learned also that my daughter Marie had been made Regent of Champagne. Her husband was away on pilgrimage in the Holy Lands. People already spoke of how her influence upon the court of Champagne had brought it to literary and musical heights. Andreas Capellanus, a famous author of our times, served her court, and Marie, literate in French and Latin, led her people in a glorious revolution of thought and word. I heard too that Alix was doing well in her marriage; she had already four children, all of whom were boys, and her husband, who was also speaking of travelling to the Holy Lands, had named her regent in the event he was absent from his lands, or if her son ascended whilst still a child. My two eldest daughters were doing well, but it was their half-brother of France everyone was speaking about.

At Winchester I heard much of the new King of France. He was the thing all mouths talked of. It is that way when anything new happens. For many people, Louis had been the only King of France they had ever known. For good or ill, he was a stable presence in their lives. They knew he might make war and trouble, and they knew he might make peace and keep treaties. Now, there was an unknown on the throne of France and since it was a neighbouring country, and often a hostile one, this was interesting news to dissect.

Of course, I knew a few things about Philip already. I had been alive for the entirety of his life and had read about his character and intellect in missives from France, but even though I knew some things, I had known them about a prince standing in the background of a king, a king I had indeed been most close to, so he was bound to obscure my vision somewhat. People we know are like that, they tend to take up most of what we notice. But now Louis had fallen behind, not dead, but so ill he could not come out – I heard he could barely move – and his son had stepped forth. Something in me thought that, had circumstances been different, Philip could have been my son. Perhaps he would have been a little different, with some of my influence upon him, but perhaps not.

"I hear the new King has great ambition to break down the empire of the King of England and absorb your husband's domains as well as yours into the Kingdom of France," Ranulf said to me one evening as we shared some wine at my fire.

"That is usually the first suspicion anyone has about a new king," I said, "that they are after their neighbours' lands."

"You think the idea wrong, my lady?"

"Indeed not, my friend, the reason it is the first suspicion held by many people is because frequently it happens to be true," I smiled. "Greed, ambition, hatred for one's neighbours, these are frightening attributes in a ruler nearby us, but they are not uncommon traits. What is truly interesting to watch is, what is he actually capable of? What are his strengths and how might he use them? He might have these ambitions for conquest, but many men do. The real question is, can he achieve them?"

"He is young." Ranulf rubbed his chin. "Untried in battle, though I hear he has courage."

I cocked my head and lifted my eyebrows. "Men say that of all rulers. When he was lost in the forest before he fell to fever, I heard this courageous prince was blubbing like a lost babe. His ambitions make him potentially dangerous, but I wonder at all the tales we are told of him."

"I hear he is, in build, stocky, with a red face and keeps his hair most unkempt," said Ranulf. "I hear too he will not bathe, lacks humour and charm and some say intelligence too."

I nodded. "My men, not long ago, when I still was free, told me they thought him more astute than his father, but that is not saying much. A blind sheep trapped in a pen would have been more astute than Louis of France. Yet they said they thought Philip a realist, a pragmatist, and that is an unusual thing for a young man to be."

Ranulf sipped his wine. "They say he will only ever ride a docile horse and is quite paranoid. He thinks assassins are about every corner and under every bush."

"Which says to me again that he is a pragmatist indeed, particularly with regards to the horse. How many young men die on wild beasts they have picked merely because the mount looks impressive? Yet here we have a young king who chooses sensible animals to ride rather than ones selected to amaze his friends. And it is not paranoid to imagine that assassins might be after a ruler, they might well be."

"He is of limited military ability."

"That will change, sooner than any of us think, I would imagine. His ability is limited because of his age, and because he has been under the boot of his father thus far. Now he is King, he will gain experience fast. If he survives, ability will follow. If it does not, he will lose his throne or his life, or both."

"Your son Geoffrey is his constant companion now, so I hear. During the coronation celebrations they were ever arm in arm."

I nodded thoughtfully. "That, above all other bits of news or theories on the new prince, tells me much," I said. "That means it is worth keeping a close eye on the new King of France."

"Because he is friends with one of your sons, my lady?" Ranulf chuckled a little.

"Because he is friends with *Geoffrey*. Out of all my boys, Geoffrey is perhaps the cleverest, and the wiliest. If he and Philip of France are close friends, that tells me a great deal about the new King. Like calls to like, my friend, and deep to deep."

"You think then the new King will be wily and intelligent?"

I smiled. "I think he will be cunning, and underhanded."

Chapter Twenty-Six

Winchester

Hampshire

1180

"I will miss you," I said to my custodian. Ranulf Glanville was to be replaced. He was going on to become Justiciar in the place of Richard de Lucy who was retiring from his post, having served the King loyally for almost a quarter of a century. I did not lie when I said I would miss him, over the past few years we had become close, often talking late into the night or meeting in the morning. He had taken my good advice on how to further his career and clearly it had worked, since he was being promoted.

I also had the feeling that he might be being replaced because he and I had become good friends. Henry did not want anyone too affectionate towards me guarding me. He thought I might escape, but there are other ways to escape a prison, as I knew well by that time. My mind was never a prisoner of the King, and besides Ranulf was moving into a useful position for me. Having men about the King who would be sympathetic to my cause was never a bad thing.

"I am to retain responsibility for all the King's prisoners, my lady," he said, kissing my hand, "and I have decided to delegate to Ralph FitzStephen my custody of you. I have chosen with care, my lady, he is a good man, and I am told that you will remain at Winchester from now on."

"I certainly am glad not to be sent back to windy Sarum," I smiled. "My bones will be glad to rest here, where there is a little sunlight."

"God keep you, Majesty."

"He has kept me well and hale thus far, my friend and will continue to do so. I think the Almighty is not done with telling my story yet."

*

As April dawned and spring fell upon England, young Henry returned and came with a warning on his lips. "He says to the King that the new King of France is not a king as his father was," Ralph, my new custodian, told me.

Where it had taken months to gain the trust of Ranulf, Ralph had immediately taken up the place his predecessor had held, I suspected because Ranulf had told him of the ease of our friendship and the benefits I could offer in terms of advice. I had, quite inadvertently, become as Dangerosa had to Petronilla and me when we were small, an elder offering advice and aid, teaching others about the world. I rather relished this new phase of my life. Because of my years and the increasing amounts of silver of my golden hair, people looked upon me as if I were a sage. There is much one can get away with, much one can learn, when everyone supposes one to be an erudite elder.

"I am not sure what that means," I said. "Not a king as Louis was? But we knew this, did we not? No man is the same as another."

"Perhaps he means the new King will make war where his father made peace."

"Louis of France made war often enough against England, and Normandy." I chuckled. "If Philip makes war he follows in the footsteps of his father."

"People remember Louis more for peace, my lady."

"Remember..." I said sadly. "We all speak of him in the past, yet he is not yet dead." I sighed. "People may remember Louis for whatever they wish, my lord, all men are, after all, made up of all they have done in a lifetime and many times Louis made peace, it is true, but you forget, friend, that I watched him try to take Toulouse, Champagne, I was with him on the crusade. I watched as he made war on my second husband time and time again, sometimes in collaboration with my sons. Remember him for peace all you want but forget not he was entirely capable of war."

Perhaps my son told my husband more details than the rest of us received, however, details which scared him about Philip of France, for the Old King decided that the two kings of England should go together to meet Philip in the hope of maintaining friendship between England and

France. Young Henry told his father this was unlikely, which led his father to think there was something underhanded going on, so first, before they went anywhere, Henry took our son to the tomb of Henry I at Reading Abbey, where the bones of my first son William also lay, and there he made our son swear on the presence of his ancestors and on holy relics that he would follow his father's instructions in all things. Young Henry swore, and they crossed to France, the Old King from Portsmouth and the young from Dover. Together they celebrated Easter in Le Mans and in June met Philip at Gisors, and there the peace Henry had made with Louis was renewed with Louis' son.

"Perhaps there is not so much to fear," said Ralph. He stared at my impassive face. "You think otherwise, my lady?"

"I think that when the world feels too still, there is a storm coming," I said.

*

"So, you are dead," I whispered to the letter in my hands.

Paper may bring much to us, otherwise unknown. A book may spill the secrets of a mind which left the world hundreds of years before. A letter may bring news of births. This one brought news of another kind.

The letter told me that a week before, in Paris on the 18th of September, my first husband Louis VII of France, who during the last month of his life had given away all his wealth to the poor of his country, had died. His son had succeeded him as Philip II, King of France.

I thought death might make Louis happier than he had been in life, for in death his body was clad in a monk's habit and lay in state at Notre Dame before it was taken to the Cistercian Abbey of Barbieux. A glorious tomb commissioned by his widow Adela of Champagne, the only woman who had given him all he wanted, which was a son, held the body of this man I had known so long, and understood so little.

I thought of Louis much that day. I suppose it is only natural that when someone passes from our life a ghost of them comes to infest our minds. I wondered what I thought of it. I felt grief, and relief at his death too. Perhaps it was only to be expected. For some time after I had left him, I had always feared he might find a way to annul our annulment and claim me back as his wife. It might sound lunacy, but Louis had often not been an entirely rational man. His death put an end to this possibility ever arising.

For the most part I felt a remote sense of sorrow, for I had not seen him for many years, and yet when I thought of some of the good things, which were few, which had passed between us, and even of some bad times which were numerous, the grief felt immediate and raw, as if I had lost someone I truly cared for, someone I loved.

I had.

I had loved him once, I remembered. It was long ago, and I had been a girl, a child in truth, but that did not negate the feeling. I had loved my mother, brother, my father when I was a child. My age did not dim the brightness of the emotion felt for them. Even if my love for Louis had been foolish, it was still love.

He had not been an easy man when I lived with him and I doubt he had changed a great deal, kings often do not. Their whims are indulged, their temper ever appeased so they tend to pursue the worst of themselves rather than the best. There was plenty in Louis that could have been good yet there was also plenty in him that was akin to a cossetted infant, a spoiled child in a man's body, something most dangerous.

I thought of our time together when we were first married, when I had looked up on that first day I had met him by the river, and, seeing this golden prince so handsome, so well-formed walk towards me, I thought myself the luckiest woman in all the world. I had expected I would marry some old, decrepit troll and be set into a foul bed, never to be loved, yet this perfect prince of promise had come to me and I had fallen in love. Yet I had fallen in love with an image of Louis I had dreamed up, not with the true man I saw. There was potential in Louis, and I loved his outward form well, vapid young girl that I was. I loved what I thought I could see him become.

It is a dangerous thing to love what someone might become. You do not know, do not ever know that the image you have in your head of how wondrous and great they could be is ever something they have imagined for themselves. Even if you see someone in a certain way and know in your heart that they could become great that doesn't mean they have any intention of living up to your ideals of them. Why should they?

Some become not great, not the best they could be out of mere contrariness, some because they do not want to be great or good. Many people have their own notions about what they want to become which have nothing to do with you, some believe not in themselves so never believe they can be as great as others think they can. But for whatever reason, we cannot change other people, and we cannot change their destinies. God or fate or our own choices create a destiny. We can only ever alter ourselves and our path, never those of others.

And so, it is a dangerous thing indeed to fall in love with potential, with an illusion, for potential is squandered by many a person; and illusions? Illusions are as fragmentary and brief as the breath expelled when someone sighs.

Had I done the same with Henry? Perhaps. I had I seen what our love could potentially become had he allowed it to blossom between us in full. In truth, I had not learned from Louis. I had fallen in love with the potential of another man when I loved Henry. Had he not spent all his time seeking out others, we might have had a chance. Had he not spent all his fire on Thomas Becket, we might have kept our spark. Had he trusted enough to let me into his heart, we might have had a love that people would wonder at, but it was not to be. He made his own choices and followed his own path, and that path was not the one I was on.

Perhaps it was simply my fate that men I offered my heart to were bound to not take care of that heart, but my heart was better off with others, with my children. Without those two men, I would not have my children, so I never could regret being their wife. I had people enough to share my heart with, and if those people were not the men I had married, it mattered not, for my children were my flesh and my bone. My children were the surging blood of my heart.

That love was a greater love than I had with any man I ever married, and I thanked God for it every day. Sometimes when we look at life it is easy to see only what we do not have. I could have dwelled upon my lack of freedom, my lack of power, my meagre allowance, on my separation from my children and indeed day-to-day all of those things did come to me. Sometimes the emptiness in me threatened to open wider, to become a mouth which would consume me.

But what held that emptiness back was a feeling which was rising in my heart, especially as I heard of Louis' death. It was an understanding that even as I was in this present state of being a prisoner, being powerless, having little money and few companions, I was more fortunate than so many people in this world and one of the people I was more fortunate than was my husband Henry, the King of England.

My children loved me, even though they could not find me, even though they could not touch me or be near me, my children were close to me in heart, in mind and in loyalty. It was something I would ever be grateful for, and it was also something their father, with all his wealth, his court and his vast lands and freedom, did not possess.

Chapter Twenty-Seven

Winchester

Hampshire

1181

As summer dawned on Winchester and blackbirds hopped through the gardens on hurried feet, seeking worms, as winter lambs grew to become as big as their parents, Geoffrey was finally married to Constance of Brittany, securing himself as Duke of that land. After the wedding celebrations, my husband returned to England to appoint another Geoffrey, his bastard son, as Chancellor of England. That Geoffrey, however, had not yet been consecrated as Bishop of Lincoln and the Pope was insisting that he be consecrated immediately or else resign the See. The Chancellor was usually a post held by a man of the clergy, such as Becket had been.

"Geoffrey has declared that he prefers horses and dogs to books and priests, has resigned the See and expressed his wish to live unhindered by the Church," Ralph informed me.

"When he was a boy, all he wanted was to be a knight, like his brothers." I smiled to remember the young, earnest lad I had known. "He never once expressed a desire for the Church."

"The King wanted him there, of course."

"Of course, so he could try to place another he thought he could trust in the Church and have them work for him. He could also give his bastard son power in the Church, of course, such as Geoffrey would not have in the material world because of his birth, but all the same, Geoffrey should not have been pushed into the clergy. He had no calling for it and it was not what he wanted." I shook my head. "The King too often tries to manipulate the world, changing people, their fates. It will not work. Eventually all things we try to shift into positions unnatural shift back, fall into place as they were supposed to. The King is too arrogant to see this, but time will teach him well. It always does."

The King, whilst annoyed that yet another plan to install someone he believed he could trust, or manipulate, into Church and government had not come to fruition, still wished to reward Geoffrey, so made him Archdeacon of Rouen and treasurer of York Minster as well as giving him two castles in Anjou.

"There is news in the town, my lady, your son the Young King as well as Duke Richard and Duke Geoffrey have supported King Philip in a war against Philip of Flanders," Amaria told me, breathless from running up the stairs to bring me the news, "and they were successful."

"Of course they were," I chuckled. "Although I consider my sons skilled at warfare, and am proud of them for such... all those men and countries against one? Against Flanders alone? It sounds to me that Philip of lonely Flanders was outnumbered." I paused. "What is more interesting, is why did they fall out? Young Henry and the Count of Flanders were close last year, so what has changed?"

"No one in the market mentioned anything of that, my lady." Amaria panted, leaning on her knees as her breath returned to normal.

"I doubt they would know. Probably it was a private matter. It must have been something of interest, however. I wonder if the rise of Philip of France to power has aught to do with it?" Amaria was looking at me with a worried expression as if I expected her to know, or find out the truth and I laughed, rising from my seat and taking her chin in my hand. "I muse aloud, that is all. I do not expect you to conjure the answer from thin air, child."

"I do so like to make sure you know all, though, my lady." Her tone was earnest. "It is a shame that you cannot be near your sons, your daughters too, though they are wives now and far off, but your sons you could be with, yet you cannot be because still, and after all these years, the King will not forgive you."

I chuckled. "The King has no right to forgive me. He can do so if he wishes, but it means nothing to me. I did as I saw was right, I stood for my children, and I would choose the do the same again. It is not a matter of forgiveness or otherwise which holds me here. At first, I would have called it spite alone, and there is still some merit to that. The King wishes to punish me and thinks it his right to do so, but there is another reason."

"What is that, my lady?"

"He is afraid of me, of what I might do if I were free, of who I might influence, of what I might encourage my sons to do or simply of my support for them. It is not a lack of forgiveness which prevents him freeing me. It is fear and every year he holds me here his terror of me deepens, for with every month and day and year that passes he knows I have more to resent, and more time to think on what I might do."

*

"I bring grievous news, Majesty." Ralph FitzStephen stood in my chamber, a missive unwelcome in his hand. Thankfully he did not pause long enough for me to run through each of my children in my mind, wondering which was dead. "I am sorry to tell you your daughter Joanna bore a son Bohemond, who died soon after birth."

I paused a moment, my heart aching deep for my daughter's loss, before asking. "My daughter, is she well?"

"It would appear she is still in fine health, although sad as any natural woman would be to lose a son but I am afraid there is further bad news. Your daughter Matilda's husband Henry the Lion, Duke of Saxony, has quarrelled with the Emperor Frederick Barbarossa."

"What is the nature of this quarrel?"

"It would appear the Lion of Saxony has been, unjustly most men agree, held responsible for the failure of a campaign in Italy by the Emperor, and the Emperor in response has confiscated all your son-in-law's estates and given them to his own supporters. He has declared the Lion of Saxony an outlaw, my lady. There is word they will have to flee their lands."

"It sounds to me as if the Emperor is intimidated by the Lion of Saxony." I frowned. "Do you know what has happened to my daughter and her husband? Have they been chased from their lands already?"

At that moment no one knew anything, not where they were or how much danger they were in. Later, in November we heard that Henry the Lion had submitted to Emperor Frederick but still found himself exiled for seven years. Matilda and her husband were forced to flee from their lands in Saxony, and there was word they might try seeking refuge either in France, Denmark or, as I hoped, in our own England.

I walked to my writing desk. "Ask the King if I may send a letter to my daughter Joanna," I said to Ralph, "I want to tell her how sorry I am for the loss of her child. I will write it now, so he may inspect it, for I want no delay in it being sent."

"I will ask Ranulf Glanville to take it to the King," said Ralph. "His Majesty will listen to him."

I smiled, thinking it was a good thing indeed to have a friend in position near the King. "Good, and please find someone to get me news of my good daughter Matilda. I shall send another letter to the King, pleading that she must be offered sanctuary in our lands."

"I shall ensure both letters are accepted by the King, there are men I know who will bring him to reason to accept your missives, my lady." Ralph sounded entirely confident, and I smiled as I went to my desk. I had no freedom of movement but every day, with every person's trust I won in captivity, I was getting closer to liberty.

Chapter Twenty-Eight

Winchester

Hampshire

1182

In the first days of March, I heard the Old King had returned to Normandy to keep an eye on affairs in the south. There had been developments which had alarmed many.

"I think that means he is alarmed by Richard's success in the south," I said to Ralph.

"It is said that Duke Richard's harsh rule has provoked virulent hatred amongst his vassals, and the lords of Aquitaine are once more plotting revolt. They hope to overthrow him and offer their allegiance instead to the Young King, Majesty."

"I never entirely believe information which benefits my husband," I mused, thinking on this news. "And if he is worried about how well Richard has done, such plots might well benefit the King. He may think to try to replace Richard with Henry in Aquitaine. But, at the same time it may be true that my people rise against their lord, my son. My people can be a rebellious lot at times. They may well think young Henry would be an easier master, certainly easier to manipulate than Richard, so might support him. Do you know who is behind this latest revolt?"

"Many are mentioning the name Bertran de Born," Ralph told me.

I hissed through my teeth. "When Richard was a boy, Bertran was ever in support of him, but de Born is a troublemaker, seemingly always in delight of stirring unrest."

Ralph tugged on his cloak, a little awry on his shoulders. "It would appear de Born has talked the Young King into joining with the rebels against your son Richard. It was said that de Born taunted your eldest son with the title 'Lord of little land' and thus provoked his jealousy against Richard."

I pinched the bridge of my nose in agitation. In truth the hardest thing to bear about captivity was how impotent I felt. "My son Henry lashes out at the wrong person. It is not Richard's fault that I gave him the lands and property which he was due and young Henry was not granted the same by his father. But the Young King cannot move against his father, so he strikes for his brother instead." If I could talk to young Henry, I knew I could get him to see sense. But I could not talk to him and if his father was indeed trying to oust Richard from his ducal seat, fearing his abilities as a warlord, he would not let me send a letter to young Henry counselling restraint.

"The Young King's grievances have made him easy to manipulate. I am told Bertran has inflamed public opinion in many areas of Aquitaine and Poitou against Richard, by using satirical songs against him. I am sad to tell you also, my lady, that Duke Geoffrey has joined the Young King. Together they have amassed an army of mercenaries and fortune seekers and are poised to invade Poitou. This is why your husband has gone to the Continent."

"My husband has gone to prevent this happening?" I lifted an eyebrow. I knew Henry too well to not consider there was another reason, something confirmed by the uncomfortable expression which flickered across Ralph's face.

"I would not lie to you, my lady," he said, "it may be that your husband has gone merely to keep an eye on what is going on, and it may also be that he supports the Young King and Duke Geoffrey against Richard."

I remained silent, my expression pinched. Ralph rushed on, as people often do when the other person in a room remains silent. It can be a thing most useful, knowing when to still one's tongue. People reveal so much more than they intend in the face of a silence they think they must fill.

"It seems that your husband may indeed be in some fright about his son Lord Richard. His military conquests are becoming famed about the world and are spoken of widely and with great respect. It is said his achievements easily rival those of his father. It seems that the King might think his son Richard is becoming too bold and may have given encouragement to the Young King and to Duke Geoffrey to somewhat dampen Lord Richard's pride."

"Do you mean… my husband gave two of my sons permission to rebel against their brother?"

"Not in so many words, my lady, but that may be what was implied by your husband."

Oh… did we all not know the dangers of what Henry merely *implied*? Becket had died for such.

"So rather than having them united against him, my husband would set his own sons against each other?" I arched an eyebrow. "Fear moves the hand of my husband to work evil."

As it transpired, Henry could not go any further into our dominions in order to keep an eye on or do anything else about this strife erupting between our sons, as he was forced to go back to Normandy. Duke Henry the Lion of Saxony and Duchess Matilda our daughter arrived to seek refuge at Henry's court at Rouen. No one else would offer them asylum.

I was glad to hear that Henry welcomed them with great hospitality and took them under his protection although I am sure he extracted something in return. He proceeded through diplomatic channels to negotiate with the Emperor for the peaceful return to Saxony of his daughter and her husband. Apparently, he took a great interest in their children, since they were the first of our grandchildren that he had seen. Three were boys, Otto, Henry and Lothaire, and four girls, Richenza – who would later change her name to Matilda – Gertrude, Ingibiorg, and last a little baby, named Eleanor after me.

I wondered if my husband was uncomfortable to have to explain in person to Matilda why he was keeping me a prisoner.

*

As the season fit for war came to an end, Henry summoned the Young King to Rouen, ostensibly to greet his sister Matilda and her husband, but really so he could keep an eye on young Henry. There was, no doubt, worry growing in my husband's heart that even if he had sent young Henry off against Richard, our eldest son might well decide his brother was not the target he should be aiming for. Young Henry came unwillingly to court and once there demanded again that his father cede Normandy or Anjou to him, saying that he wanted a seat where he and his Queen could rule, without interference. My husband of course prevaricated and the Young King stormed away in a temper to Paris where he told all his troubles to King Philip, who lent a sympathetic ear to his complaints.

Fired up by Philip, the Young King returned to Rouen and there dramatically declared that he would prefer to be banished or to take the Cross than ever again accept the subordinate role which his father appeared to have decreed for him to follow for the rest of his life. When Henry once more ignored him, my son threatened to kill himself.

"Will my husband ever take his son seriously?" I asked. The Young King was a man now, getting older every year and still without anything to call his own. It was a mark of desperation that he threatened to kill himself, and I believed him, even knowing that it would damn his soul into Hell for all eternity. He might have thought it preferable to the limbo in which he existed here, in life.

Perhaps this threat moved my husband slightly, for he offered young Henry a generous allowance as well as apartments in the Argentan castle where my daughter Matilda was presently staying with her children whilst her husband had gone on pilgrimage to Compostela. Henry's father also offered him a year's pay for his soldiers. The Young King accepted and swore an oath to remain loyal to the King and make no further demands.

"A promise he will not keep," I said. I felt unhappiness consume me. I had done all I could for my son and in my present state could do little more, but there has to come a time in any parent's life where they understand that they have indeed done all they are capable of, and the rest is up to their child.

*

"Your husband sends word, Majesty, that he hopes you will enjoy a good Christmas," said Ralph one day.

I lifted my eyebrows and threw him a look which clearly said I knew Henry did not care what kind of Christmas I passed, but the message was interesting for it meant that perhaps my husband needed something from me. There was no other reason for him to start, out of the blue, to send pleasantries to his prisoner.

Perhaps he had finally realised that setting all his sons one against another was not the best plan and he might need someone to peace-keep for him. He had often enough times blamed me for how our sons had turned out, yet now that he was alone with them, he could make them behave no better. Of course, it did not help that he was stirring up jealousy and bad feeling between all of them.

Ralph went on. "Your husband, the King, intended to come home for Christmas to England but concern over the Young King and the grave situation rising in Aquitaine has kept him on the Continent. He is to spend Christmas this year in the new castle of the Norman Exchequer at Caen."

"I do not much care where my husband spends his Christmas," I said bluntly, "I would rather know of my sons."

There was little to be told. Richard and Geoffrey both were officially engaged in war against each other but there was no fighting since it was winter. But there was a fair amount to be told of young Henry, who arrived at the Christmas court in a mood most foul. My husband's winter court was said to be a glittering occasion, easily able to rival Philip's first full court held in Paris that year, and our Norman one had been presided over by the young Queen Marguerite. All should have been well but apparently the behaviour of my eldest son struck against all this finery as a black cloud against a blue sky.

Clearly still not satisfied with his father's settlement, young Henry also arrived without William the Marshal, who up until that point had been his constant companion and was still the master of his household. Combined with this the fact that young Henry would not speak to his wife, a rumour soon sprang up that Marshal had either had an affair with Marguerite or had dared to look upon the Queen with eyes of love. Hearing that slander was being spoken about him and the Queen, William the Marshal hastened to court and demanded that the King allow him to prove his innocence by ordeal of combat, he would challenge those who had spread such rumours to be his opponents in a three-day tournament. If he won, Marshal declared, he asked no reward apart from the vindication of his honour and if he lost, he would be hanged for his crime.

"And what was the outcome?" I asked Ralph.

"None dared take up his challenge, my lady, not one man would step forth, and sadly, unable to prove himself, Marshal left court in great distress. Soon afterwards, I am told, he departed on a pilgrimage to the shrine of the Magi at Cologne."

I was worried about this. Marshal was in truth the one person I had always leaned on as a source of reassurance that young Henry would be safe. He was the one good influence on my son amongst all his silly friends, the one thing that kept him from tumbling into madness and recklessness, and now he was not with young Henry anymore. I breathed in, trying to steady my nerves for I could feel them fraying as I thought about what young Henry would do, now alone.

In truth, it was no wonder the Old King and the young did not get on, they were too similar in character to ever be content in each other's company. Both reckless, both unheeding of others' counsel, suspicious of those closest to them, and both their own worst enemy.

I feared for my son.

Ralph broke through my thoughts. "I am also told that Bertran de Born has been stirring up further trouble between the Young King and Lord Richard. He is now calling young Henry the 'Prince of Cravens' and has suggested that if Geoffrey had been made Duke of Normandy, he would have known how to enforce his rights better than the Young King does. De Born has reminded young Henry, also, that Richard has built the strongly fortified Castle of Clairvaux on the Young King's side of the border between Anjou and Poitou, and this has made your eldest son even more annoyed."

It did indeed. Young Henry erupted in a choleric outburst against his father and threatened again to renounce his titles and take the Cross if Henry did not either allow him more power or order Richard to dismantle his castle. I was told my husband was moved by his son's tears but was also fearful that Philip might exploit any rift between them, so Henry made a move which was most foolish.

"He did what?" I asked when the news came.

My husband had decided to make Richard and Geoffrey do homage to their brother Henry as their overlord. Geoffrey agreed to do so but Richard refused outright, saying that he owed allegiance only to King Philip for his dominions and had had those lands not from his father, or his brother but as a gift from his mother.

"He also, apparently lost in rage, my lady, publicly berated his father for keeping you a prisoner." Ralph looked uncomfortable, as if he should have been the one to scold Henry for my continued imprisonment. This was good, it meant the man was fully on my side.

"Richard always did have a temper," I said, "it took a lot for him to lose it, and he was never in full position of his wits when it was unleashed."

"And sadly, my lady, it went further for with regards to the Young King, Duke Richard declared if he wanted land 'let him go and fight for it' as he, Richard, had had to do. After this it was said Richard would not sit at the same table as his brother. Your husband broke up his Christmas court in anger and withdrew to Le Mans with his offspring, trying to bring peace between them."

"But there was no peace to be had."

"There was not, my lady, for the Old King asked the Young King to concede that Aquitaine belonged to Richard and his heirs. Your eldest son said that he would not incur his father's displeasure and would do as he asked, as long as Richard would swear fealty to him, but Richard exploded in further wrath and stalked out."

"I imagine he would. The Young King was trying to get Richard to swear fealty to him, recognise him as his overlord, again, and Richard had already said he would not." Again, I thought how similar my eldest son was becoming to his father, the nature of a deceiver rising in him.

"Not long after this, my lady, the vassals of the Young King and Duke Richard began fighting in the halls of court and Richard left and went into his own lands. Your husband was annoyed about Richard's behaviour and has said to his other sons, young Henry and Geoffrey, that they might reduce that pride somewhat."

"You mean he has given them permission, clear and obvious this time, to rise against their brother?"

"I do mean that, my lady, and I am most sorry to have to tell you that once again your sons are at war. Richard and his loyal men are to stand against young Henry, Geoffrey, and the rebel barons of Aquitaine."

"My sons are at war, sanctioned by their own father," I said.

"They are, my lady."

I cannot tell you of my heart then. Of the terrors there, lurking in the dark corners of my soul, waiting for a moment to overcome me. Allow them a moment to haunt me, and I would not survive. I would be swallowed by my fears. I had to stand fast, hold myself up, for if I fell apart now, there would be no putting myself back together. Henry had set our children against each other, and torn my heart and our family apart.

Young Henry drew together a vast army, and ordered all his allies to come to him, ready for war. When allies such as Duke Philip of Burgundy and Raymond of Toulouse joined him, however, when the rebels started petitioning England for aid, the Old King grew nervous.

What if this army meant to march against him, rather than Richard?

Chapter Twenty-Nine

Winchester, Hampshire and

Sarum, Salisbury

1182 – 1183

Telling Richard to dismantle his castle just to appease young Henry was ill thought out at best, and no doubt my husband had performed the command without anything approaching tact too. It did occur to me, however, that my husband might have gone along with these demands made by the Young King because he wished to try to rile further trouble between his sons.

I had many reports now that all said my husband was growing ever more wary of Richard and his emergent abilities as a warlord. Perhaps the Old King wanted, had indeed intended, to provoke Richard enough that my second eldest son might explode, thereby granting their father an excuse to send his other sons and their men against Richard. Perhaps the old lion, worried by a younger male hovering outside the group, had found a way to strike at him before he came for his pride.

Pride, a telling name to give to many lions with their great manes and feline grace so obvious. I often looked at engravings of them in books and thought them ridiculous creatures, puffed up with their own wondrousness. As kings are often described as lions too, it betrays a great deal about them. Some of them. Not all men are so suffused with this substance that so often causes trouble aplenty, this substance they often are blinded by, but my husband was. Pride and fear rode him, making him their donkey as he aged.

So, he pitted our children against each other, turning brother on brother. I sometimes wondered if it was fear of single combat that truly scared my husband. His skills in war remained undimmed, but it must have come to his mind that his sons might, if the fight was one to one, thrash him.

What fools are men who fear their sons! They make of them a prophesy which self-fulfils by treating their children with suspicion until they turn traitor.

"The King has gathered the feudal levies of England, sent orders that all dissidents are to be arrested and detained, and has marched south on the Continent to meet with the Young King and talk to him," Ralph told me.

Fearful of the Young King's ability to raise troops on the Continent, my husband had decided to go and check whether our eldest son meant to fight Richard or pit himself against his father. There was no reason to gather the levies of England or arrest suspicious people here before leaving for the Continent, unless Henry thought that in his absence there might be an uprising against him in support of the Young King.

"When one throws a wasp nest to the ground, one cannot control where the wasps fly," I smoothed my dress, enjoying the sensation of the softer material against my fingers, another boon of my 'kinder' captivity, "nor whom they sting. This is something my foolish husband will learn now. He has unleashed a nest of angry beasts, and now he tries to catch wasps in his fingers and still the air with his words." I shook my head. "He never thinks of what could come of these outbursts of temper. Never considers that he has the ability to change the world, affect so much for so many. He has the ability to bring death upon us all, with a word."

"You think the King cannot control the Young King? Will not be able to reason with him?"

"I think my husband sought to make trouble for one of his sons and in doing so has made it for himself, a common theme in his reign. One might even say it is God trying to teach him a lesson he never does learn."

*

Henry arrived before the walls of Limoges, where his eldest son was based, and although it was said it was an accident, the Young King's soldiers took a shot at the Old King. An arrow narrowly missed the King and cut instead through his cloak.

Later, when tales of this were all over the camps, the Young King rode out to say that this wild flying arrow was a mistake, but I thought it not. His soldiers must have seen the banners of the King of England fluttering in the wind.

"I would imagine the Young King told his soldiers to fire upon the Old King," I said. "If he dies, young Henry gets all he ever wanted. He will have no more need to prove himself, to demand anything, and although he might feel some guilt I doubt he will truly miss his father much."

"It would be a wicked thing, to kill his father, my lady." Amaria looked a little shocked.

"Perhaps, but what if that father is wicked? Then, no matter that he is a father, he still is a bad man, doing bad things. Would it not be more noble to kill a wicked man when he is your father, for then you do it truly for higher reasons, love not holding you back from justice?"

She looked most disturbed by my question and asked no more. Perhaps she did not like what she thought I might say. It can be worrying to those who think in terms of plain good and evil to understand there are shadows in between. Even more worrying to know that some of us are comfortable in the shadows, perhaps prefer them to the light or the dark alone.

This first incident was passed over as an accident but then it happened again. The King, upon coming back to his son's castle, was again shot at. On both occasions the Old King only very narrowly escaped being killed. After the second occasion young Henry apologised again but it was becoming entirely obvious to everyone that the Young King desired his father's death.

"Where is my third son whilst my eldest is trying to kill his father?" I asked Ralph, and I was told that Geoffrey was running about that area pillaging and looting, mainly from the Church, with the approval of his eldest brother.

In an attempt to curtail the activities of the Young King, because eventually even my husband had to accept the idea that his eldest son might be trying to kill him, the Old King stopped his allowance. Young

Henry ran out of funds quickly, having nothing with which to pay his army. Young Henry's limited purse was one of the reasons why Geoffrey had been sacking and plundering monasteries and shrines and terrorising local communities, and after his brother's allowance was stopped his efforts only increased. Eventually the Young King joined him. People said my eldest son had become a leader of villains who consorted with outlaws and excommunicates.

In honesty, the truth was poor enough. I know not if Young Henry was consorting with excommunicates, did it matter? He was at war with everyone, at once, not knowing whether to turn on his father or his brother, striking at our people, their shrines, their places of worship and safety. Much blame I could place on my husband's shoulders, yet some had to be put on my son's.

I could not even blame this recklessness on his separation from William the Marshal, for the man was back in Henry's favour and at my son's side. This sequence of events was bound to end badly, and it did.

Early in June that year the Young King and his men looted the altar treasure and famous sword of the hero Roland from the shrine of Rocamadour. Crowds of horrified pilgrims watched as my son sacked this sacred site. People said it was this which sealed his fate. Perhaps it was. I would never know what was in God's mind, for sometimes He took people who had done no harm early to His kingdom, and sometimes He took those who had done plenty of ill acts. Was it that the wicked were punished with death, or the innocent were rewarded with Heaven? I came to think death was not a reward or a curse. It was merely what happened, like the sun rising, like the rain falling. A raindrop might fall on one patch of earth and not another, just as death might fall on one person, at a certain time, and not another.

Like my son.

I knew that something had happened before I was told. I had a dream. It was not like the one I had about my father when he died and yet it was so very similar, in some way inexplicable. When my father had died, I had seen a hand shaking and pale reaching out for the door of a church and I saw none of that this time, but as I lay in my bed the next morning after the new dream had passed, I could remember it so clearly, just as I could the one of my father.

I saw my son Henry lying on a couch, his hands pressed together as if he was praying. As I looked down upon him, I realised how greatly his form resembled an effigy on a tomb. His skin was white as marble. On his finger was a great ring made of sapphire and above his white face, so very pale, there hovered two crowns. The first crown was the one he had worn at his coronation, made of gold with precious stones, but the second was entirely unlike this crown that men may place on other men. It was a circle of pure white light that shone with incomparable brightness.

I saw nothing more than this yet when I awoke, I turned to Amaria and I said, "I think my oldest son is set to die."

"My lady..." She rose from the covers, blinking at me, still half asleep, "... you dream dreams which are not real. I promise you, there have been no reports of illness amongst any of your sons."

"I know." I sat forwards and put my face in my hands in weariness, but no tears came. "And yet I know it, Amaria. I think if he is not gone already, this world is soon to lose my boy."

In all those years, she had never seen me weep. I had not cried once for myself, for my own fate, for this ongoing and apparently never-ending punishment for defending my sons. All these years and whilst they had risen to my eyes, I had never shed a tear for myself, but for my son, for his life ending so soon, before he had a chance to do anything with it, for his wasted potential, this wasted life that could have been great and now never would be, yes, for that I wept. For my child I wept.

It was not long after that Thomas Agnell the Archdeacon of Wells came to my dismal chamber at Sarum, where I was once more staying. Henry had moved me there when he left, part of his plan to secure England before he left to go to the Continent. Apparently, it was safer in case of invasion, which really meant I would be harder to rescue should any of my sons cease warring with one another and come for me.

When the Archbishop entered the chamber, his face so grave, I looked up at him. "My son Henry is dead," I said in a calm, flat voice. "That is what you have come to tell me."

"Majesty... how did you know?" he gasped, "I have only just this moment heard, and I was the first the King sent news to in England."

"I had a dream." I told him of it, explaining about the two crowns I had seen about young Henry's head. "I see no other meaning than eternal bliss that can be ascribed to a crown upon his head which has no beginning and no end, Eminence. I knew that nothing else could such brightness signify, so pure and so resplendent, if it was not everlasting joy that had come to rest upon my son. The second crown was more beautiful than anything which can manifest itself to our senses here on Earth. As the gospel says, my lord, eyes have not seen nor heard nor have entered into the heart of man the things which God has prepared for them that love Him."

I looked away a moment, sorrow overcoming me. He fell silent as I composed myself, but I would not weep again, only before those I trusted would I do such a thing.

"How did he die?" My voice was quiet but dignified. "This, I did not see."

He told me. After my son and his men had pillaged the shrine of Roland, young Henry had fallen violently ill with fever and a flux of the bowels. He was in company with only a few men and tried to reach his castle stronghold once more, but at the village of Martel in Quercy my son had fallen so sick he had taken lodgings in a house belonging to a burgher. The Bishop of Agen had managed to make it to my son and young Henry had made a confession of his sins. As men realised that his condition was hopeless, and he was close to death, the Bishop was sent to fetch the King.

My son was denied the comfort of his father at the moment of his death, for Henry suspected the tale of his son's illness was a trap. Instead of going himself to the bedside of his dying son, the King sent money and a sapphire ring which had belonged to Henry I.

"The ring, was it the ring I saw?" I asked.

"I believe it must have been, Majesty," said Thomas in a quiet voice.

"He wanted to feel his father close to him, so wore his gift." My throat ached with the tears held there. "If only my son could have had his father with him as he faced the last darkness. It would have been a comfort to him, I know, and it would have given me comfort too. But no, my son was alone when he faced that dark chasm."

I thought of when William had died, my little boy. I thought of how I had held him and how, when I had said to Henry that I felt useless in the maw of death, he had told me I had done all I could for our boy, because I had been there at his side, ensuring he did not face death alone. Henry could have been there to do this for our son, and he had not. My son had died without the comfort of a parent with him at his side, letting him know he was not facing this by himself, letting him know that he was loved, that he was cherished.

Into that darkness my little boy had fallen, utterly alone.

I would never forgive Henry for that, never.

On the 11th of June, the Young King had known he was dying and was overcome with remorse for his sins. He asked to be garbed in a hair shirt and a crusader's cloak and told his followers to lay him out on a bed of ashes upon the floor, a noose around his neck and bare stones at his head and feet, as benefited a penitent. He had sworn once he was to go to the Holy Land on crusade and had never fulfilled this vow. I supposed his last requests about clothing were to demonstrate to God he was willing, had he had more time, to fulfil his vows. William the Marshal, good man that he was, promised to fulfil the oath and take young Henry's place on crusade.

"One of his last requests, my lady, was that your husband would show grace and mercy to you. Your son said you had been held now in captivity for too long and he asked that all his companions plead with the Old King to set you at liberty."

I nodded, unable to say anything. Was I glad that in his last moments my son thought of me? I was indeed, but I wished I could have been there to hold his hand.

The Young King asked also that his father provide for the needs of Queen Marguerite, and commanded that all of his possessions apart from the ring his father had given him were be distributed to the poor. A monk who had come to hear his last confession asked why he did not give away the ring also and young Henry said, "because I wish my judge and Lord God to know that my father sent it to me as a token of forgiveness." He died late that evening.

"He was only twenty-eight years old," I murmured.

None of my son's companions dared take the King the news, so a monk of Grandmont was dispatched to break it to him instead. The King heard of how his son had died and threw himself upon the ground. All said he greatly bewailed the death of his son. He was so distraught in fact that a man reproved him for excess of grief. It was a mirror of when Becket died.

"There is no such thing as an excess of grief," I said, "What grief is enough? When the wailing of our mouths and the rain of our tears is enough to fill the void inside our hearts formed when someone we love dies, that is when grief is enough. But tears are water which slip away and wailing a sound which drifts on the wind. They cannot fill the void. It stands empty in us, gaping and baggy and open, flapping raw and ugly in the wind."

I was sure my husband's excesses of grief were only partly true in any case. I am sure he felt guilt, Henry was all too capable of that under the right circumstances, and he had refused to see his son upon his deathbed so hopefully something of regret tugged at his soul, but the descriptions of his demonstrations of sorrow were too like those for Becket. I was sure a part of Henry was relieved our eldest son was dead.

One fewer man for him to fight.

At my son's request his eyes, brain and entrails were buried alongside the grave site in the monastery of Grandmont which he had so recently sacked and pillaged. He asked for his body to be buried in Rouen Cathedral but as his funeral procession passed through Le Mans, citizens seized the body and buried it in their own cathedral. Indignant people of Rouen threatened to burn Le Mans to the ground if the body of my son was not surrendered to them and the King intervened in their favour, commanding that his son should be buried where he himself had chosen to lie. The Young King, who never was destined to rule, was set on the northern side of the high altar.

I was sixty-one when my second son died. As he passed from life I thought much about William, my first son. I wondered much about how young Henry would have turned out had William lived, that perhaps he would not have been so obsessed with all that was due to him if he had been placed second in the succession, perhaps he would have had a greater chance at life had he not been so aware of everything he was lacking, perhaps he would have counted his blessings rather than always listed all that he never had. But it was not all his fault that his life turned out this way.

Oh, how my heart burned against my husband! My son Henry could have turned out to be a good man, a good leader and a great king, I was sure of that. People followed him even when he had little, he had inspired people. There was so much in him that held potential. He had never had a chance, and now he never would have.

I was silent for some days after I heard Henry was dead. I thought of him, prayed for his soul, and then I tried to set my mind to what must happen next. It did not mean I ceased to grieve. I grieved for my sons, both I had lost and another child whose sex I never had known, every day. Every morning when I woke, I thought of them. I thought of them as babies, as mere sensations inside my body, as children I had held and sung to, the scent of their heads creeping up my nose, perfuming my mind with the bliss of the love of motherhood. If I closed my eyes, I still could smell each of my babies now.

I thought of all we had shared, and all we never would share. Every morning and every night they were with me, my children, my lost little ones, so close I could almost touch them. In the daytime I felt them too. In some ways their presence eased my pain, and in some ways made it worse.

But I tried, for the sake of my sanity, to think of my children still alive. It would be easy here at Sarum, still shut away from life, to descend into a depression most dark and waste away. I would not do such a thing. My children still alive needed me, just as the dead did. Time of each day I offered to each set of my children, to the living and the dead. It was fair, was it not? Prayers and thoughts each had, and I tried, with all the strength and courage I had left, I tried to stay alive for the children who were still living.

A strong part of me wanted to join the dead.

My son Richard was now, in the eyes of most men, the undisputed heir to England, Normandy, Anjou and my lands of Aquitaine, Poitou and Gascony. The rebel coalition in the south collapsed, and my son made sure they would not rise again. He executed many and had others blinded or maimed as an example to all those who would rise against him.

I wondered if his father would allow him to become the named heir. The truth was, Henry had feared Richard before, when he was heir to only Aquitaine, and now he was heir to so much more.

Marguerite of France, my son's widow, was permitted to retain some of her dower properties in Normandy and Anjou. Eventually she would return to Paris after marrying for a second time to Bela III the King of Hungary. Many years later, she died on pilgrimage to the Holy Lands. I was sad to hear of it. She was as a daughter to me.

People said my son had deserved the fate that fell upon him because he rose against his father. God had punished him and perhaps this was true, but I think the punishments of God more subtle than men imagine. Perhaps it was not the Young King, in truth, who was being punished with death.

Perhaps it was my husband.

The Old King had feared his son Richard more than young Henry, and now Richard was the man standing closest to his throne.

Chapter Thirty

Sarum and

Normandy

Summer – Autumn 1183

It was in the late summer of that year, the year I lost my son, that my husband summoned me to Normandy.

I had not been anywhere but Winchester or Sarum for ten years. Ten years I had been the prisoner of my husband, and now as our son died, he wanted me to come to him. Was it for grief? To fulfil a promise inspired by the last words of our eldest son, begging that his father set me free?

I doubted it.

Henry was up to something, that was as much as I knew. If he wanted me close to him, there was a reason. He wanted something from me, or he needed me for something. That was the truth. It had nothing to do with guilt over how I had been kept a captive for ten years, and nothing to do with the death of our son. Perhaps he was to have another try at getting me to agree to an annulment? The last few attempts had not worked, but I had been allowed 'privileges' since and my son had died so perhaps I should be more willing now to retire from life? Spend my last days praying for young Henry's soul?

If he thought I would abandon Richard now, he was a fool.

All the same, a trip to the sea, a jaunt on a ship, these were more enthralling moments than I had had for a decade, so I made sure I enjoyed them. Amaria was terrified of the sea, she had only once been upon it and had not wanted to repeat the experience, but I insisted she come on deck with me, look at the waves.

"It all touches." I spread my hands out to the water, feeling droplets of waves rise through the wind to touch my skin. The smell of salt and seaweed was intoxicating. "All this water, child, it reaches about the land on which we stand, about the boats we sail on, it touches the ends of our world and stretches to other lands, those we know of and those we do not. The water lapping on our boat here will travel to the other side of the world on wind and wave. Everything here becomes part of everything elsewhere, the present, the past, the future, all touch here, all connect, in the oceans of the world."

"The water is... the memory of the world?" Her teeth had ceased to rattle in her head for fear, and there was a spark of interest in her eyes.

"That is the way I have always thought of it," I smiled at her. "Here, I remember my sister, my uncle Raymond, trips taken long ago."

"Are there are monsters in the waves?" Amaria's wide eyes stared down, into the belly of the oceans as if she expected there to see a mouth opening, ready to swallow her.

"There may be, but I have never seen them. Once I saw great fish, bigger than the boat or so it seemed, but they paid no heed to us. They were on their own paths and did not cross ours. Men tell tales of monsters, but men tell tales of many things."

Amaria looked up at me. "Why are we going to Normandy, my lady?"

"Because a man needs something I have." I smiled wider, my eyes glinting. "And we will see if that is something I wish to give or hold back."

*

"My lord husband," I said upon entering his room. I descended to a graceful curtsey and held it some moments before standing straight upright and staring my captor in his blue eyes.

Henry blinked as he looked at me. I was sixty-one, had been held in captivity many years and many of those years had been spent at Sarum, a place most detrimental to the health, yet I still looked like a woman of thirty years. I cannot claim any form of magic or prayer brought this about, my line were long lived and the women in it were preserved well. It had always been that way. Dangerosa had been a rare beauty all her life.

To this longevity luck I had added my own choices, for I had ever been a spare eater and drinker, so my form was still lithe despite all the children I had borne, and the fire of anger had kept me company and maintained the colour in my cheeks. My skin was clear and my wrinkles few. My golden hair was now lit by the sheen of silver, which made my skin and eyes seem only brighter. I was no more the grand beauty I had been in my youth but now in age I possessed a different kind of beauty, less fragile than my beauty of youth had been. My beauty of age was stronger, more resilient, there was steel in me where once there had been water, and it shone from me. I was well aware I was still a deeply attractive woman. But if I was aging well, my husband was not.

It had been a long time since I had seen him and none of that time had been kind. Henry was fifty now and aged much beyond his years. His locks were mostly grey, patchy and unsure looked the hair on his head, as if it had thought aging a good idea but then had changed its mind. His stocky body had become fat, and all those years of sitting in the saddle, racing around after one enemy or another, had made him bowlegged. He also was limping, lame in one leg thanks to a horse kicking him, as I later learned. He did not look hale; his skin was pale with that kind of pallor that men have when a long illness has assailed them. I looked upon this old man, in the winter of his life, and although I was older I felt like autumn when near him, glorious golden autumn where the sun kisses the trees and the rain plumps the earth. Henry was as bare and raw as winter's last storm. I felt hope surge in me. Henry did not look well. Perhaps it would not be long now until my son Richard sat on the throne of England, and I would be free.

Although that, apparently, was what I had been brought here for. Henry had an offer to make to me, an offer of more freedom than I was presently allowed. There was, naturally, a cost.

"I want to resume our partnership," my husband announced, his voice pious, as if he thought he was performing a great sacrifice. "Although it will be hard to trust you."

"You need me, is what you mean," I said smoothly. "France lays claim to lands that once were mine, and to refute this claim you need to bring me out of prison."

Ralph kept me well informed. Upon arriving here he had learnt that Philip of France had been insisting that certain properties within the duchy belonged to Queen Marguerite by right of her late husband. My husband had adamantly refused to hand them over, declaring that they had once in fact belonged to me and I had assigned them to our son Henry *only* for his lifetime, after which they would revert once more to me. With Henry gone into the arms of the Lord, my husband had brought me to Normandy so that I could visit those lands in order to reassert my right to them. I was correct when he said he needed me.

"Do you wish to stay in captivity instead?" Henry was eyeing me with suspicion and amazement. No doubt he had expected that an *old* woman like me would have lost some of her wits by now, yet here I was, still as sharp as I had been in youth, perhaps sharper. I knew more of the world and of men than I had before.

"I do not, but I would prefer there to be honesty in what we do here and now, rather than you insulting me by pretending affection or forgiveness when the truth is you merely need me again, as another pawn on your board. The arrangement is sufficient as it is, I do not need flattery or promises of affection or love which I no longer have any need or regard for from you; I help you and I gain more freedom. Do not pretend friendship or love to me, I know it is false." I paused. "And so we are clear, I trust you not either. Too many times you have made promises to me or our children, then broken them. Your word is worth an ounce of grain, nothing more."

He frowned at me. I am sure, at least partially, in his mind he believed his own lies, but I did not. "Very well," he said in a tone stiff as a starchy root, "you will assume your place as Queen once more and we will appear together on occasion. There will be no need for us to reside together in the same castle, but I do need you to visit the lands which Philip of France is attempting to lay claim to so that we can retain them for our own family."

I smiled without humour. I knew this offer of resuming my place as Queen was only temporary. "Does it not feel better when truth comes from your mouth rather than lies?" I asked sweetly. "This arrangement is suitable, although it will end should you put your whore, Alys of France, in the same house as me."

He blinked again, obviously unaware I had been told that he had a new mistress.

"She is the bride of our son," he said.

"She is the *promised* bride of our son, that is so." I smoothed my gown. "But from what I hear it would not do Richard any good to marry a woman who has already lain with his father and borne him children. Tell what lies you wish to the outside world, but I will not share a room with that girl anymore, nor will I walk in the same halls as her."

"As you wish," he said.

I had a thought in my head, you see, that if I met with her, Henry might try to find some way to have me accept her in public, something leading to her replacing me as his wife. He had also sworn, when first we were married, not to parade mistresses before me, so I would not be shamed in public, and I had in truth grown some ill feelings about the girl. Although I knew it likely she had been talked into her position as Henry's mistress, I had still come to think if truly she had loved my son, she would have refused my husband. Perhaps this was unworthy of me, as I was well aware she had most likely been manipulated but still, part of me harboured resentment on behalf of Richard.

I did not have to worry for a while about Alys. She was kept under guard at Winchester. I think Henry had been concerned that she would be carried off to France. Her brother Philip had been insisting that my husband honour the agreements made when peace was agreed with France and marry Alys to Richard with immediate effect, but Henry of course stalled. Even had Alys not been his mistress he hardly wanted Richard, who many saw now as his heir though nothing had been announced, to be allied by marriage to the French King.

"We have larger concerns anyway at this time," Henry's voice rumbled, as his cheeks were recovering from going a little red. At least he had some shame. "We must make peace between our sons."

"What you mean is you want me to make peace between your sons after you made war between them."

"Do you wish to go back to Sarum?" he growled. I assume it was supposed to be menacing, but he scared me no more. Even if he beat me or killed me, he did not intimidate me. I looked on Henry now and I saw a man pathetic, a falling king who did not know he was standing in the last flicker of his light. The torch had been his, but it was ready to pass to another hand. He did not know how feeble his grip was.

"It matters not where you send me." I stood straight and stared him in the eyes. "I will ever be the same no matter what geographical location I happened to be in. Do not think you can intimidate me with the idea of imprisonment, my lord. I have been ten years a captive and I know how to survive, as you see. Besides, you must truly need me here most direly, otherwise you would not have brought me out of hiding, so your threats are hollow and ineffectual because I know you will not send me away, not until you have what you want, that is."

"Are you going to be this troublesome all the time?"

"Probably, I have ten years of captivity to make up for."

I almost thought he was going to smile. Perhaps the old Henry would have, the one I had met so many years ago. That Henry had loved my rebelliousness, my courage and my sharp tongue. This one though, he did not like them. He did not like me.

That was fine. I had no affection left for this man either.

Yet that moment of an almost-smile, it was interesting. It meant somewhere in there the man I had known still existed. He was buried under this old goat, under layers of hard suspicion and deep sourness over life's trials. Perhaps somewhere in there, the Henry I had met first was screaming to be let out. But there is no going back when we have left something behind. The Henry I loved was dead. This thing wearing his face was the person I had to deal with.

He outlined his thoughts. Henry had decided to apparently make a "fairer" division of his empire between Richard and John. Geoffrey was not being taken into consideration for he had his own lands already and Brittany was enough for him, so my husband thought. It was John he wanted to have more. John was the important one to Henry, the son he loved the most and he wanted his last son, the youngest, to have much.

And that meant taking it from Richard.

John was at present only to have Ireland, as well as some estates in England and on the Continent. His father had taken it upon himself to give him a nickname because of this; John *lackland*, which John resented and hated. Henry explained to me that he wanted John to have my lands, Aquitaine and Poitou, and John would do homage to Richard for them.

I said nothing, and my husband took this as an agreement to his plans.

*

John was without doubt the favourite of his father, being the only son who had never rebelled against him. My youngest son was now sixteen. I was to see him the next day, and a stranger who apparently adored me walked into my chamber.

"Mother," he said. "How I have longed to see you."

"My son." I held out my hand for him to kiss. "Your father tells me much of your studies."

As he straightened, I took a look at him. John was shorter than my other sons and looked rather like Geoffrey. His hair was thick and dark red and had a curl to it. He possessed a strongly built body like his father's, though he looked a little gangly. He had been educated well, first at Fontevraud then in the household of his older brother the Young King, and lastly, he had been in that of the Justiciar, my old custodian Ranulf Glanville.

As we talked, I saw his eyes on me, as curious about me as I was about him. In truth, we had little known each other. Resentment I would have expected, and it was there, I could see it, but there was also a shrewd light in the eyes of my youngest son. Something of the fox, one hungry and without a hole to call home, was in my child. I could see it.

He set me on edge, truth be told. It was nothing I could put a finger on, but a warning sense crept in my spine, telling me there was something dangerous here, and it was sitting across from me, expressing love for me, holding my hand.

John had a sharp mind, curious about many things and he read a great deal, but for all of this he much preferred lighter pursuits in life. In a short conversation it was easy to see that my husband had indulged him. He had all the marks of it. John had all the self-indulgence and greed of his oldest brother Henry, and little of his charm. Like all my sons he loved hunting and hawking but also admitted he gambled prodigiously. He boasted to me about his conquests with women and apparently thought no wife belonged to her husband if he wanted her. He had several bastards even by that young age and in life he would go on to have at least seven, probably more. He was wildly promiscuous. He also had the temper common to all men in my family.

"What of your wife to be?" I asked. "This Hawise?"

He shrugged, "At court they call her Isobel. She is not pretty, I hardly see her," then he got on with boasting about other things.

John was never a warrior like Richard or even Geoffrey. He did not like war and thought tournaments petty things, beneath his attention. I knew him the least of all my sons for he had been taken out of my household when he was still a baby, but I knew one thing; whilst he appeared to return the affection of his father, John liked Henry no more than my other sons did. When he spoke of his father, his lips curled, just a little, with contempt. I doubt he knew he was doing it, but his feelings were plain on his face, and spoke as loud as if those lips had expressed hatred in words.

I doubted he would have much affection for me, either, after I did what I was about to do, but I could not help that.

*

My husband summoned Richard, Geoffrey and John to Angers, issuing orders they were to make peace with each other. I was brought to them, but we were not permitted to talk. There were barons there, as witnesses. Henry meant to make this official before them, this stealing of the lands of my son. As Richard entered the room, I saw him look my way and start. Their father had plainly not warned Geoffrey or Richard that I would be there, perhaps to catch them off guard. John had of course seen me. He had been sent to me to charm me so I would think Henry's plan a good one, that was why we had been allowed time together, so he could win me over.

To own the truth, with age sometimes it feels as if blinders have been taken from your eyes. When we are young people are so hard to see through, but in age each person may be read as easily as a book left open on a chair. Henry, and so many others who tried to fool me, probably thought their actions were unreadable. They probably thought because of my age that I was an old fool, who could be duped with ease. They never knew how I saw through them. Ice on a pond they were, everything they thought was betrayed to me. When I was young, I was so easily fooled. I thought myself wise, but I fell for so much, and mainly because I chose too often to think the best of someone. That time had passed. In age, people had to prove themselves to me, then I would decide if they were worthy of my trust. This was something Henry still did not understand, much as he never understood that my love for my sons, especially Richard, was greater than my desire to know freedom again.

Henry proposed the new division of lands, told Richard to cede Aquitaine to John, and commanded John to swear fealty to Richard.

"Your mother supports this," my husband announced, looking delighted with himself.

I stood from my stool. "I support nothing of the kind."

Henry stared at me, stunned. My sons too all looked surprised, but a slight twitch appeared on Richard's lips, and I realised he was trying to keep himself from laughing out loud at his father.

"I will not allow my lands to be given to another heir other than Richard," I announced. "He was the child I trained for this role, the one that was promised to me. He is the only lord I will support whilst he lives to inherit and rule my lands."

"What are you doing?" Henry hissed. "You agreed to this."

"I did not. I said nothing, which you took as agreement to your plans, but silence is not consent, my lord."

"I will send you to hell!" His voice was ragged with disbelief.

"Send me wherever you wish, but I still will not agree with you," I said. "Not only has Richard been promised those lands since I birthed him into the world, he has fought for them, over and over and time and time again, fought to regain control and keep rebels in order. For that service alone he deserves to be given the inheritance he was promised, and since those lands are mine, I shall never agree to them being given elsewhere."

I looked to John, who had turned a little white at the thought of his vanishing inheritance. "I am sorry, my son, but considering your age and present experience, you cannot hold the south as Richard can. I know not why your father thinks to present you with this, but you being handed Aquitaine and Poitou now, in your present condition of being untried in war and politics, would be a disaster, for the lands and for you. This gift you think he gives you; it would not be a gift. It would be a curse and might well end in your death. I want more than this for you."

John stared at me a while, and I could see my words sinking into his mind, making him wonder why his father might be doing this indeed. Slowly he nodded to me.

I turned to my husband. "You have other lands, Normandy, Maine, Anjou, any of which John could rule for Richard in his stead, swearing fealty to him, but the south is Richard's, and ever has it been."

"I will not surrender any of my lands," Richard announced. "I am the heir to our empire now."

I inclined my head. "That is your choice, as heir to your father."

"I have not named him my heir!" Henry screamed.

All of us stared at him.

"So, you wish Richard to surrender Aquitaine but will not promise him your other lands?" I asked, incredulous. "You would strip lands from Richard to give to John and offer nothing in return?"

"They are *my* lands!" screamed Henry.

I knew then. Henry meant to make Richard cede his lands to John as a stepping stone to the next part of his plan, which was to make John his heir and disinherit Richard entirely. That was what he was up to. I glanced at Richard, and I could see he had understood this plainly too.

Richard, who was quite rightly appalled, did not even answer his father, and left the next morning. Once he arrived back in Poitou, he sent my husband a message which declared that under no circumstances would he yield any part of his inheritance to anyone.

I was marched to a chamber after that meeting, guards on the door again, and I was told I had no freedom of the castle. I did not care. I sat on my stool and laughed out loud at the memory of Henry's aghast face as I had announced I would not go along with his plan. What did freedom of the castle matter? I had my way. Richard would not be set aside for John. All the lords and barons there present as well as my sons had heard my refusal, it was public and would be recorded. I felt buoyant, in truth, despite the darker plot we had all seen that lay in the heart of Henry. At least Richard and I were aware of what he was up to now.

I would probably be sent back to Sarum for this, I might even be killed, but that was a small price to pay to keep Richard as my heir.

And it was a small price to pay too, for the delicious memory I would hold within me now always, of the disbelief in Henry's eyes when his prisoner of ten years had stood up and defied him openly.

*

Soon we heard that Richard had further call to be annoyed with his father. Philip of France had come to believe that the repeated postponement of Richard's marriage to Alys meant but one thing, that Henry intended to set me aside and dispossess his sons. Philip believed Henry meant to marry Alys himself, and begin a new family with her. Richard, I think, knew there would be problems if he married Alys since he was well aware that she was the long-term mistress of his father, but setting her to one side would offend Philip of France who could be a powerful ally. Perhaps he also still harboured some feelings for her, despite all that had happened. Therefore Richard appealed to the Church, asking them to support his match with Alys, and Philip asked my husband for a meeting to discuss the matter of what was to be done with his sister.

In December the kings of England and France met once more at Gisors, and there Henry declared firstly that he could not assign our dead son's lands in Normandy and Anjou to Marguerite of France because they belonged to me and he could show this beyond doubt. To prove it, he gave evidence I was in those lands now, receiving homage for them.

When Philip asked what was to become of his sister Alys, Henry promised that if she was not immediately married to Richard then she would soon be married... to John.

"I do not want to marry that whore," John said some days later, in my company and his father's.

I knew Richard would also be alarmed, for this move appeared to confirm suspicions that Henry intended to make John his heir. This might well have been the case, but it seemed to me another stalling tactic and that really what my husband wanted still was to marry Alys and begin a new family of entirely loyal sons with her.

"If I command you, will marry her," Henry said to John.

"I will not take wasted scraps from your table!" my last son shouted. "You have a son with her, my half-brother, and you would have me wed her?"

As I watched John storm from the room, I turned to my husband. "When you make peace with another king," I said in a conversational tone, "do you not negotiate? Make terms which mutually benefit each other in order to bring about alliance?"

Henry did not answer me, so I continued. "For this peace you seek with your own sons you make no allowance for their wishes. You try to form the world as you see it, as you want it and peace is only ever on your terms. You will find no peace with your sons nor anything lasting unless you compromise with them. They are all men grown and you must find a way to respect that."

"You will return to England upon the New Year," he snapped and left the room.

"That is the last time I will offer advice freely," I said to his departing shadow. "In the future, it will have a cost."

Chapter Thirty-One

Winchester, Berkhamsted and

Woodstock

1184

I returned to England in early 1184. Despite my defiance, I was allowed more freedom. I supposed this was because I had done as Henry had wanted, in part at least, by aiding him in holding on to our threatened territories, but I believed Henry still wanted my help, hoped to eventually get me to support his plan of John's inheritance, especially if I was shown what treats could be mine if I was a good, obedient wife. He also needed to drag me out any time Philip of France tried to lay claim to Marguerite's dower lands, which Henry had no intention of handing over, so I was not assassinated just yet and my location had to be easier to reach. I was not, therefore, sent back to Sarum.

That Easter I was at Becket's former castle of Berkhamsted when my daughter Matilda came to me, seven months gone with child. When I had word that she was to stay with me I was surprised, but I supposed she was another enticement to good behaviour, as Henry saw it. Since I knew not how long I would have my daughter, I was determined to make the most of it.

"Maman," she cried in a rush as we met in the great hall. There was not even time for either of us to think about curtseying, as we crashed into one another's embrace. Her husband was not far behind her, smiling as his wife fell into my arms.

"My daughter," I whispered in her ear. "I am sorry for the circumstances that have brought you here, but more happy than I can express that I am allowed to see you again."

"Maman," she said, unable to say more as tears filled her voice.

We managed the formal introductions after we had ceased to hold one another. It took a while. The feel of her warmth against me, the sensation of the beating of her heart. I had thought I never would see her again in life, and now here she was, in my arms. People who witnessed the meeting of daughter and mother were not shocked by our lack of correctness. Ralph told me afterwards that all were singing praises of the natural affection Matilda and I showed to one another, and when I looked about the hall after our embrace, I had seen many a witness there dabbing their eyes to wipe away tears.

She had gone so far to be married, I never thought I would see her or her husband, this great, tall man who spoke to me like a gentle dove might coo, or her children, who, one by one, came forth to put their hands in mine.

"They are beautiful, all of them," I said as we walked in the gardens where once Becket and Henry had wandered, arm in arm.

"They take after you, Maman." My daughter slipped her arm in mine. "I expected to find you more morose, after all that has happened."

"After I aided your brothers to rebel and your father took me prisoner, you mean?"

"I do indeed mean that."

I laughed. "I have been morose," I admitted. "But now is not the time for that, for I have you here, and those grandchildren of mine too. How can I be sad at such a time?"

"But you have been sad? When first you were imprisoned, it cannot have been easy, and Henry, my brother..."

I stopped her, putting my hand on hers. "I will miss your brother every single hour I live on without him. And when first I was taken from everyone, from the world, it was indeed hard, it still is. But do you remember what I told you, before you left to marry this impressive giant of yours?" I gazed admiringly at Matilda's husband. I could see why people named him a lion, he was physically most striking, and he even had golden hair.

Matilda squeezed my arm. "You told me many things. You said life is a path we walk, and sometimes the road is hard, and we struggle upwards wondering if we will have the energy to continue, then there comes a slope and walking it is so easy we fly along, without a care. Sometimes there are rocks we do not see, and we trip, and fall, and this hurts. What is important, you said, what marks a person as courageous and resilient, is managing to climb to our feet once more after we have fallen, and to keep moving on along that path. However slowly we get up, however much we limp, we keep going, our eyes on the end of the path, for there is what is important enough to keep us moving."

I smiled. "Did I say it that well? I *am* wise."

She grinned. "You *are* wise. You also said that your children, all of us, were at the end of the path and we were what you kept your eyes on. You said we gave you the strength to continue to walk, even when it hurt. It was your children and your country, you said, that you continued on for."

"And nothing has changed," I said. "Do you remember what else I said?"

"A mistake is not true failure, but not learning from a mistake and doing it again is."

"You remember well all I said, how do you remember so well?"

My daughter smiled. "Your words I repeated over and over to myself, when times were good, when they were bad, when I was scared and when I was bold. They became as a prayer to me, offering strength when I need it."

I patted her hand, and we started to walk again. "I did not keep to my own advice, for I made a mistake. I was a prisoner once before, and I am again. This shows even your wise mother may sometimes take time to learn her lessons, but I will tell you something, daughter, I have learnt this lesson this time, but your father is a worse scholar than me; he never does learn."

*

Oh, the opulence of freedom I was offered when Matilda was with me. I began to suspect Henry wanted it to appear to our daughter and her potentially powerful husband, if he was ever forgiven in his own country, that I was indeed free, and this rumour of imprisonment was but a myth. I was allowed more freedom of movement but was still in the custody of Ralph, if custody you could call being with a friend, and after Easter my household and I moved to Woodstock where we stayed until the summer. There were strolls in the countryside to be had, as Matilda's husband went hunting and hawking and her children learned their lessons and played. There were long nights where my daughter and I tucked ourselves into bed together and talked late into the night before falling asleep in each other's arms. There were evenings in the dusky blue gloaming where we sat at the fireside and told each other everything we had missed in our lives. There were my daughter's tales of her babe, resting under her heart, and there were times we wrapped our arms about each other and wept for Henry, her brother and my son. It was a good summer.

In June Henry returned to his kingdom and within a few days of his arrival at Winchester, Matilda bore a son whom she named William. The boy would be brought up in England and I was permitted to be present for the confinement, something which gave me great comfort, and yet something my husband thought I should be grateful for even though it was a natural right of any mother to be present at the birth of her grandchild.

I allowed the midwives to do their jobs, for although I had been present at many a birth, I had been the one being ordered about. Being on the other side, I knew it was important not to get in their way, and to support all they told my daughter to do. Of course, she had already borne babes, but each birth is different. This one was of mercifully short duration and as I held the baby, wiped clean of blood with wine and honey and handed to me, I showed him to his exhausted mother. "Your fine son," I said, moved enough that tears came to my eyes as I sat on the bed next to her, wiping away hair stuck to her face with sweat.

"William is a good name," she said.

"After your brother?"

"After him, so his name continues to be spoken, Maman, by others aside from you."

*

There had been other signs Henry was trying to win me over. My household had been augmented and gifts had been sent by the King. One was of a new scarlet gown lined with grey miniver, much as we had had before, and as before Amaria was presented with the same gown as me, which offended my daughter Matilda. "You should have cloth or furs a grade better, at least!" she exclaimed, staring at the gowns as if they offended the world and his wife by merely existing.

I chuckled. "Your father thinks to try to please and punish me at the same time. It will not work. This is a tease, you see. If I obey him and disinherit your brother, better cloth will follow, my rank may be respected. He thinks me so shallow that material comfort could mean more to me than notions of justice or love for my children. Your father knows me not at all. This cloth is finer than anything I have had for years, and I would rather wear sackcloth or walk naked in the streets than betray Richard or my people by giving them a lesser man as their ruler."

I also had a saddle trimmed with gold and fur, embroidered cushions and more items for my maid Amaria which I had asked for myself, since the girl had been entirely loyal and a good companion.

Henry, true enough to his promise, had kept Alys of France at Winchester, away from me, but he had another mistress at this time too called Bellebelle, a ridiculous name and one which I surmised since it was so infantile meant she was young, perhaps only just of an age to be bedded. To her he sent rich gifts as he did to me and to Alys. I knew this for Ralph told me. Henry ordered them all at the same time, had them made all at the same time. It was business for him, you see, taking care of the women in his life, prisoners and lovers alike.

Probably we all were wearing the exact same gown.

Chapter Thirty-Two

Berkhamsted and

Westminster

1184

That July Matilda and her husband, as well as their children and I, moved to the Castle of Berkhamsted once more, where we remained for the rest of the summer, and a fine summer it was. Many was the time I took William from his cradle and walked with him, outside if the weather was clement, in the great hall if it rained, talking to him, telling him of my son, his namesake, who had died. Many more times did I play in the gardens with Matilda, who was still recovering so we took care with her, and her children, hiding in the bushes from one another.

I came to think it is a shame we all must grow up. To be a child is an existence most perfect, where the simple sight of a perfect rock found on the ground, the possibility of a game where we might hide and hunt one another, or the sight of an eagle cresting in the skies become things of wonder. See through the eyes of children as an adult, and the world becomes new and exciting, untarnished by all we have seen and done, and all that has been done to us. As I raced in pursuit of my grandchildren in feral games they taught me, this often came to my mind, and I thought how fortunate I was. I had survived long enough to play with them. I was still quick enough to catch them and hear them squeal with fright and pleasure combined as I wrapped my arms about them. Not everyone has that joy.

*

Henry's attempt to assign Poitou and Aquitaine to John had led to other rifts forming.

"Geoffrey has allied himself with John now, and together they have moved into Poitou to raid." Matilda was reading from a letter sent by her father. She put the paper down and looked at me with desperation in her eyes.

"No doubt they have done this with your father's blessing," I mentioned.

"Why is Father doing such things? What has happened to him in the years that I have been gone?"

I inhaled and let it out, pausing a while before I spoke. It was too easy to curse and rail at times. Sometimes, in my head, I had arguments with Henry where I berated him for all he had done, to all of us, where I excused all I had done. Trying to be balanced can be taxing when you have had a thousand fights in your mind with someone who is not there and knows not what you have said to their phantom.

"Everything that he does now, everything he is, it was there in him already," I said, sitting near her and taking her hand. "All men contain good and bad, and characteristics in between, just as we carry the light and the dark within us. Your father is not a wholly bad man, nor is he a bad king, but what he has done to his sons, yes, that I cannot forgive. That he gave my daughters away without asking me, too, is another thing I do not forgive, and I do not need to. There are some acts that are unforgiveable. Some say we will become stuck in resentment if we do not forgive, but I disagree. Some people do not deserve our forgiveness, and we dishonour our own values to tell them otherwise."

"But this setting my brothers off against each other, what does he hope it will do?"

I shrugged. "Keep them so occupied with each other that they will not come for him? He views each of them as men who desire his kingdom and will come for it. His sons are his enemies. Perhaps Becket taught him not to trust those he thinks of as friends. Perhaps his brother Geoffrey taught him that those close to him will try to take his lands. Perhaps after a lifetime of fighting, it is all he knows and understands. I think it barely matters why he is doing it, only that he is." I drew in another breath.

"But you see, he has chosen this path. These things he believes, they are what he has chosen to believe. Your father had another brother, one who never tried to take anything from him. He had others close to him, like me, who would have kept his trust safe had he left it in our hands. He had a mother who gave up her own claim to the throne of England to rest it upon him, and his own father did the same for him with Normandy. He has brought about great peace and took England in a peaceful settlement, so not all of his life was war. Your father has chosen to look at the bad things, the poor things, the betrayals and the distrust in his life and concentrate so hard on that, that he cannot see how much good there was in his life too. There is nothing we can do for someone who has stared so long into the darkness that they have blinded themselves to the light."

"You think this will never be resolved?" Her hands were cold as they clutched mine.

"I think it will be resolved," I said. "All things are, in the end."

In response to his brothers invading his lands, Richard plundered Brittany, and he was a far greater warlord than any of his younger brothers so did more damage.

I was growing tired of this. Now I was a little more at liberty, now I had seen my sons again I wanted to take them by the ear as I had when they had thrown tantrums as children and tell them this was not the way. They were playing into their father's hands and destroying their own lands in the process. But I had no way of reaching them. I was not allowed to write to them. It did also occur to me that my husband might have stirred this latest trouble to convince me that John should be given more lands, or my sons would rip each other apart trying to snatch them from each other. Perhaps this had been done, this latest conflict where any of them might die, had been put into action because Henry wanted to convince me to support his original plan. Had I even had a finger free to intervene with, I might be playing into his hands too.

That November Henry commanded his sons to come to England and cease warring against each other. Then he brought me to him, for he told me he intended for both of us to bring peace between our sons. On the 30th of November, Saint Andrew's Day, I was reunited with my sons. Commanded to join Henry and our children at a court convened at Westminster which was intended to bring about peace through negotiation, I found myself looking into the eyes of my three living sons again.

The secondary reason for the council meeting was to elect a new Archbishop of Canterbury, an event I was not present for and was done quickly. Then came the main event.

I was summoned to the council chamber where I was seated in a place of honour and watched as Richard, Geoffrey and John were called forth to make peace in public with one another and give each other the kiss of peace. I looked at each of them in turn.

Richard looked thin, probably caused by weeks in the saddle defending his lands. Geoffrey looked well, pillaging and warring against his brother clearly suited him, and John was the surprise. He should have been merry, perhaps, but he looked nervous, on edge, and not because he was standing near Richard, with whom he had been so recently at war. I realised John was nervous because he was not sure what his father was going to do. Despite it appearing to all the world that John was his favourite, I understood then that John did not trust his father any more than any of his brothers did. He could not predict what Henry was going to do. He was nervous his father was not going to support him.

Then came the moment I knew had been coming.

"As part of this settlement of peace, I call upon my wife Queen Eleanor, as Duchess of Aquitaine to approve the assignment of Poitou and Aquitaine to our son Lord John," brayed my husband, "I believe that she will agree this constitutes a much fairer distribution of our empire, which will prevent the further warring of our lands."

What would prevent the further warring of our lands would be for you to cease starting wars between our sons, I said in my mind.

Too true, sister, said Petronilla.

Those blue eyes, now of ice, were resting on me. Once I had thought them like the ocean, but they were far colder now than any sea. Henry thought I would go along with him, because we were in public, before all these lords, because he had sent me so many treats, allowed me liberty, because he was announcing this was the only way to peace. He thought wrong, again.

"I refuse to approve the assignment of my lands to my third son, Lord John," I announced loudly, so all there could hear me.

"I too refuse to accept this," said Richard, glancing at me with gratitude in his eyes.

"My lord, I also believe this to be a mistake," chimed in the newly elected Archbishop Baldwin of Canterbury. I tried not to smile as in my heart I blessed the man.

As voices such as these broke in the hall, lords of the council joined in as well, protesting. Many objected, and in truth I think many were baffled. Why assign lands so important, so rebellious, to the youngest son of all? Why disinherit Richard, who was a grown man, who was clearly able to hold those lands and was already the named Duke?

"If this reallocation of lands proceeds, I will petition my overlord King Philip of France to intervene," I announced, my voice booming above the wrangling in the hall. "He is my guardian, as his father was before him. I will put my case to him if I am not heard here."

At this moment Henry, glowering, his face black as night, capitulated and stalked away.

Later he called me to him.

"I have returned you to your seat as Queen and this is how I am repaid!"

I stared down my nose at this man beneath me in so many ways. "You have returned me to nothing. That seat is mine for I am wife of the King, so you cannot give it or take it away, and neither can you take away the rights of our son. You may hold my body prisoner, husband, but my mind you have no control over, and never shall you!"

"What if you were to disappear, Eleanor? You are old, many would accept you had simply died." His eyes were blue gimlets, dangerous and vile.

I laughed. "Many might accept, but not my children, my lord. Go ahead, threaten to kill me. All it shows me is how very desperate you are."

"And if I actually give the order?"

"Then I will become as a martyr to our children, and win again, just as Becket triumphed over you."

The shock on his face was delightful as that comment hit him in the pride. Henry left the chamber, and I laughed out loud.

*

It seemed Henry was not done causing strife between his sons. Just before that Christmastide began the King sent Geoffrey back to Normandy to take control of the duchy in his absence. It was a move which astonished all people and led to many rumours flying about court that Christmas that the Old King was contemplating naming Geoffrey as his heir.

"It is entirely possible," I said to Richard when he was allowed to visit me, "for since Geoffrey now has an heir it may be that your father believes he can persuade the lords of England to support this appointment, for whilst this child was a daughter others may follow."

Constance had recently given birth to this daughter who had been named in honour of me, but my sons had not many legitimate offspring between them. That Geoffrey and his wife were breeding now was a sign many might take as a good one, stability for the future.

Henry never seemed that fond of Geoffrey, however, and I wondered sometimes about William, Matilda's son, who was being raised in England. I wondered if Henry perhaps meant to name him his heir. A young child could be moulded as he wished. His sons, grown men who already resented and did not trust their father, could not be so anymore.

"You must return to your lands." I set my hands on Richard's arms, a distant embrace. "If there is any other plot forming from this, that Geoffrey should perhaps attempt to take your lands whilst on the Continent, you need to be there to defend them."

He sighed. "I know, but I do not want to leave you, Maman, not like this. Years it has been since I saw you properly, and now to see you after all this time and to leave again so soon..."

"There will come a time when we will not be parted by my imprisonment." I squeezed his shoulders with both my hands. "A time when you are free too, to exercise your will upon these lands. In all you have done, I have been watching and I am proud of you, Richard. I may not be able to tell you this always in person, but I am proud. You have risen to every challenge and faced every foe. There is nothing more I could have taught you in any case, so you did not need me by your side."

He leaned in and kissed my cheek. "I did not need you there, it is true," he said. "But I always shall want you there, Maman. You ever were not only my tutor, but my best and most trusted advisor. I love you."

I smiled. "As I love you. And now you must go, but know that if you wish that post filled in the future, of best advisor, I will happily take it as long as my wits are still as sharp as they are now."

"Yours grow sharper with age." He grinned like a proud cat. "There is nothing Father ever can do that would dull you, Maman. You glint like Spanish steel." He kissed me again. "When we both are free, much will be changed."

Not long after Christmas Richard returned to Poitiers. I remained in England, of course, but to my pleasure I was at Winchester in the company of Matilda and her growing family. My quarters were far from those of Alys of France who was housed there at that time. Henry's promise still kept true, somewhat.

I never saw her. We might have walked the same halls, but never at the same time. I wondered, at times, if she was afraid of me, and the thought made me grin.

Chapter Thirty-Three

Winchester

Hampshire

1185

"There is news…" Matilda told me as she entered my chamber, the guards standing politely aside. I barely noted them anymore, "… from Jerusalem. King Baldwin IV is dying of leprosy, and I am told that the patriarch of Jerusalem is to lead an assembly to England offering our father the throne of Jerusalem for my brother John."

"It would be an honour for him to take that position." I stood from my chair where I had been sewing and rubbed my back. Many times, I felt as young as I had once been, but sit long enough in a chair and something always would remind me I was not young anymore. Often it was my hips and sometimes it was my back, but these were slight things. There were not many people of my age who were in as fine a fettle as I was. "And it would solve the issue of his inheritance."

Later I went to my son, then housed at Winchester, and asked him if this was what he wanted.

"It is." John surprised me by dropping to one knee before me and taking my hands. He had a penchant for the dramatic. "Mother, by the time I was born there was little land apart from Ireland left to hand out to me and I want Ireland not." He scowled. "But Father would not send me so far away as Jerusalem. He says he cannot do without me, but in truth I think he trusts none of us to stand far from where his eyes can see us."

"Your father often protests his love for you." I pulled my son up to sit on a stool beside me. "If you go before him in public and beg for this honour to be yours, there is a possibility he will agree."

"In public?" A strange smile curved up his lips.

"Indeed, for then more men will know of the great honour accorded to you in this offer, and hopefully more men you will have on your side."

He laughed. "You are a cunning woman, Mother."

"My sons inherited that from me," I said with a smile. "You do not think you got it from your father, do you?"

"Indeed not, he is the 's' in subtle, but you are the 'b'." He kissed my hand.

John went on his knees again, this time before his father, and begged him to allow him to accept the offer of the throne of Jerusalem. Henry refused. Instead, on the 31st of March that year he knighted his son at Windsor and arrangements were made for John to depart for Ireland. On the 25th of April the Pope himself sent my son a golden crown decorated with peacock feathers and asked that his father should have him crowned King of Ireland.

None of this appeased John.

I was unsurprised. Jerusalem, dangerous though the area could be, was the stuff of legends to young men, and it was rich, the sun was hot and the lands exciting. Ireland was not a warm place, and John, much like all men of England at that time, had a habit of regarding it as a brutal and primitive island, lost in mist and rain. They might have had a point about the rain, but I knew well enough that Ireland bred great warriors, the land was rich and fertile. A man could make a great living out of it, had he the vim to stay there and rule, get the various warlords and princes on his side, but John had no such ambition. He had wanted Jerusalem, and I knew before he went to Ireland that he was going to make a mess of it on purpose. Rather than demonstrate he could rule well, which might have led to more men supporting him over Jerusalem, he would rule badly, to show his father his dissatisfaction.

If cunning was inherited from me, spite was the trait many of my sons received from their father.

I think Henry did not trust John enough to send him all the way to Jerusalem, so far out of his control, and besides the post was a prestigious one, and the crown would make John his equal. Henry could not have that. To all outward eyes, when one saw Henry and John together it appeared Henry loved John more than anyone, but I knew it was not so, not in truth. It was not all on my son's side, either, this distrust, this false affection.

At Winchester there was a chamber where one panel which had for years been left blank, but by the time I was there it had been filled in. There was an eagle painted there, four young eaglets perched upon that eagle, one on each wing and a third sat upon its back. All of them were tearing at the parent with their talons and beaks. The fourth eaglet sat upon his father's neck, waiting but for the moment to come when, weakened enough by the others, it could pick out his parent's eyes.

When some of the King's close friends had asked him what the meaning of the picture was, he told him the four eaglets were his sons who would "never cease to persecute me even unto death. My youngest, even whom now I embrace with such tender affection, will someday afflict me more grievously and perilously than all the others."

Henry declared that he loved John more than all his other sons, but the truth was he trusted him no more than the others. He feared him a little less than Richard, but only because John was still young, still untried, untested.

Henry said that painting was a prophesy, but when I looked upon that picture, I saw a man who had made a prophecy about himself and would see it fulfilled, even if it meant his own destruction, just to prove himself right. It had been the same in his fight with Becket. In the end it had not mattered what their fight did to them, to others, to the country they both protested they cared for. It mattered who was right, that was all.

And so, our son John set sail to this country he wanted not, and I knew it would not go well. John was not one to do things he was disinclined to do, and although the idea of him ruling Ireland had been mooted for some time, I knew it was an honour he wanted not.

"Another dissatisfied son," I said to myself. "Oh, Henry, you break sticks from the tree with which to whip yourself."

There came in April a mighty shaking of the earth which was felt throughout the realm of England. Lincoln Cathedral collapsed and many houses in many towns were left in ruins. People said it was a portent and I believe they were probably right. Just what the Almighty was trying to tell us, however, was not clear.

On the day after the earthquake Henry left England, even though his people were in fright and disarray. He had decided he was to bring Richard to heel. In late April I was summoned to the Continent as were Matilda and her husband. When we arrived, we had a shock.

"Richard has been sent a command by Father that he must without delay surrender the whole of Poitou to *you*, Maman," my daughter said, reading from a letter sent to intercept me as I arrived, "because it is your inheritance and not his. Richard has been further told that if he delays in fulfilling this command or denies it then you, my lady mother, will make it your business to ravage the land with a great host."

My daughter had found a way to communicate with Richard, because she knew I needed to. This letter was from Richard, sent in secret.

"A great host commanded by my husband, I suppose." I took off my riding gloves and handed them to Amaria. She alone was with us; I would have no others knowing I was in communication with my son. "What is your father up to?"

Richard must have known that I was not likely to invade his lands and do battle with him myself. This letter was not sent as a protest but a warning of what my husband was up to. Henry obviously meant to bring my lands under his full control again, and if Richard surrendered them to me, then Henry was made master of them again, as my husband. I pondered what to do.

I was certain that my liberties would be restricted again if I refused to go along with this plan. I believed the idea was that I might well die soon, being an elderly woman without much time left, or I might be done away with by some dire, dark means, and then my homeland, in the hands of my husband, could be left to one of my sons, and I was certain I knew which son. No doubt a will would be produced, with my seal, proclaiming I had assigned my kingdom to John.

This was a way of reassigning the lands, just as Henry had planned before, a way to circumvent my protestation about it. This time, however, the Old King was threatening all-out war on Richard, in my name.

Think as I might, I could not find of a way out of it. If Richard refused to hand these lands over, Henry would march upon him. If Richard was to stand against his father he needed more men, more support and allies, more time, and he did not have them.

I sent secret word to my son. I told him to go along with this plan and cede his lands to me and when I was able to, I would return them into his hands. *"Return as if you are a penitent son,"* I wrote *"for we must have you named heir to the kingdoms of our empire. I believe that without this sacrifice on your part, your father will never agree to it."*

He might not in any case. Henry wanted his way and to get this was now threatening war on my son, not done in his name by another son, but done directly. I had faith in Richard's skill as a warlord, but I had to admit Henry's might well be greater. He was older now, less able in the fight personally, but he had years of experience Richard did not possess, and Richard might well end up facing his brothers also. Henry seemed able to turn Geoffrey and John on Richard with ease, promising them much in return.

We had been challenged, and it was time for a tactical retreat.

Upon my word, Richard went further even than I asked, surrendering not only Poitou but the whole of Aquitaine to me, and he returned to his father's court in Normandy acting the part of the dutiful son.

"We play the long game now, my son," I said to Richard. "You father cannot last forever, and he is not a well man. Let us wait him out, and get you upon the throne, where you belong."

Chapter Thirty-Four

Bordeaux, Rouen,

Fontevraud

1185 – 1186

"Would that you had been born a boy," I said to Matilda before she departed for Saxony. At last, she and her husband had made peace with the Emperor and were allowed to go home. They were leaving several of their children with me, however, to be raised at the English court. "If you had been a boy, you would have been more rational than all your brothers, and I would not have to talk sense into you all the time."

"I think it's a good thing I was not, Maman," she said, "for then you would be forced to choose between me and Richard as your heir. He has sense and listens to you."

"I suppose that is true. But you would have made a fine ruler of Aquitaine."

"That was not my destiny, but Saxony is." She smiled, kissing my cheek. "I would you could come one day and see it, the land is beautiful, the forests glorious. One day, if you are able, come to me. We will sit at the fireside for a winter and catch up on all the doings of my brothers, all their silly stories, and I will tell you of my life and you will tell me of yours."

"I would like that, very much."

She took me in her arms. "And now I will say to you what you said to me, Maman. Life is a path we walk, and sometimes the road is hard, and we fall. What marks a person as courageous and resilient, is managing to climb to our feet once more after we have fallen, and to keep moving on along that path." She kissed my cheek. "Never give up on your feet, Maman. You have come far but for the sake of all of us and yourself, you have further to go."

"How could I give up," I asked her, "when you are here to spur me on?"

I was entirely correct about John and Ireland. As soon as he arrived and attempted to establish his authority, my son decided to act in a way even more childish than his father and even less wise than his older brother Henry. It was quite an achievement in arrogant foolishness, if such a thing can be an achievement. John was there for eight months and during that time he succeeded in offending all native Irish kings and all of our Norman lords who lived there as well. A remarkable feat and I had no doubt it was done on purpose. He wanted to send a message to his father.

"We are told, my lady, that when the kings of Ireland came to pay homage to Lord John, he and his entourage of young lords began pulling at their long beards and openly laughing and sneering at them," Ralph told me.

"I thought something of this kind might occur," I said. "I did not think he would pull beards, but I knew he had something in mind."

"You think this deliberate, rather than the foolishness of youth?"

"It is entirely deliberate." I shook my head. "John is one of the brightest of my sons. He is not the bravest, nor is he the most likeable and he has many ill qualities, perhaps more than all his brothers and none of my sons are perfect men, my friend, much as it saddens me to say it, but a fool he is not. He is punishing his father by acting like this, for men, much as you appear to be right now, will be shocked and shamed by such behaviour from a prince of England."

"But if his father thinks him irresponsible and foolish, what more would he give Lord John to rule over? This would not lead to another kingdom being granted to him, surely."

"Sometimes, we go out of our way to prove people right who think the worst of us," I said sadly. "It does not help us, of course, but still we do it and that is what John does here. He was not trusted to rule Jerusalem? So, he will prove he cannot be trusted to rule Ireland. Sometimes it is easier to prove those who do not believe in us right, than it is to do anything about what is wrong with us."

"My lady, do you love your sons?" His question came from nowhere.

I smiled without humour. "You ask because I speak honestly of them? Because I do not dote and see only perfection as a mother is expected to?" I narrowed my eyes. "I love all my sons, my lord, that does not mean I like them all the time. I see all that is good in them, but also all that is bad. It is proof of my love that I see all this, and still I love. My love is perhaps deeper than those who look on their children and see only perfection. They are blind, as is their love. My love has its eyes wide open."

It only got worse in Ireland. John seized land, apparently on whatever whim took him that day, from Norman settlers and handed it out to his favourites. In time even Irish Kings who had been at war with one another began to unite against him. There was going to be great trouble if Henry did not call John home soon. By December he had returned, complaining it was everyone's fault but his that he had not succeeded.

While this was going on, I was travelling about the Continent with my husband and my son Richard. Both Richard and I were busily acting the parts of the dutiful son and obedient wife of the King of England. We were busy watching and waiting, to see what time would bring us of opportunity.

With Richard under his heel, Henry seemed happier with our son and that was good, for another son had started to complain. Geoffrey decided he was not satisfied with Brittany and wanted more land. Anjou was the country he demanded.

"It is because you do not share your plans for the future of the empire," I said to my husband when he came to complain about Geoffrey, who had, until that moment, been in high favour. They all were favourites, until they expressed an opinion of their own, then they were enemies. "You make them insecure, Henry, and I am sure that was your notion in the first place, but insecure men lash out, they do violent acts. You reap what you sow, and what you sow with your sons here is discord. Your crop is chaos, my lord husband."

He said nothing and left, which I took to mean at least part of him believed I was correct.

Since I was permitted more money at this time, I gave to the Abbey of Fontevraud and all the nuns serving God there a rent of one hundred pounds and all the proceeds from a tax of wine. I said it was so that they might do the soul of my lord the King some good, but I also asked them to pray for my soul and for that of Richard and all my other sons and daughters.

"My sons, now dead," I said to the Abbess, pressing her hands in mine. "For them I would have prayer sung each evening, at dusk. It was the time I used to sing them to sleep, so let them be sung into heaven by voices more glorious than mine."

*

"Geoffrey has moved to Paris?" I asked when Richard told me the news one day.

"I think it is so he and King Philip may share a bed," said Richard in a dry tone, and grinned.

"Even if your brother had temptations of that kind, which I do not believe he does, having seen him with the women of court," I said, "I do not think that would be the reason he has gone to Paris. He wants the support of Philip. Geoffrey is not satisfied with Brittany and has already said to your father he wants Anjou. He and Philip are close, it may be he can persuade him to make war on your father in return for more land."

"Philip and Geoffrey are close, it is true." Richard stretched his strong arms upwards. He always complained that too long out of the saddle or away from the sword made him stiff. "They found themselves birds of like feathers and wish to remain together."

I tapped my fingernails on the table. "Uniting with the King of France will not aid him. We need to keep an eye on your father, that much is obvious, but I think Geoffrey will find no great support from Philip of France. The man only does what benefits him."

In the spring of that year my husband and I held court at Normandy and then in March Philip again came to Henry to talk of his sister. Perhaps worried about Geoffrey and Philip's relationship and what an alliance could mean, Henry agreed to sign a treaty which provided for Alys to be married to Richard with the Vexin as her dowry.

"Father has installed his own custodians in the very strongest of my former castles in Aquitaine, and he has ordered me to go and deal with Raymond of Toulouse who is acting in a hostile fashion towards Father." Richard looked annoyed. "I am his dog, sent out to guard lands of his, and not my own anymore."

"Go and do as he wills," I said, "and make no complaint. We will have you named heir if it is the last thing I do."

"I do not want that to be the last thing you do," Richard said, smiling. "When I am King, I want you there to advise me."

*

On the 27th of April, it being said he had put his kingdom to peace, my husband sailed from Barfleur to Southampton, and I was on the same ship as him. Whilst I often relished a voyage upon the sea and loved to see the waters of the oceans spread out before me, I did not come up on deck that time. I told Henry I was unwell but in truth I did not want to stand with him on the deck of another ship, watching England come into view as we had once when first we were married, coming to England to claim his throne and mine.

Then, I had been proud to stand beside him, but not now. Now, I wanted nothing of him close to me.

Love for him had died in my heart but that did not mean that memories of what we could have had, what we could have possessed, did not chime a chord and ring a bell inside my soul, reminding me of all the sweet feelings I had once had for this man. But he was not that man anymore.

It is a thing remarkable, you see, that death may part us from many people and that is the natural way of course, but what is more remarkable is to understand that a person can die whilst they are still living and become instead a revenant, something which walks the earth wearing their skin and looking like them, even using their voice, even holding their memories and yet the person you knew is dead and all that is left is a shell.

There were enough empty shells in the sea or on the beach for me to lift to my ear and hear the hollow ocean. I did not need to stand beside one, hearing the hollowness of his heart echo in my ear.

*

When we arrived back in Winchester, I was told that Ralph was being taken from me as my custodian and a man named Henry of Berneval was to take his place. Berneval seemed most interested in me and my doings immediately, and I surmised that my husband had grown suspicious about how humble and obedient I had become, perhaps about Richard too. Berneval was a spy in my household.

"I will be sorry to see you go, my friend," I said to Ralph. "I think my husband has decided we have been too close friends and this he does not trust."

"He tells me it is because I need relief from the job, my lady," Ralph kissed my hand, "and yet I have never felt you to be a burden in any part of my life. Though your husband would not welcome this, I would say to you that I wish this role I have played would be retired. You should be restored to be Queen in full, for never was there a better lady who ruled over us than you. You are the only one who might keep your sons in check, too, for God knows their father cannot."

"Thank you, my friend. I have no intention of all my days being a prisoner, and whilst I am sure sometimes that my husband wishes for my death, I have no intention of dying. There is much left to be done, so much left to be seen."

Soon it seemed there was too much.

Geoffrey had remained in Paris throughout that summer, and it was said he was up to much with Philip, but whatever the two had been planning never came to be. In August my son died. It was sudden, it was violent and then he was gone.

It was during a tournament. Geoffrey came unseated in the melee. Under the horses and under the hooves my son fell. He was trampled to death.

I had no dream about Geoffrey. I saw no light shining about his head, no hand shaking at a church door. There was no warning this time. Men came to tell me he was dead, and into a chair I slumped, shocked and horrified.

"My lady, are you well?" asked Henry Berneval my new custodian, seeing my condition, and he called for some wine to be brought to me. "Drink, my lady," he said, and as I stared glassy eyed into his face, I saw genuine concern. It occurred to me that the spy might be won over, just as his predecessors had been.

With a shaking hand I picked up the wine, but I did not drink it. I stared into the goblet where red wine sat like blood, and I imagined the bloody death of my son. I never until now had a reason to dislike tournaments, yet in that moment I did suddenly see why people called them foolish, for had my son not being engaged in games of war for the entertainment of others he would still be alive.

I looked up at Berneval. "His wife is with child," I said in an empty voice. "I hope that whoever goes to tell her of Geoffrey's death will take care in the way they inform her. Such a shock could bring on early birth or the loss of a child. She lost one, not long ago, did you know? I would not have her lose another, not after this. I think she loved my son."

I broke into tears and the spy set his arms about me.

My son Geoffrey was buried in the choir of Notre Dame. I felt guilt at his death, not only because I should have been with him, but because he, of all my sons, was the one most overlooked. I had known it, had I not? Even as he had lived with me, I had given more time and attention to Richard. I understood why I had done so, why it was necessary, but as Geoffrey died, I knew I had failed my boy. I know not how I could have fixed this, but when he died, I knew I never would have the chance to.

His father had small regrets, saying Geoffrey had ever been an unfaithful son, but someone mourned. King Philip of France was driven insane with grief, and it was said that he had to be held back by all his men to prevent him from throwing himself upon the coffin and its open tomb.

"I am glad that someone was there to mourn him properly," I said to Amaria. "My daughter Marie, Countess of Champagne was also present, and she gave money for Masses to be said for his soul."

It seemed that Constance had been told carefully, for she continued to hold Geoffrey's child within her. Eventually she would bear a son, named Arthur. Henry was not pleased, he had wanted the boy named after him, but in a strike of defiance I rather admired, Constance named her son for Arthur the legendary King of Bretons.

That Christmas my husband sent only for John, no others, and they celebrated at Guildford Castle in Surrey. I was not sent for. I had no wish to be there in any case. If Geoffrey had not been so disastrously dissatisfied with his lot in life, he would not have gone to France to conspire with Philip, then he would not have died in that foolish way.

And yet all this I could have forgiven Henry for, but I did not forgive him for keeping a merry Christmas at court as yet another son was taken to God.

Chapter Thirty-Five

Winchester

Hampshire

1187

In February of that year, while snow still was falling upon England, Henry returned to Normandy and left me in England. I suppose he had all he needed from me at that time, so I remained at Winchester. On the 29th of March Constance bore Geoffrey's son. The son he never would know he had, until they met in Heaven.

"King Philip has claimed Arthur's overlordship and insisted the infant Duke of Brittany is to be his ward," Berneval informed me, "but your husband has of course refused this. Constance is to be named as regent for her son, and Brittany goes under the protection of England and Normandy."

Berneval and I had become friends much as Ralph and I had. I was careful what I said, however, since I knew he must still be reporting to his lord, my husband, but I had a feeling his friendship was becoming genuine. My husband's plans for putting men who could not be swayed by my charms in place never had worked. I always found a way. I think the only men I had failed to charm so were Bernard of Clairvaux and Becket.

Berneval was also no simpleton. There were many rumours of the ill health of the King. If Henry died, Richard was still the man most likely to become King and all knew he and I were close. It paid to play both sides of the game at this time, keeping my husband appeased but sharing plenty with me, too.

"Of course." In truth I agreed with my husband on this point for if King Philip managed to gain such a foothold in Brittany as having a ward there, he would eventually claim it as his own. "You said that Constance of Brittany will act as Regent for her son?" I asked. "I wonder that the King supported that."

I had never been entirely sure about Constance of Brittany; in so many ways she was an entirely suitable wife for my son Geoffrey for she was just as canny and duplicitous as he. On that basis she might make a good ruler, but a good neighbour she would not be. Henry had never trusted her either. The very next year proving his distrust, my husband had Constance married to a loyal vassal on whom he could depend named Ranulf de Blundeville, Earl of Chester, the idea being he would rule her and her lands. It did not work. The Bretons excluded the Earl from governance of the duchy and turned to their lady instead. The Earl never managed any kind of control, for the simple reason all of Brittany wanted Constance and her son, not some foreign puppet set up there by a foreign King.

But this was of the future.

Tensions over Constance's son was only part of the growing problems between Henry and Philip and there was talk once more of war. The French King was growing ever more indignant about Henry refusing to marry Alys to Richard and was starting to demand that she, and her dowry of Berry and the Vexin be immediately returned to him. Henry once more suggested that Alys be married instead to John and he would name him Duke of Aquitaine if this went ahead, but Philip refused to believe any more promises of his sister being married to any son of the King. He marched at the head of a great army into Berry and took Châteauroux. My husband and Richard joined forces, and, fearing Richard perhaps even more than his father, Philip requested a space for negotiation. In the middle of summer that year they concluded a reluctant truce.

I am not sure what passed between my husband and my son during the time they were allied but it could not have been anything wondrous. It is possible that Richard was, for a time, ignorant of the idea that his father had offered again to wed Alys to John and make him Duke of Aquitaine. If he found out as the truce was announced it would make sense, for immediately afterwards Richard rode to Paris and allied himself with Philip. Much as Philip and Geoffrey had been close friends, so Richard and Philip became the same, perhaps closer. They ate at the same table, shared the same dish and at night they even shared a bed. Many said there was more between them than friendship and it was possible, but I had never noted Richard taking any interest in men in such a way. I do believe that the two of them became great friends for they had a great enemy and knew how dangerous Henry could be.

And indeed, Henry was much alarmed by this new friendship. Anything which made his heir more powerful, he would fear.

*

Not long after, in the summer of that year, war of another kind broke out on the 4th of July. At the Horns of Hattin near the Sea of Galilee an army of the King of Jerusalem was destroyed by forces of Turks led by Saladin. Soon after Saladin invaded Jerusalem and managed to occupy it. I suddenly thought better of the idea to send John there. It had been his wish to go, it was true, and men must choose their own fates, but had he gone, he would be in the hands of Saladin now, one of the most feared commanders the world had known.

Saladin had already taken Damascus, although peacefully, as well as Hama and Homs, and after the Battle of the Horns of Hama some years before he had been named Sultan of Egypt and Syria. Two assassination attempts he had escaped, and many more campaigns he had fought, including conquering Aleppo, and now the Battle of Hattin was done he was master of the Holy City and the Levant. His people worshipped him as a wise, fierce ruler, and the men of Christendom feared him for the same reasons.

"All that is left now of our crusader kingdoms are three seaports," I noted to Berneval.

"The Pope is to proclaim a new crusade, my lady." He read from a missive, scratching his nose at the same time with his free hand. "The duty of all leaders of Christendom are clear. They must unite once more to free the Holy Lands from the infidel."

I lifted my eyebrows, as I did whenever anyone suggested crusade. Having been present on the disastrous second crusade myself, I knew it was not as easy as some men liked to think it was. I also sometimes wondered that we would call the enemy infidel. Mistake me not, I knew Saladin's men performed atrocities in war, but so did ours, so did my sons. Either we all were infidel, or none were. The horrors man is capable of never are restricted to one side in war. God be praised if one side could indeed be the angels and the other the devils, but I have neither heard nor seen any war where this was true. Sometimes one side has a cause which is just, or *more* just than the other, but that does not stop acts of horror occurring on both sides, and often those who think themselves the most angelic are in truth the most blind to the devil within, and the demons unleashed.

I was further horrified when I heard that Richard himself had taken the Cross from the Archbishop of Tours. Richard proclaimed himself the champion of Jerusalem and vowed that he would dedicate his life to liberating the Holy City. He had not of course consulted his father, since they were at odds again, or me, because I was in England. I certainly did not want my son riding off on crusade when he was needed here in order to hold his lands and claim his kingdom when the time came. I thought this a grand mistake. I suspected my husband would use this time of crusade, while Richard was far away, to steal his lands and hand his titles to John.

It was said Henry was so consumed with grief about Richard taking the Cross that he locked himself in his chamber for four days and refused to see anyone. I did not believe this was honest. Henry might well be delighted that his son was to run off on crusade and perhaps would be more delighted if he never came back.

I came to rest a little easier when Richard declared he could not commit himself to the venture entire until his father assured him that he was to become heir to the entire Angevin empire. Henry once more refused to do so, which I suppose kept Richard in our domain rather than riding off on crusade, but it also kept our son Richard in suspicion that his father intended to leave everything to John.

Not long after Richard took the Cross there was a series of uprisings which broke out in Aquitaine and Toulouse. "Widely it is rumoured that the King is behind them," Henry Berneval told me.

"He has encouraged rebellion against Richard, again?" I asked.

"I hear, my lady, the notion is to divert Lord Richard from not only taking up the Cross but from allying himself further with France."

"Once again my husband proves himself a wild and reckless King," I said.

"There is, however, no sure evidence that he is behind this, my lady."

"My dear lord," I arched an eyebrow, "if I only ever operated on what was sure knowledge in this world then I would be hoodwinked at every turn and deceived in every venture. Even sometimes when we do not know for sure if someone is behind something there is a feeling inside us, arising in our gut, which some men call intuition and others may call wisdom, and it is that feeling we should always listen to if we do not want to be known as the fools of the wide world."

"You would trust your intuition in this case, my lady?"

"I would, for it has many years been warning me about the same man, and many years I told that little voice to be quiet and still, but it was right. All the time it was right. Never ignore the voice telling you something or someone is dangerous, my friend. If the little voice is wrong, all you have done is suspect someone unnecessarily. But if that voice is right, and you ignore it, you may walk into the maw of death, as innocent and trusting as a calf may walk to the slaughter at Martinmas."

Chapter Thirty-Six

Winchester

Hampshire

January 1188

After another meeting at the end of January between Henry and Philip once more at Gisors under the elm tree, they received the Archbishop of Tyre who happened to be going about Europe at that time gathering knights for the crusade against Saladin.

"Apparently the man was most persuasive," said Berneval, staring out of my window to the grounds below. From where he stood, he could see the oak tree where I used to play with William, and with Henry, when they were small. I wondered if Berneval could see, as I could whenever I looked there, the pale ghosts of my children, laughing as they ran about the trunk, escaping me.

"Apparently so," I agreed. On impulse, after hearing the Archbishop, both kings had taken the Cross and had sworn that they would maintain their truce whilst campaigning together in the Holy Land. I thought it was a feint, another way to engender support from the Church, but my husband returned to England on the 30th of January to raise money for this crusade. There was a tax imposed named the Saladin tithe.

Unity did not last long. That spring Henry and Philip began again bickering over Alys and her dowry, and in June Philip attacked Henry's border strongholds in Berry. In response Henry gathered an army of English and Welsh soldiers and left England to invade France, yet before his departure he came to see me. You might think this was a show of affection, but it was not. He had deprived me once again of my freedoms, fearing that I would support Richard against him.

"What reason do you have this time to keep me in my chambers and not allow me out?" I demanded as he came through the door. "What have I done?"

"Your son is entirely too devoted to the King of France." Henry's face wobbled as he spoke. He had grown corpulent, unhealthily so, and he looked pallid under the skin, reddened by riding in the sun and wind, of his face.

"I ask again, what have *I* done? You list a grievance against another man, not against me."

He laughed. "Do not think I do not know that everything Richard does he does because he thinks it will grant happiness to you."

I drew myself up and shook my head. "All these years, Henry, and you never can stop trying to blame me for your trouble with our sons. When will you find a new refrain?"

"You encouraged them to rebel against me!"

"They needed no encouragement. They were ready, had been ready for years to rise up against you. I saw it was coming and I tried to ensure they were safe. That is my duty as a mother, and you can hardly blame me for all they have done since I became your prisoner. Whatever has passed between you, that is down to you and to them. I will accept culpability for my own sins, my lord, but not for those of others."

"You cannot be trusted, and so you will remain in stricter keeping." He turned for the door. He was walking curiously, as if in pain. I surmised the conversation was over and that, apparently, was all I was going to gain from him in terms of information as to my supposed crimes.

I had the strangest sense as he went to walk out the door. I knew not what it was at the time, but I missed him suddenly. This was odd, for I did not even like him.

As I was kept in further confinement, Amaria my only maid once more and my information from outside apparently restricted, though from my guards and my custodian I still heard much, Henry arrived on the Continent only to find that Richard had quarrelled with Philip, had left the company of the French King and had led a force against the French soldiers in Berry, driving them out. You might think word would be sent to allow me freedoms again, since my husband's fears had been proved unfounded, but no such order came.

On the 16th of August Henry and Philip met again at Gisors to once again attempt to resolve their trouble, which went nowhere. It probably did not help that Philip spent three days lecturing Henry on Alys, her dowry, his promises and on all the scandalous ways in which he was treating a Princess of France and daughter of the royal family. Henry maintained that the Vexin, part of the dowry they were arguing about, was his. Both kings withdrew without meeting an agreement.

Philip later ordered that the ancient Elm of Gisors should be cut down. When Henry saw the stump that was left of this ancient meeting place he declared war on his rival.

*

"The King is not in a good state of health, my lady," I was told by my custodian. "He has many ailments, one of them being a wound in his rear end which gives him much trouble when he tries to ride."

"I saw him walking a little oddly when he was here," I said, remembering, "but he said nothing of it. Probably he is embarrassed."

The truth was that Henry was ageing fast beyond his years and had grown grossly corpulent. This might not be a problem for a king living in times of peace, one who sat in his hall laughing with his men rather than going to war, but since my husband kept trying to start wars with anyone who passed by him, that meant riding out to *make* war on men, taking part in battles, leading soldiers. This was a problem. The stress of all the extra weight he was carrying was obvious in the broken veins in his cheeks, in the way his breath huffed and puffed as he moved. It caused him to age before his time, rode his heart hard and his bones too. Add to all this an anal fistula, which was what I was eventually informed was the trouble he had with his rear, and Henry was in truth a mess and in no state to be making war.

That did not matter to him, however. He had worked the impossible more than once, why not again? The trouble is, there is always a first time to fail at making the impossible possible. Those who succeed too often forget how to fail. They know not how to get up again when they have fallen down.

That was what I hoped this time, in any case.

*

Henry invaded France, assaulting castles near Montes. Fighting broke out in Normandy and Anjou, and Henry had an early victory in managing to woo away allies of Philip, the counts of Blois and Flanders. It seemed for a while as if he was winning, yet Henry was ever his own worst enemy for at this point either Philip managed to persuade Richard to come back to him, or Richard and his father fell out. I can guess which one was the more likely.

My son deserted the forces of his father for the forces of his friend and liege lord once more. Many condemned my son, but Philip was his overlord, more so than Henry was, and Philip had not spent all his life making promises and then breaking them. We reap what we sow.

That November, as winter approached and it would be unwise to continue to make war, the two kings met again, not at the ruined stump of the tree but at Bonsmoulins to attempt to make peace. Richard, who was with Philip, demanded that Henry name him his heir and give him immediate authority over Anjou, Maine and Touraine. He also asked him to allow his marriage to Alys to take place immediately. Henry refused all the demands of his son to which Richard shouted, "Now at last I believe what heretofore has seemed incredible!"

I sometimes wondered what he meant by that. Whether it was that Alys was the mistress of his father, but that he must have known, or whether it was that his father truly intended to dispossess him as heir. Perhaps it was all of these things, perhaps more besides. Perhaps Richard finally believed his father meant him only harm.

Richard knelt before Philip, and, proclaiming himself the heir to Henry's Continental fiefs, paid homage to the French King as his liege lord for all those dominions. He added "saving his father's lands while he lived, and the loyalty which he owed his father," but the transfer of allegiance was clear, as was his intention. If his father was not to name him heir, he would take his inheritance for himself.

French barons, angered at Henry's refusal to name Richard his heir, drew their swords and attacked the King and his entourage. They were forced to withdraw to a nearby castle.

"Despite all this unrest, they will not do anything about it this year," I mentioned to Berneval as we spoke of the event, "the campaigning season is at an end. Only fools make war through winter."

I was right enough. A truce lasting until Easter was agreed. Richard withdrew with Philip, and Henry went alone to Le Mans. It was reported Henry was ill and depressed in spirits, saddened by his son deserting him, but some men desert because it has become impossible to remain loyal. Some men leave because they cannot stay.

During that winter the Pope's legate and a host of bishops used all their skills to try to bring about a peace settlement so the crusade could go ahead with both the kings leading it, but they had no success. The kings were unified no more.

When the thaw came, so would war.

Chapter Thirty-Seven

Sarum and

Winchester

March 1189

When winter eased, I was sent to Sarum again. Again, because war was coming, Henry wanted me contained.

Yet war dragged its heels on the way to battle.

When the truce expired at Easter, Henry could not meet with Philip and Richard to discuss either continuing war or a settlement of peace. He was too ill.

Finally, they did meet on the 4th of June at La Ferté-Bernard, and although he was sick in body and clearly low of spirits Henry refused again to compromise and again proposed that Alys of France be married to John. Richard refused the terms, and Philip did too. Once more the two sides rode away with no resolution, and war began anew.

Philip and Richard immediately reopened hostilities by invading Henry's lands and they were highly successful, taking castle after castle. "The King's barons in Maine, Touraine and Anjou have begun to desert him, my lady," Berneval told me, glancing at a letter he had received that morning from Normandy. I could see he was weighing up his own choices anew too.

"Do they say why?" I could guess, but I wanted to know.

"There are rumours his men are tired of his tyranny and lack of compromise. Rumours that the King has been desperately ill over the winter have spread everywhere."

"People start to believe there is a chance Richard and his allies might win this time."

They were not alone. The deliberations of Berneval had come to some interesting conclusions, I found.

"My lady, although you know I cannot go against the wishes of His Majesty, for should he prevail I would be in great trouble," said my custodian a day later, "I would like to offer that should you wish to have letters taken from this place and into the wider world without being opened by me or the King's men, it might be possible for me to do this."

His tone, never disrespectful, had taken on a deeper note of esteem. Berneval was no fool, he knew that there was a chance I might well not be a prisoner much longer, if reports on the King's health were true. It was not long after this that we moved from Sarum to Winchester too. A rumour was set about that my quarters at Sarum had been damaged by a storm, but it was not true. Berneval knew I would like to be closer to the seat of power in England when the time came, and it seemed the time was coming fast.

*

When Philip's army appeared before the walls of Le Mans, where Henry had so long ago been born, the English King set fire to a whole quarter of the city trying to stop them, but the wind fanned the flames and the city itself caught light, allowing Philip and his men to breach its defences.

I thought of that event so long ago when another husband of mine, Louis, thought to set fire to Vitry and had ended up killing hundreds who burned, trapped within its church. I wondered at the synchronicity of life. That event had altered Louis's destiny, the path of it. That event, more than even the promise made to his brother on his deathbed, had sent him on the crusade where I had lost what little respect I had for him, and where he had lost his way, again. These choices we make in life, which seem so slight, they never are. We never know which events will alter everything, and which will fade into the past, forgotten as dreams of the night before.

The French stormed into the city and Henry and his men were forced to make a hasty escape. It was said that as he pulled up his horse on a hilltop overlooking the city, watching it burn and the French sacking it, the King shouted, "Oh God, thou hast vilely taken away the city I loved best on earth! I will pay thee back as best I can. I will rob thee of the thing thou lovest best in me, my soul."

"It is said he uttered more, my lady, but his men will not repeat what was said. It was too blasphemous." Berneval, not a man to look easily shocked, did.

"Men should not challenge God." I was staring out of the window. At the oak in the gardens, I could see memories of my children, my sons, now dead and lost to me, my daughters now so far away, playing. If I tilted my ear, I could hear their laughter. Sometimes I thought I could see Petronilla with them. It comforted me, the dead waiting, just on the edge of our vision, waiting for a time to be with us again.

I turned to Berneval. "Sometimes men think they are God, I believe, for the Bible tells us we were made in His image, or men were at least. This makes them think they are divine and all-powerful but God, whilst He has learned to be kind and accepting, once knew only vengeance and retribution. Sometimes I think that element of God still rises up. Men should be careful when they choose to challenge God, for they have not the power to stand against His wrath when it is roused."

As Henry raced away from his enemies, I had poor news.

"It cannot be," I murmured. "She was well when she was here."

Earlier that month my daughter Matilda had died. She was thirty-four. Her grieving people buried her in the cathedral church in Brunswick which she had co-founded.

I had thought, if there was a chance, if Henry did not survive this engagement or Richard were to win, I might have been able to take up her invitation to go to Saxony. It had been a long time since I had seen the world, had travelled, and though I was old now there was little wrong with my body. My bones ached at times, my joints too, but I was not about to let any infirmity stop me doing anything when finally I was at liberty. I was still light on my feet, still able to ride and certainly to be carried in a litter. I would have been eager, keen to take another trip to see another land, and I would have loved to see my daughter and the country she had been sent to and had fallen in love with.

But the chance to see her again had gone, for she was lost to life. This captivity had prevented me seeing another child, before they left the world. We would not spend that winter at the fireside, telling tales of life, that she had imagined for us. That chance was gone now. I had to tell her children, those living in my household. God forbid that anyone else should ever have to do such a thing as I did that day when I told them she was gone. Many hard things I had done in life, but that was one of the hardest.

"Wait for me at another fire," I whispered in my prayers, "and there in the warmth of eternity, there we shall tell each other of all the doings of our life, daughter, every single one of them."

*

As I grieved my daughter, my husband was having untold troubles. Attempting to make for Normandy, which was still loyal to him, Henry ordered William the Marshal, who had remained with him after the Young King's death, and a squadron of knights to cover his escape. It was not long after when Marshal met Richard. My son was leading a contingent of the French army, chasing his father. The two forces came to blows and Marshal came face to face with Richard. Marshal levelled his lance in readiness and Richard cried out, "By God's legs, Marshal, do not kill me! I wear no hauberk."

This was the only time that I ever heard of when Richard pleaded with another man for his life, a fitting testament to the skill he knew was within William the Marshal.

"May the devil kill you," cried Marshal, "for I will not!" and with that he thrust his lance into Richard's horse. This unseated my son, but Marshal would not kill Richard, there was too much affection between them. So, he turned his horse and rode to warn his King of Richard's approach, which allowed my husband to escape from a direct confrontation with his son.

"That is some comfort at least," I said, "much as I am sure it would solve many things if they met each other face to face, I do not want to contend with the idea of my husband killing my son, or my son killing my husband. What a curse it would be on all our family." *As if we do not have enough already*, I thought.

The weather was perilously hot at that time and as the King and his men made their escape into Normandy, many of Henry's knights fell to flux of the bowels or fatigue and died by the wayside. The King meant to press on to Normandy but his trouble in his rear was giving him untold pain and he was unable to go any further. He dispatched some of his knights to Alençon to bring back reinforcements, and with his bastard son Geoffrey and William the Marshal, Henry retreated to Chinon, leaving Touraine wide open to be occupied by his son and Philip of France.

I was told later he was worried about what had become of his son John who had been with him but had mysteriously disappeared.

"I can guess what happened to John." I stared at Berneval as he read notes from reports sent from the Continent. "He has joined Richard, has he not? When it looked as if his brother would win, he joined him."

"It only says here that no one knew where he was."

"I know where he was."

By that time, it was clear that Henry's campaign was failing. On the 4th of July Tours fell to the French and on that day, Henry pulled himself from his sick bed and rode to a meeting with his enemies at Colombières, a small village. He was forced on the way to take rest at a House of the Knights Templar where he told them, "My whole body is on fire."

"His blood was infested," I said. "I know those signs."

His knights rode ahead to inform Philip that Henry was ill, but Richard insisted it was a trick. It was the same that Henry had said of young Henry, when he too was dying.

"We reap what we sow," I whispered.

Hearing that his son had said this, Henry, sick unto death and weak as a kitten, had his man hold him up on his horse. In a thunderstorm he rode into the village. Seeing him so obviously unwell, the King of France offered to have a cloak spread upon the ground for him to sit on, but Henry tautly refused this, saying he had not come to sit but to learn the price he must pay for peace. He stayed on his horse with men holding him upright, as for perhaps the first time in his life and the last time he agreed to undertake whatever another man demanded of him.

The King of France, determined to shame his enemy, demanded that the terms of peace with France were that Henry was to pay homage to Philip for all his Continental domains and must agree to leave all his lands including England to Richard. He was to command his barons on both sides of the Channel to swear fealty to Richard as his father's heir and was to pardon all those who had fought for Richard.

He was also to promise to go on crusade by Lent of the following year, was to immediately surrender Alys of France into her brother's custody, and arrange without delay or excuse her marriage to Richard once he had returned from Jerusalem. Finally, Henry was to place himself at Philip's will, pay 20,000 marks and surrender three strongholds in Anjou or the Vexin as tokens of good faith.

These were crushing terms, much like those Henry had inflicted on other men when he had won over them.

At all other times in his life Henry would have refused but knowing he was defeated, Henry accepted the terms without argument. He went to leave but Philip called him back and insisted that he give Richard the kiss of peace. My husband reluctantly did so but as he drew away from the cheek of his son his words were, "God grant that I may not die until I have had a fitting revenge on you."

Thunder rolled in the skies as the King of England and Duke of Normandy was set into a litter and carried back to Chinon. All the way he called down the wrath of God upon his son Richard, cursing all his sons as well as himself, and the day he was born.

"It is said he spoke many blasphemies, my lady," Berneval said, "which I will not trouble your ears with."

"Blasphemy will not harm me, my lord, they are not words I have spoken." I straightened my shoulders. "What did my husband say?"

"He shouted, 'Why should I worship Christ? Why should I deign to honour Him who takes my earthly honour and allows me to be ignominiously confounded by a mere boy?'"

When he reached Chinon the Archbishop of Canterbury was shocked by his words and made the King go to the chapel and make peace with God by confessing his sins and receiving absolution and communion.

"At least someone was thinking of his soul," I said, "for he was not."

Sick in his castle, on the 5th of July Henry had the news he had no doubt been dreading. His vice-chancellor brought him a list of vassals who had supported Richard and would be spared punishment due to the demands of Philip. "May Jesus Christ help me, sire," exclaimed the man. "The first name here is Count John, your son."

"Is it true that John, my heart John, whom I loved more than all my sons and for whose gain I have suffered all these evils has forsaken me?" Henry wailed in a piteous voice. I know not why he was shocked; he must have guessed where his son was. "Say no more now, let the rest go as it will. I care no more for myself nor aught for this world."

I shrugged. "John was ever one to do what was best for him, much as his father was. Of all my sons, John was his father's son the most." As for saying he had done all this for John, it simply was not true. Henry had done this for himself.

I think John's desertion was the last weight which unbalanced the scales. Henry always had a notion that people *should* love him, that he needed to do nothing in order for them to show him loyalty and give him their hearts. He thought that was what being a king and a father, a husband or lord or friend was, unconditional love and obedience.

But there are conditions to love. It should be reciprocal. It should be infused with respect. It should be something honoured and not used against another. Yes, there should be conditions to love.

And Henry had a habit of loving the wrong men. Becket, John, they were not men to love another deeply. Perhaps Henry saw something of himself in them, and that was what he loved.

John was destined always to eventually seek out that which he thought would benefit him most, the side most likely to win. Support his father, after all, and he might well find himself disinherited, just as Henry had tried to do many times to his older brothers, if Henry found a younger heir to replace John with.

Henry underestimated yet another son and paid the price for it.

He only had hours left to live. During that time, he slept or fell into fevered delirium, groaning with pain and with grief. His bastard son Geoffrey stayed with him, held Henry's head in his hands, spoke soothing words and kept flies away from the dying man. In one moment of clarity Henry declared blessings upon his son, crying out that Geoffrey was the only one of all his children who had remained true to him. He asked that he be made Archbishop of York and gave Geoffrey his signet ring, which had two leopards upon it. After this he became delirious once more.

His last words were, "Shame! Shame on a conquered King!" before he fell to his dreams of fever.

Henry of England, the second of his name, died on the 6th of July 1189, and Geoffrey stayed with him until the end. As soon as Geoffrey left the chamber the dead King's attendants stole all Henry's personal effects, including the clothes he wore. The King was stripped naked, and it was left to a young knight to cover his corpse with a short cloak.

"Curt mantle," I said, remembering sadly a moment we were in bed together, when first we came to England, full of plans and passion, "that was what they called him when first he came to England."

Geoffrey and William the Marshal managed to gather goods enough so that their master was not humiliated in death as he had been in life. A woman gave them a fillet of gold embroidery to use as a crown and they managed to locate a ring and a sceptre. On the morning of his death my husband was carried out for burial in regal pomp, the golden crown of embroidery upon his head, gloves on his hands, a golden ring on his finger, his hands holding a sceptre, wearing shoes of gold fabric with spurs on his feet, and girded with a sword. His body was covered, his dignity restored, and he lay with his face exposed, so the world could see him one last time.

William the Marshal went to Richard and told him his father was dead and Richard went to Henry. I was told that as he looked upon the body, no one could tell whether my son felt joy or sorrow, grief or anger or satisfaction. I would imagine in all honesty he felt all of those things. People often describe moments of high emotion as being ones of anger or sadness or joy, but we are creatures more complicated than even we believe at times, capable of holding so many emotions raging through us all at once. We are as a riverbank dried in the heat, through which a flashing flood may pour, and in those waters may be carried branches and twigs and leaves, rocks and sand and root and all these things make up the rushing tide of the water that flows through us.

Richard knelt to pray at his side but not for long. When he rose from his prayer, blood began to flow from the nostrils of the dead King and would not cease to flow while his son remained there.

"Is this true or is it a tale?" I asked with a sceptical tone, for the story of corpses bleeding was often told. It was a sign, people said, that the murderer of that person was close. I believe this was a tale told to try to cast Richard in a bad light, as the killer of his father. In truth, his father had done this to himself, the choices he had made had led to this death.

Richard accompanied the body of his father to Fontevraud, where on the 10th of July he had him buried in the nuns' choir. It was not where Henry had asked to be buried, he wanted to lie at Grandmont, but Richard thought Fontevraud a more fitting place.

There was in time an epitaph engraved upon the tomb of my husband:

I am Henry the king. To me

Divers realms were subject.

I was Duke and Count of many provinces.

Eight feet of ground is now enough for me

Whom many kingdoms failed to satisfy.

Who reads these lines let him reflect

Upon the narrowness of death,

And in my case behold

The image of our mortal lot.

This country tomb doth now suffice

For whom the earth was not enough.

With the news that there was a new King of England, with the news that my husband was dead, there came an order to my custodian, sent by my beloved son Richard. William the Marshal brought it to us. Always the trusted man of my son, then my husband, he now served Richard.

"You are no more a prisoner of the state, my lady," he said upon entering my chamber.

"I never was." I stood tall. "I was the prisoner of my husband, but now his time is done." I smiled up at William. "And mine has just begun."

Chapter Thirty-Eight

Winchester

Hampshire

1189

In truth, by the time William the Marshal arrived, I was already free and busy setting up my court. People had begun to flock to me, knowing that the moment my son was in power I would be too.

Even before word came of Henry's death, no one dared keep me captive anymore. Many of them had no wish to in any case, their affection having been won by me in the years of my imprisonment.

"I am both surprised and pleased to find you here already at liberty and so happy, my lady," said William, glancing about at the milling crowds of people already at Winchester.

Some were petitioners, some were my household, some were friends I had not seen for years. My uncle Raoul, old and in ill health had nonetheless made the trip to England as soon as he was certain I was free. To be in his embrace again was something of magic.

"How I feared for you, all these years," he had told me after embracing me so hard he knocked the patch from his eye, revealing the pink and silver scar underneath.

"As I feared for you, uncle, when I heard Henry had taken your castle." I looked on him, all his hair white as snow now, his face wrinkled and worn, and I felt love infuse me, fill me to the core and to the tips of my toes.

"Your son has granted it back, for true service during the troubles. It will be good to go home again."

I laughed, slipping my arm into his. "France did not agree with you?"

"Sometimes it did, and sometimes we argued." He grinned, his mouth baggy now, his teeth few. "But I want to go home. My end draws close, I think, but God has granted me the chance to see you again, and to go home. That is all I asked."

"Do not speak of death, I need you now, uncle."

He had looked about. "You are already Queen of your own court again, Lenor. Your son is King. Let me rest my bones where I may when the time comes."

"Let that time not be yet."

I hoped he would remain with me, but I could see Raoul's time was close, as he could. I was touched he had taken a swift ship to me the moment he heard I was free. There were many there at Winchester, but he meant more than so many ever could.

I looked on William Marshal and smiled. "You are no longer the boy I remember, but a fine man you have become. My people here, they were already in affection for me and resented, as all good people did, my imprisonment by my husband. The moment we heard that King Henry was dead I knew my son would send word to set me free and so did they, so they set me free. My custodian knows the love King Richard has for his mother and so I told him that it was time, and he heartily agreed." I waved my hand at my hastily assembled court; many more were arriving daily in order to pay their respects to me now that I was free again.

William held out a paper to me. "I am to inform you, my lady, that you have been named Regent of England by your son King Richard. Indeed he has issued instructions, which I bear with me in my hand, to all princes of the realm and lords. It is in the style almost of a general edict and it states that your word should be law in all matters."

All hail the Queen Regent, whispered the voice of my sister in my mind.

I smiled, allowed a laugh to escape my lips. "From prisoner one day, to my word being law the next. The wonders of life never cease, do they? And I should know, for I am an old woman now."

William laughed a little. "In truth, my lady, you look as young as I remember you, so many years ago, when you ordered me to go to your son, the Young King."

I paused and when my voice came it was rough with sorrow. "I want to thank you for all you did for him, Marshal." I clasped his hand in mine. "His life was a brutal waste, he never was allowed to become the man I think he could have been, but many things that were good in him, they were things you brought out in him."

"He was my good friend, my lady." William's eyes sparkled with grief. I put my hand on his shoulder.

"And I am grateful, every day, that he had something good in his life," I said. "And that something was you."

I looked out on the world. I was sixty-seven and the Regent of England. I had now outlived both husbands I had married and finally I had in my life a man who respected me enough to give me the freedom and the power I always had desired. That man was not a husband but was my son.

The truth was, much as his father had needed me at various times, my son needed me too now. Richard simply had the grace to admit it and treat me with respect.

My son cared not a fig for England, he had said it often enough and people here knew that. Aquitaine was in Richard's heart but now he was to be ruler of a vast empire, and he would need help, trusted people to hold his lands for him. I was one of those people.

"Come," I said to William the Marshal. "We must organise meetings, my lord."

Whenever I sprang to life and announced something, Marshal would look at me most curiously. I think he was somewhat surprised I had not lost my wits whilst in captivity. I wondered what rumours had gone around about me, perhaps spread by my husband, that I was old or a dotard, that I had lost my mind or my energy but none of it was true. I had, in the time I was separated from the world and under the power of my husband, had a great deal of time to consider what I would do when Richard became King, as I was sure he would. Faith had kept me alive, and belief in myself had kept my mind sharp. I was ready for all that was to come, and more than that, I was eager for it.

The first matter would be that England's people needed to know and love their King. They had fallen out of love with the Old King but now there was a new one, a fresh start, and we needed to begin an affair between Richard and England that the pages of history would sigh over, with his people so deep in love with him that they looked at none of the bad moments or times. That was what I wanted for my son. What little the people of England knew of Richard they knew from Henry; therefore, they would see him as a traitor, a deserter and someone who was untrue to his father, but all of that would change.

I would make it change.

A king, you see, is as much a story as he is a person, and from the barest fragments can a story most glorious be made. I was going to ensure that England's people were entirely loyal to their King, and I would do that by making stories about my son so I could from the fragments left behind by his father weave another story entire, one of the great warrior king, Richard of England. If people believe the stories, then they will believe in their king. There was to tale to be told, and I would be its author.

"There is a new King of England, but his people know him not." I took Marshal's arm as we walked up the stairs to the council chambers. "This, we will alter, beginning today."

"It is good to see you inspired and ready for the task in hand, my lady," he said.

I nodded. "Eagle of the broken covenant, they called me once. I suppose I broke one promise, to my husband but I kept another, to my children." I stopped walking and smiled at him. "We are never what other people think we are, in truth, Marshal. We are what we know we are in our hearts, our souls. Eagle, they called me, and yet phoenix have I become."

Here ends *Eaglets*, book three in the story of Eleanor of Aquitaine.

In book four, *The Narrowness of Death*, Eleanor will aid her son

Richard in his rule, as dangers from outside the realm and inside

press upon the royal family.

Author's Notes

Did Henry II order the murder of Thomas Becket? Was Eleanor of Aquitaine the main instigator in the revolt of her sons against her husband? Some things we may never know for certain, and that, I believe, is what makes history interesting. There is always a little mystery to be solved. Sometimes we just have to take our best guess.

At the time, certainly, many believed Henry guilty, and plenty of contemporary sources hold Eleanor accountable as the brain behind the pact with France, the escape of the Young King and the war which followed. As I have presented in this book, however, perhaps this is only partly true.

Certainly, I think it possible Henry said something incautious, as Eleanor believes in the book, and this led to the murder of the Archbishop. I think too that Henry probably wanted Becket dead by this point, he was proving most troublesome after all. In the same way I think Eleanor was the one who arranged the escape of her son from the clutches of her husband, and she must have known it might well lead to war, but I think the decision to go ahead with the revolt came from her son. He had a choice, once he got to France, to make war or to try to bargain with his father and he chose war. Once this was done Eleanor supported her son in all ways she could, something she is often condemned for, but I understand, and I think many others will too that she knew the dangers her sons were facing and decided they needed her. Frequently she is accused of being the one who urged her sons to war with her husband, but I think some accountability must fall on others, on her sons and indeed on Henry II himself, who in many ways pushed his sons into actions most desperate against him.

Some people might be surprised that Thomas Becket (I may have said so before, but he never was Thomas *a* Becket. The "a" which sometimes appears in his name is a later addition, quite possibly a very old spelling mistake which managed to stick and appeared afterwards added to his name for a very long time) is presented as not a very saintly man, mainly because I do not believe he was. Others may form other opinions, but I think he was motivated by self-interest and the pursuit of acclaim. Perhaps becoming a martyr was his crowning glory in the end.

It is worth noting that Henry II probably never shouted, "Who will rid me of this turbulent priest?" He said some things close to this, but this particular phrase appears to be again a later addition to the tale and was first used in 1740. For Henry's words at the time, I used the quotation cited by Edward Grim (who was a contemporary of Henry's, but since he was present at the murder of Becket, he can't have heard what Henry said firsthand either) in his book on the life of Thomas Becket.

We may argue about other things, such as did Eleanor deserve to be locked away, a prisoner, for so many years due to her choice to support her sons rather than her husband? Some will think it justice, perhaps, but even at the time many thought it a disgrace she was held so long, particularly when all the male leaders of the rebellion had been freed and many restored to favour. Perhaps it was, as Eleanor says, a measure of how deeply Henry feared her, but he also knew he could use her, as a prisoner, as a weapon, against her sons.

Amaria's origins are not noted in any source I can find. There is little on her at all, in truth, but I decided to give her a backstory which would allow her and Eleanor to have something in common, so set her birth in Constantinople. One origin of the name is Greek, another possibly Hebrew, but Amaria could have been from anywhere.

Many people were surprised when Eleanor was released that she was in such good health and in complete control of her faculties. She was not old by our modern standards, but for the time she would have been considered so. This, added to her long imprisonment is why people were probably surprised. That she endured so much time shut away from all she loved, her homeland and children in particular, and emerged victorious, is a testament to the strong will within this Queen of England and Duchess of Aquitaine. It was an inner strength and light which she did not allow her husband to dim, no matter what he did, and her repeated refusal to hand her lands to John and disinherit Richard demonstrate this too. Whatever power she still had, she wielded, and she worked for the preservation and protection of her children wherever she could. The same could not be said of her husband, who spent most of his time pitting his sons against each other. Yet so often Eleanor is condemned for the ways her sons turned out and for their actions, where Henry is not held accountable at all. To my mind, his refusal to allow his sons, particularly young Henry, true power in his lifetime led to many of the events described in this book. Had he shared power, as his father and mother did with him, many of these events might have been different.

But who can say? Perhaps the sons would have warred only more against each other.

There is much in this family that we would today deem deeply dysfunctional, and quite rightly so, and Eleanor certainly made mistakes, but if one thing shone out at me from the research I did for this book it was that she loved her children, and would, to the last, stand up for them. That, I think, along with Eleanor not only surviving decades of imprisonment but emerging with vim and lust for life, is something to be admired.

Thank You

…to so many people for helping me make this book possible… to my proofreader, Julia Gibbs, who gave me her time, her wonderful guidance and also her encouragement. To my family for their ongoing love and support. To my friend Petra. To my friend Nessa for her support and affection, and to another friend, Anne, who has done so much for me. To Sue and Annette, more friends who read my books and cheer me on. To Terry for getting me into writing and indie publishing in the first place. To Katie and Jooles, Macer, Pip, Linda, Fe, Pete and Heather, people there in times of trial. And to all my wonderful readers, who took a chance on an unknown author, and have followed my career and books since.

To those who have left reviews or contacted me by email or on social media, I give great thanks, as you have shown support for my career as an author and enabled me to continue writing. Thank you for allowing me to live my dream.

Thank you to all of you; you'll never know how much you've helped me, but I know what I owe to you.

Gemma Lawrence
Wales
2024

About The Author

I find people talking about themselves in the third person to be entirely unsettling, so, since this section is written by me, I will use my own voice rather than try to make you believe that another person is writing about me to make me sound terribly important.

I am an independent author, publishing my books by myself, with the help of my lovely proofreader. I left my day job in 2016 and am now a fully-fledged, full-time author, and proud to be so.

My passion for history began early in life. As a child I lived in Croydon, near London, and my schools were lucky enough to be close to such glorious places as Hampton Court and the Tower of London, allowing field trips to take us to those castles. I write historical fiction for the main part, but I also have a fascination with ghost stories and fantasy, and I hope this book was one you enjoyed. I want to divert you as readers, to please you with my writing and to have you join me on these adventures.

A book is nothing without a reader.

As to the rest of me, I am in my forties and live in Wales with a rescued cat (who often sits on my lap when I write, which can make typing more of a challenge). I studied Literature at University after I fell in love with books as a small child. When I was little, I could often be found nestled halfway up the stairs with a pile of books in my lap and my head lost in another world. There is nothing more satisfying to me than finding a new book I adore, to place next to the multitudes I own and love… and nothing more disappointing to me to find a book I am willing to never open again. I do hope that this book was not a disappointment to you. I loved writing it and I hope that showed through the pages.

If you would like to contact me, please do so. I can be found in quite a few places!

On Twitter, (I am not calling it X) I am @TudorTweep.

You can also find me on Instagram as tudorgram1500. I am new to Mastodon as G. Lawrence Tudor Tooter,

@TudorTweep@mastodonapp.uk, and Counter Social as TudorSocial1500.

On Facebook my page is just simply G. Lawrence, and on TikTok and Threads I am tudorgram1500, the same as Instagram. I've just joined Bluesky as G. Lawrence too. Often, I have a picture of the young Elizabeth I as my avatar, or there's me leaning up against a wall in Pembroke Castle.

I am also now writing on Substack, where my account is called G. Lawrence in the Book Nook. On there I publish articles, reviews, advice for other writers and I'm publishing a book there chapter by chapter each week. Join me there!

Via email, I am tudortweep@gmail.com a dedicated email account for my readers to reach me on. I'll try and reply within a few days.

Thank you for taking a risk with an unknown author and reading my book. I do hope now that you've read one, you'll want to read more. If you'd like to leave me a review, that would be very much appreciated also!

Gemma Lawrence
Wales
2024

Printed in Great Britain
by Amazon

48230532R00165